ONLY HUMAN

ONLY HUMAN

Beryl Kingston

This first world edition published in Great Britain 2001 by
SEVERN HOUSE PUBLISHERS LTD of
9–15 High Street, Sutton, Surrey SM1 1DF.
This first world edition published in the USA 2001 by
SEVERN HOUSE PUBLISHERS INC of
595 Madison Avenue, New York, N.Y. 10022.

Copyright © 2001 by Beryl Kingston

British Library Cataloguing in Publication Data

Kingston, Beryl
    Only human
    1.   Historical fiction
    I.   Title
    823.9'14 [F]

    ISBN 0-7278-5714-2

Typeset by Palimpsest Book Production Ltd.,
Polmont, Stirlingshire, Scotland.
Printed and bound in Great Britain by
MPG Books Ltd., Bodmin, Cornwall.

One

After the prolonged snowfall of the winter, spring was late arriving that year, even in the south of England. The earth was sullen and waterlogged, so there was a great deal of heavy work to be done about the farm: sticky fields to be ploughed, clogged ditches cleared, thatch repaired, fences mended. Crops were slow to appear, lambs slow to thrive, and Farmer Lambton's prized soft fruits were little more than bare twigs and looked more dead than alive.

The sloth of the season was a daily irritation to Suki Brown now that she'd set her heart on that vital trip to Bristol. It was nearly nineteen months since she'd last seen the Captain, and in private moments, alone at night with the household sleeping around her, she was beginning to wonder whether she would ever see him again. His ship could have been lost at sea or taken by the French. Anything could have happened. It troubled her that her memories of him had begun to blur and were now a disquieting blend of uncomfortably sharp focus and wavering unreality. She could remember the persuasive passion of his eyes – those beautiful, dark-fringed, brown eyes that could provoke love by a glance – but there were times when she couldn't picture the rest of his face at all or recall what they'd said to one another. Only their last despairing conversation remained clear in her mind and

1

that was because it had been so fraught with loss and finality.

"I must leave you, sweetheart," he'd said gazing down at her from the height of that great horse of his.

"Not now!" she'd cried, breathless with the shock of hearing such an awful thing so suddenly.

"Aye. Now. I ride to London this evening."

"When to return?"

"Well as to that," he'd said carelessly. "I couldn't say. 'Tis uncommon hard to estimate such matters. There are things to be done. Money to be earned. You'll not say no to a trinket or two, I'll warrant, when I return."

Trinkets meant nothing to her. "I'll wait for 'ee," she'd promised earnestly.

"Aye. Be sure to."

"How shall you find me, when you return?" she'd asked. The season was nearly over and her employers would be leaving Bath at any time.

"Don't worry your pretty head on that account," he'd said when she told him. "If you lose one mistress another beckons. 'Tis the way of the world. Go to Lady Bradbury on South Parade, should you need employ. She will hire you."

"But . . ."

He'd leant from his horse to kiss her. "Sweetheart," he'd said. And he'd smiled into her eyes, straightened his spine and ridden away. Out of her life for nineteen months.

At her lowest ebb, when the house creaked and the air she breathed was ice cold on the back of her throat, she would get up and tiptoe across the room to the chest of drawers where she kept his precious silk kerchief. She would take it back to her pillow to comfort herself with its softness under her cheek. Oh my dearest, she thought, my dearest darling Captain. When shall I see you again? It seemed to her in those dark night moments as if the spring would never come, as if she would never get to Bristol, never make enquiries, never find out what she wanted to know.

We must go a-marketing soon, she fretted. But however pointedly she watched the weather, the days passed and nothing was said. She tried throwing out hints, remarking on how low their stocks were getting, which was demonstrably true, for the family sugar loaf had dwindled to a sad little mound in its dish, like the blob of a burnt-out candle, and she was sure that their stock of tea was low too, for when Mrs Lambton unlocked the caddy, she had to dig deep for her careful spoonful. But Annie was unmoved, pointing out that there was still half a side of bacon hanging from the rafters, apples in the barrel and a good supply of flour, swedes, leeks and potatoes in the larder, "which will serve a deal longer, I think."

She was more concerned about little Constant who was over four months old now but still spent most of his day lying listlessly in his cradle, pale and unsmiling, and showed no signs of wanting to sit up and see the world. She knew he wasn't growing as he should and there was no strength in his little back at all. He sagged and wept when she sat him on her knee and wouldn't be comforted until he was allowed to lie down again, which was plainly wrong, even in a baby who was slow to develop.

William had been sitting up and taking notice when he and Suki arrived, as she remembered very well, and now he was standing and taking his first tottering steps from chair to chair or crawling about the kitchen at great speed and with the strongest determination. There were times when his healthy presence in the house felt like a rebuke to her. Oh no, she certainly couldn't leave her Precious yet awhile.

In the middle of March a mail man arrived with two letters for Suki, for which he asked double the going rate, "being the roads is a treachery hereabouts."

The first was from Lady Bradbury, informing her that "her dear Ariadne" was engaged to be married "to the grandson of the Duke of Errymouth" and would consequently require her services as lady's maid on their return to Bath, and asking, almost as an afterthought, for news of "her dear William" for whom she enclosed a bank note for five pounds, which she said was to be used to buy him new clothes, "as I am sure he will have grown since my last *billet.*"

The second and longer letter was from Ariadne. It contained a scathing description of her fiancé, a rambling paragraph deploring the way her mother and father were fawning upon him, "which 'twould sicken you to see," and ended with a lengthy postscript.

> I mean to follow my heart and marry the man of
> my choice since that is plainly the right true thing
> to do. No man has the right to determine my life
> for me. My body is my own. 'Tis not my father's
> nor my husband's nor any other's. I shall bestow
> it upon a lover who has earned it and deserves it.
> We shall talk further of these things since we have
> said nothing of consequence since we last spoke
> and there is much of consequence.

"She means to marry her lover then," Annie observed, when Suki had read the letter to her. "'Twill not be easy, I fear, nor likely."

4

"She has great spirit," Suki said. "If any are to do it, she'll be the one. I'd lay money on it."

Annie couldn't concentrate on such an improbability. She was grappling with the fact that Suki would be leaving her in the summer and wondering whether this would be a good thing or a bad. On the one hand she would be glad to have William's rude health out of the house, on the other she knew Constant would miss Suki's "good feed" at night time, so she hoped it wouldn't be too soon. "When do they want 'ee to go to Bath?"

"In the summer," Suki said. "'Twill be June, I daresay. That's when the knights of sugar come to town. Meantime, I got to buy material to make new clothes for William. 'Twill mean a trip to Bristol, don't 'ee think?" And she looked at her mistress with a hopeful question on her face.

Annie agreed that it would, but it was the first week of April before she finally decided that the cart should be prepared for them.

"This aren't a journey to be took in haste," she explained, "not with two babbas dependent upon us."

Her preparations were slow and meticulous. Suki's sister Molly was summoned to look after the babies, a bowl of gruel was prepared for them and left to be warmed on the fire, a shopping list was written, bonnets and mantles brushed clean and ready, the mare groomed, the cart swept clean. It was past nine o'clock before Constant had been fed and settled and nearly half past before he and William were considered to be in a fit state to be left, even with a confident ten-year-old who said she was sure they'd be no trouble at all.

"I don't like to go without un just the same," Annie said, looking back anxiously as the cart joggled her away

5

from the farmhouse. "What if he should try to sit up and tumble?"

"Don't you go a-worriting, ma'am," Suki comforted. "He'll be right as rain, you'll see. Our Molly's got the knack, same as me. An' we'll be back in no time. 'Twon't take more'n a minute to get our purchases. 'Tis a fine fair place, as I remember, and shops a-plenty." And a shipping office somewhere on the quay to tell me what I want to know.

The sun was quite warm by the time they arrived and the High Street was pungent with the smell of newly ground coffee, fresh-brewed tea and newly killed meat. One butcher's shop was doing a fly-burdened trade in "offal and suchlike delicacies", another was hung about with sausages that dangled from their hooks like long fat beads in every colour from gum pink to blood black, the baker's shops were floury with the last bread of the morning, and down by the Exchange, sugar loaves stood to attention in the grocer's shop window like a row of glistening white skittles.

By this time Suki was in such a fever of impatience to find the shipping office that she couldn't stand still. "How if we were to go our separate ways, ma'am?" she asked, hopping from foot to foot. "You won't need my help with the sugar on account of Mr Jones'll carry it to the cart. I could be choosing the cloth while you'm a-marketing here. 'Twould save us a deal of time, don't 'ee think."

Annie agreed readily. Anything to enable them to get home quickly. "Yes," she said, her eyes on the sugar. "That might be politic."

Suki was gone before she could look up at her, tripping towards Broad Quay, her skirts swinging with the urgency of her walk. Now, now, now! At last!

The quay resounded with its usual important bustle. The first of the sugar ships had come in the previous day and was being unloaded under the shrewd eyes and knowledgeable comments of half the sugar merchants in town, there were cargoes of wood and sea coal and spices scenting the air, carts and drays blocking the cobbles, men bellowing, timbers knocking, dogs barking with excitement or squealing as they were kicked, and down by the coal barge two avid boys were tying a lighted candle to the tail of a scrawny black cat that was writhing to escape them and screaming in terror.

For a second, Suki was so bewildered by the rush and noise, that she had to stand still to get her bearings. She could see lines of warehouses on both sides of the quay, but nothing that looked like a shipping office. If only they'd leave that poor cat alone, she thought, I could think what to do. The noise it was making was so pitiful it was putting her in a muddle. And then, as if that weren't enough, a horse starting screaming too. She looked towards the sound to see what was happening.

It was a large bay stallion, rearing up, front legs flailing, mouth foaming, showing the whites of his eyes, as three rough men pulled at him, swearing and sweating. One was a huge fellow in his shirt sleeves, who was in a furious temper, whipping the animal with all his force and struggling to catch his flying bridle. There was something familiar about the stallion's head and neck, something she knew, and as pity rose in her, she realised what it was. This horse was Beau, Jack's precious stallion that he loved so much.

Without stopping to think, she stormed to the animal's defence, eyes blazing. "Stop that at once," she ordered and pushed the man aside.

7

He was so amazed to be attacked by a slip of a girl that for a second he didn't know how to respond, and that gave her a chance to catch the bridle and begin to gentle the horse down, speaking to him as Jack would have done, using the same words and the same tone. "Easy now. Easy. That's my boy. Gently does it. You'm all right now. I got you."

The fellow was impressed despite himself and that gave him the strength to attack. "Clear off out of it," he ordered, making a grab for the bridle. "What business is it of yourn?"

She stood her ground, furiously, as Beau trembled beside her. "'Tis my husband's horse an' you've no right to whip him. Look what you've done to un. I'll have the law on you." Now that the horse was still she could see what a bad state he was in, his mouth torn and bleeding, whip marks on his rump, hooves caked in mud, mane and tail matted, eyes staring in terror. "You got no right to treat him so."

The man sneered. "Well that's where you'm wrong, my lover. 'Tis *my* horse. I paid for un fair an' square, an' I can do as I please with un."

The news took her back a bit, but she had an answer for him. "Then you'll have a bill of sale."

He hadn't expected knowledge of the horse trade from such a young woman. "Not about my person, no," he blustered. "But he'm mine, fair an' square. Depend on it." The argument had gathered a crowd and some of them were egging him on. "Tha's right, Johnny-Jo, you tell 'er."

"I don't depend on nothing," Suki told him trenchantly. "Not when 'tis a matter of money. If he'm yourn an' you've a-paid for him, you'll come with me to a notary and show the bill of sale. 'Twill have my

husband's signature upon it, which I shall know, depend
on it, and *then* 'twill be fair an' square."

"Now look 'ee here," the man said, beginning to sense
that he was getting out of his depth. "I bought un from
a good stables. Reputable. Mr Wenham's Livery stables
on Broad Quay. He'll tell 'ee."

"Very well," Suki said. "We'll go there an' see." And
she began to lead the horse away as if she knew where
she was going.

"Now look 'ee here," the man said again, but he had
to follow her whether he would or no and the crowd
followed him, eager to see the end of the drama.

The stable was easy to find. She could have sniffed
it out, even without Mr Wenham's brightly painted sign
to point the way, and when the gentleman himself was
called for and appeared, curry-comb in hand, swarthy
and tousle-headed, in his fustian breeches and his leather
apron, she knew at once and by instinct that however hard
this fight might prove to be, she was going to win it.

"Yes," he agreed, "'tis the Captain's horse. No mistaking."

"Which you sold to me," Johnny-Jo said, pushing himself forward. "Fair an' square. Six pounds ten shillin'."

The crowd burst into a chorus of comment. "Now
we'm a-comin' to it." "Tha's got her, Johnny-Jo. You
tell 'er."

Encouraged, Johnny-Jo repeated his claim. "Which
you sold to me."

"Which I never did nothin' of the sort," Mr Wenham
said. "I hired un out to 'ee. No more."

Johnny-Jo was blustering too much to make sense.
"You told me . . . What I means for to say . . . 'Tain't
handsome, Mr Wenham."

Suki swept his incoherence aside and made a direct

appeal to their audience. "The one thing I do know about my husband," she told them, "is he never would've sold this horse. Never. 'Tweren't in his nature. He loved un too much. 'Tis a rare fine horse. Anyone can see that with half an eye. And another thing. You'd never buy an animal of this quality for six pounds. Look at him. I ask you. Six pounds? Sixty maybe. That 'ud be more the mark. But six? Never in a month a' Sundays. He's making it up an' that's the truth of it."

"I knows what I knows," Johnny-Jo said stubbornly. "This horse was sold to me, fair an' square. I defy Mr Wenham to say any different. Six pounds fifteen shillings. In the Seven Stars."

"You hired un," Mr Wenham said. "That was all. Onny you don't recollect the manner of it on account of you was drunk."

The blustering rose to spitting point. "I remembers every blamed word, Mr Wenham. We shook hands on't."

"You was drunk."

"I was not."

They were glowering at one another now, red in the face and panting. Suki sprang her clinching argument into the pause. "Then where's your bill of sale?"

The chorus swayed, in both senses of the word. "She got the right of it there." "Ought to be a bill of sale." "After all, she knows her own husband. Stands to reason."

It was all over bar the shouting, which went on for ten more minutes and got louder and more and more ridiculous. When Johnny-Jo finally left the stables he was shouting that he'd "have the law on Mr Wenham and that witch there. Which I means to say that witch should be set in the stocks. Flayed alive and ate she

10

should be. I wouldn't touch her with a red hot poker. Nor the horse neither. 'Tis a vicious aminal. If you want my opinion of it, 'tis blamed injustice, that's what. I'll have the law on the whole blamed lot of you."

The crowd booed him off the premises and were quite disappointed when he'd gone. Soon they began to drift away, there being nothing left to see and hear except horses.

"So, Mr Wenham," Suki said, brisk and to the point. "This horse was stabled here by Captain Jack, and you been a-hirin' him out. Is that the right of it?"

"'Twas all agreed upon," Mr Wenham told her, speaking respectfully, having learnt that she was a woman who got her own way. "We come to an arrangement, on account of the price of hay, which he eats monstrous. He's a reg'lar trencher, you might say. Which I 'aven't had no more money for his keep since your Jack set sail, which is a good long time since, as you know."

It was time to make a decision and an offer. "I got a bank note for five pounds in my pocket," she said, pulling it out and displaying it, "what say this horse is mine and his fodder well paid for? How say you to that?"

Twenty crowns was a fair and immediate profit even for a horse that had been steadily earning his keep. Not to be sniffed at certainly. "Aye," the stableman said. "I'd be agreeable."

"Then we must have a bill of sale," Suki told him and sensing that the lack of one in Johnny-Jo's case was due to Mr Wenham's illiteracy, she offered, "I'll write un for you if you wish, if you'll fetch pen and paper."

It was fetched and a careful document written, agreeing . . .

The bay stallion known as Beau is henceforth

the property of Suki Brown of Lambton farm in
Twerton, having been stabled with Mr Wenham of
Wenham's Stables Broad Quay for . . .

"How many months, did you say?"

"Now as to that," Mr Wenham said, thinking so hard
he had to hold his face with both hands to keep it from
nodding, "'twould be around six, as I recall. He left in
harvest time. October, 'twas. They were in a parlous
hurry to get the ship away on account of the trade
winds."

"Which ship was that?" Suki asked, seizing her chance
for more information. "Do you recall the name?"

He was delighted to think that his knowledge was
greater than hers. "Don't 'ee know?" He tried mocking
her a little. "I'd ha' thought you'd ha' knowed your own
husband's ship."

It was a tricky moment, but she spoke through it
easily. "He sails on so many ships," she said. "I forgets
the names of 'em. He do tell me, but I forgets."

"I got a better memory than you then, me dear, for
I remembers it clear. Every blamed detail. The *Bonny
Beaufoy*. That was the ship. Belongs to Mr Smith the
banker. I remembers his name too. Mr Jedediah Smith.
Sailed *with* her, as I recall, which I don't see the sense
of, bein' 'tis a mortal hard crossing."

The details were being written.

. . . having sailed on the *Bonny Beaufoy* out of
Bristol being the ship of one Mr Smith, banker.
All costs of fodder ate by the stallion Beau, are
now clear and paid for.

"There you are Mr Wenham, if you'll put your mark

12

just here below where I've signed, 'twill be all cor-
rect."

"Which I s'pose you'll want to ride un home," Mr
Wenham said, when he'd appended his cross.

She hadn't thought of riding this great beast – ambling
along on Farmer Lambton's old mare had been difficult
enough – but now it was being suggested she had to agree
to it, even though it meant hoisting up her skirts in the
most immodest way in order to sit astride Jack's high
saddle. What did it matter? She had bought the horse and
she would find his owner. It was just a matter of seeking
out the shipping office and asking the right questions.

Pretending to horsemanship, she clicked Beau into
walking, touching his flanks gently with her heels,
remembering how easily Jack had ridden him, all those
months ago. To her delight, he went where she led
and stopped quietly when she reined him in outside
the shipping office, which had been easy to find from
such a splendidly high vantage point. She was charmed
to notice that he came to a halt right beside the mounting
block where he stood obediently, almost as though he
knew she would need the use of it.

The office was so crowded she required a fierce face
and considerable pushing to fight her way to the counter.
But once there, her request was taken seriously.

"Yes," the shipping clerk confirmed, consulting his
ledger. "We do have news of the vessel. The *Bonny
Beaufoy*. Yes. Here 'tis. Sailed in October and left the
slave coast in February. The owner had letters from the
Bissagos Islands to that effect. She'm expected back in
Bristol some time between May and July, depending."

She thanked him rapturously – May! May! Next
month! A matter of weeks – and rode back to the high
street, singing with pure joy.

13

Annie was sitting in the cart waiting anxiously and crossly. "Where you been, you bad gal?" she said. "What you doin' on that great horse?"

Suki was still bubbling with happiness. "I bought un."

"What nonsense!" Annie said, and her voice was sour. "I thought you were supposed to be buyin' cloth for your babba. You can't just go about buying horses. 'Taren't fitting."

"Well I've bought un," Suki said, stroking the horse's neck. "He's mine. Arn't you Beau?"

"Where d'you get the money from?"

"I used the bank note."

Annie's eyes widened in astonishment and disbelief. "All that money on a horse. You must have took leave of your senses. You'll not have a penny piece to spend all spring and summer. And William growing so. I wonder at 'ee Suki Brown. I truly do. And what will 'ee do with it, now you've got it? Tell me that. 'Twill need stabling an' fodder an' grooming. Have 'ee thought of that?"

Suki hadn't thought of anything except rescue. "I shall speak to Mr Lambton," she decided. He had stable room a-plenty and would understand what a fine horse Beau was and what a bargain she'd got. Wouldn't he?

Annie was coughing with distress and annoyance. "You've made us late," she complained, "an those two poor babbas awaitin', an' all you've done is buy a horse! Walk on Mr Jones, if you please. I don't know what Mr Lambton will say."

Mr Lambton laughed out loud, his brown face wrinkled with delight at her daring. "What a spirit you have," he said. "We never know what to expect of 'ee." He agreed that Beau was a fine strong horse and saw how badly he'd been treated. "He'll be out of place on a

14

farm," he pointed out, "for he'll not pull plough or cart. But I could ride him to market, I daresay. And so could you."

So Beau was given stable room "until you gets sent for or the Captain comes for him". And Suki's immediate problems seemed to be resolved.

Annie wasn't pleased. She was weary after her day on the road and her conscience was troubling her for leaving her Precious all on his own for so long – even if he *did* have Molly with him. "Have you thought of the expense, Mr Lambton?" she asked and the question was a complaint. "'Twill cost us dear, a great horse like that."

"He shall cover our young mare, while he's here," the farmer said. "We could get a fine strong foal out of him. Think of that, my dear."

Annie wasn't mollified. "I think 'twill be a good thing when she'm sent for and goes off to join those fine Bradburys of hers," she said. "Horse indeed. She'm a sight too bold for the likes of us."

"You were glad of her company when Constant was born," the farmer pointed out, "and pleaded for her to stay when I would have had her move on."

But she was coughing too much to answer him, so he let the matter drop out of pity for her. A strong foal would more than make up for a few weeks' fodder and Suki herself would soon be off with the Bradburys, and might well take the animal with her, which would solve all their problems.

Suki's fine Sir George Bradbury was actually in Bristol that very afternoon. He'd travelled down with Sir Arnold Willoughby and the Honourable Sir Humphrey de Thespia in order to inspect their biggest and most impressive privateer, the three-masted frigate called *Yorick*, and to give instructions to her master for her first sailing, which was to be to Nevis to escort the Bradburys' sugar crop home and protect it from the French.

The ship had been transformed since Sir George first saw her languishing at the head of Broad Quay. Now, agleam with new black paint, her decks scrubbed white, her rigging fresh, her sails neatly furled and with the formidable addition of sixteen brass cannon, she looked every inch the man-o'-war and a most impressive vessel. It gratified them all that she was the centre of admiration and gossip the length of the quay.

"She's proved a handsome purchase, Georgie," Sir Arnold said. "Damme if she ain't. She'll do well for us." Her second sailing was to be to Portugal to protect the cargo of oak beams and quality cloth that he and Sir Humphrey were currently amassing in the port of London, so his interest was keen.

Fitting her out had cost a great deal more than Sir George's original estimate, which considering the depleted state of his finances should have given him cause for concern, especially as he had a wedding to pay for in the autumn. But in fact, he was glowingly content, beaming at their fine ship and rubbing his hands with satisfaction. Taking financial risks excited him. It made him aware of his acumen and courage. And besides, he was basking in the reflected glory of his prospective son-in-law's dazzling company, having learned during the last six months that the young man was renowned and feared and admired wherever he went.

He seemed to have an influential relation in every town and city they visited. Today he had arrived with his impressive retinue to take up temporary residence with an aunt who lived in one of the prestigious new houses in Queen's Square, and had insisted that his two friends should join him there for dinner, which sent the poor old lady into a tizzy of anxiety. Now stooping delicately backwards as he ascended the gangplank of their splendid ship, he was the focus of all eyes, like the principal actor at a play.

Sir George and Sir Arnold followed at a respectful distance, Sir George looking back over his shoulder to address some happy remark to his old friends and to enjoy the stir they were causing. As he turned he caught sight of a face he thought he recognised.

"Who's that?" he said. "Feller in a brown bob wig. Looks familiar, damme if he don't."

Sir Arnold glanced back too. "Not a man of my acquaintance, me dear," he said. "Nor yours neither, judging by the look of him."

There was something disquieting about the man's pointed stare, something that made Sir George think of being beaten about the head and stitched by some fool surgeon. He frowned and bit his lip, trying to remember. "He looks this way."

"Ignore him," Sir Arnold advised. "'Tis an idle fellow. A poor tradesman or a bounty hunter or some such. Suchlike wretches are ten a penny hereabouts."

They could hear Sir Humphrey drawling a greeting to the ship's master. "Mr Swann, your sarvant sir." So they had to join him and leave the man in the brown wig behind. But his disturbance echoed in Sir George's mind.

The master was given orders to sail to Nevis with all speed, to wait there until the sugar ships were loaded and to escort the cargo home. He was moreover, as Sir George told him happily, "to engage such French ships as should put in an appearance and give 'em a good trouncing." He expressed himself mindful of the importance of his mission and promised to obey it "to the letter, sirs, to the very letter."

"We wish 'ee God speed," Sir Humphrey said, bowing in his exquisite style.

"Aye sir," Sir George echoed. "So we do sir. That's the ticket, damme. Fair winds, fine weather and God speed." And he found himself wondering what speed the *Bonny Beaufoy* was making, and how many slaves she'd lost, and what sort of price they would make in the Windwards, and how well old Jedediah was managing to ration the food stocks. I'm a man of action, he thought, mopping the sweat from his forehead, damme if I ain't.

Two

The *Bonny Beaufoy* was becalmed. She'd sat in the same flat, filthy patch of water for the last seven days, waiting for a breeze that never came and now the sea was beginning to rot around her. Strands of thick weed lay heaped and motionless on the surface of the water, brown and oily and entangled, and above her empty masts the sky burned in an endless, maddening blue, with no cloud to soften its glare.

Without movement, the heat was intense and the smell from the holds so nauseating that Jack had been allowing the slaves out on deck for most of the day, even though their sores festered in the sunlight and the smell they carried with them was as miasmic above decks as below. After three more storms and an outbreak of shaking sickness, they'd lost six of the crew and were down to a hundred and sixty-two male slaves – all unshackled save for six who were too violent – and forty-one females, which made for an impossible crush on deck. But at least the holds could be sweetened a little in their absence, and that was done every day, although their stock of vinegar was running parlously low. Lack of vinegar was the least of their worries. Their drinking water was coated with green slime, the maize barrel was full of weevils, and their diet was much reduced because all their livestock had been killed and eaten long ago. Slaves and crew alike were unshaven and unwashed for there was no wish to add to the debris floating beside them. Consequently many of them were suffering from boils and many more were too weak and lethargic to do more than sit in what little shade they could find and wait.

The dead days passed in slow hot enervating seconds. Buckets were emptied at the heads every morning but the filth lay in the weed and didn't disperse. The decks were foul for lack of a good scrub and sluice, the gunwales brown with grease. On the fourth day swarms of black flies arrived to crawl over the decks and breed in the weedstrewn water, and soon obscene grey grubs and worms like blood-threads emerged from the leathery coils to creep and wriggle as they fed upon the filth.

By day they buzzed and rustled and the noise of their pressing lives echoed through the ship as though they were consuming the very planks. At night they lit the thickened darkness of the weed with small sharp pulses of light, blood red, rheum yellow and poison green. It was as if they were laying seige to the ship and everything in it, gathering force to consume it, plank by shrinking plank, wood, brass, canvas, blood, flesh and bone, swelling bruises, running sores, rotting corpses and all. For, as if their predicament weren't bad enough, there were three dead slaves stinking in the weed a mere four hundred yards away, still lying in the spot where they had been dumped over the side on that first becalmed day when they all thought the lull was going to be temporary.

To Jack Daventry, every moment was an extension of the nightmare that had begun when the big feller was torn apart by the sharks. At the start of the voyage, when he'd been knocked breathless by the force of the first gales, he'd prayed in terror for a calm sea. Now, with the sails slack and without a breath of wind, with nausea racking him night and day, and a continual stink in his nostrils, he yearned for full sails and leaping speed and would have given all his earnings for the slap of a wave against the hull. Sometimes, as tempers frayed and sharp angry arguments broke out among the crew, and females were used so roughly that they wept, and slaves were kicked out of the way for no other reason than that they were there, he felt as though the world had been turned inside out, that reason and civilised behaviour were lost, and that they were all descending into the savagery they deplored. Occasionally and even more pessimistically he suspected that everything would go by opposites and grow steadily worse, and that they would die stuck in this hellhole.

Nothing in this voyage had turned out as he'd expected. He'd taken the job to make an easy fortune and so far all that had happened to him was that he'd worked a deal too hard and come a deal too close to losing his life. He'd expected to be the master of these slaves and had become little more than their servant, cleaning their filth, shaving their chins, feeding them their two meals a day, even disposing of their dead bodies. He'd expected speed and adventure and success, and had found an eternity of stinking boredom. It was a daily torment, impossible and cruel, and he could have been completely cast down by it, if it hadn't have been for the baby.

On the fourth day of the lull, the blue-eyed boy climbed out of the hatch with a new-born baby in his arms. All that day, he and his mother crouched by the fo'castle, sheltering the little creature with a torn piece of tarpaulin as it lay in its mother's lap and watching over it with a purity of concern that was totally at odds with the filth and stink around it. From time to time, it gave

21

an odd mewing cry and was lifted gently until it could find its mother's nipple and feed, but apart from that the only sound from the group of women clustered around it was a flutter of hands brushing the flies away, a murmur of admiration and approval, a gentling of baby worship that was plainly sustaining them. Until that day, they'd been taut and full of alarm, afraid of their captors and scolding their children if they dared to move so much as an inch away. Now they all moved about with a peculiar ease. Even the corn mill ground more gently.

By the seventh day, the infant had become a sort of talisman. Jack found himself watching for it every morning, scanning the woolly heads of the females as they emerged from the hatch and holding all his emotions in reserve until the blue-eyed boy had eased out with his little kicking burden. He was delighted when the infant grew, privately applauding as its new-born wrinkles smoothed and its little stick legs grew more rounded, and watching it suckle was comforting. It reminded him of all the peaceful beasts he'd seen in the farms and fields when he was a child: of cats suckling kittens, calves nudging their mothers' teats, lambs leaping long-tailed and stiff-legged to be fed. He couldn't help feeling that if this infant could survive, the lull would lift and they would sail again. He recognised that the idea was mere superstition but he thought it daily just the same.

Unfortunately, his crewmates didn't share his opinion. The cook complained that there was no call to give the woman extra portions. "'Twill all go to waste," he said, slopping the stew pot down on its trivet on the deck. "The brat will die, sure as God made little apples, an' the sooner the better to my way of thinking. I can't be doing with 'em, nasty squally critturs."

The purser had an even tougher opinion. "We should

22

chuck it over the side," he said. "Here an' now. The sooner 'tis gone, the sooner she can get back to earning her keep, which she should've been a-doin' long since. As 'tis, she'm a waste of space and fodder."

The lull had sharpened Jack's perceptions. He saw at once that the purser wanted to use her himself and that he would kill the infant without a second thought. "Belike," he allowed. "But I'd rather keep it alive until we move. Three bodies a-rottin' alongside is enough for me. Or for any man else, I dare swear."

Mr Smith was looking at the blue-eyed slave, calculating. "If the female's out of bounds, damme," he said, flicking away a pair of flies that were coupling on his forearm, "I'll have him. I've got the itch something prodigious. It must be met one way or another."

In other days and other places, Jack would have accepted the man's decision as evidence of his human need, perverted but not open to question. Here, with his own sensibilities sharpened to snapping point, he opposed it, instinctively and with abhorrence. "No sir," he said. "I think not."

The purser swore at him. "'Od's bowels! Am I to be allowed no pleasure at all?" And as Jack hesitated. "Answer me that!"

There would have to be a reason and a good one, as Jack was well aware. It was in his mouth before the purser had finished roaring. "The slave is mine."

That was a surprise. "How yours?"

"He is my entitlement. My choice."

"Then you'm a bigger fool than you look," the purser roared, delighted to be able to say so. "He'm a half-caste, damme. And a child moreover. You'll not get any sort of price for him, if you can sell him at all. I tell 'ee what, sir, swap him for one of those big strong fellers an' I'll take him off your hands for you and no hard feelings."

"No, sir," Jack insisted stubbornly. "He's mine and will remain so."

"Then let me throw the brat over the side and take the female."

Jack set his jaw. "No, sir. You know my mind. 'Tain't to be done and there's an end on it."

It was not. Nor could it be. The purser's authority had been challenged and, as part-owner of the ship, that couldn't be permitted. He returned to the attack at every opportunity and in every sort of company, from the surgeon to the captain.

Mr Dix was no help to him. He'd heard that there was a dispute between the purser and Mr Daventry and was disposed to take the younger man's part.

"I'd throw it overboard if 'twere fractious," he told the purser, having cast a professional eye over the new-born. "But 'tis quiet enough for the time bein' an' a fine healthy child, in all conscience, which 'twould be a pity to waste. He could add to the price of the female."

Mr Tomson was more direct. "I leaves all such matters to my slave master," he said, twiddling the ringlets in his beard, "bein' as that's what we pays him for. Which I'd advise you to do the same, sir, and leave well alone."

The lull continued: heat, stink and bad temper increased; the infant fed and thrived, and was beneficently quiet; and the quarrel simmered on.

Soon they were into their eleventh day of inaction. That morning they woke to a new smell and a new fear.

Mr Dix had been below making one of his regular inspections while the first fifty slaves were fed and watered on deck. When he emerged from the hold, his expression was so grave and the stink that rose with him so sour that Jack knew at once that his news would be bad. The old medicine man was blind in one eye, which had "clouded over since yesterday" and there were four slaves in a fever with vomiting and the flux.

"Bloody?" Jack asked, having heard enough about this disease to fear it.

"Not yet," the surgeon said grimly, "but 'twill be proved so by nightfall, I fear."

They went to report their findings to the captain, who said he'd feared as much too, "being I could smell it from here. What's to be done, Mr Dix?"

"I've dosed 'em with chalk," the surgeon said, "but I doubt 'twill serve."

"Will it spread, think 'ee?"

"Aye sir, I fear so. There is little we can do to prevent it in such foul air."

Mr Tomson considered, pulling his beard, and then made one of his rapid decisions. "Bring 'em out of the hold, Mr Daventry, if you please. Put 'em by the heads. They'll not last long and 'twill be easier to dispose of 'em from there."

By the time two suitable pieces of canvas had been found, one to act as a ground sheet and shroud, the other to use as a sling, there was a fifth casualty groaning below deck and the bad news had spread through the ship.

Late that night, Jedediah Smith came down to the heads to join Jack and Mr Dix and to demand action. He took care to maintain a sensible distance between himself and the stink for fear of taking infection and he covered his mouth with a scented kerchief, but his order was clear despite his muffled speech.

"'Twill spread like wildfire," he said, his eyes popping

with angry alarm. "Have 'em over the side here and now Mr Dix and have done with it."

"With respect Mr Smith, sir," the surgeon protested, "they ain't dead yet."

"They soon will be," the purser told him. "Hell's teeth Mr Dix. Are we to wait till they've infected us all?"

"I hopes not, sir."

"Very well then. Over the side with 'em. You chucked the baby out quick enough and that was still living, as I recall."

"A brat's one thing," the surgeon said, stung by the reminder. "Five grown slaves is another, being they'm worth good money if we can recover 'em."

"And if we can't, they will infect us all. You can't deny it. We shall die out here in this stinking cesspit with none to help us and none to know of it. Where's the profit in that? Have 'em over the side."

The surgeon did the only thing that was possible in the circumstances. He turned to the slave master. "How say you, Mr Daventry?"

"Yes, sir," the purser echoed. "How say you?"

To be deferred to by these two men was a moment of almost pure elation to Jack Daventry. It was inopportune, there was no denying that. He would rather they'd consulted him on any other matter and at any other time, but it was rewarding nevertheless – well earned, long overdue. Remembered scenes tumbled pride and justification in his mind. The insufferable lordliness of the purser when he'd first come aboard, his odious behaviour over the female and the blue-eyed boy, his greed at table – and now he was reduced to asking advice of Jack Daventry, praise be.

"The scraggy one is dead already, if I'm any judge," he said, bending to examine his charges. "And t'other is far gone. He don't groan you notice. I agree with Mr Dix. We shall have two corpses to be rid of by sundown."

"Be rid of all five," Mr Smith insisted, "or we might as well sign our own death warrants here and now."

The thought of throwing a live man over the side made Jack flinch. "We will wait till darkness," he decided. "'Tain't a thing to be done in daylight. The rest will be below, save for the watch, and there will be enough of a moon to see by. I will make a final decision then, sir."

The purser actually called him a "stout feller".

They lowered the longboat at a little after midnight, taking a crew of six to row them and all five slaves, wrapped in their canvas sheet – two dead, one dying and two so far gone in delirium that they couldn't see, although their eyes were open. The weed was so thick that rowing was extremely difficult but the moon was as bright as a chandelier and dropped a straight silver path across the black water to guide them on their way.

Jack sat in the stern, between the surgeon and the purser, silent and brooding, with a loaded pistol in his belt and murder in his heart. To throw a live creature overboard to drown was a sin whichever way he looked at it, but did he have the right to refuse to do it when all the other lives in the ship depended upon it being done? If the worst came to the worst and the creatures struggled, he could give the *coup de grâce* with a shot from his pistol. There was risk in it, for the sound of the shots would wake the ship. And 'twould be murder assuredly. But they would die in any event. They were as good as dead already. Not like to survive the night. And if they did 'twould only be for a day or two. And yet . . .

Images of the big feller tore at his mind. He saw him again, threshing and screaming in that obscene whirlpool of blood and spume, fighting for his life as his limbs were ripped from his body. He cringed again under his own dreadful powerlessness, was seared by the knowledge of his responsibility, ached to weep at the remembered terror of it.

"Well, sir?" the purser asked.

They had travelled the appointed distance. It was time. The thing had to be done. He had to decide to do it.

"Put in the ballast," he ordered, and when that was done and none of the creatures struggled. "Bind 'em up."

"All of 'em, sir?" one of the seamen asked.

"Aye, sir. All of 'em. None will last till morning. They're best out of their misery."

But for all his air of authority and calm decision, he was shaking as the heavy canvas was rolled over the side. And that night he lay wakeful in his bunk, afraid to sleep for fear of the nightmare that was pressing down upon him. He was glad when the daylight broke and he could creep up on deck and smoke a calming pipe. Like everything else on board, his stock of tobacco was running low, but that morning need was greater than prudence. He sat with his back against the main mast and his pistol reassuringly against his thigh and tried to prepare himself for whatever the day might bring.

At the change of the watch, he went below to check the slaves. There was no sound of groaning, which was encouraging, and no sign of the flux. The medicine man's eyes were oozing pus and the stink of the buckets was as foul as usual but there was nothing worse. Much relieved he walked to the galley to check stocks for the morning meal, and found that they were inadequate and that the cook was complaining, but that was usual too. So far so good. Back on deck, he opened the hatches to the female quarter and watched for the blue-eyed boy and his talisman child to emerge, which they did, both well and lively. The day took another quiet movement into normality.

By mid-morning, when he was feeding the second batch of males their limited meal, he had shaken the nightmare from his mind and was quite himself again. So he was unprepared for the sudden outburst that erupted by the fo'castle. The screams were so piercing that he left the porridge pot and ran to see what was happening.

Mr Jedediah Smith was standing over the tarpaulin that sheltered the infant, although it was impossible to see whether the child was still there, because the women were standing in an angry phalanx all around it, screaming at him as he tried to punch them out of the way. "I'll take the cat to 'ee!" he yelled at them. "Devil take it, get out of my way or you'll know the worst."

The noise had already attracted the crew, and several of them had ambled over in hope of seeing a flogging. Jack had to push through quite a crowd before he could reach the scene.

"How now?" he said, when he was standing beside the purser. "What's this?"

Mr Smith turned a flushed face towards him. "The brat is sick," he said, "and must be dealt with. She'll not hand it over."

Jack looked round for the baby and his mother. The females were bristling with protective anger and stood so close together that it was impossible to see beyond their bodies. The blue-eyed boy was crouched on the deck at their feet. He carried his head with the tremulous alertness of an animal that knows it is hunted, and he was looking around him, his odd blue eyes darting from side to side. He's searching for his mother and the baby, Jack thought. Checking that they're still safe. But where were they?

Then he saw the female. She was sitting calmly behind the protective wall of all those determined legs with the baby cuddled against her breast and she was murmuring to it and gazing at it with an expression of such melting tenderness that Jack felt his bowels yearn at the sight. Oh to be cared for like that. Gentled so. Loved so. He was charged with envy and admiration, pricked by regret for the callousness of the previous night, stirred to anger at the ugly greed of the purser, spurred to a sudden, irrational determination to protect this child and his mother come what may. In one second his emotions coalesced into action.

"On whose authority, sir?" he said.

Mr Smith recognised that battle had been joined and answered powerfully. "Mine, sir, since I own this ship and everything that sails in her. If I say the child is to be handed over, I'm to be obeyed."

"No, sir," Jack said, standing astride and in front of the slaves, with his fingers on the handle of the pistol. "I think not. You don't own me, sir, nor do you have authority over these slaves, not while I am slave master."

"Hell's teeth! Am I to be told me business by a jumped-up puppy with no breeding? I think not, sir. I think not. Damn your eyes! Now get out of my way, sir. 'Tis my slave and I mean to have her. You'll not bar me from my rights. If I say the brat is to be dealt with, I shall deal with it, and you'll not prevent it. Make way I tell 'ee. Damn your eyes!"

Jack refused to move. "The child is not sick," he said, his face set, "and consequently needs no attention. He is to be left with his mother."

"Mother! Mother!" the purser mocked. "What do they know of motherhood? They're just cattle."

30

"No, sir," Jack said hotly. "You are wrong. They are human. As you and I are human."

The purser roared with delighted horror to hear anything so preposterous. "The feller's mad!" he said to his audience. "I never heard the like. Human! The very idea!"

They agreed with him, mocking and cat-calling. Whoever heard the like? To call a savage human. The feller *was* mad. "Took the heat, I shouldn't wonder," the bosun said.

Much encouraged, the purser turned to bullying. "Get out of my way, lunatic," he shouted, looking back at his audience to enjoy the impression he was making, "or I'll have 'ee sent to Bedlam, damme."

Jack pulled the pistol from his belt, cocked it and held it towards the purser's head. It was done so quickly and with such expertise that Mr Smith missed it altogether while he was looking for admiration, and few of the seamen realised what was happening until the gun was levelled. But none of them could miss the chill of command in his voice.

"I think not, sir," he said quietly. "Nor will you take this baby."

"Hell's teeth!" the purser said and this time it was no mean oath. "I'll have you in irons, sir." And he turned to the nearest sailor and gave his own commands. "Seize him!"

The sailor hesitated. Looked at Jack. And didn't move.

"Don't just stand there," the purser roared at him. "Seize him, you dog! Why do you wait?"

"Well, sir, 'tis like this here, sir," the sailor explained, avoiding his master's eyes but making his point notwithstanding. "If we puts the slave master in irons for 'ee, sir, who'll do his work? 'Tis mortal hard work he'm a-doing."

The purser was spitting with anger. "Devil take 'ee! Do as I say or I'll have 'ee flogged sir."

This time, the sailor shifted as though he was about to take a step forward but, as soon as he moved, Jack turned the pistol in his direction. "Lay so much as a finger on me, sir," he said, "and I'll blow your head off."

Flogging was to be preferred to decapitation.

"'Od's bowels!" the purser roared. "Ain't there a one of you man enough to take him?"

Apparently not. "Not with that there pistol in his hand, sir."

It was impasse and it froze them all into inaction, slave and master alike. They were so still that they could hear the insects buzzing and clicking in the weed, and the little lick, lick of water against the hull.

The little lick, lick of water! "There's a breeze, me hearties!" Mr Reuben yelled. "We've got a breeze!"

The captain was among them, giving orders. "Clear the decks! Get those slaves below! Set the spinnaker, Mr Reuben."

The quarrel was forgotten in instant activity, the slaves hustled below, fed or not, sails unfurled and set to catch the least movement in the air. And at last, at long, long, exhausted last they began to move, inch by tantalising inch, timbers groaning. The lull was over.

Within an hour, they were beginning to pick up a little speed and had left their filth behind. Within two, they were under full sail. By the end of the afternoon, they were back in the bounding force of the trade winds.

The transformation aboard ship was total, as they relaxed in the triple blessing of fair weather, abundant clean water and a strong slip-stream. Nobody was flogged, the cook didn't grumble about his poor rations, the crew obeyed orders without demur. Soon the decks had been scrubbed until they were white again and the gunwales were scraped clean. Everybody on board took it in turns to wash and the barber worked all day and every day until there wasn't an unwanted beard to be seen in any part of the ship and all the male slaves were youthfully clean-shaven. Boils healed and tempers calmed. The infant lay in a cooling breeze and was fed and admired. The blue-eyed boy took to following Jack about, eager for odd jobs, which was sometimes useful and occasionally embarrassing. Best of all, nobody mentioned the stand-to. It was almost as if they'd forgotten all about it.

Except for the purser himself. He took his complaint to the captain as soon as the ship was comfortably under way.

Mr Tomson heard him out and then gave his considered judgement. "Well now, sir, Mr Smith," he said. "I takes your point and so forth, but the fact of the matter is this. The man does a good job of work with our cattle, no matter what his lunatic opinion of 'em, and so forth. If we was to put un in irons, who'd look after the cattle an' feed 'em and doctor 'em and clean 'em up, an' so forth? I tell you plainly, sir, I'd not do the work for all the tea in China, and I doubt you'd volunteer for it neither. No, sir, the way I looks at it is this. Leave him be to work on for the rest of the voyage. Then when he'm landed and the slaves are sold, you can have him back to England in as many irons as you choose and bring him afore a magistrate and so forth, to your heart's content."

It wasn't the answer the purser wanted and he argued long and angrily against it, pointing out that the man had pulled a gun on him and wasn't to be trusted, that he was

33

running mad and a danger to the ship. But the captain was adamant and in the end Jedediah had to accept his decision whether he would or no.

"You want to watch your back," Mr Reuben warned, early one morning, when he and Jack were on watch together. "You made an enemy with that there pistol of yourn."

Jack had already faced the fact that there would be consequences to his defiance, so he could afford to be casual about it. "What of it?"

"Watch your back, that's all," the bosun repeated. "'Tis a mean-minded old swabber and means to have 'ee in irons. Take advice from one what knows."

"I've got his measure, Mr Reuben, don't 'ee worry. He'll not get the better of me. Have I not come through the jungle fever and outbid old Wan Four and cleaned the holds more times than I've had hot suppers? I'll not be put down by a purser, no matter how much money he's got a-jingling in his breeches."

"What of the boy?" Mr Reuben asked, looking at the blue-eyed slave, who was sitting at Jack's feet as he usually did these days. "He follows you about like a little pet dog. Shall you keep him?"

"Well as to that," Jack said patting the child's woolly head, "I shall see."

"Watch you don't get bit," the bosun warned, alarmed by such contact. "I wouldn't touch narry a one of 'em, if I was you."

Jack looked at his slave, who was smiling seraphically, his teeth like ivory between wide dark lips, his face moulded into placatory circles. "Not this one," he said. "He'll not bite. Will you, sir?"

Then an extraordinary thing happened. The slave looked up as though he was listening, and suddenly spoke, not with the usual clicking, gonging sounds that they expected but with a single, recognisably English word. "Bite?" he said. "Bite?" The questioning inflection was plain.

Jack was so surprised that for a moment he couldn't answer. Did this child understand what was being said? Could he speak English? Or was he mimicking like a poll parrot? If a bird could do such a thing, could a savage?

The word was repeated, this time with more insistence. "Bite?" There was no doubt about his understanding now.

"Bite," Jack explained, and he put his hand to his mouth and mimed, taking his forefinger between his teeth and pretending to snap at it. "Bite. Snap, snap."

"Bite," the slave said with satisfaction and smiled his broad smile. "Bite. Snap, snap."

He's quick, Jack thought and before he could stop to consider the propriety of what he was doing, he spoke again. "Jack," he said pointing to himself. "I am Jack."

The slave seemed to understand that too. "Jack," he repeated and beating a black hand against his own rib cage, "Oleanda."

"Well blow me down!" Mr Reuben said. "Here's a thing! Is that his name d'you reckon?"

"I shall never remember it, if 'tis," Jack laughed. "Howsomever that's a matter can be remedied." He turned to the slave again. "I am Jack," he repeated. "You are Blue. Understand. Blue. You are Blue."

"Blue," the slave said, smiling again. "Oleanda Blue."

The ship's bell was ringing the end of the watch. "Come with me, Blue," Jack said. "We've work to do." He didn't beckon, because there was no need. He knew he would be understood. "I reckon I could teach him to speak like a linguist, Mr Reuben. What

35

do 'ee think to that? He be a trifle more than a pet then."

The boy worked all morning with the rest of the slaves, swabbing the decks with sea water and brushing vigorously. From time to time, he would look up from the streams of water at his feet, hold his arm to his mouth and say "Bite! Bite!" laughing aloud as though the very idea was an irresistible joke. "Bite! Bite!"

As the days passed the impromptu lessons continued and became more frequent, for as Jack soon discovered the newly named Blue had a thirst for learning and wanted every object named, touching sails, mast and spars with a query on his face, bringing lesser objects to lay at Jack's feet. "Marlin spike", "belaying pin", "spoon", "bowl", repeating the words until he could pronounce them properly. He learnt fast. By the end of that first free-sailing week, he had accepted his new name and understood the use of the personal pronoun: "I Blue, you Jack, she Umumi." By the end of a fortnight he understood "up" and "down", "here" and "there", and had begun to use verbs. "You thirst?" "I thirst." He had even ventured into the complications of the English auxiliary verb. "You are thirsty?"

At the start of the third week, they managed their first conversation.

The evening meal was over and the tubs and spoons were being collected, when one of the male slaves walked across to the empty stew pot and began to beat a rhythm on its side with his wooden spoon as if it was a drum. It was an infectious sound and since the cook wasn't on deck to complain and Jack raised no objections, another man walked over and joined in, this time drumming the side of the pot with both hands and in a different rhythm. The sound instantly became faster and more complicated. The stew pot throbbed as both men beat with their hands and stamped with their feet. The slaves gathered, at first hesitantly, then with a happy insistence, until they'd formed a semi-circle before the drummers. A third man drifted to join them, his mouth slightly open as if he was in a trance, and for a moment on-beats and off-beats seemed to be working against each other, nudging and colliding. Then they suddenly came together in a single pounding rhythm and a woman began to dance.

The effect was electrifying for as she threw herself into the rhythm, arms raised and feet stamping, all the other women began to clap, swaying from side to side like a chorus. More and more hands joined in, and the speed of their syncopated rhythm grew faster and faster as the noise increased. Soon the woman was dancing bent double, with her body thrust forward, and her outstretched arms flailing, and her knees rising almost to her chin with every pounding step. She looked like a huge brown bird, struggling to fly.

She must stop soon, Jack thought, or she'll be exhausted. She can't go on like this for ever. But even as the thought was in his head, she let her arms drop and fell back laughing into the crowd, and another woman took her place, dancing in the same way and with the same total abandon. After that, the women threw themselves into the circle one after the other, some in twos and threes, some on their own, but all dancing in the same way, arms outstretched and feet pounding. Now and then the drummers would stop in mid-beat and pause to rest, and the dancers would be carried by the clapping of the crowd. Sweat poured down their faces, their arms fanned the air, and still the drummers beat and still they danced.

37

"They are like birds," Jack said. And was instantly asked to explain the word to his slave. "Bird," he said, miming flight. "Bird," pointing up at the sky. "They fly. Up there. Up and away."

Blue understood him completely. "Yes," he said. "She is bird. She is not here. She is bird. She fly."

"As I thought to do once," Jack told him. "I thought I was an eagle." He remembered the evening the *Bonny Beaufoy* had left Bristol and how he'd felt he was flying into the setting sun. "'Twas all folly, Blue. I was never an eagle." The pistol was heavy against his thigh. "A fighting cock perhaps, but not an eagle."

Blue had listened without comprehension. "What is eagle?" he asked.

"A great bird," Jack told him. "And we are but earthbound men. Human. Not birds. For we cannot fly away." And it seemed to him that he had said something profoundly true.

Three

It was June and the city of Bath was preening itself for the start of the summer season. The king was in Windsor and the ton were entertaining at their summer retreats, but the slave-owning gentry were assembling in their customary watering place and the city stood ready to receive them. Sunshine filled the welcoming honeycomb of the Pump Room, and slanted in above the King's Bath to stripe the walls with brightness and make the gilded columns shine. It was June.

Sir George Bradbury was still in London with Sir Humphrey, supervising the loading of their third cargo for Lisbon, which had been purchased from the profits of the first two and which they hoped would prove even more lucrative. But Lady Bradbury had arrived in South Parade the previous afternoon, and now, having taken the tinny waters for the first disagreeable time, was happily cleansing her palate with tea and bath buns, while she regaled her dear friend Arabella with news of Ariadne's conquest.

Arabella was the most rewarding of friends. As the little orchestra produced its neat patterns of sound behind them and teacups clinked and voices rose in giggling cadences, she expressed her happiness at Ariadne's good fortune, with every indication that she meant what she said. Hermione felt she had never begun a summer so well.

"Where do you intend to hold the wedding?" Arabella asked, knowing that this was just what Hermione would want to divulge.

"At the Church of St James, in Piccadilly, at the end of September," Hermione said with studied carelessness. She had written to her father to tell him the good news and had received an acknowledgement, which was uncommon gratifying, and the promise that the wedding "would be attended". He hadn't actually specified who would attend but the promise was enough and might well turn out to be the first step towards the reconciliation she desired so much. "The Daventry family are usually married at St James, as you know. We could hardly break with tradition."

Arabella agreed at once and sipped her tea. "I trust we shall see the bride in Bath this summer," she said. "And Melissa, too, of course. How happy she must be for her dear sister!"

"I left them sleeping," Hermione said, assuming a smile of motherly concern. "The journey down was most fatiguing. But they have promised on their honour that they will join me here within the hour."

She would have been surprised to know that Ariadne was up, dressed, and ready to leave the house and that Hepzie, who had been given strict instructions to accompany her wherever she went, was now being given peremptory and contradicting commands.

"Melissa will be awake directly," Ariadne said, prodding her sleeping sister in the ribs. "You are to stay here and help her to dress. Be quick about it or she'll be late for the baths."

Hepzie was aggrieved. "Your mama wished me to attend upon *you*," she said." How may I do that if I am to dress Miss Melissa?"

"The wet nurse shall accompany me," Ariadne said casually. "She is to be my personal maid. 'Tis all agreed. Were you not told? She has returned here, has she not?"

Hepzie professed not to know, although she'd watched the wretched girl walk into the kitchen not five minutes ago. Ain't that just like her, she thought angrily. Sticking her oar in. *I'm* the lady's maid. Her place is in the nursery.

In fact, Suki was still in the kitchen and doing her best to wash her son in case milady wanted to see him. It was difficult because he was doing *his* best to wriggle away from her. He was nearly fourteen months old and a strong plump baby with a lusty voice and great determination. And as he'd been toddling for several weeks, he was irked by all this unnecessarily immobilising hygiene.

"Come along, William," Suki coaxed. "Have your pretty face washed like a good boy, an' then you shall have some nice titty to make up for it."

"He'll go off bang, one of these days, you keep on feedin' him the way you do," Barnaby rebuked.

"Don't you pay that Barnaby no mind," Cook said, pumping water vigorously. "You give the little thing all the titty he can take. Pretty soul! Lor, what a mess this kitchen is. Don't they scour nothin' here in wintertime? That's a temptation to cockroaches, that is. Now where's that gel? Bessie! Dawdlin' again. You'll miss the pick of the market, you don't get off direct. And what milady'll say then, I do not dare to think."

Bessie had slept badly after her journey and was drooping with fatigue. "I does me best, mum, I'm sure," she pleaded. "Can't do no more."

"We'll go to market together," Suki promised. "Many hands make light work." It was the chance to slip across

41

to the Captain's lodgings. If his ship had returned, he might even be at home. Oh she couldn't wait.

"I'm that grateful, Suki," Bessie said, as they pushed their way into the crowds. "That market fair sets my head to spinnin'. I can't get accustomed to a multitude. That I can't. Not nohow."

They'd certainly chosen a squashed moment to set off. The streets were crowded with perspiring chairs packed against straining carriages, and pedestrians, passengers, horses and bearers cramped into strife and confusion because the day's beasts were being driven past them to be butchered: bewildered lambs with coats like clotted cream; sheep bleating piteously, their fleeces matted and bedraggled; frantic pigs squealing between the greasy legs of their red-faced drovers. Above the animals' frightened heads, the rich fat faces that were so soon to devour them complained loudly and arrogantly that their presence was a nuisance.

The market was noisome, too. It had been raining heavily for the past three days, so the ground was slushy with churned-up mud, and the goods were splashed and spotted. It took a long time for the two girls to find fruit and vegetables that were still wholesome enough to suit Cook's most particular palate, and by the time both baskets were full, their skirts were hemmed with mud, despite the fact that they were both wearing pattens. And William had grown uncomfortably heavy on Suki's back.

"Get you off home," she ordered. "I'll follow later. I've another errand to run. I shan't be long." And as soon as Bessie was out of sight, run she did, despite William's weight on her back, as fast as she could to Mrs Roper's.

The inn at the corner of Nowhere Lane was just as

she remembered it, crowded with drovers, who lounged
in the doorway and waded in and out of the churned mud
in the alley, clutching beer mugs and loud with greeting
and argument. But the lodging house was changed. The
front door had been pulled off its hinges, the windows
were open and curtainless, and inside the hall, which
was pungent with the sharp damp smell of new-mixed
plaster, three workmen were busy at the walls, whistling
as they smeared. Beyond their rhythmic arms Suki could
see that the rooms were empty and the staircase ridged
with mud. It was obvious that nobody had been living
in the house for a considerable time and none of the
workmen had heard of Mrs Roper.

"Wasn't the name of the party was it, Jess?" the
foreman said, and the other two shook their heads
without much interest.

"Clerk of the works is upstairs," one said. "You could
try him if you've a mind. Not that he'd know a deal
more'n us."

He turned out to be a short stout man in a well-worn
suit of stained brown fustian and an ancient bob wig
made of very coarse horsehair. He was studying a
crumpled plan, which he'd spread out on the trestle table
before him and pinned into position with four pewter
candlesticks, and he wasn't pleased to be interrupted.

"Be off with 'ee!" he ordered at once, barely giving
her a glance.

"I came to enquire for lodgings, an't please you,
sir," she tried politely, bobbing a curtsey. "My mistress
sent me."

He was partially placated. "No lodgings here, Mistress," he said. "Nor will be till we've made all sound."

"I wonder Mrs Roper didn't send a *billet* to inform my
mistress," Suki tried, as he seemed a little more affable.

43

"Mrs Roper!" he laughed. "My life, you *are* behind the times! Sold out and gone has Mrs Roper. Belongs to Chappell and Winthrop now for all the good it'll do us."

Suki couldn't conceal her annoyance, but she did her best to fish for more information. "What has become of her tenants?" she said.

"Prison belike," the man said. "Or Bedlam, I shouldn't wonder. They were a low crowd, thieves an' card sharpers an' gentlemen of the road, by all accounts. Don't you go bothering your pretty head about tenants. Tell your mistress, Mrs Roper's gone to London. Shut up shop an' gone. Christmas it was. I wonder she didn't write."

Suki was so cross she couldn't bear to stay in the house a minute longer. She banged down the stairs and out into the street, and once there she gave the unhinged door a good kicking to relieve her feelings. What a foolish, stupid woman, she thought, as she shifted William's weight on her back and set off on the long walk back to South Parade. What folly to up sticks and go. Now how am I going to find the Captain? I can hardly ride into Bristol every five minutes to check arrivals, especially now I'm back with the Bradburys and Beau's still on the farm. But how else can I find out if he'm back? I shall need to invent a good excuse to slip away. I wonder whether Miss Ariadne would help me.

And at that moment, she came to Orchard Street and the theatre.

The stage door was firmly shut against the mud, but she could hear banging and shouting from inside the building. Of course, she thought, I'll ask the actors. I never had a chance to ask them last summer and I'm sure they'll help me if they can. He was always in the theatre and they'm uncommon friendly. Encouraged and hopeful again, she beat upon the door.

It was opened by a goblin in red boots, stockings and an ancient leather jerkin so slashed and cut about that it looked more like wickerwork than a pelt. "Are you the eggs?" he demanded, cocking his head to one side, his eyes as bright as a bird's.

Suki told him who she was.

"A pretty demoiselle, be Our Lady," the goblin said, peering at her face. "But witless. Well come in child, come in, if you're a-coming."

"Is it the eggs?" said a voice from the stage, as Suki kicked the mud from her shoes before she stepped inside. It was all as she remembered it from the year before, dusty costumes, tattered scenery, unwashed children, the smell of greasepaint, shrieks and screams. A bower was being dismantled on stage between the pillars, and two of the players were throwing costumes into a skip. The leading lady sat on the edge of the stage in her chemise, eating a loaf of bread and looking fatter than ever.

"We shall starve to death, Charlie, I hope you realise," she complained. "The eggs not come. 'Tis uncommon hard."

The man she was addressing took off his wig and polished his bald head with a yellow handkerchief. "Eggs!" he moaned, rolling his eyes dramatically. "Here's Mr Clements gone a-promenading, the Lord knows where, the Lord knows why, and just when we're packing up, and the cart short by a good two feet – although how that could *possibly* have come about I cannot imagine – and the new scripts not arrived from the copier, and he'm supposed to be the *best* in Bath and promised to deliver 'em before we left, and you speak to me of *eggs*.

S'blood woman, have you no wit to worry me so?" He gave his wig a good shaking, and replaced it with an air so martyred you would have thought it made of thorns. "And what have you come here for, pray," he said to Suki, "if it ain't for eggs?"

"An't please you, sir, I'm looking for Captain Jack. He used to come to the play."

"S'blood!" Charlie drawled, and he threw his head back at such a ridiculous angle that his wig immediately began to slip off his pate, and made a dramatic exit into the wings, sighing like a bellows.

"Brute!" the leading lady roared. "Have you no heart, Charlie? Where would we be without heart? I ask myself. Why nowhere and nothing." And she assumed her stage expression and began to rehearse her lines. "Ah love, sweet love, that blighteth many a heart!" she intoned, clasping her fat hands to her fatter bosom. "Queen of all passions, patroness of pride."

"How I do agree, ma'am," Suki said, seizing the moment. "Without heart, we are truly nothing."

The lady looked at her as though she was having trouble focusing her eyes. "What is it?" she said. "What do you want?"

"You haven't seen Captain Jack about anywhere?" Suki asked, pressing on although the odd look discouraged her.

"No, no," the lady said vaguely, pausing in her speech to flick the words away from her like the irritation they were. "How like th'avenging angel dost thou ride . . . Run along dear, there's a good creature. We open in Bristol tomorrow and there ain't a minute to spare."

She don't care for me a bit, Suki thought, watching the performance. "Where would we be without heart?" indeed. They make a great palaver, blowing kisses from the stage and saying how much they love us all, but 'tis all show.

She shifted William on her back again and wandered away from the empty words and out of the theatre. The actress didn't even see her go.

It was chill in Orchard Street, for the little alley was too narrow for the sun to penetrate and the cold air made her feel lonely. She gave herself a hug for warmth and comfort, but that only made her shiver. And William was unconscionably heavy.

Down at the end of the street were the steps where Old Sheena had told fortunes and, as Suki glanced towards them, she saw that the top step was occupied by a pair of lovers. They stood together as close as statues, wrapped in each other's arms – he bending his head towards her so that their foreheads were almost touching, she gazing rapturously at the mouth so near her own. Suki had responded to them with jealous fellow feeling before she realised who they were. Then she had a moment of alarm, for the girl was Miss Ariadne and the man Mr Clements, the actor. Had she forgotten that she was being spied upon? Hepzie could come round the corner at any moment and surprise them. She must warn them, and quickly, before harm was done.

Her approach was so abrupt that they jumped apart, turning guilty faces towards her. Then Ariadne recognised her and ran to seize her by the arm.

"Say nothing!" she ordered. And when Suki answered, saying that she wouldn't breathe a word, Ariadne was eager to tell her tale. "I have followed your teaching to the letter. This is my dear Mr Clements, who has declared his love for me. We have been writing to each other ever since I went to London, as you know, dear Suki. We are much beholden to you for all you did to bring our correspondence about. Are we not, Mr Clements?" The actor looked sheepish, but she pulled him towards her, smiling into his eyes. "Now we are to marry," she declared. "Papa may think I am betrothed to his horrible Sir Humphrey but the man is an abomination and ain't fit to be considered. I cannot marry where I do not love and there's an end on't."

"Quite right!" Suki applauded, thrilled by her courage.

"My body is my own, is't not?" Ariadne said boldly, rehearsing her new opinion and enjoying the power of what she was saying, watching for Suki's approving nod. "Nobody has any rights upon it save me. I have chosen the man I will marry and nothing will deter me from the path I have chosen. So here we are to await our carriage. How say you to this for a wedding gown?" She smoothed the saffron silk of her bodice, blushing with pleasure.

"I wish you joy," Suki said, "but should you not keep better hidden till the carriage is come? Hepzibah—"

"Is taken care of," Ariadne said, "and the carriage will be here presently."

It was being reined up at the bottom of the steps as she spoke, with a great clatter of wheels and much snorting and blowing from the coachman and his horses. Mr Clements was off to meet it so quickly that he could have been running a race.

Ariadne tripped gaily after him, her yellow pumps bright against the grey pavement. "I have left Mamma a note," she called, as the carriage step was lowered. "'Tis well hid. 'Twill not be found until the room is cleaned and we are far away." And she climbed aboard and was gone, in a rush of dark curls, yellow silk and giggling happiness.

The note was discovered as soon as Lady Bradbury returned to the house.

She'd gone straight to her daughters' bedroom to find out why they had been so tardy. "Fie upon you, slug-abed!" she said to Melissa, who was still sitting at her dressing table with Hepzie arranging her hair. "You promised to join me at the baths within the hour and here you are still at your *toilette*. Where is your sister?"

"Gone out, I believe," Melissa said, almost artlessly. "She left you a *billet*. 'Tis behind the blue vase on the mantelpiece." She'd watched it being written and hidden, while pretending to be asleep, and she knew from her sister's agitation that it was something scurrilous.

"Out?" Hermione said, her long face creased with suspicion. "Out where?"

"I'm sure I couldn't say, Mamma," Melissa told her smugly. "Hepzibah offered to accompany her – did you not, Hepzibah? – but she'd none of it."

"'Tis the truth, ma'am," Hepzie confirmed. "She said she'd rather have the wet nurse for company. She said 'twas arranged.

Hermione narrowed her eyes at their maid as she broke the seal on her daughter's letter. "I hope she ain't contemplating a visit of any consequence," she observed. "We dine with Lady Fosdyke at three and her father will be here before noon with Sir Humphrey, who will be anxious to see her, I do not doubt." Then she read the letter. And read it again, her mouth trembling. And sat down heavily in the nearest chair, her fingers pressed to lips grown suddenly pale, her face aged with distress. "Leave what you are doing, Hepzibah," she instructed, "and go and fetch Mr Jessup to me directly. And the wet nurse, if you can find her."

Melissa was delighted to have caused such disquiet.

She assumed a solicitous expression as well as she could. "Is it bad news, Mamma?" she asked when Hepzibah was gone.

"The worst," her mother said. "Oh my dear child, the very, very worst. I hardly know how to tell you. If I try I fear I may run distract. Oh, oh! The shame of it! The shame! I'm sure I don't know what I ever did to be so cruelly treated. How could she do such a dreadful, dreadful thing? To her own dear mamma! 'Tis beyond mortal comprehension. She has run off with an actor, and on the very day when we are to dine with Lady Fosdyke! We shall be shamed for ever. Jessup must see to it."

They could hear his feet measuring the tread of the back stairs, his careful cough before he knocked – krmm, krmm – and behind him the babbling of a baby and a voice saying, "Hush now, my William. Be a good boy." And then the room was full of servants, Mr Jessup discrete in black, Hepzibah in her floral cotton, looking smug, and behind them Suki Brown, bright as sunshine in a yellow dimity gown trimmed with pink ribbons, with William toddling beside her, a blue padded cap on his curls to protect his head from tumbles, blue leather boots on his feet and his little fat legs stomping manfully beneath a froth of blue and white petticoats.

"Heavens!" Melissa said. "Is that my brother?"

Hermione barely looked at him. After one cursory glance, she fixed her gimlet eyes on Suki. "Ah!" she said. "I am informed that you accompanied Miss Ariadne when she left the house this morning. Is my information reliable?"

"No, ma'am," Suki said, looking her straight in the eye. "I only just got here, ma'am, an't please you. I came by way of the market in Farmer Lambton's cart. I haven't seen Miss Ariadne yet. Nor Miss Melissa. Good morning, Miss Melissa."

Lady Bradbury digested this, thinking deeply. Then she turned to her butler. "Mr Jessup," she said. "When the master returns, ask him if he will be so good as to attend upon me directly. I shall be in my boudoir. Sir Humphrey will no doubt wish to be attended *in his own room.* After his travels, he will be fatigued."

Jessup went off at once to obey her, but it was already too late. Sir George was in the house and bounding up the stairs, loud with success. His wig was over one eye and his fine suit creased and crumpled from his journey but he paid no heed to any of it. He pushed Jessup out of the way and roared up stairs, two at a time, "Hermione! Where are you? We've had such a time of it. Never knew such a time. Wait till I tell you. The *Yorick*'s launched at last, all shipshape and seaworthy and ready to sail!" He crashed into her boudoir, bursting through the door with such force that flakes of plaster fell from the ceiling.

Hermione was out of the bedroom and across the landing so quickly that the sack back of her day gown hissed against the floorboards. There was no time for greeting or courtesy. "Read that," she said, and thrust the note into her husband's hand.

Then, and too late, she realised that Sir Humphrey was making his languid progress up the stairs, pelvis tilted, white hand trailing the banister, powdered face raised towards her in concern and enquiry.

"My dear lady," he breathed, avid for scandal. "What is it?"

She was caught in such an acute state of embarrassment that her throat constricted. To be facing this man, at this time, when she'd courted him so assiduously and the marriage was arranged and everything was going so well . . . 'Twas more than she could bear. She wanted to faint or die or vanish into thin air. But she remembered her breeding and struggled to find breath and words to answer him. "My dear Sir Humphrey," she said weakly, "I trust I see you well. 'Tis nothing." Her voice was growing fainter. "Nothing." Fainter still. "Of no consequence . . ."

She was wasting what little breath she had, for Sir George was bellowing, in a voice that would be heard all over the house, "'Od's bones and brains! You've bred a harlot, ma'am. A harlot."

"Abate your tone, my love, I do entreat you," Hermione whispered, glancing anxiously at the door to the backstairs, where the servants hid to eavesdrop.

Her husband saw no point in subterfuge. "'Twill be all over town by dinnertime," he roared. "Had you no control upon her at all, ma'am? What were you thinking of to let her wander free?"

She tried to fight back. And to warn him. "I take it hard, my love, that you should think to lay the blame at *my* door," she said. "As you yourself observed, 'twas a wench improved. We were deceived! That is the truth of the matter. We were deceived and *we* should make an end of it."

He was too angry to take the hint. "*You* may have been deceived, ma'am. *I* was not. She's a monstrous imp of wickedness, and should have been kept within doors at all hours. Day and night. Bad blood will out, ma'am, and there's the truth on't. We all know where it comes from. Not *my* side of the family, as you'll allow. There ain't an ounce of bad blood on *my* side of the family. Not an ounce. 'Od's my life, not an ounce. And as to that actor fellow, devil take him, he should be horsewhipped. Let me once catch hold of him, I'll cudgel him! I'll blow his brains out, so help me!" Then he noticed Sir Humphrey's enquiring expression. "Run off with an actor, sir, if you ever heard the like." And to Hermione's horror, he passed Ariadne's note to her fiancé. "Read that."

Her humiliation was complete. Cheeks burning, she tried to offer an apology. "I can scarce lift my eyes to look at you," she whispered, "for very shame. What must you think of us?"

The Honourable Humphrey suggested them both into her boudoir, away from listening ears, and once there, made suitably comforting noises. "There is no need of apology," he said smoothly. "'Tis your daughter who is at fault, not your good self."

"You are kind to say so," Hermione murmured, thinking what good breeding he had. And all gone to nothing. The pity of it! She cast about to find something else to say but at that point Benjy stirred from a snorting sleep on the *chaise-longue* and lumbered to his feet to investigate the newcomer, giving a few preliminary growls by way of greeting.

Sir Humphrey lifted him deftly on the toe of one elegant shoe, deposited him outside the door, and shut it firmly. "I think not, sir," he said. "We have enough to contend with, have we not, dear lady?"

The dear lady had to agree, partly because she was hardly in a position to do otherwise and partly because the awful nature of their social commitments had come pressing back into her mind. "'Od's my life!" she said, her fingers to her lips in dismay. "We are due to dine with Lady Fosdyke at three. What is to be done? 'Tis too late to cancel, I fear."

"Cancel? My dear lady!" Sir Humphrey said, aghast at the very idea. "By no means cancel. Face it out, me dear.

'Tis the only possible way, We will make apologies for your daughter's absence – a chill perhaps, you will know the likeliest cause – enjoy our meal, as much as we are able, which I fear will be little, given the circumstances, and return. We shall have news before nightfall, depend upon it."

She wasn't comforted. "I do not see how. She has fled."

"There are two roads out of Bath," he explained, "and farms a-plenty all along the way. Fee'd posts, dear lady, set in position, ready to serve. Offer the right fee and I'll lay any money, you will hear of your runaway by morning."

Hermione deferred to her husband. "What do you think, my love?"

He raised his shoulders and his eyebrows in despair. "Think?" he said. "I'm past thought. I doubt if I shall ever think again." But he tried to be gracious, even in desperation. "Howsomever, he may be right."

"Never doubt it," Sir Humphrey said warmly. "Send two men, with good horses and full purses, and you shall see how well we fare. If they are flown 'twill be to Bristol or London, and either way we shall follow."

Sir George sighed. "But what then?"

"The new law will stop a hasty marriage. Unwed, the lady will return to sense. If we move swiftly, a scandal may yet be averted."

"Would it could be so," Sir George said, "but you forget the player, arrant rogue, that he is."

"All men have a price," Sir Humphrey drawled. "We shall find his. Send for her maid and enquire what dresses are taken. I'll lay she's worn her best, and a good bold colour with any luck. Then send your man."

Nobody below stairs was the least bit surprised to hear

of Sir Humphrey's treacherous advice and, to Suki's dismay, most of them shared his worldly opinion.

"He's onny an actor," Cook said, "an' gold's uncommon persuasive to the acting trade. They'll buy him off as easy as winking."

Suki sprang to his defence before she could stop to think of the consequences. "Not if he loves her," she said stoutly. "If he loves her, he'll stick to her through thick and thin. Love ain't open to bribery."

"If 'tis love, I might agree with 'ee," Hepzie sneered. "But she's took her best silk gown and twenty crowns. So money is of some consequence, I should hazard."

"If that's the case," the newest kitchen maid said. "He'm after her money. Poor soul. 'Tis the same the world over."

"You know nothing of it," Suki said angrily. "So hold your peace." Then, and too late, she realised that they were all looking at her, some much surprised and some a deal too knowing, and she wished she'd stayed silent.

"Hoity-toity!" Hepzie mocked. "Are you paid to defend 'em? Is that it?"

It was a straight question and had to be answered. "No I arn't. An' if I were 'tis none of your concern."

"I might make it my concern," Hepzie warned and was delighted when Suki blushed. "Seems to me you know a deal more than you should. Seems to me you had a hand in it."

Suki fought back hard, remembering her lie to milady. "I only just this minute arrived," she said. "I 'aven't had time to have a hand in nothin."

They bristled at one another, both thinking of a retort.

"'Tis my belief," the new maid said, chopping parsley vigorously, "there arn't no such thing as true love. 'Tis a

55

concoction of poets. Most of us marry for money when
all's said an' done. I know I would."

"Her father got a powerful rich husband for her by all
accounts," Cook said. "A duke or some such. She should
ha' stayed home an' married *him*. She don't know when
she'm well off, an' that's my opinion of it."

"But if she loves the actor," Bessie offered, her face
anxious.

"Nobody marries for love," Hepzie told her. "That
ain't the way of the world. You marry where your father
chooses for you if you've any sense. An' if you ain't got
a father to look out for you, you marry the richest man
you can find to offer. That's what I mean to do. Love
don't come into it."

"Well then you'm wrong," Suki said. "Love's the most
important thing and nobody has the right to choose your
husband for you. That's your affair. Yours an' his."

"Oh, oh! So that's the size of it!" Hepzie mocked.
"You're still singing *that* old song. I'd ha' thought
you'd've learned better by now. Well let me tell you,
Suki Brown, there ain't another person in this house
would say such foolish things."

"That aren't foolish," Suki fought on, "'tis right. Our
fathers don't own us."

"Since when? Course they own us. Our fathers own
us an' our husbands own us an' our employers own us.
'Tis the way things are. If we 'ave any power in anything
'tis by stealth and well you know it. 'Tis the way of the
world."

"Then the world's wrong. Ask any true lover an'
they'll tell you different."

"An' you're a true lover, I suppose," Hepzie said
tartly. "An' that husband of yours, we all hear so much
about and never see, he's a true lover, too. You love

56

him an' he loves you. We don't exactly see him rushin' homewards to his true love, do we, though? 'Tis my belief he don't exist."

"He do," Suki said, eyes flashing. "He'll come home soon. You'll see. 'Tis a matter of time, that's all."

"He's been gone years, to my certain knowledge."

"He'm on a slaver. They take years."

"Aye," Hepzie sneered. "So you say."

"They'm a-ringing for you, Hepzibah," Cook said, glancing up at the bell board, and glad of an excuse to bring the quarrel to an end. Hepzie had right on her side, but she could be uncommon sharp.

'Twas a mistake to speak out so, Suki thought, as Hepzie flounced from the room. I should have held my peace. Now she'm suspicious and will tell tales. She still felt embattled, even though her adversary was gone, for the scullery maids were looking at her most oddly. "How hot 'tis in this kitchen," she said, fanning her cheeks. "I shall take William out in the air for an hour or two to cool un. Milady aren't like to call for us again being they're out at the Fosdykes'."

"'Tis a-comin on to rain," Cook warned.

But Suki already had her bonnet on. Now that she'd made up her mind, she couldn't stop in the house a minute longer. I shall visit the Spring Gardens, she said to herself. There wouldn't be anyone there to talk to, so she wouldn't say the wrong things. 'Twould be peaceful there. "'Tis a pretty place. William likes pretty flowers. Don't you, my pet lamb? I'll be back in time to help with supper."

Four

The Spring Gardens were in full summer bloom and looked extremely fine, every flower peculiarly brightly coloured under a grape blue sky and every bed perfectly symmetrical. There wasn't a leaf out of line, nor a shrub out of place. Arcades stretched to north and south: tree-lined walks paved with gravel, and each with its own leafy arch, led in every direction; and in the central rotunda a band played soothing music beneath a ceiling painted to resemble the sky at night. It was the hour of the afternoon promenade and the parades were crowded with new arrivals, all trimmed and titivated ready for admiration, the ladies exquisite in embroidered gowns, the gentlemen dazzling in velvet coats and silk breeches.

As Suki arrived, they were gathering beside the rotunda where three rows of gilded seats had been set to receive them. 'Twill be some marvel to attract 'em so, Suki thought, so she joined the crowd too, standing behind the little chairs at a respectful distance from their finery. Her entry ticket had cost more than she'd expected, so she might as well take her money's worth and an hour's idle entertainment was just what she needed to take her mind from her troubles.

The marvel was an extremely fat person who dressed like a man and sang like a woman, with a high-pitched echoing voice that Suki didn't like at all. But the sugar merchants were enraptured by him and applauded his first offering most enthusiastically, so she stayed where she was at the edge of the crowd to see what would happen next. After a while, a flautist arrived in a patched coat and a moth-eaten wig, and he and the singer rearranged themselves in front of the band with a great deal of hand waving and chair scraping. Then the singer polished his forehead with a kerchief as large as a pillow case, and the introduction to the second aria began.

Suki was wondering idly whether the flautist would be better or worse than the singer when she became aware that a group of rough-looking men had taken up positions immediately behind her, and were standing a deal too close for comfort. She edged sideways through the crowd so as to avoid them, but they followed, pressing so hard against her back that she feared for William's safety. Pick-pockets, she thought, and was surprised that she felt no fear. But she'd hardly taken another step before a rough arm grabbed her round the waist and an even rougher hand was fumbling at her petticoat. Her parasol hung unopened on her left arm, and it made a splendid weapon. She stabbed it backwards against the legs of her assailant, and while he shifted round to avoid her blows, she ran, dodging through the crowd despite their displeasure. The merchants, seated in their glittering circle around the stage, took no notice whatsoever.

The walk was almost empty, so she ran like a greyhound, straight down the centre, her lungs straining and William bobbing on her back. Within seconds, her bonnet flew from her head and was lost in the bushes, but she couldn't stop to retrieve it because she could hear feet thudding after her and a rough voice yelling, "Grab her, Johnny. She got somethin' worth the taking or she wouldn't run."

She wondered briefly whether to turn and argue with them but it was too late, they had already caught up with her, three swarthy, sweating men, in stained coats and soiled linen, pulling at her skirts to impede her, thrusting their odious faces at her, mouthing at her with stinking breath.

"Leave me be," she panted, struggling out of their grip.

"Why, 'tis the Captain's wench," one said, holding her face in the vice of his fingers. "Look 'ee here, Spider."

Her thoughts were muddled with fear and loathing. "Leave me be," she said again, "or I shall tell the Captain how you treat me. Do way your hands."

A mouthful of broken teeth moved into her line of vision and another voice said, "You won't tell the Captain nothing, you stupid wench. On account of he ain't here, an' he ain't the man for the likes of you. He's a gentleman of the road, is the Captain, an' may take any wench he chooses."

He had a hand down inside her bodice fumbling her breasts – how dare he! – and William was screaming in sharp staccato cries that roused her to a surge of protective fury. How dare he do this! How dare he frighten her baby! Odious filthy creature! She turned in a storm of fear and anger and beat him about the ears with her parasol, kicking and screaming, so that a group of promenaders, who'd just turned into the walk, were stopped in their stride and began to gather about them. At that, her attackers drew back and hesitated, and that gave her the chance she needed. She ducked beneath the nearest arm and ran for the exit. Beyond the bushes she could see the ferrymen casting off. If she could only run fast enough, she could be aboard and away before they caught up with her again.

"Wait!" she yelled as she ran. "Oh wait for me, do!" And to her great relief, the ferryman waited, steadying his narrow skiff as the river waves slapped against its sides, and he and his passengers watched as she tumbled down the bank and scrambled aboard, panting and weeping. But safe.

They were all mightily interested in her adventure and said it was a crying shame for pockets to be picked in broad daylight, so it was, and something should be done about it. And gradually their sympathy eased her distress. Soon she was telling them the tale, and being commended for her level-headedness as they creaked their way back across the river. But when they landed in Boat Stalle Lane, she knew that the attack had exhausted her. She was compelled to sit on the bank with William on her lap for comfort and try to recover a little. It had been a disastrous outing.

"Oh my William," she said as she cuddled his damp face against her cheek. "I haven't seen so bad a day as this for many a year. First Mrs Roper up and gone, and then the actors uncaring and Hepzie hateful – and now this. We got the stars against us today an' no mistake." And as if to underscore her misery, it began to rain.

Short though it was, the walk back to South Parade stretched before her like a five-mile march. "Come now," she said to herself as she hoisted William on to her back again. "This will never do." And she began to sing as she trudged, to cheer them both up. "Oh up she got, and home did trot, as fast as she could caper." But she was still so cast down that she paid no attention to the people who jostled beside her, nor to the carts and horses in the road. Even when a voice called her name in a questioning way, she didn't bother to look up.

But it called again. And again. "Suki Brown! Do you walk to South Parade?" And she looked up at last and saw that it was Farmer Lambton, sitting astride the Captain's beautiful horse and looking down at her with patient concern.

"Oh, Farmer Lambton," she said and, despite herself, her eyes filled with tears. "I've had such a day of it, you never would believe. I been set upon by pick-pockets in the Spring Gardens, of all places. You can't imagine how good it is to see you!"

He dismounted carefully and lifted her into the saddle, without a word, sitting her astride with William before her. Then, as he walked beside her through the crowded street, he questioned her gently. What had happened? Was ought stolen? Was she harmed? And satisfied that she was only shaken, he led them through the Abbey Gardens to the nearest tea house and bought a dish for them both, and a sop for William.

"A restorative," he said as the steaming bowls were laid before them. "Sip it slowly. 'Twill be of more benefit that way. William will sit on my knee for a minute or two." Which William did and was as good as gold, back with a familiar face, sucking his sop and regarding the company. So Suki recovered sip by sip, and the colour washed back into her cheeks, the frown eased from her forehead and she became her pretty self again.

"Time for home," he said as she set down her empty cup.

"'Tis uncommon kind of you, sir," she thanked him as he lifted her on to Beau's back again. It was raining harder now and their clothes were getting damp. She opened her parasol, hoping it would give William some protection. "I've put you out of your way, I fear."

"No," he said, settling William in front of her and untying the reins. "My way is yours this afternoon. I've come to see your master."

'Twill be on account of Beau being left on the farm, Suki thought. He wants to know when I'll be able to take him. "I haven't had a chance to talk about the horse," she volunteered, holding the parasol over her son's head. "We been at sixes an' sevens today."

"Aye," he said, "so I understand. That's why I'm here. I've come to see Sir George about his daughter."

Her heart sank. "Not Miss Ariadne?"

"She passed the farm this afternoon," he told her. The rain was dripping from the brim of his hat but he paid no attention to it at all. "She and her lover. Tipped into the ditch, down by Seven Acre Field, some time around noon. One wheel stuck fast. I sent your father down with Ned to haul them out. I knowed who they were the minute I clapped eyes on 'em, for I saw them both at the theatre the night I took Mrs Lambton to the play. Which I daresay you remember. So when Sir George's man come a-riding by, asking if we'd any knowledge of 'em, I knew 'twas my duty to report it."

Suki was aghast. She had to dissuade him quickly, before they reached the house. She couldn't have them hunted down. "'Tis a love match," she said. "They've run away to marry."

That didn't alter his purpose at all. "Belike," he said, and he spoke the word carelessly.

She looked at him earnestly through the rain. The parasol had split and was now leaking water all over William's head. "Then you won't peach on 'em," she said as she tried to turn it into a better position.

"It ain't a matter of peaching," he told her seriously. "She is engaged to marry another."

"But she don't love him." The water was pouring over her own head now and running off the bridge of her nose.

"Marriage is too important to be left to mere liking," he said, stolidly leading the horse. "Her father has made a good match for her, so 'tis his plain duty to bring her home to honour her commitments. Any father would do the same. My plain duty is to help in any way I can. They are runaways."

How can he do such a thing? Suki thought mutinously. Mr Lambton of all people. Mr Lambton, the stolid, dependable, sensible . . . Why don't he understand? "Oh Mr Lambton," she pleaded. "Pray don't peach on 'em, I beg you. They love each other. They really do."

"That's as maybe," he said in his unruffled way. "But whether they do or not, 'tis no concern of mine, nor should it be of yours. Her father wants her found and that is all we need to know. He is fearful of Mr Clement's intentions."

"He has no cause to be. 'Tis an honest match."

He gave her his patient look. "If 'twere an honest match," he said. "Mr Clements would have spoken to Sir George and asked for her hand in the proper way. This was never done, Suki, as you must know, for Sir George's man was well aware of it and told me of it roundly. No. Marriage on the gad is rarely to the maid's advantage. Marriage on the gad to a man so far below her in rank and wealth and opinion would be the ruination of your Miss Ariadne."

"They love each other," Suki repeated. His righteousness was making her stubborn. She shook the rain from the parasol, feeling angry with it. It had split in so many places it was no use to flesh or fowl. Dratted thing! Oh, she must make him understand. "'Tis a love match."

"If *that* is the case," he said, "and Sir George is agreeable to it, they will wed and no harm done. If 'tis not, Sir George will bring the lady home."

"But . . ."

They had arrived in South Parade and there was little time left for argument. It was raining in earnest and they were all thoroughly damp. He gave her his hand to lift her down from the saddle, as Beau twitched his ears against the wet. "Beyond the giving of information, this matter is no concern either to thee or me," he said, and his tone was a rebuke. "We must allow our betters to settle their own affairs."

She made one last appeal. "Delay for a day," she begged as the rain ran out of her hair and down her face. "'Twould do no harm. If 'tis in the stars for 'em to be found, he'll find 'em, depend on it, sooner or later. Tell him tomorrow when you come to market. That would be time enough, surely."

"Oh Suki!" he said, smiling at her. "What a spirit you have! But 'tis all gone to waste, I fear. I saw Sir George an hour ago. He's on his way to Bristol this very minute."

Five

Frederick Bradbury had dined late that afternoon. Very late indeed. In fact, by the time the table-cloth had been removed and the port set deferentially beside his elbow, it was past five o'clock. Because he was an excessively mild-mannered man and mindful of the susceptibilities of his cook, he made no comment upon the delay and asked no questions. But it upset him nevertheless and, when the meal was over, he found himself fatigued. He had the fire made up, propped his heels upon a footstool, and covering his face with a clean napkin, settled down for a late afternoon snooze.

He was considerably put out when his valet crept into the room some twenty minutes later to inform him that his brother's coach had arrived.

"Very well," he said wearily. "Fetch the chocks, Morgan." And he straightened his wig and dusted his coat and went downstairs to greet his guest and all the noise and confusion he would bring with him.

It was all as he expected. Rain was spitting into the open doorway and a chill wind tossing coat-tails up into the air in the most unseemly fashion, the two greys were steaming after their exertions up the hill, Barnaby was fairly scraping the chocks into position under the wheels and Sir George was cussing and swearing as he emerged from his unsteady door on to the sloping pavement.

"Damme Frederick," he complained, "why must you live on a hill?"

"A pleasure to greet 'ee, me dear," Frederick said and tried to sound as though he meant it. "What brings you to town at this hour? Is there news of the *Yorick*?"

Then he noticed Sir Humphrey, who was stepping delicately from the coach, wincing at the rain. "Sir Humphrey. A pleasure, sir, I give you good evening."

"Mr Bradbury, sir," acknowledged Sir Humphrey. "I wish you could, sir. Plague me if I don't."

"Come into the powder room, brother," Sir George said, looking at the valet's ears. He spoke so urgently and his expression was so fraught that Frederick escorted both his guests into the house at once and took them straight to the little closet beside the door, certain of bad news, and there amid spare wigs and dustsheets, face cones and bellows, Sir George told the tale of Ariadne's elopement, pacing the little chamber with furious strides and to the imminent danger of everything in it. "'Od's bowels, did you ever hear the like?"

Frederick was instantly solicitous of the Honourable Sir Humphrey, aware of what a mortal blow this must have been to his delicate constitution. "My very dear sir," he said earnestly, "pray allow me to offer my most sincere apologies. My niece must have taken leave of her senses to do such a thing. I cannot tell you how grieved it makes me."

Sir Humphrey raised his eyes to the ceiling and sighed elegantly.

"Needs a good thrashing," Sir George said furiously, charging at the wigs. "That's my opinion."

"She is a female creature when all is said and done," Frederick sighed. "Little more can be expected of that sex, I fear. 'Tis a different breed altogether." And seeing

67

that the face cones were scattered and the wigs knocked awry, "Pray do be seated, brother. Have you cause to think she is in Bristol?"

"Her carriage overturned at Twerton," Sir George explained, still prowling. "Seen by a farmer. Reported to me. In a yellow silk gown, if you please. Brazen hussy!"

"They may well take ship on the morning tide," Frederick said, "and if that is to be the case, 'twere well to be prepared against it. There were many arrivals today but few sailings, praise be, which is one mercy, you'll allow. Tomorrow morning we will walk to the Custom House and see the controller." He rescued the cones deftly and replaced them on the shelf behind him.

Sir George was too impatient to wait for morning. "We must start now, damme," he said. "The sooner we find 'em, the less time for niggling. I've trouble enough without bastards."

Frederick sighed again, and this time more heavily, for it was plain that his evening was to be ruined. Given his brother's anger and the distress of his illustrious guest, there was nothing for it but to take a trip down to the Backs, rain or no rain. "We'll to the Seven Stars," he said, "and offer twenty crowns for information."

"Aye, but shall we get it, think 'ee?"

"In a city devoted to trade," Frederick said sagely, "money buys busy tongues."

So the valet was sent for a lantern and a woollen cloak, and presently the three men set off down the hill into the drizzling darkness. The two rivers were crowded with ships, resting in their lines, hull against hull, the forest of their bare masts black against the lights of the quay. The sight of such an immense fleet made Sir George scowl, for if his errant daughter were already embarked and aboard, how could he possibly tell where she would be hidden?

Frederick, on the other hand, gave them scant attention. He was already cold and damp, and he intended to walk to the Backs as quickly as he could, conclude his business there and return at speed.

Fortunately, the Seven Stars was crowded with likely customers, and the news that the Bradbury brothers were on the look-out for information regarding a pair of runaways brought immediate interest and scores of itching palms. Details were sought and given, of age, appearance, colour of dress, lack of wig, time of arrival, and the brothers were eagerly assured that finding such a dainty lady, even in a city of this size, would merely be a matter of time.

"I shall give this note of hand to the landlord," Sir George declared, reading as he wrote. "My note of hand for twenty crowns for any man who can provide me with information leading to the discovery of my daughter and a certain Mr Clements, actor." He signed with a flourish of calligraphy and Brussels lace, and added, "You may find me at my brother's house, which is, I believe, known to you."

Then they returned to the house, through driving rain but in better spirits. Their capes were set to dry and a dish of tea ordered to sustain them, and they settled down to wait.

An hour passed. And then another. And nobody came. Frederick ensured that Sir Humphrey sat in the most comfortable chair before the fire with his feet propped on the fender, and did his best to make intelligent conversation, discoursing on the latest play and the latest books, the news from the Commons and even the price of sugar. But Sir George prowled the room like one of the lions in the Tower, scowling through the curtains, scuffing the edge of the carpet, flinging himself into every unoccupied chair and sofa in the room, cursing the weather, his daughter, actors, theatres, ships and Hermione, incessantly and indiscriminately.

At last, a little before midnight, Morgan came gently into the room to tell them that a seafaring gentleman was waiting in the hall, and had sent word that he had "solid information, and required them most humble-like that they would see him below in the hall, on account of his leg didn't take too kindly to stairs."

They went down at once.

The seafaring gentleman was an outlandish look-ing personage, with a gnarled wooden leg and a pair of tattered crutches. He seemed to have had a life-long propensity for heat, for he smelt most vilely of sweat, rum and gunpowder, and his skin was burnt as brown as old leather. He wore his own hair, which was black and greasy and hung behind him in a short pigtail tied at the ends into a straight pouch of cracked black leather, and his suit was rubbed shiny with age, the right leg of his breeches tied with fraying rope just below the stump of his knee. He was totally out of place in Frederick's elegant hall, like a bug in a cradle.

"A villain, damme," Sir George whispered as he and Frederick descended the stairs.

But Frederick thought that a good thing. "Takes a thief to catch a thief," he said.

The seafaring man leant on his crutches and regarded them with shrewd black eyes. "God gi'ee good e'en," he said. "Which of you two gennulmen does oi 'ave the honour of sarvin'?"

"Speak to me," Sir George said. "Where is the lady?"

70

"The lady's hard by, in a manner of speakin'. Farr an' twenny crowns, oi do believe thee offered."

"Twenty," Sir George said stiffly. "That was my note of hand."

"Ar," the man said, and he sucked his brown lips and gave the matter ostentatious thought. "'Tis a marrtal bad night fer twenny."

"Twenty," Sir George repeated. "An' you've to earn it, damme."

"Ar," the man said again, breathing decay upon them. "Twenny-two'd be dandy."

"Have us there within the quarter," Frederick said, consulting his hunter, "and twenty-two it shall be."

So the bargain was struck and their disreputable guide took up his lantern and wrapped himself in his cloak, and they all set out into the rain again. He moved remarkably quickly for a man so badly crippled, lolloping downhill, past the sleeping houses of the sugar and slave merchants, past Red Lodge brooding blackly under the rain, and down Pipe Lane into the sloping terraces where the knifesmiths plied their trade. At the knifesmiths' steps, he paused to rearrange his crutches and then he was off again, swinging precipitately down into the wet unlit chasm, crutches scraping, while the brothers followed, their lanterns bobbing before them and their shoes squeaking on the wet stone of the stairs. It was indeed a mortal bad night.

As they crossed the Frome, Sir George realised that their guide was leading them into the old town, but neither he nor his brother felt any need to speak of it. They filed through the filthy archway of St John's Gate, where beggars sat against the walls snoring in their own stink, and then they were in the narrow alley called Broad Street, where ancient houses leant towards one another in

71

the darkness, obscuring what little light there was. The seafaring man was a simian shape swinging on ahead of them over the cobbles, and now he was going at such a speed that from time to time the brothers had to run to keep up with him.

Without warning, he turned out of Broad Street into an alley smelling of piss and decay and so narrow that they had to walk it in single file, and even then they were splashed by water pouring out of gulleys on either side of them. The houses here were all built in the old style with high gabled roofs, windows dangerously out of alignment and overhanging jetties bulging down above their heads. Creaking, ancient, bug-ridden, uncivilised hovels, Sir George thought, holding his handkerchief before his nose, and just the sort of place that this foul man would use to hide his folly in.

Sure enough they stopped at the end of the alley and the seafaring man knocked at the window with his crutch, and presently a candle wavered into view behind the glass and a rough voice said, "'Oo's that?"

"'Tis oi. A matter of farr crown," the seafaring man said, with his mouth to the window, and the candle said, "Ar!" and wavered away again. They waited in the rain and the torrent from the gulley until the front door was eased open and the candle flickered before them in the hands of a grizzled man in a brown bob wig. "Come froo denn," he said and, as that seemed to be permission to enter, they trailed their wetness into the house.

"Where are they?" Sir George said. The smell in that narrow hall was overpowering. It was neither the time nor the place for ceremony.

The candle led the way up a very dark staircase, illuminating a pale halo on the stained ceiling above it and leaving the brothers to stumble up in the darkness behind it as well as they could. At the top of the stairs was a candle stand with a double-headed candlestick upon it and, once this extra pair were lit and all their lights were gathered together, they could see that they were standing before a brown door, and that the man in the brown wig was pushing it open with his foot. Sir George seized the candlestick and strode into the room shedding light as he went.

The saffron gown lay abandoned across a wicker chair with Ariadne's yellow pumps beside it on a tumble of petticoats, and the high bed set against the slope of the ceiling was mounded with sleeping bodies. Without a second's hesitation Sir George seized the matted blanket in his free hand and pulled it from the bed, yelling "Up strumpet!" at the top of his voice.

The actor slept on, with his mouth open and one knee in the air, but Ariadne woke at once and made a grab at the retreating bedclothes to try and cover herself. She was in her shift, but one breast and both legs were bare, and a garment so voluminous did little to protect her from the immodest gaze of a room suddenly and inexplicably full of men. She was afraid and bewildered, and she looked it. Then understanding cleared the fogs of sleep and she saw that she was facing her father and her fiancé, and that they were both glaring at her – Sir George puce with anger, Sir Humphrey chalk white with disdain.

"Papa!" she begged, clutching at the blankets, "I prithee don't!"

"Cease your wallowing, slut," her father said, tossing the saffron gown at her struggling body. "Wallowing is the sport of pigs! Rise from this foul den of corruption. 'Od's blood, it makes my brain boil, so it does! Clothe yourself for the love of God!"

Ariadne contrived to cover herself by a combination

of gown and blanket, but by now she had remembered her lover and was pulling at his shoulder to rouse him. "Mr Clements! Dearest love! Pray bestir yourself. My father and Sir Humphrey are here."

The actor stirred in his sleep, mumbled a little, scratched his close cropped head and slept on. She persisted, "Mr Clements! Dearest love!" And at last he opened his eyes and looked up at the turkey red face glowering down upon him.

"'Od's my life!" he said in alarm.

"If you have harmed one hair on my daughter's head, sir," bellowed Sir George, "I shall have the law upon you. So help me if I don't. 'Od's blood and bones and bowels, brother Frederick, restrain me, or I shall run distract and do this villain some mischief."

The actor stumbled from the bed and reached for his clothes. "Your daughter, sir," he said with as much dignity as he could muster, "your daughter and I intend to marry, I would have you know. The banns will be called on Sunday for the first time of three. All legal and above board, you will allow, and according to the new Act. In three weeks' time, we shall be man and wife."

"Pardon me, sir," Sir George said fiercely. "In three weeks' time, you will be no such thing. In three weeks' time, sir, you could be incarcerated in the nearest Bridewell. In three weeks' time, sir, you could die on a dunghill."

"Papa! Papa!" Ariadne cried, sitting up in the bed, the straw beneath her crackling as she moved and the blanket clutched to her throat. "You lacerate my feelings!" To be caught so soon and so easily and here in this filthy place was making her blush with a shame so acute that she felt as though her cheeks were afire. "Please, Papa!"

Her father had no pity for her at all. "Your feelings have no bearing upon the matter," he said. His eyes never left the actor, who was pulling on his wig and making a very poor job of it. "'Od's bowels! Have you no shame?"

Ariadne drew breath to answer him but, before she could speak, Sir Humphrey stepped coolly forward and poised between them, superbly elegant in the squalor of the room. He took over, ignoring her and speaking directly to her lover.

"Mr Clements, sir," he drawled. "Your servant."

The actor was surprised, impressed, suspicious – all at the same time – but he gave Sir Humphrey the expected greeting and doffed an imaginary cap out of courtesy.

"We have business to discuss, sir, I believe," Sir Humphrey said smoothly.

Now it was Ariadne's turn to look wary and to feel afraid. What business could there be between her lover and the man she had wronged? Terrible possibilities filled her mind. A duel, a summons for damages, imprisonment, a stabbing.

Mr Clements tucked his shirt into his breeches with trembling hands. "I think not, sir," he said. "What business could there be? What's done is done."

"I think you will find we have," Sir Humphrey told him, milky smooth, "most profitable business. The best that has ever come *your* way, sir, or is ever likely to."

The actor was puzzled. "What business, sir?" he asked.

"Why theatre business, Mr Clements. Acting business. What else?" The hook was baited. The actor was intrigued. "What would 'ee say, sir, to a part in the new play at Mr Garrick's new theatre in Drury Lane in London?"

That was so unexpected that the actor gaped. "You jest, sir."

"I never jest in matters of commerce." Sir Humphrey told him sternly.

"*Could* this be done?"

"Aye, sir, you have my word on't."

Mr Clements licked his lips.

"So what say you?" Sir Humphrey went on. "'Twould be easy enough to accomplish, I daresay. Dependin' upon my word of recommendation, you understand."

"Aye," the actor said, understanding perfectly.

"Well then, sir, think on't. I could scarce recommend a libertine for such employ, or a runaway rake, or any other such idle fellow. That you'll allow."

The two men looked at one another for a long moment, while the rising yellow light patterned their faces and molten wax ran down the sides of the candles like fat white tears. The room was so quiet they could hear the mice scratching in the wainscot. Sir George scowled by the bed. Frederick and the landlord stood still as stones in the doorway, their faces pale and grotesquely shadowed by the candle held between them. Ariadne sat in the shadows and trembled. Mr Clements was the first to drop his gaze.

"Five minutes for 'ee to dress," Sir George said coldly, lifting the rest of his daughter's clothes from the chair and dumping them on the bed.

She turned away from him and held out her hands to her beloved, imploring, "Mr Clements, I beg you!"

"'Tis the chance," the actor said, trying to hold her hands and finding the blanket a great encumbrance, "the chance, Addy my love."

"Have you no care for me?" she said. "But two hours since I was your own true love, most dear to you in all the world. Have you forgot so soon?"

"Five minutes for this to be concluded," Sir Humphrey warned, "or peradventure I may change my mind on't."

"Put on your gown, my dearest," the actor urged, touching Ariadne's anguished cheeks with placating fingers. "I think it best. For any but Mr Garrick, I might resist, but this . . . Oh my dearest Addy . . . I prithee put on your gown. Go with your father."

She flung his fingers aside as though they had stung her and rose from the bed, still draped in her filthy blanket but wearing it with the dignity of a queen. "If you betray me now," she warned, "I'll ne'er speak again. No, not to you, nor yet to any man. Consider it well."

"'Tis my trade," he said and now his voice was cold and he had turned his body away from her.

She let the blanket fall and began to dress herself, without a word and without modesty, as though she were alone in the room. And at that Frederick ushered the landlord out of the room and, taking the candles from his brother, stood with his back to her so as to afford her the decency of darkness. And Sir Humphrey took a card from his pocket and handed it across to his defeated adversary, and the matter was settled.

It was blacker than ever in the alley and the walk home was pierced with rain, but Ariadne was in a trance of misery and rejection and noticed nothing. She crossed the bridge and climbed the hill without speaking and, when they were all safe within doors again, she stood quite still in the hall, gazing into space with a face so expressionless it quite chilled her uncle to see it. When he asked her if she would care to retire, she went silently to the room he indicated and, although he wished her goodnight, she made no response whatever.

"Poor soul!" he said, as the door closed behind her. "She is much wounded, I fear."

"And so she should be," her father said irritably. She had shamed him before a member of the prestigious de Thespia family, and now the marriage was lost. Hermione would be angered and there were endless and embarrassing difficulties ahead of him. "She will recover."

Frederick was all solicitous concern. "Should I have a room prepared for you, Sir Humphrey?" he asked.

But Sir Humphrey declined the offer, explaining that his constitution was so delicate that he could only sleep upon a mattress made to his particular design "and then only for a matter of hours, don'tcher know." He would prefer to sit up until daybreak, which was only an hour or two away, in all conscience. As soon as there was sufficient light to travel in safety, he would return to Bath. "Sir George will sit up with me and keep me company," he said. "We have matters to discuss, have we not?"

Sir George agreed that they had, secretly wishing that he could avoid it. So the fire was made up, Frederick retired at last and the two men were left to their vigil.

"A bad business," Sir George apologised. "Would t'were not so. She'll be punished for it, I promise you."

Sir Humphrey waved his long fingers. "'Tis of no consequence," he said, easily. "I cannot marry her, you understand, the fault being too public, but we have avoided a scandal which is nine-tenths of the matter."

"If the actor don't blab."

Sir Humphrey was sanguine about it. "Oh I dare swear

he'll hold his peace," he said, "with such a prize to be earned. We need have no fear of that."

"The folly of it!" Sir George grieved. "The wretched iniquitous folly. I thought to make you my son-in-law and now her foolishness brings all to ruination."

"Courage, sir," commiserated Sir Humphrey. "You have another daughter, have you not? And one, if I am any judge, too young and sensible for foolishness. How of a match there? With a suitable dowry, naturally."

Sir George widened his eyes. "A capital idea!" he said. "Would your father approve, think 'ee?"

Knowing how much the Bradbury money meant to his family and how necessary it was for him to marry into it so as to buy off his creditors, Sir Humphrey was happy to assure his prospective father-in-law that the new arrangement would almost certainly find favour. "There is much to be gained on both sides by this alliance," he pointed out. "Our two families being business partners already, and in no small enterprise, as I need hardly say."

"A capital idea!" Sir George repeated. His relief was so intense that for the moment he couldn't think of anything else to say.

Dawn was staining the lower edge of the window glass with green light, the trees and shrubs in the garden were gathering dark shape, and down below them they could see the first faint gleam of river water. "Time to be on the road, I believe," Sir Humphrey said.

So Barnaby was roared for and Morgan roused from the shelf in the kitchen where he slept. A jug of water was brought to both gentlemen to cleanse their hands, and cold beef, bread and beer provided to sustain them. Barnaby was sent to wake Ariadne.

She came into the drawing-room ten minutes later, dressed and neat, quiet and withdrawn. She sat down

79

when told to do so, took a dish of tea when ordered, but she didn't speak and she didn't look up. She might have been a statue or some life-sized mechanical toy. Neither of the men paid her any attention at all. They were far too busy discussing the excellent conversion of the *Yorick* and the fire power of her guns.

"Force, sir," said Sir Humphrey. "That's the only language they understand."

Six

S uki Brown was busy dicing potatoes by the area window in the kitchen at South Parade when she was distracted by the sound of grinding wheels and looked up to see Ariadne's tattered yellow pumps stepping down from Sir George's carriage. She was instantly burning with pity for the poor lady and furious at Farmer Lambton. 'Tis all his fault, she thought angrily. They'd never have found her so soon if it hadn't been for him a-telling tales. I knew 'twould be so.

Alerted by the sound of the carriage, the rest of the servants came to join her at the window. "Well that's put paid to that old actor feller then," Cook said cheerfully.

The scullery maid had her nose pressed against the pane and was squinting upwards to get a better view. "They'm a-coming in," she reported. "I wonder what's happened."

"Perhaps they fought a duel," Bessie suggested ghoulishly, "and the master killed 'im. What d'you think?"

He certainly sounded fierce enough. They could hear him in the hall, bellowing like a bull, "Hermione! Deuce take it! Hermione! Where is the woman?"

"Oh go on then," Cook said, as the three girls looked hopefully at her. "There'll be no peace till you've found out what's happened."

So they crept up the back stairs to eavesdrop.

Lady Bradbury was skimming towards the foot of the stairs, one lace-edged hand gliding over the banisters and her new sack-back gown billowing behind her like a sail, and she was scolding furiously. "You wicked, wicked girl! How you could do such a thing to your *dear* parents who so *truly* love you? 'Tis past my comprehension. Ain't you ashamed to be so wicked?"

"You'll get no answer, ma'am, so you may as well spare your breath," Sir George said, brusque with anger and incomprehension. "The wench is dumb."

"How? Dumb?" her mother demanded. "What nonsense! She will speak to her mother." She put out her hands to turn her daughter towards her, shaking her angrily. But Ariadne stood as still as a stone, mute and apart, looking into nothing. She might as well have been a corpse.

"Ain't spoke a word since I found her, and that's the truth of it, damme," Sir George said, scowling at her.

Crouched behind the servants' door, Suki and Bessie looked at one another in amazement. She couldn't be dumb, surely. Something terrible must have happened. But before they could say anything, they heard Mr Jessup coughing in the passageway below them, so they had to tiptoe back to the kitchen.

"We shall know about it soon enough," Bessie said. "That I'm certain sure, for 'tis mortal bad to be struck dumb."

Above their heads, Hermione was still holding Ariadne's unresponsive shoulders, peering into her empty face. Now she looked more anxious than angry. "What ails her?" she said. "Is she hurt? Is that it?"

Sir George was on his way upstairs, bellowing for Jessup.

"If she is ill," Hermione called after him, "we must send for a surgeon."

"You may do as you please, ma'am," he called back coldly, pausing briefly in his ascent. "'Tis all one with me. I've done my part. If 'twere the old days she'd ha' been whipped, which she would do well to remember. She deserves as much. I wash my hands of the whole affair. I shall change my clothes, whilst they're attending the horses, and then I'm off to the tables." A spot of gambling would cheer him. "'Od's bowels! It makes my blood boil to look upon her!"

"My heart is palpitating!" Hermione complained to his disappearing back. "I shall run distract!" But he took no notice of her, even though she put her kerchief to her forehead and closed her eyes. When she opened them again, Jessup was standing politely before her, so she recovered herself and became practical. "Pray run for Mr McKinnon," she ordered, "and send Hepzibah to me, and the wet nurse to attend to Miss Ariadne. You see how things are with us. We are too ill to stand." And she sailed away towards her boudoir, with Ariadne walking stiffly and obediently behind her.

Just at that moment, Melissa returned from the baths, brick red and sweaty inside her steaming chair, and was carried into the hall, ready for Hepzie to assist her to her bed and the full sweat she needed and had now begun.

"Mamma!" she called petulantly from the damp side window. "Pray send Hepzibah to me directly!"

"You must make shift for yourself," her mother said, waving her kerchief weakly in the general direction of the chair. "Your sister is returned and we are all too ill and upset for words!"

"'Od's blood!" Melissa said angrily. "It's come to something when a person may not be treated civilly in a person's own house." She struggled out of the chair on her own, and began to puff up the stairs after her mother, very red in the face and dripping water from her bathgown as she went. "I see I must be a runaway if I wish to be treated civilly. Those who stay at home and behave with propriety are not worth the candle in this world."

But at that point, her father put his red face over the banisters to address her and what he had to say stilled all complaint and even startled her mother to silence. "Ah!" he boomed. "Melissa! You're there, are yer? You're to marry Sir Humphrey de Thespia. What d'you say to that?"

As a proposal, it lacked a certain style but Melissa was enchanted by it, thrilled, uplifted, and cattily rewarded. She had stolen her sister's fiancé, which was triumph enough, in all conscience, and all without lifting a finger or batting an eyelid. And now she would be the first daughter to marry, which meant that Ariadne would have to dance at her wedding while she would be the queen of the hour. And she would have a rich husband and fine clothes and a diamond necklace and the best food and a town house and a country house and a carriage with a coat of arms . . .

"I am honoured, Papa," she said and dropped him a dripping curtsey to prove it.

Her father was as pleased with her answer as she'd been with his question. "That, mark 'ee, Lady Bradbury," he said, "is the proper way for a daughter to behave. Would you had two who knew it. 'Tis settled then, Melissa. You're engaged to dine with him at Lady Fosdyke's this afternoon."

Hermione was thinking fast. 'Twas wondrous to know that her alliance with the great de Thespia family was still intact, but there would be all manner of problems to be solved. She would have to write to her own family, for a start, with some acceptable reason for the change of bride, or they would sense a scandal and refuse to attend. She could say 'twas a love match, perchance, that none had the heart to deny. She could stress Ariadne's generosity in standing aside for the happiness of her sister.

She was so busy with her thoughts that she forgot to applaud her younger daughter, who had to remind her. "Mamma, am I not worth congratulation?"

"Indeed," she said, remembering herself, "my dearest child. 'Tis a most happy match and one that does you honour."

"I shall need a lady's maid," Melissa said, remembering how her sister had been treated.

"You shall have Hepzibah."

"And new gowns?"

"As many as you wish."

Melissa looked smugly at her sister's unresponsive back. "And I suppose Ariadne will have to dance at my wedding?"

It was a minor detail to her mother. "Yes," she said, vaguely. "Belike. But first we must cure her of this present infirmity." And she led them both upstairs.

Below stairs, the household was in such uproar that there was barely time to pass on the gossip. The bells in the kitchen rang like church chimes, jumping and jangling until Cook declared they'd shake the board off the wall if they didn't give over. Barnaby was dispatched to fetch a barber, Jessup had gone for the surgeon, Hepzie was told to make a cold compress, Bessie was required to provide hot water, fresh towels, sal volatile, a clean chamber pot, and a complete change of linen for Sir

George – in that order and with considerable difficulty, for Benjy was beside himself with so much traffic on the stairs and was soon running berserk, nipping ankles and barking himself into a froth.

Suki went straight upstairs to Miss Ariadne. She found her sitting on her bed as still as a statue and totally mute. Her eyes flickered towards her friend, but without recognition, and there was no expression on her face at all. The sight of her was so upsetting that it was all Suki could do not to cry. 'Tis my fault, she thought. I was the one what spoke of choosing your own lover. I told her 'twas the proper thing to do. She remembered Ariadne's excitement and the pretty flush on her cheeks as she'd leant towards her lover. "I have followed your teaching to the letter."

"Oh Miss Ariadne," she said. "I'd do anything to help 'ee. Truly I would."

"An infusion of sage tea, perchance," Lady Bradbury said from the doorway. She was holding the cold compress delicately on to her forehead with one lace-trimmed hand but her face and her voice were distracted.

"'Tis a comfortable drink, ma'am," Suki said, still watching Ariadne, "with no harm in it." And no response to it either.

"I believe my daughter is bewitched," the lady said. "How I shall sustain this suffering I truly do not know. Oh, would Mr McKinnon were here. He is taking an unconscionable time, is he not?"

Mr McKinnon had been at the Cross Baths attending a dowager, and so he made less speed than he could have wished. It was nearly half an hour before his bearers finally brought him to South Parade. But he made up for his tardiness by elaborate manifestations of concern and the provision of three different medicaments in as many minutes. All for Lady Bradbury, naturally, since she held the purse strings. She was prescribed a restorative powder for her weakened pulse, asafoetida for her swooning fits, and a blackcurrant cordial to rouse her spirits. But Ariadne was a puzzle, as the gentleman himself confessed with much learned shaking of his fine new full-bottomed wig. "An enigma, ma'am, I'll own it. But we will accept this case, fear not. 'Tis a challenge."

"We?" Hermione queried faintly, sipping his restorative.

"Indeed so, ma'am," the doctor said, assuming his most deeply concerned expression. "'Tis a case will require the combined wit and learning of at least . . . three . . . doctors. I have never seen the like, ma'am." Then as he foresaw a possible loss of faith in his judgement, he continued quickly. "A similar on one occasion, which I do assure you was treated to a most successful conclusion. Most successful. Howsomever, since there are differences in this case – the lady being, shall we say, mute – I do maintain we should proceed with the utmost caution. The utmost caution. I will do myself the honour, ma'am, to call upon you again before dinner, with two of my esteemed colleagues. Did you wish me to attend upon your husband whilst I am in the house?"

Within an hour, Sir George had changed his linen, taken tea and a clyster and departed for the gaming house, leaving the foetid smell of his relief behind him. Within an hour and a half, Mr McKinnon had come back again with his two opportunist colleagues, one short and obsequious, bearing a jar of very fat leeches from Bordeaux, the other tall and taciturn with a lancet protruding from his top pocket.

They examined their intriguing patient pompously and at length, conversing with one another throughout in hushed whispers and incomprehensible terminology. A sample of her urine was considered by daylight and candle-light; skin was scraped from her arm and hairs plucked from her head; they counted her pulse and measured her tongue and looked down her throat and took swabs from her nostrils. Finally they declared themselves of the opinion that she was suffering from one of three possible ailments, the Straight Fives, the Rising of the Lights, or Hockogrocle, and that all or any of the three could prove fatal unless professionally and expensively treated.

"We do most seriously advise, dear lady, that treatment be commenced without delay," Mr McKinnon said.

"Oh, what calamity!" Hermione said. "My husband and I are due to dine with Lady Fosdyke within this half-hour. What is to be done?"

The doctors, being professional men, were equal to such a challenge. Without question, Lady Bradbury should honour her social commitments, they said. Her poor sick daughter could be left quite safely in their care, providing a trustworthy servant could be found to sit with her. They would commence the treatments that very afternoon. There was not a minute to lose.

So Suki was called from the nursery to be witness to Miss Ariadne's medication, and a thoroughly unpleasant, cruel business it was. On that first afternoon, they bled her until her cheeks were white and then prescribed Tartar Emetic mixed with a slimy broth made from the strained fluid of twelve boiled snails. Ariadne was heaving after the first mouthful, but they forced the whole noxious mess down her throat with a funnel, and were delighted when she was monstrously and strainingly sick. Then they gave orders that she was to be kept in bed until their return in the morning, when they were perfectly confident that speech would be restored to her, and left her, panting, exhausted and mute, to recover as well as she could.

Suki helped her into bed and covered her cold limbs with blankets. Then she went off to fill a warming pan. She was furious at their cruelty. "Poor soul!" she said to Cook as she heaped the copper pan with hot coals. "'Tis torture no less, and more than any mortal soul deserves."

"Aye, but do she speak?" Cook said. "That's the aim an' purpose on't."

"No she doesn't," Suki said. "An' no more would I, if 'twere done to me. Tartar Emetic indeed."

The next morning the torturers returned with a fresh supply of leeches, and a strong clyster. But despite all their efforts, Ariadne's silence was unbroken by speech, although this time she groaned as she was sick, and this they proclaimed to be encouraging progress.

Suki was angrier than ever at such foolishness. "The poor soul can hardly swallow tea," she said, 'an here they are a-pourin' poison down her throat. They'll send her to her grave, that's what they'll do. I wonder they can't see it. What she'm a-suffering from is a broken heart. Poor lady."

But the doctors continued to treat the Rising of the Lights and Hockogrocle.

On the fourth day of their administrations, since neither clysters nor emetics, nor bleeding by leech, nor even prolonged cupping had so far had the desired effect, they decided that the time had come for them to apply the very latest and most efficacious treatment of galvanisation. They arrived that afternoon with so much equipment that they needed a coach and horses to haul it to the door. The first leather case contained four identical glass bowls, which were taken carefully out of their wrappings and stood upon the carpet. Jessup and Barnaby were commandeered to lift Hermione's day bed into the air and lower it inch by inch until all four legs were inside their own glass container. Then the miraculous instrument itself was unpacked and set on a table beside the bed. It was a very curious instrument, consisting of a brass cylinder with a neat wooden handle attached to it, a large rod made of golden amber and a collecting jar, coated in lead and lined, impressively and expensively, with no less an article than gold leaf.

Jessup and Barnaby were impressed by it and Lady Bradbury looked at it with suspicious interest but Ariadne ignored it as if it was of no consequence whatever, and when she was ordered to lie down upon the day bed, she did so meekly, her face still blank. Hepzie and Suki were instructed to stand one on each side of her and be prepared to hold down her arms, should she start to struggle. Then the machine was set in motion, and while Lady Bradbury watched, the amber rod was held against the cylinder while the handle was rotated vigorously by Mr McKinnon. To Suki's mistrustful eye, the whole thing looked sinister in the extreme, but even she wasn't prepared for what followed.

The rod was suddenly plunged against Ariadne's face. Blue sparks flew into the air, and there was a sizzling noise, like a snake striking its prey. Ariadne arched her back, and groaned as though she was falling into a deep swoon. Then her arms and legs began to twitch, horribly and uncontrollably, like death throes. Her eyes were open but completely without sight, and when the rod was finally taken away they remained open and her limbs went on twitching but she was deeply and terrifyingly unconscious.

"What have you done to her?" Hermione shrieked. "My poor child! You've killed her!"

"Calm yourself, madam," Mr McKinnon said. "'Tis all as it should be. The nature of the treatment is—"

But Hermione wasn't listening to him. She was on her knees beside her convulsive daughter, slapping her pallid cheeks and weeping, "Arouse yourself! Wake up! Oh, I prithee wake! Ariadne, my dear, my dear, wake I beg you!"

The taciturn doctor endeavoured to take his patient's pulse, and Suki noticed that even he was looking a little anxious, despite his professional calm. Ariadne went on twitching.

"I suggest we cover the patient and await the return of consciousness, which will, I can assure you, dear lady, bring the power of speech within its train," Mr McKinnon said, ebullient as ever. And Ariadne turned her head and was violently sick all over his breeches.

At that, and to everybody's relief, all three medical men decided to retreat. Jessup and Barnaby were dispatched to escort them to the door, and Hepzie and Suki were sent to the kitchen for cloths and warm water to clean up the mess. But it was many long minutes before Ariadne groaned her way back to the world, and then she was so weak she couldn't raise her hands from the bed, even to have them sponged clean.

"Speak to me, child," her mother begged. "For the love of God, have pity. A word, that's all I ask. Just one word." But Ariadne was still dumb. Tears welled from her blank eyes and washed across her nose and on to her pillow, but there was no answer, no recognition, no sound.

"How does she fare, think 'ee?" Hermione asked, wiping her daughter's clammy forehead. "I am mortal afeard."

"We shall recover her, ma'am," Hepzie said. She was on her knees and busy with the scrubbing brush, but she knew the right thing to say.

But Suki was still too overwhelmed by pity and terror to consider her words. "They could have killed her, poor lady," she said heatedly. "Them an' their galvanisation. 'Tis quackery to my way of thinkin' an' more like to kill than cure. Why just look at the poor creature. She's no more strength to her than a babe new-born. Show 'em the door, ma'am, and let's have no more on 'em."

Hermione looked up at the flushed furious face beside her, thinking what spirit the girl had and how honestly she spoke. "You may be right," she admitted. "Howsomever, Sir George would take it ill."

"Sir George arn't 'ere," Suki pointed out. The gentleman was out gaming again with his good friend Sir Humphrey. "Beggin' your pardon, ma'am."

Hermione stood up, and smoothed her wrinkled petticoat, and made a decision. "She shall have a day's rest," she said. "The surgeons need not call again. You shall sit with her and keep her company and care for her. You will report to me if there is any change, you understand. Tomorrow she shall travel to Appleton and you with her. 'Tis quiet there."

It was a turn of events that Suki hadn't anticipated and it didn't please her at all. She'd faced the fact that it was going to be difficult to ride into Bristol now that she was in Bath but if she were sent out into the country, it would be impossible. Worse still, how would he find her if he came a-searching? Appleton was more than fifty miles away. Oh no, she didn't want to be sent out there.

"How of the baby?" she asked. "Should I not stay here with him?"

Hermione tossed the excuse aside with a flick of her long white fingers. "He can travel with you," she said. "'Tis a fine strong child and will take no harm of a journey."

And at that she swept out of the room and into the necessary organisation. Within half an hour, everything had been arranged. Suki's truckle bed and William's cradle had been carried upstairs and installed in Ariadne's bedroom, and the dog cart was ordered for six o'clock the next morning.

It annoyed Suki to have been so easily overridden but, once the beds had been moved, there was nothing for it but to comply. Somebody had to look after poor Miss Ariadne and she was the best and most proper to do it. That couldn't be denied. So she made up a good fire – because the day had been chill with mist – took plenty of candles, the smallest kettle and a selection of cold meats from the kitchen, and persuaded Lady Bradbury to allow her a teapot already primed with tea in case her daughter required refreshment during the evening. Then she suckled William to settle him for the night, put him sleepily to bed, and settled down to her vigil, watching from the window as the house emptied.

First to leave were Sir George, Lady Bradbury and Melissa who were off to the masked ball at the Assembly Rooms, with Hepzie smirkingly in attendance, then the local servants went, tired but well laden and, after them, Mr Jessup, coughing like a steam engine and with his hat pulled well down over his eyes. Soon the parade was quite empty and the sky had darkened to a most oppressive grey and there was nothing to do except draw the curtains and light the candles and sit by the fire and wait. William's little silk coat had a tiny tear in the sleeve, so she took her needle and thread from her pocket and began to mend it, holding the fine work close to the candle.

There was hardly a sound in the room, except for the quiet rasp of her needle, the flicker of the coals, and William's gentle breathing, so when Ariadne began to cry the sound filled the room. Suki put down her mending at once and rushed to comfort her.

"Don't cry," she urged, flinging her arms round her poor friend. "'Tis all over. I promise 'ee. Plaguey doctors to hurt 'ee so! 'Twas more than human flesh and blood could stand. Well, there's to be no more on't. They'm all dismissed. Every plaguey one of 'em. You aren't to be tortured no more."

"Oh!" Ariadne said, leaning her head against the comfortable warmth of Suki's bosom. "I wish I were dead. I wish I were dead. I am shamed and ruined and sore and nobody loves me, nor is ever like to. I wish I were dead."

It didn't surprise Suki to hear her speak, but she was shocked by her despair. No wonder the poor lady played dumb.

"He said he loved me more than all the world," Ariadne wept. "'Twas a lie. He said we should never part. I should be his for ever. I was his one true love in all the world. 'Twas a lie, a lie! I wish I were dead!"

Suki was full of tender concern. Something must be done to comfort the poor lady. Some creature comfort maybe. "Could 'ee fancy a dish uv tea?" she suggested. "Or are you still too sore? They pulled you about most cruel, plaguey critturs."

94

"Aye," Ariadne said, as though she was surprised to be saying it. "I *do* thirst."

So the tea was made and Ariadne trembled out of bed and sat by the fire to drink it, and was tempted to a little custard cup, which Suki assured her would "slide down her poor throat, smooth as silk". And presently she talked again, at great length and weeping freely but gradually with more sadness than passion. Soon Suki had heard the full story of courtship, proposal and betrayal.

"I shall never love again," Ariadne mourned, gazing at the fire. "The game ain't worth the candle. 'Tis a brave thing to vow to marry where you love, but if love ain't returned you are lost before you begin."

"There were still some men of honour in the world," Suki told her earnestly. "They arn't all rogues and vagabonds. Some has a most tender concern for their womenfolk. Captain Jack was always—"

The use of the past tense alerted Ariadne to question. "Have you not found him?"

Suki made a grimace. "Not yet," she confessed. "He'm still at sea. Due back any day, so they says at the shipping office."

That was a surprise. How bold this girl was! "You've been to the shipping office? All the way to Bristol?"

"Aye," Suki said, grinning at the memory. "And bought a horse there."

So that story was told and much enjoyed. By the end of it, Ariadne was still sad, but had recovered enough to be philosophical. "What is to become of us?" she said, half resigned and half teasing. "My lover faithless, yours at sea. Could we look into the future what *should* we see?"

"There's only one I know what could do that," Suki told her, "and that's Old Sheena, the gypsy. She read your palm outside the theatre. Do you recall? And Miss Melissa's too."

Ariadne remembered very well. "Aye, she did, and saw uncommon clear."

The idea struck them both in the same instant. "How if we were to call her here?" Ariadne said. "Would she come think 'ee?"

"If we offered her silver," Suki said knowledgeably. "She'm uncommon fond of silver."

"We would need care," Ariadne warned. "None must know of it." The thought of arranging something so deliciously illicit was cheering her visibly, bringing colour to her cheeks at last. How angry her mother would be if she knew what they were planning.

"I shan't breathe a word," Suki promised. "'Twould be our secret. Could you keep the door?"

"Of course. There's silver in my petticoat. Fetch me scissors and I will unpick the pocket."

Which she did and found three silver groats and two pennies. Seconds later, Suki was on her way to the theatre.

She reached it just as the doors were being opened and the first rush of warm, stale, evocative air emitted, and a potent mixture it was, of candle wax and greasepaint, dust and orange peel, strong perfumes and stronger sweat. For a second, she stood beside the steps remembering how happy she'd been sitting in the stalls beside her darling, all those long months ago. But there was no time to stand about. Sheena must be tempted before the playgoers could dominate her.

She was in her usual place at the top of the stairs and there was already an eager crowd around her, but it was easy enough to push to the front and a simple thing to catch the gypsy's eye.

"Here's a groat says you would be welcome at a lady's house for a private consultation," Suki said, revealing the coin tucked under her fingertips. "And more to come when 'tis given."

Sheena looked at her shrewdly. "Was that one consultation or more, gel?"

"Two," Suki said, feeling that this answer might be more acceptable.

"Palm or crystal?"

"Both, mayhap."

Sheena flicked the corner of her long shawl across her shoulder and removed her attention from all the other eager hands stretched out towards her. It was a bargain.

The parade was very dark and completely deserted. As the gypsy followed her down the area steps, Suki wondered whether Ariadne would have the strength to come down and open the door to them. But there she was, and with a pretty flush on her cheeks. "Come in! Come in!" she said to Sheena. "You are welcome here."

They climbed the back stairs like three shadows and opened the door quietly to the warmth of Ariadne's room. She was obviously feeling a deal better, for she had placed the card table before the fire, with an armchair on one side of it for Sheena and the nursing chair on the other for herself. It was a cunning arrangement, Suki thought, worthy of her mother, for it put the gypsy on a higher level than her client, and that was both flattering and suitably deferential.

The crystal was agreed on and a second groat expended, and Sheena put her hand under her apron and produced a small globe of grey glass, clouded with what appeared to be vapour of some sort. She set it in the middle of the card table and held it between her hands as though she was warming it, the bells at her wrists whispering softly as she moved her fingers.

"I give you warning, young miss," she said, "my sight is uncommon clear tonight. I 'ent to be trifled with."

"I do not trifle, I assure you," Ariadne said earnestly, leaning forward and looking up into the gypsy's dark face.

"Pain," Sheena said. "Sorrow. Tears. A great love lost, or missing or both. For here is money a-plenty, but not thine, aren't that right? And here's a handsome face, turned quite away. Such heaviness. Such sorrow." The clouds in the crystal were shifting as though they were in the sky, and Sheena's face was taut with concentration. "It changes. I can see nothing. Only heaviness. And tears are falling."

"True. All true," Ariadne told her. "Would 'twere not."

"Now here's a sea journey," Sheena said. "Much water. A long sea journey. Very long. To the Indies, I'll be bound, for here's a storm, and white sand, and water full of bright fishes, and here's sea under moonlight and blue sea and weed and sails becalmed. Oh yes, a very long journey, my pretty."

"I know of no such journey," Ariadne said. "But it *is* possible. My father has plantations in the Indies."

This was no news to Old Sheena. "Spare no tears for what is lost and gone," she intoned, still gazing raptly at the crystal. "An old love lost, a new one found," and she flicked a rapid glance at her client to see how she was doing. "Here comes the face again, young missy. And a fair fine handsome face, set between curtains of some heavy red stuff. Not a window, that I'm certain sure. A theatre, could it be?"

"Oh yes. Yes," Ariadne whispered. "What of the face? What can you see?"

"Dishonesty," the gypsy said firmly. "'Tis a fair face but a hard heart. Here's greed under that smile, and money in that hand. Woe to his black heart, I say."

"Amen!" Ariadne agreed. "Can you see more? I would know more if I could." Her tone was almost humble, her face pleading.

But the gypsy seemed to have finished. "Well as to that," Old Sheena said. "I can't say. See how the clouds thicken." And it was true. They could see swirling shapes filling the little globe. "No. No. There is no more to see."

Suki would have loved to have offered her palm, for she felt sure that the sea journey was the one the Captain was making at that moment, but the gypsy was already standing up and wrapping her shawls around her head and shoulders. She was looking around her in the most peculiar way, her nostrils flaring almost as though she was smelling the air. The firelight made flickering patterns on the brown skin of her forehead and the long hoops of her earrings glittered as she turned her head from side to side. "Change!" she said suddenly. "That's what 'tis. I 'ent felt it so strong in many a long year. There'm change a-coming."

Her words were so unexpected and so dramatically delivered that they made the hair rise on Suki's neck. Ariadne looked as though she'd been bewitched. The room was full of pulsing shadows and redolent with the gypsy's heavy, oily scent and the strong smell of wood smoke that rose from her clothes. But she looked so fierce, they daren't question her, and presently she left the room without another word. Suki had to run after her to see her off the premises.

"What do 'ee think?" Ariadne asked the minute she returned. "Did she speak true?"

"'Twas likely," Suki said cautiously, because she was still feeling distinctly disturbed.

"How well she described Mr Clements. A black-hearted lover. How could she know it?"

"Change is a-coming," Suki said. "She had that to rights and no mistake, for we'm off to Appleton in the morning."

"Would 'twere change for the better," Ariadne said sadly.

"We'll make it so," Suki promised. "We'm young yet and the world is wide." There were voices in the street below. "Milady's back," she reported from the window. "Shall you speak to her now?"

"No," Ariadne said firmly. "I shall not. She ain't worthy of speech. Besides," and she assumed Old Sheena's tone and manner, "'twould take a powerful amount of spirit, that would."

Seven

O n the other side of the wide world, the *Bonny Beaufoy* lay at anchor just off the coast of Nevis, rocking gently on a peacock-green sea, while the island steamed and shimmered at a tantalising distance. The last leg of their nightmare journey had been a long stinking slog. A raging fever had killed another seven slaves and four of the crew, and those who were left were too weary to clean the place properly – even with Jack to urge them on – so the smell of shit and vomit pervaded the ship. Their food stocks were so low and so badly contaminated that even the captain had been given short commons and, now, after one hundred and seventeen wretched days at sea, there wasn't a man aboard who wasn't frantic to get ashore. They ached to put fresh food in their bellies, clean air in their lungs, firm earth under their feet, an expanse of clear water between themselves and their stinking cesspit of a ship.

Like everyone else, Jack Daventry was standing at the ship's rail waiting for the local surgeon who was being rowed out from Jamestown – at an exasperatingly leisurely pace – to examine the cargo and give the ship a clean bill of health, or not as the case may be. He was uncommon well dressed for a surgeon, in buff breeches, an embroidered waistcoat and a black silk jacket, fashionably unbuttoned but, as his boat gradually drew nearer, Jack could see that he wore his own hair and that it was shoulder length, sandy-coloured and very dishevelled, that his cravat was poorly tied and none too clean and that his tricorn hat was faded and stained, which detracted somewhat from his first appearance. Even so, he was plainly a man to be reckoned with, for he carried a gold-topped cane and an air of heavy authority.

Before he climbed aboard the *Bonny Beaufoy*, he took an old-fashioned nose cone from his medicine bag and tied it over his nose and mouth. He was instantly and ridiculously transformed, for it made him look like some huge ungainly bird with a brown beak and tufts of ginger feathers sticking out on either side of his hat.

"Can't be too careful," he called up to Jack, his voice muffled as though he were shouting from the back of a cave. "We can smell you on shore. D'you have no vinegar, damme?"

Jack explained that they'd been becalmed.

That didn't impress the surgeon. "You didn't buy enough in the first place, that's the truth of it," he said. "Ah well, lead on. The sooner 'tis done, the sooner we can get back to civilisation."

His examination was perfunctory, which was just as well, for his extraordinary appearance struck terror into the slaves, who were already anxious at the new sounds and smells they were encountering, and had been preparing themselves for fresh horrors ever since the ship hove to. The women were so afraid of him that they cowered and shook and did their best to squirm away when he stuck his beak over the edge of the hatch and peered down into the darkness. But he had no intention of exposing himself to any infections below deck. He stayed where he was, muttering questions. "Flux? No.

Good. Good. Pox? No. Good. Good. How many did 'ee lose on the journey? Good. Good. That old feller's stone blind. Did 'ee know that? You'll not sell him."

After half an hour, he was ready to sign the clearance paper and declare the ship fit to come into port. Then he turned his mind to business.

"Now sir," he said. "I need eight of your best for the Bradbury plantation. Six field-hands and two for the house."

Jack was surprised and annoyed by such a peremptory demand. "I was told nothing of this, sir," he protested. "I was given written instructions from Mr Bradbury himself. I can show them to you if you wish. There was no mention of slaves being handed over for the plantation."

That didn't concern the surgeon. "Was there not?" he said easily. "'Tis no matter. Mr Bradbury knows of it. Mr Ferguson will sign for 'em. Those two big buck niggers in the corner would do for a start."

Jack was in two minds. During the last days of the voyage he'd been checking the current price of slaves with Mr Tomson and Mr Reuben, who were the most knowledgeable men aboard, so he knew that his would command between two hundred and fifty and two hundred and seventy pounds each, so eight slaves translated into a deal of money to be handing over without argument. Over two thousand pounds. If he queried the arrangement, he would cause a delay and nobody would thank him for that. On the other hand, if he allowed it to go ahead, 'twould mean two thousand pounds less profit for the Bradburys and Mr Jedediah Smith, which wouldn't please *them*. The purser had been studiously polite in the last few weeks, but he knew that the animosity between them was still simmering and could be dangerous.

The surgeon took his silence as consent and went on choosing his slaves. It took him longer than his examination had done but at last he seemed to be satisfied.

"Bring 'em up on deck," he instructed. "Put 'em in irons. They can travel back with me. 'Tis but a short distance and I've a musket aboard to pacify 'em."

Jack despatched two crew men to do as he required. "Shall you see the captain, while you wait?" he asked, following protocol.

The surgeon had no desire to stay on the ship a minute longer than was necessary. "No, no," he said. "We shall meet tonight at the banquet. To which you are all invited, by the bye. 'Twill be a fine occasion. A chance for you to meet your escorts."

That was news to Jack, too.

"She arrived last week," the surgeon said, pointing at the harbour. "See her? The three-masted frigate. Fine ship, damme. The *Yorick*. Out of Bristol. First-rate fire power. You'll be safe enough with her."

This time, Jack felt he could question. "Safe?"

"Aye, sir," the surgeon boomed, adjusting his nose cone. "We're at war with France, damme. Have been since May. They took Minorca so 'tis said, on account of some pesky admiral who don't know one end of a ship from another. Left the place wide open for 'em, by all accounts. Name of Byng. Much good may it do him. Should be hung drawn and quartered. That's my opinion of him. Howsomever, the end result is that we're at war at last. And not a minute before time. Pesky Frenchies! Now we can give 'em a dammed good trouncing, which they've long deserved. Good afternoon to 'ee, sir." His slaves now loaded, he swung one buckled foot over the side and descended the ladder.

"He's a rum sort of cove," Jack said to the bosun as the laden boat creaked away. "You'd have thought he'd have seen the captain – for the sake of politeness, if nothing else."

"There's no accountin'," Mr Reuben said, sucking in his cheeks. "I likes the sound of that there banquet."

In fact, the captain wouldn't have welcomed the interruption had the surgeon wished to see him because he was in the middle of an argument with Mr Jedediah Smith.

"You gave me your word of honour," the purser was saying, "as a gentleman, that he was to be clapped in irons the minute we arrived. The minute we arrived, sir."

"Well now, as to that, sir," the captain said, "'twas afore we were becalmed, as you'll allow, which have made a deal of difference to the circumstances and so forth. A deal of difference. They'm all a deal leaner than we'd intended, on account of the low state of our provisions and so forth. 'Twill take a week to fatten 'em for market, at the very least, as you'll allow, and then there's the hold to be scalded and so forth. I'd not wish my slave master in irons with such a deal of work to be done. And neither would you, I dare swear."

The purser's face was dark with frustration. To have his wishes overridden was irritation enough, worse there were no arguments he could use to prevent it, for the captain seemed to have an answer to everything, worse still there was no higher authority that he could appeal to, so far from home. "If I agree to this delay," he said, "I'd have you know 'tis against my better judgement."

"You shall have him in irons the moment we sail," Mr Tomson promised. "You have my word on't. A slave master's so much waste of space on the return journey."

Mr Smith looked at him sourly. "He's been a waste of space, sir," he said, "since the day he turned his pistol on his betters."

"Ah!" Mr Tomson said, turning his attention to the departing surgeon. "They'm off. Now we can put into harbour. If you'll excuse me, sir."

So the *Bonny Beaufoy* sailed into harbour at last, and Jack and the rest of the crew staggered ashore, unsteady on legs accustomed to the pitch and toss of the sea, and light-headed with euphoria at their sudden release. It was like walking into paradise, for the air was warm and clean and scented with spices and the entire island lush with trees, most of them bearing fruit. There were branches bright with oranges, lemons and limes, and others dropping huge bunches of green fruits curved like scimitars; there were trees hiding an odd-looking golden fruit that they afterwards learnt was called a pomegranate; and all along the edge of the beach, a line of tall palms waved huge feathery fronds, shushing and whispering in the cooling air of an on-shore breeze.

There was a house slave waiting on the quay, who said he'd been sent to lead them to their quarters, and two more wilting patiently beside a two-horse carriage that had been sent to carry Mr Tomson and the purser. Behind them, more than a dozen slaves were waiting in the shade with seven huge barrels from which they drew coconut shells full of water for the newcomers to drink. And uncommon welcome it was, for they were parched with heat and waiting.

Jack noticed that all their new attendants were males, that they all wore blue striped cotton breeches and that they understood what was said to them. When he asked them where the new slaves were to be housed, they rushed to point the way to the slave compound, which was sturdily built with a high stockade to prevent escape and provide shade.

But bringing the slaves ashore took him a very long time, even though he had Mr Reuben and six of the crew to help him and Blue to translate his instructions. Being in a new situation renewed their mistrust and, although Blue tried to persuade them that no harm would come to them, they struggled when they were hauled from the holds and fought with all their strength to avoid being pushed down into the longboats. Once they were safely inside the compound, thirst drove them to obedience, but they were still dirty and afraid and smelled most vilely.

"We'll get 'em washed down tomorrow," Jack said to Mr Reuben. For the moment, he was glad to walk away from them.

Their guide was still waiting for them on the quay and having ascertained that there were "no more English a-coming", he set off at a brisk pace following the cobbled path uphill. They arrived at the plantation house out of breath and sweating but even Mr Reuben had to agree that it was worth the climb, for it was an impressive building with a view over the entire estate – from hillside to bay. And even though it was made of wood, it had all the refinements of an English country house, being two storeys high, with elegant shuttered windows, a deal of fine carving, and an imposing flight of stairs leading up to a long veranda and a front door which was the equal of any Jack had seen in London or Bristol.

"My eye!" Dickon said. "They live like lords here-abouts, I see. Are we to stay here, think 'ee?"

Apparently not. There was another lesser building to the right and slightly behind the main house, which their guide told them was "de gues' house" and to which he led them. It was a long single-storey hut, blessedly cool but confusingly dark after the blaze of sunlight outside. At first sight, it seemed to be full of slaves. Their guide led them to the long room which they were to occupy, and they were brought ewers of water and cakes of soap so that they could wash. They were shown the pallets on which they would sleep and the long trestle tables at which they were to dine. "But not tonight, massas. Tonight is de banquet." There were even, as they discovered when they began to clean themselves, small children sitting outside the door waiting to take their soiled clothes away to be laundered.

The thought of being well dressed and clean again lifted Jack's spirits at once. He was the first to strip, the first to pour water from the ewer, the first to pick up the soap.

"This is the life!" he said, as he scrubbed away the filth of the voyage. Oh the pleasure of stepping away from the stink of his sea clothes, the joy of seeing his hands return to their normal colour. "If the banquet is one half as splendid as the house, we shall dine well tonight."

It was more splendid than anything any of them had ever seen and it began with two receptions, one on the lawn for the seamen, the other – to which Jack was invited – in a small front parlour for the officers of both ships. There they were served rum punch, sherry and canary wine and felt themselves uncommon fine dogs, and were greeted by the factor of the estate, who was a rough-faced Scotsman with broad shoulders and sandy hair, not unlike the surgeon to look at, but dressed like a lord, in shoes with silver buckles, green satin breeches and a brocade coat that was the very height of London fashion.

"Your sarvent, sirs," he said as his guests were

announced and made their entrances. "Angus Ferguson, sirs. Uncommon pleased to meet you, damme."

It wasn't long before they'd all been introduced to one another and were well on their way to a cheerful inebriation. Jack was back in his element, talking to everyone and instantly befriending the master of the *Yorick* and his second mate, who was called Jack Jerome and had, so he said, been "born and bred in Brissol" and consequently knew all the more shady watering holes along the quay. They were a splendid pair of swaggering rogues and reminded Jack of Quin Cutpurse and the company of the road. It was quite a disappointment to him when they moved on to make small-talk with the purser. But 'tis the way in such gatherings, he thought, as he, too, moved on. There would be other opportunities to improve on the acquaintance. Now was the time to exercise the art of conversation. Within two paces he was talking to the three surgeons about the fevers common in the tropics, within two minutes he found himself discussing slaves and sugar crops with the factor and his wife.

"You've some fine cattle aboard, I'm told," the factor said.

"Aye sir, I believe so. Eight of our best were chosen for this estate."

"Yes indeed," the factor said, but his voice was vague as if the matter didn't interest him.

Jack decided to push him a little. "You've seen 'em, I daresay, sir."

"Not yet, sir," Mr Ferguson admitted. "'Twill wait till morning. I can trust Mr Mackie's judgement."

This seemed a little suspicious to Jack. If I'd spent two thousand pounds on merchandise, he thought, I'd want to see it for myself and be sure of the bargain. But there was no time to pursue the matter further for at that moment a slave in off-white breeches and a snow-white wig appeared in the doorway to beat on the floor with an ebony cane and announce that dinner was served. So, still clutching glasses, they progressed from the press and noise of the little parlour into the candle-lit splendour of a large chandelier-hung dining-room.

At its centre was a sumptuous table covered in a white linen cloth and set for sixteen guests with elaborate glasses and a great deal of fine blue-and-white china. There were three plates for every guest, a medley of glasses by every set of plates, and so many heaped platters and steaming dishes in the centre of the table that they'd been placed rim to rim in order to find room for them all. Jack tried to count them and gave up after fourteen, having established that they were all beef of some kind and very well cooked. There were several roast joints: a rump and a chine in particular, a tongue curled and flattened and set about with herbs, a beef pie, steaming most succulently, a dish of tripe, another of marrow bones, even the cheeks, baked, eyes and all, and set side by side with a mound of minced beef between them and two large leaves curved on either side of them like ears. After the paucity of food aboard the *Bonny Beaufoy*, it was positively regal and, as soon as the first toasts had been drunk – to "William Pitt, God bless him" and "The sugar trade, long may it prosper" – they set to with a will. And uncommon good eating it made.

For the first twenty minutes, conversation was limited to grunts, but once they had taken the edge off their hunger, their host turned them to the topics of the hour, and the French took a roasting as thorough as the one that had been given to the beef. While the story of the miserable Admiral Byng was passed along the table, and breeches were unbuttoned and wind passed, the remains of the feast were cleared from the table and the second course brought on.

To their amazement, it was a second banquet and as lavish as the first had been, with just as many dishes. There were potato puddings and meat pasties, a roast leg of pork, the shoulder of a young goat and an entire kid with a pudding in its belly, a sucking pig swimming in claret wine and flavoured with sage and nutmeg, a loin of veal with a sauce made of lemons and limes, a shoulder of mutton lying on a bed of dark leaves, three boiled chickens, four ducklings, eight turtle doves and three rabbits, spread across the dishes in which they'd been cooked with their skinned legs at full stretch as if they were running away. Which is what most of the guests thought of doing, for their sea-starved bellies were uncomfortably distended by the first course and the thought of chomping through a second made most of them feel decidedly nauseous.

Except for Jack. He was looking quizzically at the factor, wondering how he could afford such a costly feast. 'Twould tax the pockets of a prince and he was a mere servant, factor or no, yet there he sat, sprawled in his chair as if he were the prince himself. Did Mr Bradbury know of his opulence? Or was it done without his knowledge? Was he billed to provide it? Or did this man have other means?

The factor caught the tail-end of Jack's calculating expression. "You've not seen such a spread, I daresay, Mr Daventry," he said and there was a mocking edge to his voice.

"No, sir," Jack said coolly, pleased that he was about to contradict the man. "Quite the reverse. I've sat at many such tables in England. Too numerous to count. My grandfather was a duke, don'tcher know, and a leading member of the ton besides, so hospitable extravagance was expected of him. *De rigueur*, you might say."

The information caused the stir he intended: Mr Tomson was surprised, Mr Dix envious, and Jack Jerome winked at him across the table, raising his glass in admiration.

Mr Jedediah Smith turned his head to speak to Mr Tomson from behind his hand. "Insolent puppy," he said, and mocked, "His grandfather a duke indeed. And we are to sit here and listen to such nonsense. The man should be in irons."

"I'm surprised you undertook such a voyage," Mr Ferguson said, "if that's the humour of it."

"My family deplores idleness," Jack told him easily, "and a man must see the world, don'tcher know."

"You don't fear the hazards of it then, Mr Daventry?" Jack Jerome asked.

"Life is a hazard," Jack said, easily.

Jedediah Smith scowled at him. As you will discover, he thought.

"Good appetite!" the factor said, returning their attention to the food. "Let's have all those glasses filled, if you please, Joshua!"

So his guests settled to their second repast and, with plenty of wine to wash it all down and endless toasts to give them pause for breath, most of them did justice to it, although they ate a great deal more slowly than they'd done when their appetites were keen. By the time they reached the third course, most of them were so befuddled with drink and rich food that they no longer knew nor cared what they were putting into their mouths, and simply spooned through custards and creams, cheesecakes, puff-pastries, guavas, plantines, pineapples and water melons without pausing. The talk grew ribald and ridiculous, the belching louder and more extravagant. When they finally staggered from the table, it was past three o'clock in the morning.

"Uncommon fine banquet," Mr Smith told his host thickly. "Thank 'ee mos' . . . mos' . . . squisly. Mos' esqui . . . surlally." And giggled. "You know what I mean, damme!"

Even Jack, who'd always claimed a strong head for drink, was too confused to think. He managed to remove his clothes, and to check that his pistols were still in his locker but, after that, he fell across the mattress and slept as though he'd been knocked unconscious. His messmates shuffled in and out of the hut for the rest of the night, to piddle or to ease themselves by vomiting, but he slept on, groaning and dead to the world. The sun was at full strength and directly overhead before he woke and then it was with such a sore head and such an overloaded stomach that it took an effort to creep from the hut. Then, and with shame, he remembered the slaves and realised that they hadn't been fed or watered since the previous evening. How could he have been so unfeeling? He set off to the stockade at once to attend to them.

To his relief, they were sitting in the shade of the high fences eating the broken meats of the banquet. Most of it was already sour, and a lot was rotting and high, but they were picking it over, hungrily, their hands full and their chins dripping with sauces and gravy. After a night away from them and an evening of good food and civilised living, the sight of them appalled him. They were an affront, filthy, naked, half-starved, covered in weeping sores. Most of them were so thin, he could see their ribs and the jutting bones of their haunches, and the children were pot-bellied and snotty, with a thick crust of rheum, crawling with flies, between their nostrils and their food-smeared lips. Savages, every single one. And at that moment, Blue looked up at him from the group to his left and greeted him with his familiar wide smile. "Good morning, Mr Jack."

He was caught between the revulsion that was still riding strong in him and shame at what he'd been thinking. Had he not stood on the deck of the *Bonny Beaufoy*, pistol in hand, bellowing that they were human? "You must be cleaned," he shouted, as if the volume of his voice would make amends. "I cannot allow this squalor. 'Tis insupportable." And he strode off at once to arrange for it to be done.

For the rest of the day, he took his charges down to the river, twenty at a time, with six musketeers to prevent escape, and stood on the bank while they rubbed all the encrusted filth from their bodies. And that evening he made sure that a stew was cooked for them with ground maize and fresh vegetables.

"How long afore they'm a-ready for sale?" Mr Tomson asked that evening.

"Ten days at the very least," Jack told him. "They're parlously thin. A fortnight would be my preference."

"'Twill take a week for to scald and load," the captain said. "So a fortnight 'tis. I shall send instructions for notes of sale to be printed and posted for two weeks tomorrow. I daresay we can wait so long, what do 'ee think, my hearties?"

"You can take as long as you likes over it, Mr Tomson," Mr Reuben grinned. "'Tis all one with me. Some swabber'll find me employment, I daresay. Or if that aren't the humour of it, I can allus sit in the shade and rest my bones and drink a tot of rum or two an' wait for 'em. As I sez to 'ee, 'tis all one with me."

That was the general happy opinion round the table.

"'Tis a fortunate island to be idle in, Mr Tomson, sir," Dickon said. "Women a-plenty, food a-plenty, grog a-plenty. What could a man desire more?"

In Jack's case, as he discovered before the fortnight was spent, it was action. The fittest of the slaves had been set to work and the holds had been scrubbed and scoured and sweetened with vinegar. The sugar was being loaded under Mr Smith's close supervision. The slaves were fattening visibly. There was nothing left for him to do but sit in the shade with Mr Reuben and drink rum punch but, as always, enforced idleness made him restless.

"I've a mind to take a look at the plantation," he said to the bosun.

"You'll do it alone if that's the humour of it," Mr Reuben warned. "I've no desire to go a-clambering about in this heat."

"Nor no facility neither," Jack teased him. But now that he'd thought of it, the excursion was imperative. "Come, Blue. Let us see what can be seen."

It was a long hot climb, for the Bradbury plantation was more than halfway up the hill, separated from its neighbour by a large banana grove, and the path that led to it was overgrown and in poor repair. The afternoon sunlight columned in upon them through the banana trees, sulphur yellow, muddy and voluptuous. The air was furnace hot and oppressed their lungs. Soon they were streaming with sweat and their skin had acquired a coating of thick sticky brown dust. Sugar dust, as Jack discovered when he licked his lips.

They pushed past fields of sugar cane, where teams of slaves stooped and sweated, hauling away the tangled undergrowth and hacking at the heavy canes with vicious-looking machetes as the sugar dust rose about them in clouds of sickly sweetness. The plants were taller than they were and the smell of their sweat in that enclosed steamy field was stronger than the scent of the crushed cane. It might be an uncommon fine island for idleness, Jack thought as he and Blue struggled on, but 'twas a fearsome place to work in.

Presently they came to the factory, which had been built in a clearing and consisted of a huge mill where the cane was being crushed, a stone gulley to carry the juice from the mill to the shed for boiling down, and the shed itself, a long wooden structure with a roof but no walls, which was full of huge cast-iron vats in which the juice was being boiled. The heat from the fires was so intense, it made the very air buckle and waver. Slaves stooped in from the fields, bent double under the weight of the cane they carried. Some pushed and groaned as they turned the mill-stone, others, streaming sweat, stirred the boiling sugar, their feet leaving black perspiration marks on the trodden earth as they moved from vat to vat. There were scores of foremen about the place, all of them carrying whips and using them remorselessly.

"Nothing like a whip to get some work out of 'em," one foreman explained to Jack, nodding with satisfaction at the last back he'd striped with blood. "They're lazy beggars, d'you see, sir, every man jack of 'em. They'd be idle if they could. That's a likely looking tyke you got there, sir. I never seen a nigger with blue eyes afore."

The blue eyes were transfixed with horror at what they were seeing.

"How long do they work each day?" Jack asked.

"All day and every day," the foreman told him. "Sun-up to sun-down, you might say. They enjoys it. 'Tis all they're fit for."

Jack was impressed by their stamina. "I couldn't

stand such labour for an hour," he said, "leave alone a day."

"Ah well no, sir," the foreman said, "a' course not. You're a white man. 'Tis different for the likes of us."

'Tis the same prejudice, Jack thought, and he ventured a sly question to prove it. "You don't think they are human as we are?"

"Human, sir?" the man laughed. "Lord love 'ee, sir, a' course not. They're slaves."

It was too hot to argue with the man – and too dangerous. "I'd like to see their quarters," Jack said.

They were out in the fields a mere three hundred yards from the factory, four long wooden huts, thatched with grass and set at right angles to one another to contain an inner square of trodden earth. There were three women slaves simmering a stew of some kind in another cast-iron pot in the middle of the square, and gossiping to one another as they worked, but otherwise the place was deserted.

Blue went leaping off across the compound to greet them. "We speak!" he explained, glancing backwards at Jack as he ran. "We speak!" And was swept up into the arms of the nearest women and hugged and patted and bounced until, to Jack's watching eyes, his head was little more than a blur.

After the cruel assumptions of the foreman, Jack found himself unbearably touched by the scene and had to walk away from it before he revealed what he was feeling. He could see what looked like another compound a few hundred yards into the cut field and one that was occupied, what's more, for he could hear murmuring voices, so he decided to investigate, more by way of giving himself something to do than out of any burning curiosity.

It was a walled stockade, but there were sufficient cracks in the walls for him to peer through. As he suspected, there were several men and women inside, squatting on the earth and talking to one another, as they fed from a central bowl. It seemed to contain a porridge of some kind, for the food they were moulding in their fingers was meal-coloured and fairly solid, and he noticed that they were eating in a leisurely way, as if they had no real hunger. As soon as they heard him outside the stockade, they fell silent and looked around them apprehensively, and then he recognised who they were. Six men and two women. The slaves who'd been taken off the ship on that first day for use on the plantation. So why were they here? Why weren't they working with the others? They looked as though they were being fattened up, like the rest of his cargo. But why was that? Their fellows in the field were thin and hard at work. Eager to know the answers, he went straight back to the huts to find his interpreter.

It took quite a long time before Blue could discover what was going on in the other stockade, but eventually he returned to his master with some information.

"They Mr Ferguson's slaves," he explained. "You leave. Then they go Jamaica night-time. He sell them."

It was a shock but not a surprise. That accounts for his wealth, Jack thought. Two thousand pounds plucked from our cargo without the least effort on his part and no capital outlay. The thought infuriated him. We sail halfway round the world, and bargain for 'em, and feed 'em, and clean 'em, and risk death by fever and flux to boot, and in he comes at the eleventh hour, cucumber cool, to take his cut and steal our effort from us. The man's no better than a common thief. Well, Mr Ferguson, sir, your days are numbered. I shall peach

on you to Mr Bradbury the minute I set foot in Bristol.
"Does he indeed," he said grimly.

"He got sugar, too," Blue said. "Massa Ferguson's
sugar."

It was almost predictable. "Can they show me where
'tis?"

They could and did, although they led him to it
guardedly, watching for the foremen at every step of
the way. It was a large open-sided barn stacked to the
roof with cane.

"You go," Blue translated. "Other ship come. He
sell."

"Is't done with every crop?"

Oh yes. Every crop. They were sure of it.

"The man's an arrant knave," Jack said to Mr Reuben
when he told him the full story over breakfast the next
morning.

"He's grown uncommon thick with Mr Smith," the
bosun warned. "I'd watch my back if I was you, with
them two swabbers about."

But, as it turned out, there wasn't time to watch anything. There wasn't even time to collect his belongings
and return them to the ship. For as soon as breakfast
was over, Mr Dix arrived to take him to the compound
to examine the slaves, and less than an hour later, having
seen them, pronounced them fit for sale. He was hard
at work reloading them aboard the *Bonny Beaufoy*, this
time remarkably easily, for improved food and better
treatment had calmed the worst of their fears.

"Capital!" Mr Tomson said, when the last one was
aboard. "We've tide and wind favourable so we should
be in St Kitts by nightfall and so forth. All in good
time for the sale tomorrow, eh Mr Daventry? 'Tis all
a-goin' accordin' to plan. Now we shall see what price

they'm like to fetch for us, which I hopes will be high."

The sale was a hideous business and if Jack hadn't been hired for the sole purpose of undertaking it, he would have cried off as soon as it began. But Mr Tomson and Mr Smith had come ashore to watch the proceedings and as he was the slave master and knew he would be paid accordingly, and, moreover, as he needed the money if he were to survive back in England, he would have to go through with it, despite his deepening misgivings. So he stood alongside the slave owners – detesting their gaudy clothes and their vulgar manners – and urged the value of his bewildered slaves, stressing how strong they were and how well they would work. He stood aside as they were prodded and pulled about and had their lips lifted with the end of horse whips and canes, so that their prospective purchasers could examine their teeth. Lighted candles were held between their legs to search for signs of the pox, and they were required to bend over to check that they hadn't been plugged against the flux.

They use 'em like cattle, he thought, as the females howled and were whipped for it, and the children clung to their mother's legs, wide-eyed with terror. The most that could be said for the occasion was that he'd made a good profit on his cargo. Almost immediately, he'd sold eighty slaves to a local trader who was selling them on in Jamaica – the ten strongest males had gone for £285 each, and he'd even persuaded one of the slave owner's wives to buy Blue's mother and the talisman baby "as a pair." But when it was all over and the purchased slaves had been taken away, he was limp with misery and the shame of what he had done.

"What's to become of the ones that remain?" he asked

Mr Tomson, for the old medicine man and a young slave who'd been deemed "too skinny by half" were still standing in the slave ring.

"Leave 'em where they are," the captain said. "We've no use for 'em."

He was shocked by such a callous reply. "They will starve with none to feed them."

"Aye," the captain said, carelessly. "Belike. 'Tis what mostly happens to refuse slaves. They lives on the beach or in the market place and so forth. Some of the locals feed 'em, I believe, but most of 'em die off sooner or later. 'Taint our affair, as Mr Smith here will tell 'ee."

The ominous pressure of his words wasn't lost on Jack Daventry, but he was too caught up in concern for his last two slaves to heed it. "We cannot leave them here," he said hotly. "'Twould be tantamount to a death sentence and I'll not have that on my conscience. We will take them back to the plantation."

The purser's face was dark with gathering anger. "'Od's teeth!" he said. "What now? Are we to change our entire plan of campaign to suit two naked savages? Is that the humour of it? Have sense, Mr Daventry. They are old and sick and they stink the place out. If 'twere a farm they'd have been put down long since."

"Howsomever this ain't a farm, Mr Smith. Nor we farmers."

"No, sir," the purser said angrily. "We are traders and your foolishness is losing us time and money. Have done with it and come aboard and let's hear no more on't."

The young slave had slumped to the ground and was sitting with his head on his knees.

"No, sir," Jack said, his jaw set. "We'll not leave them here to die. They return with us."

"No, sir. I am the master here and I say they do not."

121

"I take responsibility."

"You, sir, will take a cuff of my cane," the purser bellowed. "'Od's bowels! Am I to be dictated to by a jumped-up jackanapes with no sense and no breeding? Your grandfather a duke! D'you take us for fools?"

Jack was stung. "'Tis gospel truth, Mr Smith, and I'll thank you to mind it."

"'Tis poppycock. And we'll hear no more on't. Come, sir. Aboard, if you please. The boat waits on us."

Jack squared his shoulders. "I'll not move without my slaves."

The purser was furious and decisive. "Then you must be forced, sir. Seize him, Mr Reuben, if you please. Frogmarch, if necessary."

The bosun was embarrassed to be asked to arrest his shipmate but he obeyed orders, that being his trade. "Best do as he say," he warned in Jack's ear. "'Tis a mean old swabber an' means to have 'ee in irons. We don't want that."

There was a pause as Jack considered whether or not to resist, the captain stood aside as if it were no concern of his, and the purser watched, tapping his breeches with his cane. Whatever is done here now, Jack thought, I shall answer for it. 'Tis too public for a brawl and I've lost the argument without my pistols. They'll be the first things I look for when I get back to shore. 'Twas folly to travel without 'em. I'll know better next time and no mistake. In the end, he followed the bosun aboard, scowling and furious but powerless to do anything else.

It was dark by the time the *Bonny Beaufoy* put in to the harbour in Nevis and as nobody, except Jack, had any urge to go ashore, the gangplank wasn't lowered. But the purser seemed to be in a good humour again, regaling Mr Dix with stories of the sale, and there was such an air of happy anticipation among the crew that it made him feel easy despite the dishonours of the day. So he decided to forget about his pistols for the moment. There would be time enough to collect them in the morning.

"We'll make our adieus at first light," Mr Tomson said, "check the cargo, water and so forth, and then we'll be off back to old England. How say 'ee to that, my lubbers?"

They lit torches and gathered on deck to sit in the cool air under a yellow moon and sing sea shanties to the accompaniment of Dickon's wheezing accordion. "For we've received orders for to sail to old Eng-er-land. And we hopes in a short time to see thee again."

Eight

J ack was awake, dressed and ready for the day as soon as the sun rose the next morning. Blue was lying in his usual place beneath the bunk, dressed in his new striped breeches and fast asleep, but he woke at the touch of his master's hand, and scrambled to his feet, shaking the sleep from his eyes and declaring he was "Ready!". So they swung up on deck together.

There was an encouraging swell running out at sea and, even within the harbour wall, the *Bonny Beaufoy* and the *Yorick* swayed away from the quay as if they were eager to be off. Their movement reminded Jack of something he'd heard in a theatre once, "they strain like greyhounds at the slip", and the words sang in his head as he and Blue set off for the gangplank and the retrieval of his precious pistols. Oh, he couldn't wait to get back to England.

The quay was awake, too, and busy. The last of the water barrels was being trundled aboard with much unnecessary heaving and shouting, and Mr Tomson was ashore, patting the ringlets of his beard as he conversed with Mr Ferguson, who had come down to supervise the loading of his parting gift, which was ten crates of newly picked fruit. It was in every respect the sort of scene common to any departure and one Jack had seen on several occasions since he joined the ship. Not worth notice.

124

Until, that is, he stepped off the gangplank to find himself instantly surrounded by half a dozen seamen from the *Yorick*, one of whom thrust a loaded musket into his chest.

He'd been holding himself in readiness for trouble of some kind, but he wasn't prepared for anything as sudden and as violent as this and the shock of it was palpable.

"How now?" he said, pushing the musket aside, and he tried to make a joke of it. "Do 'ee take me for a villain, sirrah?"

"Aye, sir," the purser's voice said. "That being exactly what you are, sir. Clap him in irons if you please, Mr Cooper."

"I think not, sir," Jack said, turning to face him, "since I have done nothing wrong to warrant it."

"I think *so*, sir," Mr Smith answered, "since you are outnumbered, sir, and have no pistols about you to threaten us with. Let's have him shackled, Mr Cooper."

"At your peril, Mr Cooper," Jack warned. "I am related to a duke of the realm, I would have you know, and my family do not take kindly to rough treatment."

The threat stopped Mr Cooper in mid-stride. He put out a hand to stay his fellows and looked across at the purser questioningly.

"The man is mad," Mr Smith said, scathingly, "and may be ignored. Depend on't. He thinks slaves are our equals, if you ever heard the like. 'Human like us.' Ain't that the way of it, Mr Daventry?"

There was a roar of happy mockery. "Hell's teeth! What sort of folly is that!" "Human like us! He'm sea-crazed, damn his eyes." "Raving mad." "Send 'im to Bedlam, the dog!"

"Aye, sir, so 'tis," Jack shouting to be heard above the uproar. "'Twould be plain to see . . ."

But he was wasting his breath for they were surging forward to seize and bind him. No, dammit, he thought, you'll not take me without a struggle, and he drew his strength together to fight them, although he knew it was useless, for he was outnumbered six to one and a musket is a heavy argument. He deflected blows, ducked, punched, struggled from their grasp, until they clubbed him to the ground with their muskets, and then he kicked and writhed against the hands that were trying to force his ankles into shackles. "Hell's teeth, sir! I'll not be treated so. I am a gentleman." The side of his face stung from their blows and there was blood in his mouth and his ears were singing with the power of his struggle. "I'll not be treated so."

But in the end he was trussed and bound, with his hands roped behind his back and leg irons locked about his ankles.

They frogmarched him up the gangplank and on to the *Yorick*, opened the hatch and flung him into the hold. The last thing he heard as he fell was the purser's gloating laughter and his voice shouting, "The equal of slaves, eh Mr Daventry? Now see how well you like their lodging."

The ignominy of it was so extreme that for a few seconds he simply lay where he'd fallen, with his head wedged against a sack of flour and his arms and legs spreadeagled, too stunned and defeated to speak. The hatch was closed with a clang, feet stamped away, darkness and dust settled around him, musty and full of menace. 'Od's bowels, 'twas not to be endured.

Anger invigorated him again. He was on his feet and raging in the darkness, in a surge of fury and hatred and impotence, acutely aware of everything around him, every sound, scent and sensation magnified as if his world had suddenly been writ large. He could hear sails being set above him, the capstan protesting, the slap of bare feet on the deck, and knew from the tone of the captain's voice that he was irritable and prone to flog. He could smell every article of the cargo, although he couldn't see beyond the nearest sack, from cornmeal to ship's biscuit, through every variation of meat, rank, salt and freshly killed pork, bacon, beef and goat. Everything was louder, more pressing, more immediate. Rats scrabbled past his feet, their claws as loud as rakes, the timbers creaked like the crack of thunder, every slap of wave against the hull was clear as a gunshot, and his leg irons burned his bare skin with every movement he made. "I'll not be treated so, hell's teeth! I'm a gentleman. I'll not be treated so."

Time was an irrelevance. There was no day, no light, no freedom, no justice. Just the need to roar, shriek, protest, demand redress. "I'll not be treated so." It was a very long time before he realised how futile it was. He *was* being treated so. No matter how loudly he roared, nobody answered. There was nothing he could do now but endure. He slumped back on to the sack of wheat, his bound hands behind him, and abandoned himself to weeping.

Presently, there was a shuffling sound somewhere to his left and he heard a soft voice calling his name. "Jack! Mr Jack!"

"Blue?"

The outline of Blue's face moved into his limited vision, a gleam of blue eyes, the line of a cheek. "Yes, Mr Jack?"

The shock of knowing him there was almost as great as the shock of being thrown into the hold. "How did you get here?"

"I run. I come down before."

The trust and affection revealed by such an action moved Jack to tears all over again. But this time, they were tears of elation. "There is more human kindness in you, Blue," he said, "than in the entire crew of this ship. The entire benighted crew, 'Od rot 'em. Undo these ropes, will 'ee. Ah! That's better. They fell upon me like wolves, Blue, like ravening wolves. They pulled me and kicked me and beat me with muskets as though I were a dog, 'Od rot 'em, whilst you . . . You treat me as one human being to another, as a friend, nay more than a friend. What friend would risk life and limb for me in this hell-pit. I was right in everything I said and you bear it out. You are human as I am human. I cannot tell you . . ." And he wept again.

The child didn't understand more than three words from such a babble, but he sat beside his master in the darkness, untying the ropes that bound him and occasionally patting his arm for comfort, for now they were like slaves together in this place and touch was possible. And Jack was glad of his comfort for his rage told him how low-spirited he was becoming.

Time passed. They felt the ship leave harbour and hit open sea and soon they were being thrown about as the vessel dipped and swung through the swell. From time to time, Blue whimpered as a particularly heavy wave sent them both lurching.

"Take heart," Jack said, and this time it was his turn to comfort. "'Tis only the sea, Blue, and the stronger the sea, the sooner we shall be home."

"Home? What is home?"

"My home, Blue. England. That's where we're going. And the sooner there the better. You shall be a free

128

man in England. I'll see to it. Providing I'm a free man myself."

The conversation was getting incomprehensible again. "Master?"

Best turn to something easier. "I am glad you are here with me."

"I am glad also."

Hours passed. And passed. And soon, what with the stuffy air, their own inertia and the rocking motion of the ship, they both slept. When they woke, they no longer knew whether it was night or day. The heat was stifling and there was a rat gnawing at Jack's shoe. He kicked it away, viciously, before he remembered that he was shackled, and the sharp movement tore the leg iron into his skin. The pain of it brought him to full consciousness. He realised that he was in urgent need of a piddle and struggled to his feet to find an empty corner of the hold.

As he was relieving himself, he heard footsteps above his head and rough voices shouting by the hatch. "Come out! Come out Jack Daventry! We wants to see yer." The hatch rose to reveal a strip of blue sky and the dark outline of three sailors, who were leaning in towards him, smelling strongly of sweat and rum. *Am I to be a sport to these ruffians?* he thought. But he straightened his breeches and swung out of the hold as well as he could for the encumbrance of his irons, calling to Blue to follow him.

"Hello!" one of the sailors said. "What's this? We got a nigger aboard. We'll have some sport now, my lubbers." He had a whip in his hand and raised it to crack within inches of Blue's hunched shoulders, grinning with delight at the pain he was going to inflict.

"Send for Mr Jerome, if you please, sir," Jack said.

"This is my servant, come aboard with me, and we'll not be flogged or I shall know the reason why."

"He'll know the reason why, will he, lousy swabber?" the sailor mocked and this time he aimed the whip directly at Jack's head. He was quick, but not quick enough. Jack lunged forward, ignoring the pain of his shackles, to catch his fist, whip and all, before the blow could fall. Then he was under a pile of bodies, one trying to pin his arms behind his back, another flailing punches, a third kicking and yelling and there was nothing in the world except a confused blur of fists and faces, a roar of voices, struggle, and the pain in his ankles.

A whistle was being blown, sharp and commanding. Other voices were yelling, "Get back you dogs! Stand clear or I'll have 'ee whipped." Mr Jerome was standing barrel-chested and splay-footed before them, bellowing that he was to be obeyed.

"Feed 'un and get 'un back below," he roared. "'Od rot it, we've no time for this sort of caper. They'm less than a league away, damme. Clear the decks."

His voice was shaking with emotion – fear, anger, agitation, pride – and his face was red as a turkey cock. Jack was instantly alerted. He saw that they were sailing in a more southerly direction than he would have expected, that there was no sign of the *Bonny Beaufoy*, that look-outs were in the rigging, decks cleared for action, gun crews standing ready. And he realised, with a rush of excitement and exhilaration, that they were heading for a sea battle and that, if he made a bold enough bid for it, he could be released from his shackles to join in the fight.

"You'll need every man jack, Mr Jerome," he said, "and I'm a man jack to equal any on board. Release me of these irons, sir, and give me a pair of pistols and I'll do you good service. I'm an uncommon fine shot and cool under fire."

Mr Jerome looked puzzled. "You'm on deck to be fed and watered, sir. No more. What folly's this?"

"No folly, sir. Believe me. An honest offer. You'll not get a better."

"'Twill be no sawdust brawl, sir. We fight the French."

"Aye, sir, as I see."

"How if you were to turn your pistols on me or the captain?"

Jack made a joke of such a suggestion, laughing, "Not an eventuality, I give you my word as an honest gentleman. For what would I do then? I'm not like to jump ship in the middle of the ocean and you've enough firearms aboard to overpower me twenty times over, which is clear to any eye. Besides, why would a man shoot his fellows when there are Frenchmen to fire upon! They will be target enough for me or any man."

The second mate was almost won over. "I like the cut of your jib, sir," he said, "damme if I don't."

"Then let it run, sir. 'Tis sound British canvas all the way from Brissol."

"Aye dammit, so 'tis. Very well then." He turned to give orders to his men, who'd drifted way from his conversation, irked that he should be taking the part of a madman. "Feed un, water un, take off those irons. No more brawling mind, which apply to all of you. If there's any flogging to be done, I shall do it, an' I'll have the skin off your backs mark 'ee. When he'm fed, send to Mr Warwick for a pistol."

They were puzzled and annoyed by such a change of tack and one of them was bold enough to protest. "But he'm a madman, Mr Jerome, sir. That there Mr Smith, he told Mr Cooper. I seen it all. I was one what brought un aboard. He'm lunatic."

"No, sir," Mr Jerome told him. "He'm never lunatic. He'm from Brissol same as me, sir. We have a different way of goin' about things. Tha's all 'tis. Aren't that the truth of it, Mr Daventry?"

So Jack and Blue were given the remains of what appeared to be the mid-morning meal, handed a mug full of grog which they shared between them, and allowed down to the heads. By that time the ships that the *Yorick* was stalking were clear on the horizon – a merchantman, heavily laden, and a frigate under limited sail.

Jack's irons were removed. The *Yorick* made good speed, visibly closing the gap between herself and the French, the wind being in her direction. The weather was warm, the sky clear. All preparations had been made, even to the production of Jack's requested pistols, balls, powder and all. It was simply a matter of sailing and waiting. Tension and irritability increased. There was much chewing of tobacco, much contemptuous spitting, much prowling and shifting of feet, more and more lurid swearing. Only Blue and Jack were calm, the boy because he had no inkling of what lay ahead, the man because he was determined to be courageous.

By three o'clock that afternoon, they were close enough to see the rims of the frigate's cannon gleaming in their portholes and to watch the French crew trimming sail so as to give the ship more manoeuvrability. The English gun crews stood to, were told to hold their fire until the signal was given, licked dry lips as the *Yorick* bore down on her prey. Their own sails were trimmed. Ropes screamed. Canvas creaked. The sea hissed from their prow. The wait was interminable, particularly as they could now see that the

French frigate was going about ready to aim her cannon.

When the order came to fire it was greeted with a whistle of relief and, as the cannon recoiled from their first roaring barrage, the crew gave a cheer. It was a moment of high drama and unalloyed glory. And was followed almost instantaneously by another of sheer terror as the French guns blazed fire from every port. For a few seconds the air between the two ships was full of hurtling missiles, then the first shots landed and a French mast was split, canvas afire and men screaming, and a ball whistled past Jack's shoulder and ripped a hole in the foredeck, as they bucked through waters grown choppy with activity and received another shot amidships as they steadied in the line of fire.

It was time for Jack to take up a vantage point if he were to make best use of his pistols. As Blue watched, he loaded each in turn, opened the flashpan, sprinkled in his powder – dry as a bone – closed the cover. Then he braced himself against the rocking of the ship, climbed the rigging, a pistol in each hand, and was ready. All he needed now was a prestigious target.

The cannons were being fired again. He could hear the thunder of their ricochet and the air was full of smoke and the smell of cordite. There was a stay falling below him, fire spurting red from the quarterdeck, a line of raised muskets gleaming, and a man's hand lying in the gunnel torn off at the wrist and still clutching a ramrod. The noise was more insistent than the pounding of African drums and heat rose with an intensity that Africa had never equalled. And there immediately below him was the French captain, white gloves neat in his epaulette, gold-topped cane elegantly in hand, directing operations and too good a target to miss. He cocked the first pistol, took aim and fired. For a few seconds, the flash completely blinded him, then the red mist of it cleared and, peering through the smoke, he saw, with a sense of total disbelief and amazement, that the captain had been hit and was lying on the deck, rolling in pain and clutching at his chest. What capital sport!

A voice yelled at him to "Look out!" and glancing down, he saw a French musket levelled in his direction and, all instinct now, he swung his body sideways away from its trajectory. After that, things happened at such speed that there was nothing but smoke and noise and action. He flung the used pistol down into Blue's outstretched hands, cocked the second, turned, aimed, fired into a muddle of half-seen figures. Missed. Plague on it! Now he must reload. But before he could move, the first pistol was handed back to him, presented by the handle what's more, and he heard Blue's voice shouting "'Tis ready, Mr Jack!" and so he turned to fire again. This time he saw a musketeer staggering backwards, screaming and falling into the smoke. Then a volley of fire peppered the sail furled below him. Oh, he was an eagle, soaring in the rigging, picking off his prey with every shot. Change hands, exchange pistols, take aim, fire, the rhythm as easy as breathing. He recognised that the *Yorick* was changing tack, and swung further aloft to take up another position, roaring with excitement and exhilaration. He was magnificent, fabulous, invincible.

Then, suddenly, it was all over. The French frigate was turning, setting all the canvas she could muster, her mainmast split and her topsail in tatters, holed at the water line and yawing heavily, admitting defeat. The merchantman was left an easy prize, without a defender and little more than half a league away. The pistol in Jack's hand was still smoking but the battle was won.

There was a flurry of doffed caps, a growling cheer, voices bellowing orders but for a while he stood above it all, unable to move because he was shaking so violently that he had to cling to the rigging for fear of falling. Blue was looking up at him, calling "Mr Jack, Mr Jack! You want more pistol?" but he hadn't got the breath to answer. 'Od's bones and brains, he thought, what a monstrous wonder it is to go to war.

"Bully for you, Jack!" Mr Jerome called up. "As pretty a piece of shooting as I ever saw."

Praise gave him back his breath. "Shall we board the merchantman?"

"Belike. Stay where you are. We may need your good aim again."

But as they drew near to the French trader, she hove to and flagged a message admitting defeat.

"Here's a thing," the second mate said. "She's to be took without a shot fired."

The captain wasn't so sure. "We'll not trust the swabbers," he said. "There could be trickery afoot an' I ain't about to be caught by it, damme."

They approached cautiously, inching towards their enemy until they could see the patches on her sails and count the members of her crew who were lined up on deck. The captain stood apart from the rest and had a distinctly piratical air about him, with a red bandanna about his neck, a black patch over one eye and a tricorn tucked under his arm. But he answered soberly when Mr Jerome took the hailer to ask if he was prepared to surrender.

"Aye, sir. We 'ave Engleesh aboard."

They were so close to one another that there was little more than a foot of water between them. "Have you indeed?" the second mate called. "How many?"

The Frenchman considered. "Twenty, thirty."

"Where are they, dammit?"

"I show."

The boarding party swung across, muskets slung across their shoulders and bristlingly alert but there were no tricks and no opposition. Watched by his enemies, the French captain led the way to the hatches, where, after a few fumbling minutes and some altercation with two of his officers, two dozen dishevelled men emerged from the hold, blinked in the sunlight and turned to wave their thanks to their rescuers. English indeed and part of the original crew of the ship.

"She was the *Mary Elizabeth* afore she was took by this 'ere load o' plaguey swabbers," their leader explained. "British ship. Out of Portsmouth. They took the officers ashore in the Windwards. We was pressed to stay on an' sail her on account of they was short of crew."

It was a common enough practice. "What's her cargo?"

Silks apparently. Some spices, which were scenting the air now that the hatch was open. Some ivory, although they couldn't say where it was stashed. "Might be some gold. They was powerful cagey about it but we was give a powerful escort, which do make 'ee wonder."

"If there's gold, we'll find un," Jack Jerome told him happily. "Cheer up, me lads. We'm your escort now, which I daresay you won't object to, on account of we've sent your Frenchie off wi' grapeshot in her ears an' her tail atween her legs. Now I'm a-here, to captain the ship for 'ee. Choose me a crew, sir, an' I'll send the rest aboard the *Yorick* for safekeeping. Here's our other ship a-coming, d'you see? We shall be good company."

The *Bonny Beaufoy* was labouring towards them, low in the water with the weight of her cargo. Signals were flagged to her and she hove to and settled to wait for them. It took another hour to do all that needed to be done, and even then the wounded were still being attended to when all three ships set off in convoy to resume their journey. But the hold of the *Yorick* was full of captured Frenchmen, the crew of the *Yorick* were assured of good prize money and Jack was a free man and something of a hero.

That night, when the blood had been scrubbed from the decks and the three most badly wounded men had had their stumps sealed with hot tar and been carried below to groan until they recovered or died, Jack dined in the wardroom as though he were one of the *Yorick*'s officers, with Blue behind his chair to wait on him and an admiring company to drink his health. "You're a plaguey fine shot, sir, damme if you ain't." By the end of the meal, since one officer had been grazed by gunshot and Mr Jerome was on other duties, he had become temporary officer of the watch, with Blue as his accepted servant. By the end of the week, he'd been accepted by the crew – grudgingly and with a deal of grumbling which was only to be expected but acknowledging that at least he was a man who'd proved his worth under fire.

Even Mr Cooper allowed that he could be gentry. "He'm raving mad when it comes to the niggers," he said. "There's narry a one of us would agree with him on that score, for 'tis plain folly when all's said an' done, but he's got 'bottom', I'll say that for him. They'm a rum lot, the gentry, an' given to folly an' suchlike, an' he do seem to go on the way they goes on, with pistols an' all. Take that nigger-boy of his'n. 'Tis the sort of thing they

137

goes in for. They has 'em like puppy dogs. I seen 'em in London."

So the voyage continued, more or less uneventfully except for the occasional drunken brawl, one of which ended in a flogging. The three ships kept close company in an empty ocean. The ship's carpenter repaired the deck. Two of the crippled men died and were buried at sea, the third made a slow recovery. Mr Jerome reported that there was no gold aboard the *Mary Elizabeth* but that the silk was of good quality and there was a deal of ivory. The weather wasn't always fair but what storms they weathered were less violent than others they'd known and there were no slaves aboard to plague Jack's conscience, and no sickness and no sign of the French. Best of all, as an officer, he had a chance to see the ship's charts and find out what speed they were making and how rapidly they were returning home.

"We shall be in England pretty soon," he told Blue, one lazy afternoon, "and then I must be taken from the ship with my hands bound, I fear." That had been established with the captain, who said he could see no way else, or Mr Smith would want to know the reason why. "You must take this note and hide it in your breeches and if things do not go well with me, you must go to the inn whose name I have written *there* and ask for the man, whose name I have written *there*. Do you understand?"

Blue looked worried. Although he could speak well and understand most of what was said to him, written instructions were beyond him.

"Should it come to the worst – which I doubt, but should it – find a kind person in fine clothes, and ask them to read it for 'ee."

Blue agreed, although dubiously. "Yes, Mr Jack."

"Cheer up, me lad," Jack said, ruffling his woolly hair. "It may all work out for the best yet. I'll run mad rather than be sent to prison or the hangman. I've done good service aboard this ship and when Mr Bradbury hears of it, he'll not punish me further. He'll see 'twas folly and mischief-making. I've yet to tell him of the factor and his scurvy tricks, which ain't a thing to be ignored. No, no, we'll come through, the pair of us, and then we'll live like lords. What do 'ee think to that?"

Blue held the paper and didn't know what to think. "What is lords?" he asked.

Nine

As soon as Suki Brown arrived in Appleton House, she searched out pen, ink and paper, settled William on her lap and wrote a letter to Farmer Lambton, explaining that she and Miss Ariadne had been banished to the country, hoping that Mrs Lambton and the baby continued well, and begging him please to tell Captain Jack where she was. "He'm bound to come to the farm, for to collect Bow, for I never knowd a man love a horse as he do that one, which I hopes is well and no trouble to you." After she'd signed her name, she was tempted to rebuke him for his part in her sudden exile, but she forbore because she was trying to be a good Christian soul – and besides, he was still stabling the horse, and until the Bradburys remembered to pay her, she had no money to send him for its fodder.

She was rather put out to discover that the letter couldn't be sent until Saturday, which was *days* away. But she couldn't complain about that either because Mrs Norris, the housekeeper, was such a kindly soul and explained it to her so patiently. "Lord love 'ee, dearie, we don't get post hereabouts. Leastways not when the master's away. 'Twill go a' Saturday, for 'ee. I'll make sure of it."

So Saturday it had to be and an irritating wait it was, for life at Appleton House was slow and enervating,

particularly after the bustle of Bath. There was plenty
of work going on all around her for the estate was at
the centre of a large apple orchard and had its own
house farm in the grounds, with a dairy for butter and
cheese, a herd of orchard pigs to be fed on the skimmed
milk and whey, a dovecote for over six hundred birds
that had to be cleaned out most religiously every week,
a sizeable stables with its own smithy, to say nothing
of all the labour in the kitchen where bread was baked
every day and ale brewed for the entire estate. But that
was no work for a lady's maid and as her particular lady
did nothing but sit silent in her room, there was little to
keep her occupied.

The house was no help to her either, for it was a dark,
old-fashioned place, with leaded windows that gave very
little light and oak panelling that was cracked and ancient
and horribly oppressive in all the main rooms. There
were no modern devices at all, not even a pump in the
kitchen, as she discovered on her second morning. All
their water had to be drawn from a well in the courtyard,
and a back-breaking job that was. As to the kitchen, that
was just a low dark cave – full of grease and fumes –
where the sun never penetrated and the stone flags were
always chill underfoot. 'Twas no wonder Miss Ariadne
was low-spirited.

Mrs Norris was most concerned about her young
mistress. "'Tain't nat'ral to sit so, day after day, poor
soul," she said to Suki at the end of their first week
together. "Shall we try her with a little junket? What do
'ee think to that? If she got a sore throat 'tis no wonder
she don't speak."

But junkets didn't work and neither did apple jelly
and after another week Mr Norris was called in from his
work in the dairy, to discuss the situation. Like his wife,

141

he was short, stout, good tempered and hard working. But he confessed himself baffled by Miss Ariadne's silence.

"Happen a walk in the air would do it," he said, scratching his tousled hair.

So a walk in the air was tried. That evening, when William had been fed and settled, the two girls put on their straw bonnets, wound their shawls about their waists – country style, since there were none nearby to rebuke Ariadne for vulgar behaviour – and set out for a stroll through the fields.

The moon was already out, flat and smudged as a white penny in a sky still daytime blue, the apple orchards were heavy with burgeoning fruit, honeysuckles breathed their languorous perfume into the evening air, and below the gentle curve of the hill, the river shimmered like shot silk.

"'Tis a cruel world," Ariadne said suddenly, "which is sad to think upon when it can be so beautiful." It was the first time she'd spoken since they arrived and her voice was husky with lack of use.

Suki's concern was more practical than philosophical. "How of your silence?" she asked. "Do 'ee mean to stay mute all summer?"

Ariadne's voice was instantly firm. "I mean to stay mute," she said, "until the time has come for me to speak."

"When will that be?"

"When I have something to say, I imagine."

"Don't 'ee fear they'll call the surgeons again?"

Ariadne grimaced. "What worse could they do than they have done already?"

"They could kill you," Suki told her hotly. "I thought they had."

"But as you see, I am still here," Ariadne said, smiling at her briefly, "though how I shall fare hereafter I cannot tell."

They walked on quietly, each busy with her own thoughts.

"We will walk every evening," Ariadne decided. "'Tis good to talk to 'ee Suki and I know I can depend upon 'ee not to tell a soul of it."

So the pattern was set and they walked every evening.

The days passed slowly, for nothing was hurried on this estate. Haymaking was long over but work in the fields still began at first light because there were cows to milk, pigs to feed, horses to groom, vegetables to tend, and it all had to be done thoroughly. After a while, Suki begged to be allowed to work in the kitchen, when William was happy to allow it, for at least kneading dough with the amiable Mrs Norris gave her something to occupy her time. William grew fatter and more handsome by the day and toddled about with her wherever she went and was admired and petted by everybody on the estate. But there were no letters from Twerton, so the Captain couldn't have come home yet, and none from London either.

"I am bored beyond belief," Ariadne complained, when they'd been there a month. "We might as well be dead and buried here, for all they care."

"But we aren't," Suki laughed, tossing William in the air and catching him, as he squealed with delight at such rough play. It had been a long hot day and he'd been too wide awake to settle, so, for once, they'd taken him along with them on their evening stroll. Now having walked as far as they could at a toddler's stumbling pace they'd stopped for a rest, Ariadne to sit in the dappled shadows of a chestnut tree, Suki to play with her child. She tossed him in the air again. "We'm *very* much alive. Aren't we my 'andsome?"

"How you do love him!" Ariadne observed.

"Well o' course," Suki said carelessly. "On account of he'm my babba. Aren't you, my little duck?"

"But he ain't, is he?" Ariadne said, equally carelessly. But then she looked up and caught a glimpse of startled fear in her friend's eyes, and her own eyes widened as she suddenly saw the implication of what had just been said. "Oh Suki! *Is* he?"

Suki was alarmed, then ashamed for allowing herself to be caught out so easily, then relieved that it was only Ariadne who would know, because they were so used to confidence now and trusted each other. "If I tell 'ee," she said, "you'll not breathe a word to a living soul."

By then, Ariadne was agog for the details. "You have my word on't."

So the story was told, from Sir George's assault, which Ariadne greeted with a snort of disgust, followed by peals of delighted laughter when she heard how Suki had dealt with it, and so past the death of that poor little frail baby, whom she had to confess she could barely remember, and then to his funeral, which she remembered uncommon clearly.

"I might ha' known it," she said, when the tale was finally told. "You've always seemed a deal too fond of our William for a wet nurse. While as to my father . . . 'Tis the sort of behaviour I would expect of him, no more nor less. The man is an oaf. When you hit him 'twas richly deserved. Would I could have been there to see it. We heard him roar, as I recall, but took little heed of it, for he roars at everything."

"He roared uncommon loud *that* morning," Suki told her, throwing William in the air again.

Ariadne smiled with satisfaction. "I'm glad on't," she said. "I hope it taught him a lesson, which he sorely needs, although I doubt he will mind it for he's uncommon settled in his opinions. He regards all women as his property. Shame upon him. We are mere cattle in his eyes, there to be bedded, or bred from, or married off to some repellant friend of his. I'm so glad you hit him."

"And now Miss Melissa is to marry his repellant friend."

"She'll get no joy of *him*," his erstwhile fiancée said. "For I never knew a man so full of himself, nor with such vile breath."

"She'll be mistress of a fine house," Suki said, adding with happy spite, "which might console her."

Ariadne was suddenly intensely serious. "Were we wrong, think 'ee, in what we said?"

"No," Suki said, with equal seriousness. "We were not. If any woman marry it should be for love. Without it, we'm no better than beasts in the field, put to breed for profit."

"How glad you will be to have your lover home," Ariadne said enviously. For Suki had told her how soon that homecoming was to be. "Would mine had been so true."

"You might love again," Suki consoled, "and find a truer man."

"I think not," Ariadne sighed. But she recovered quickly. "One thing is most certain. I'll not stay at home to belong to my father, nor marry to belong to a husband. There must be another way and I mean to find it."

Suki understood her completely. "An' stay mute till you do," she said.

Ariadne opened her mouth to agree but then turned her head, alerted by the sound of footsteps in the lane below them. "There's someone coming," she said. "How if 'twere your lover?"

Suki stood up at once with William on her hip. Could it be the Captain? Could she hope for such a thing? There was such a fluttering in her throat, like a bird in a cage, throbbing and pulsing. It couldn't be him, could it? He'd have ridden Beau. Oh let it be him. I've waited for him so long.

The footsteps drew nearer, and as the walker rounded the bend below them and emerged from the shelter of the trees, they could see that it was a stocky young man in his working clothes and that he'd walked a fair distance, for he was moving with the long-legged rhythmical stride of someone well into his journey. Suki drooped with disappointment. He wasn't the Captain. She'd have known *his* splendid stride anywhere and, besides, he was too poorly dressed.

Then he looked up towards them and she saw that he was her brother John. "Something's amiss," she said and went down at once to find out what it was.

Her brother took off his hat at their approach and wiped his forehead with it. He looked so anxious it was hardly necessary to ask him if something was the matter. "'Tis Pa," he explained. "Got hurt up the quarry yesterday. Ma says can you come?"

For a second, Suki couldn't understand what he was talking about. "The quarry?"

"Yes. Ma says can you come?"

"What was he a-doin' in a quarry?" Suki said, angered by the folly of it. "He'm a farm worker. You might ha' knowd he'd get hurt in a quarry. He'm dangerous enough with a rake."

"He was earnin' a bit of money to buy Ma a new dress."

"What do Farmer Lambton have to say about it?"

"I don't know. Can you come?"

"Is 'e bad?"

"'Aven't seen un yet, to tell the truth," John confessed, twisting his hat in his hands. "That Mr Aylock's such a tartar. He don't give you time for nothing. Ma came over this morning and persuaded un to let me come here on the stagecoach to Chipping Sodbury. If we goes back the same way tomorrow morning, we can catch Mr Jones at market, an' he'll take 'ee on to Twerton. 'Tis all arranged."

Suki wasn't interested in the stagecoach or any other travelling arrangements. Her concern was solely for her father. "What did he hurt? His back? His legs? What part of un?"

"Fingers," John enlightened her. "Fingers of his right hand. Ma says he'm bad. Can you come?"

Fingers, Suki thought. Why, fingers are nothing. He'll soon get over *that*. But she'd go and attend to him because he *was* her Pa, poor old thing – and, besides, a trip to Twerton would bring her close to Bristol and that was what she wanted more than anything. She could ride there from Twerton or tease a lift on a cart. She might even contrive to be there at the very moment when that *Bonny Beaufoy* came in. Right on the quayside, awaiting him. Oh yes, she would certainly go to Twerton.

"Come up to the house," she instructed. "Mrs Norris will find 'ee some supper an' somewhere to sleep, an' we'll go back at first light."

Given her mixed reasons for agreeing to accompany him, she was quite ashamed to see how relieved he was.

*   *   *

They set off together in the small cart with the groom to drive them, just after dawn the next morning so as to be in good time to find an inside seat on the stagecoach, but it was a long, uncomfortable, rackety journey down to Bath, even with a hamper of food and ale from Mrs Norris to sustain them on the way. The weather was sticky, the roads in poor repair, and because he was cooped up inside a coach for hours, William was fractious. He grizzled and complained and climbed all over Suki from the start of the journey to the finish. She was heartily sick of him by the time they reached Bath and very glad to find Mr Jones's nice clean airy cart waiting for her in the market.

Yes, he said, he'd been expectin' her. "Just you hop aboard, me dear. I shall be finished here in two shakes of a lamb's tail." So she kissed her brother goodbye and settled beside the dog for the last three exhausting miles to Twerton.

It was growing dark by the time they arrived at the farm, William was sound asleep and she was bone weary. But she was encouraged by the sight of her old home. The sagging thatch was gone, replaced by a splendid piece of work, close-packed and so dry and neat that the straw ends bristled in the setting sun. The door had been mended too and the walls plastered and whitened with lime wash. This must be Pa's doing, she thought, as she carried her sleeping baby towards the door. So he can't be too bad.

But then she stepped into the kitchen and the odd combination of scents and smells in that crowded room alerted her again, for besides the ones she expected, of cabbage and boiled bacon, scrubbed table, the mustiness of Mrs Havers' unwashed clothes, the sharp ammoniac smell of chicken shit, a strong odour of pig, there was an equally strong smell of blood and another, at once cloying and rank, that she couldn't identify.

Apart from the smell, the room was exactly as she remembered it. Mrs Havers was sitting in her usual place in the chimney corner, plainly in the middle of one of her grumbles, Molly and Tom were in their usual place under the table and her mother was mending stockings by the light of a single candle, holding the work up to get as much benefit from its little beam as she could.

As soon as she saw Suki she rose to her feet with a cry of welcome. "Oh my dear girl. I'm *that* pleased you'm here. Thank the Lord." And Molly and Tom scrambled out from under the table to fling their arms around her and hug and be hugged. But her father sat where he was in the shadows, cradling his bandaged right hand protectively with the fingers of his left, and Suki saw at once that he was in pain and ill. She handed her sleeping baby to Molly and crossed the room at once to attend to him.

"What you been a-doin' then, Pa?" she asked. Now that she was close to him, she could see that his bandages were heavily stained with blood and knew that the rank smell was pus.

"Little contree-tom," her father said apologetically. "I shall soon mend." He glanced quickly and anxiously towards his wife, warning Suki in the old subtle way that she wasn't to make too much fuss for fear of upsetting her mother.

"When you last have them dressings changed?" she said, practical as ever.

"They was onny put on day afore yes'day," he told her, still apologetic. His face was grey in the candle-light and his eyes strained.

149

"I'll do 'em for 'ee now."

"No, no," he protested weakly, but she was already bustling about the room to fetch a bowl of water and some clean linen.

"He'll let you see to un, I shouldn't wonder," her mother whispered, producing a flat dish from under a pile of dry clouts. "He won't let us come near un. He'm mortal bad."

"I made un a dish of penny royal," Mrs Havers complained. "An' he wouldn't so much as put his lips to it. The trouble we'm in, dearie, you wouldn't believe the half of it. There's that poor little babba been so poorly you wouldn't believe, an' we all knows the outcome of *that*, an' Mrs Lambton took to her bed, poor soul, an' now your pa. 'Tis more than human flesh an' blood can stand. I said so to your poor ma onny this morning . . ."

Suki let her ramble on and paid no attention to her, for the smell of pus had roused the most unpleasant forebodings. She poured the last of the day's water from the ewer into the kettle, set it on the fire to warm and tore a clean clout into little strips for bandages, then dabbing and soothing, she began to ease the dirty dressings from her father's fingers. She hurt him so much that he groaned despite himself.

I must be ready for it to be nasty, she thought, as she eased the last red rags from his quivering hand. But even then, half prepared as she was by his pain and her mother's concern, she was horrified at what she saw. His two middle fingers had been hacked off at the knuckle and the stumps were swollen and black with bruises and oozing yellow pus. And I said "'twas only fingers", she thought with shame. "Only fingers." My poor dear brave old Pa.

"Run up the farm and see if Farmer Lambton could

spare a mouthful of Hollands," she said to her brother.
But as he ran from the room, her father gave a shuddering
moan and fainted away.

"Hold his hand still," she told her mother, "an' we'll
clean it all we can while he don't feel nothin'."

"Poor soul!" her mother mourned. "An' never a word
of complaint! 'Tis always the same with un. He don't
like us to know how bad he is. Never did."

"You'm the bravest man alive," Suki told her father's
insensible head. She was washing his wounds as quickly
as she could, but even so she wasn't quick enough. He
came to long before she'd finished, and had to endure
several groaning minutes before Tom ran back with
the gin. Then they struggled on together, in the short
numbing time the spirits eventually bestowed.

But at last the wounds were clean and freshly bandaged and her father had been sick, which didn't surprise
any of them, and she'd sponged his face and wrapped
him in a blanket and laid him in his truckle bed.

"Don't you go a-sayin' a word, you foolish creature,"
she scolded lovingly when he tried to thank her. "Just
you get yourself warm and get yourself better. I'd do
anything at all to make you better. You know that." Then
she had to turn away from him, for pity was making
her cry.

"I'll clean up for 'ee," Mrs Havers offered, gathering
the dirty rags to burn them on the fire. "I never knowd
he was so bad an' that's a fact. Poor soul."

"Shall you stay here?" her mother whispered. "Or go
up to the farmhouse?"

Suki hadn't thought so far ahead. "I'll go to the farm,
if they'll have me," she said. "They've a cradle there for
William."

"Then you'd best know the news," her mother told

her. "The babba died last week. Poor little thing. She'm in a poor way over it."

So that was what Mrs Havers was rambling on about, Suki thought. "Poor Mrs Lambton," she said, flooded with pity for her. "What a parlous thing to happen. No wonder she'm took to her bed. They'll not want me in the house at a time like this. I shall sleep here with Molly. We can find a drawer for William, perviding 'tis long enough. I'll walk across an' see them in the morning an' say how sorry I am. What a parlous thing to happen."

Such a morning it was, golden with the promise of noonday heat, lush with birdsong, heady with the scents of summer, a morning for courtship and sweet talk, for gathering flowers and stitching bridal gowns, not visiting the sick. But she coaxed her father to a breakfast of ale and bread, fed William until his belly was as tight as a drum, left him with Molly and walked across to the farmhouse notwithstanding.

She was upset to see how neglected it looked. The floor was strewn with dirty rushes, the ashes of last night's fire were still grey in the grate, and, although there was no dust visible to the eye, the bench looked smeared and the table grubby. But it was the sight of Farmer Lambton that upset her most of all, for he seemed to have aged and shrunk and was stooping in a way she'd never noticed in him before. There were more wrinkles in his cheeks, more lines in his forehead and his eyes were bloodshot and deep shadowed. But he made her welcome and urged her to come in. "She's abed, I fear, and none too well," he explained. "But she'll be pleased to see *you*, Suki. I'm sure of that. Go you up."

Annie Lambton lay propped among her pillows in a room that smelt of blood and phlegm. There was a phial full of green liquid on the table beside the bed, an unemptied chamber pot beside it, and a small white bowl, full of blood and vomit, tipping sideways on the coverlet just out of reach of her hands. The windows were shuttered, as though air and sunlight would be injurious to her, and in the half-light that seeped through the cracks in the wood, her face looked grey and heavily lined. She had made an effort to plait her long hair but the plait was tousled and straw-dry, her eyes were shut and much sunk in their sockets and she was wincing with every indrawn breath, her chest was shrivelled and sunken, too, and her hands lay against the coverlet as if they had been discarded there.

"Oh Annie!" Suki said, forgetting the proprieties in the distress of the moment. "I'm so sorry to see you so ill."

"Not ill," Annie said, with her eyes still shut. "I'm dying, Suki. I been a-dying these seven days since my poor Connie was took."

Suki rushed to deny it, "No! No!" But the effort of speaking had provoked such a spasm of coughing that denial was useless. She held the bowl beneath her friend's straining mouth and caught the blood as she coughed it up and knew that death was tearing her down with every gasp.

"Could you fancy anything to eat?" she asked when the spasm was over. The poor lady was mortal thin and looked as though she hadn't eaten for days.

Annie was beyond food. "A stoop of ale to moisten my mouth," she whispered. And coughed again.

The ale was fetched and three sips taken painfully, the patient's face and hands were washed with a soft cloth, the bowl and the chamber pot taken down and emptied on the midden, the floor swept and sprinkled with vinegar, but no amount of loving care made any impression on Annie Lambton who had drifted into a

153

murmuring unconsciousness as soon as she lay back on the pillows.

"She'm dying," Suki said to her mother when she was back in the cottage.

"Yes," Mrs Brown said. "Poor soul. What a blessing you'm home. You'll do what's needful for her, won't you, my dear? We must pray for an easy end. Not a word of it to your pa. We'm keeping it from him, bein' he got pains enough of his own."

And so have I, Suki thought, for I wouldn't have wished such suffering on either the one of 'em, and it pains me cruelly to see it. But there was tomorrow's dough to knead and set to rise – no matter how she might be feeling – and a stew pot to fill with pot herbs and scraps of bacon, and her father to be coaxed through his supper before his wounds were cleaned and dressed again.

That night she lay awake in the narrow truckle bed beside her sister, too full of sadness to sleep. How suddenly your life can be turned about, she thought. Two days ago, I was playing with my William under the chestnut tree in Appleton without a care in the world, except for wonderin' when the Captain's like to come home and feeling cross with poor Farmer Lambton for telling tales on Miss Ariadne. And now here I am with Pa sore injured, that poor babba dead, Mrs Lambton a-dying an' the farmer like an old man. 'Tis a mortal sad world and we'm all a-tangled up in it, whether we will or no, on account of we loves each other. 'Tis only them as don't love as are free to come an' go as they choose. She knew there was no hope of a visit to Bristol now. She would have to contain her soul in patience until Jack came to Twerton of his own accord and, in the meantime, do what she could for her patients.

154

It was distressing work, for however hard she tried to help Mrs Lambton, the poor lady grew weaker by the hour, drifting in and out of consciousness, racked with coughing and too fatigued to lift her head from the pillows. The priest arrived to administer the last rites and sat with the farmer for two hours afterwards, doing his best to comfort, and the farm labourers came and went, murmuring how sorry they were and hoping the mistress would take a turn for the better, but they all knew the truth of it.

"'Twill not be long, I fear," Farmer Lambton said on Suki's seventh evening in the farm.

She was wrapping herself in her shawl ready to walk back to the cottage. "Should I stay with her overnight, think 'ee?" she asked.

"No," he said wearily. "I'll sit up with her. 'Tis the least I can do and little enough in all conscience."

It was the least and the last. The next morning when Suki came tripping back across the yard he met her at the door with the news that Annie was dead. It had been a cruel passing, with a deal of blood, and he was still stunned by it.

"I never thought to see such blood," he said, shaking his head as if he were trying to shake the vision of it away. "'Twas the blood that killed her, Suki. She died of the blood. Such blood! Could you ask Mrs Havers to come over. She'll need laying out and there's such a deal of cleaning to be done. I never thought to see such blood."

Suki was glad to run back to the cottage to fetch the old lady, for she was aching with such anguished sympathy for the farmer that the tears were streaming down her cheeks. How cruel to die so, after all she'd suffered. 'Twas monstrous. Monstrous.

It seemed even more monstrous when she and Mrs Havers arrived in the bedroom, for the bed was so badly soaked with blood that it had dripped through the feather mattress on to the floor. There were two chamber pots full of it and even the walls were scarlet spotted. "My dear life!" Mrs Havers said. "'Tis like a shambles."

They washed their dead mistress between them, mourned at how thin her body was. They dressed her in a fresh nightgown, brushed her tangled hair, and laid her on clean sheets with a wild rose between her hands. Then they emptied the chamber pots and scrubbed the floor and washed down the walls.

"I'm beholden to 'ee," Farmer Lambton said, when they came downstairs to tell him all was done. He had the necessary coins laid on the table ready to pay them but it took him a while to remember that they were there. "Ah yes," he said, when Mrs Havers looked at them and raised her eyebrows at his tardiness. "Of course, yes. I'm beholden. Is there anything else I can do for 'ee?"

"If I could have pen, ink and paper, sir, I'd be obliged," Suki said. "I should write to Miss Ariadne to tell her how I fare. She'll be a-wondering."

That night, when her father's wounds had been dressed yet again, and William had been fed and settled in his pillow-padded drawer, she wrote a long letter to her friend, describing everything that had happened, and weeping again with the anguish of it. "How oddly things do turn out," she ended.

> When I left home for to go to work in Bath, I was mightily pleased with myself and thought I could not fail to succeed and I should return for my wedding, not for Mrs Lambton's funeral. I had a poor opinion of my family then, I fear, but tis

much changed now for I see how brave Pa is and
how dearly Ma loves him. I have not been to Bristol
nor am I like to, there being so much here for me to
do. Nothing has turned out as I expected. I confess
to you that there are times when I wonder what is
to become of me and my William. I wish you and
I could be together again, if only for an afternoon.
There is no one here for me to talk to and, if there
were, there'm only sad things for to say.

Your loving friend,

Suki

When she finally put down her pen and wiped the ink
from her fingers, she found that the act of composition
had eased her but, even so, her night was fraught with
bloody dreams. When William woke her in the morning,
calling "Ma! Ma!" as he climbed out of his drawer, she
was as stiff about the neck and shoulders as if she'd
been carrying a pair of milk pails. But feeding him was
a comfort as it always was, being patted and smiled
at so lovingly with those fine brown eyes, and when
she got downstairs to the kitchen, carrying him on her
hip as she usually did these days, she found her father
already eating breakfast and looking much better and
much brighter and that cheered her even further.

"We shall soon have 'ee well again," she told him.

"Aye," he agreed, "once the funeral's over. Poor soul.
Your ma told me of it this morning. Put your pretty babba
on the stool aside me here an' he shall have some of my
bread and butter, pretty dear."

The pretty dear was a comfort to them all in the days
after the funeral, for knowing nothing of the death they'd

endured, he babbled and played and entertained them with his chirruping, as bright as a bird in a tree. And gradually, under Suki's gently determined ministrations, her father's raw stumps began to heal. On the fourth day after the funeral, the pus was finally gone, the bruises were changing colour and the swelling was quite definitely going down. Two days later, scabs began to form.

"You must sit out in the sunshine," Suki said, "and let the air heal you. See if we can't get a bit of colour back in your cheeks. Our William'll sit with 'ee, won't 'ee my 'andsome?"

That afternoon, she baked a rabbit pie for the family supper, and decorated the table with a jugful of wild flowers to celebrate his healing and to mark the gradual lifting of their long gloom. It made a sunny picture, for she had garnered a pretty armful, yellow celandine and mallow flowers as wide as poppies, fragile herb Robert and purple pansies, brown burnet and yellow trefoil, even six downy heads of hare's foot clover. And then, just as her mother was cutting the first slice from the pie, a postboy galloped into the yard to crown the feast with a letter for Miss Suki Brown. There was a happy scramble to find a coin to pay him, and then they all waited with cheerful anticipation for Suki to break the seal and read what it contained.

It was from Ariadne and her news was like a return to life.

> We are summoned to Bath for the bride is to spend a week there to be made healthy and beauteous for her wedding, although 'tis my opinion an ocean of sulphur water could not achieve such a miracle. I believe I have found the path I must take but will tell you of it when we have leisure. I shall arrive

in Bristol on the three o'clock stage on Thursday
and will wait for you an hour on the Broad Quay.
I trust your father is much improved and that I shall
hear good news when we meet.

"I've to go to Bristol a' Thursday," she said. At last!
At last!

Ten

"'Tis a fair fine ship," Frederick Bradbury said, pushing his telescope into the socket of his right eye with excitement. He'd been in a state of controlled elation since four o'clock the previous afternoon, when Mr Tomson's *billet* had been delivered. To learn that his ships had reached Eaton in Gordano and were lying at anchor waiting for the pilot was most welcome, for it meant that his cargo had come safely home, which allayed the anxiety he invariably suffered while any ship of his was at sea. To hear of the profit that had been made on the sale of his slaves was heartening, too, for he'd been anxious on that account ever since the *Bonny Beaufoy* set sail. But to be told that the *Yorick* had taken a prizeship on her very first voyage out, and with little loss of life what's more, provoked him to such raptures that he actually let out a whoop of joy, to the consternation of his valet, who had never seen his gentleman behave with such abandon. It was a triumph, a vindication of everything that he and his brother had been working for since the French attacked the *Antelope*. 'Od rot 'em. And now here was the prize herself, sailing slowly upriver between the *Bonny Beaufoy* and the *Yorick* and a fine fair ship indeed. "I must send a *billet* to my brother," he said. "He will be cock-a-hoop."

A strengthening sun was burning off the early morning

160

mist, which rose from the river in long swirling swathes. There was something theatrical about it that morning, as though it was blue gauze lifted by unseen hands, something at once familiar and otherworldly, a mark that this was an especial scene. The three ships sailed through it steadily, dipping with the tide and the breeze, their brass giving an occasional gleam as the sun touched it, their long masts alternately misted and golden. The oars of the pilot boat were gilded too and tipped with royal scarlet as they rose and plunged in perfect unison – and where the water was clear, its ripples sparkled as though they'd been sprinkled with gold dust. It was a sight to delight his mercantile soul.

"Fetch me my hat and gloves," he ordered. "I shall go down to the quay to welcome them home."

He arrived to a flurry of applause from his friends, who had come down to the quay before him, for they too had seen the advance of the three ships and the news had spread like sunrise. "A prize on your first voyage, damme!" they approved, patting his shoulders as though he had captured the ship himself. "That'll show the plaguey Frenchies." "Was there much cargo?"

"Ivory and silks," he told them happily, gazing towards his approaching booty and swelling with the pride of the moment.

Jack Daventry was back in his cabin in the *Bonny Beaufoy*. As soon as they'd dropped anchor off Eaton in Gordano, Mr Smith had sent a boat across to the *Yorick* to fetch him and since then he'd been a virtual prisoner, with his legs shackled and his hands tied behind his back. Now, as they swayed upriver, his old shipmate, Mr Reuben, had dodged into the cabin to make a few unofficial adjustments.

"There's a reception committee awaiting us," the

bosun said, as he retied the rope, "which you'd best be warned of, for 't could cut 'ee one of two ways. If they'm in a fair mood they'll not want unpleasantness to mar un, an' you might 'scape clean. Let's pray so, eh my old lubber. On t'other hand, if they'm vindictive, which jealousy do tend towards – an' there'll be a powerful amount of jealousy a-brewin' this morning – they could howl to have 'ee punished sore. You must hold fire for either eventuality, my lubber, and if you'm to run, you must jump so soon as you see a chance."

Jack explored the slip-knot with his fingers. "Trust me," he said. "I'll not be sent to the gallows, nor to prison neither, not when I've a good friend to aid me and a good horse waiting in the stables to carry me away."

"Well good luck to 'ee," the bosun said, kicking Jack's discarded leg irons under the bunk. "You'm a valiant fighter and not one to waste in a jail. What's to become of your nigger-boy?"

Blue was sitting on his heels in the corner of the cabin. "I go with Mr Jack, massa," he said.

"He's provided for," Jack said, smiling at his slave. "He knows what to do, don't 'ee Blue?" Neither of them were entirely sure that he would be able to follow his instructions but they were determinedly optimistic. "He'll wait for me."

The ship juddered as she began to go about. "We'm coming alongside," Mr Reuben said. "I'd best be off. Good luck to 'ee, Jack." And was gone like a shadow.

Left on his own in the stale air of the cabin, Jack sat on the edge of his bunk and tried to calm the agitated pounding of his heart. The wait seemed endless. He heard the captain shouting orders, felt the ship strain against her hawsers, saw feet scampering on the quayside, or braced against a heavy haul, but the wait went on long after the

162

ship had been steadied to a halt. He was fevered with tension. Soon, there were congratulatory voices booming on the quay. He recognised the weaselly tones of Mr Jedediah Smith, the Bristol burrs of Mr Tomson and Jack Jerome, the precise enunciation of the ship's surgeon, the deep-throated laugh of the *Yorick*'s captain, and knew that they were bragging of their successes. The wait went on. Perhaps they've forgotten me, he thought, and a little hope dampened his fever. Perhaps they'll all go swaggering off to dinner and leave the crew to disembark on their own. If that's the case, I can sneak off to the stables and be away before they know it.

There were feet tramping outside the cabin and the door was flung open to reveal the four musketeers who'd captured him in Nevis. "Mr Cooper, sir," he said, greeting their leader.

Mr Cooper was brusque and unfriendly. "Stow that," he said. "You'm a prisoner now. On your feet! Where's your leg irons?"

Jack decided to be polite and cool. The man was an armed guard, no more, and should be handled with care. "They were removed," he said.

Mr Cooper looked suspicious. "What for?"

"To allow me to walk, I daresay."

"I s'pose they knows what they'm a-doin' of," the musketeer said. "Well let's be having you." And he jabbed Jack forward with the muzzle of his musket.

The light out on the quay was so dazzling that for a few seconds, as he walked down the gangplank, Jack could barely see. He kept his head high and his spine straight because it was necessary to show that he was a man of "bottom", but his senses were as blurred as the faces below him. He was aware of a seething crowd: merchants in wigs and tricorns, leaning

on their canes; local women waving and calling to their
returning menfolk; dockers already unloading the prize
ship's cargo; horses shaking their harness; dogs snarling
and barking. But the reception committee was a faceless
smudge of dark colour, more felt than seen, an aura of
disapproval, a stab of needle voices that made his heart
shrink in his chest.

"There he is!" Mr Smith shouted. "Arrogant puppy!
This is the fool that thinks he may draw pistol on
his betters. Send for the constable, sir, and have him
arraigned."

Jack stepped off the gangplank, sending a quick eye
message to Blue that he was to hide behind the nearest
bollard. Mr Bradbury's anxious face swam into focus.
"Is this true, sir?" he was asking Mr Tomson. "Did he
draw a pistol?"

"He did, sir."

"Was it fired?"

"Not to my knowledge, sir," the captain said. "Just
drawd and so forth. No harm done."

"No harm!" Mr Smith shouted. Excitement was making him sweat. Jack could see beads of moisture forming
on his upper lip and running like raindrops from
underneath his wig. "He could have blown my head
off, sir, and would've done had I not been too quick
for him. Have him arraigned. 'Twas an act of rank
disobedience. He needs stringing up and the sooner the
better. Send for the constable."

"He is my slave master is he not?" Mr Bradbury
asked, peering at the captive's face. And kin to Lady
Bradbury as he recalled. 'Twould not be politic to
annoy *that* lady by arresting a kinsman. He would never
hear the end of it. And yet Mr Smith was uncommon
pressing and would need to be answered, one way or

another. What a dilemma to be in! If only brother George were here.

There was a sudden noise to the left of them as a barrel rolled from the trolley on which it was being hauled and thundered along the quay, turning on its axis, perilously near the water's edge. It was a welcome diversion and he seized it at once.

"Have a care what you're doing, sir. You must excuse me, gentlemen."

Mr Smith scowled and took out a kerchief to wipe his forehead, the seamen turned to watch the recovery of the barrel, and Jack was suddenly ignored and suddenly all instinct, alert to his finger ends. It was the moment. He must take it or be lost to the hangman. Quickly and now. He ripped the knot apart, tossed the rope aside, leapt into the quay, moving with such speed that it was all one action, the water closing cold over his head before his wrists lost the rope's sensation. He could hear people shouting while he was still underwater – their voices belling and bubbling – could see the hull of the *Bonny Beaufoy* encrusted with moon-white barnacles, the hawser ridged and rippling like some great sea-green water snake. Then his head was in the air again and he struck out for the opposite quayside, ears popping and lungs straining, as the sun broke cut-glass on the water and the outraged roaring behind him rose to a crescendo. "'Od's bowels! Stop him, somebody!"

The water was heavy, pulling him down. He was a bird caught in its toils, struggling to fly free. He could hear the thwack and splash of his feet, feel the water parting before the force of his arms. Three strokes. Two. And there was a line dangling just beyond his grasp. He plunged at it, grabbed the air, pushed again, caught it, held on, gasping for breath. Then he was climbing hand over hand with the rope steadied between his feet and water streaming from his hair and falling in great drops from his shirt and breeches. Over the gunwale, on to warm deck, sea-brown faces in his line of vision, rough hands grabbing at him, dodging, ducking, pulling away from them, six dancing paces to the gangplank and he was free, running through the crowds on the quayside, where the merchants were too preoccupied by their own affairs to pay much attention to a running man – even a wet one.

He glanced back at his pursuers, who were charging along the opposite bank towards the head of the quay, yelling encouragement at one another. It would take some time for them to reach him and Mr Wenham's livery stables were a matter of yards away. He could already smell horse flesh, already feel Beau's supple neck under his hands, see those clever ears pricking for command. As he leapt into the yard, his mind leapt ahead of him. He was already in the saddle and galloping away.

His arrival was like an explosion. Work stopped, heads turned, mouths opened. A piebald mare being led out of her stall shied in alarm, and all the horses in the yard laid back their ears and rolled their eyes.

"Quickly!" he shouted to the nearest startled face. "Get Mr Wenham! Jump to it!"

The stable lad jumped, but Mr Wenham was already walking out of the tack room – bandy legged and tousled, with a straw in his mouth and his cap on the back of his head – to ask what was amiss.

"I've come for my horse," Jack said urgently. "There's not a minute to lose." Now that he was standing still, he realised that he was shivering and that water was running from his shoes and gathering in a puddle round his feet, but there was no time to explain his appearance. "My horse, Beau. You remember. Bay stallion. Eighteen hands."

"Ah yes," Mr Wenham said, remembering. "You owes me money on that there hanimal, as I recall."

Fury burned in Jack's shivering chest. To be balked now, when the matter was so pressing! Obdurate man! "You'll be paid, sir," he said, speaking as calmly as he could. "You have my word on't. Where is he?"

"Well now as to that, sir," Mr Wenham said, "I believe we must settle accounts afore I tells 'ee."

"Deuce take it, man. This is a matter of life and death. You'll get your money when I get my horse."

"Well as to that, sir," Mr Wenham began.

There were feet pounding the cobbles somewhere outside the yard. There was no time for politeness or sense or even thought. Frantic with fear, Jack seized the stableman by the throat and thrust him against the nearest hay bale. "Tell me where he is, damme, or I'll put paid to 'ee. Damme if I won't."

Mr Wenham struggled away from him, red in the face and full of fury. Customer or no, he would *not* be handled so. Not by any man. "You can save your venom," he said. "He arn't here."

The news threw Jack into a panic. He could feel the fever of it, rising in his chest like a wave. He *had* to be here. He was needed. How could he get away if his horse were gone? "You jest!"

"I never jests, sir. He arn't here."

'Od's blood and bowels. He means it. "Then where is he?"

"Your wife took un."

"Wife?" Jack said wildly. "What folly's this? I have no wife."

"Said she was your wife. Anyways, she took un. Months ago."

Nightmare was closing in with the pounding feet. He was so hot it was hard to breathe. "Where to? I *must* find him."

Suki's carefully written note had been lost and forgotten long ago. "How should I know, sir? She'm your wife, not mine."

The feet were behind him and there was nowhere to run, nowhere to hide. He turned, his face wild, cast about for a weapon, saw a pitchfork stuck in the straw, seized it and held it before him, daring his pursuers, "Come on then, damn you. You'll not take me without a fight."

It was short and vicious and drew a happy crowd. The outcome was predictable, for the young man was hopelessly outnumbered, but he was handsome and valiant and put up a splendid struggle, defending himself most courageously with his long fork, and swearing like a trouper, until he was clubbed to the ground and gagged with a bandanna. As his captors led him away, barefooted and with his hands tightly trussed behind his back, with blood dripping from a split lip and a long gash across the top of his head, they gave him a cheer, as though he were a prizefighter. "Good luck to 'ee! We'll come to your hanging, boy, damme if we won't. 'Twill be a sight to see." And most of them trailed along after him, eager for the next excitement.

Jack acknowledged them with a nod, since he couldn't speak or wave, but he was drawn with distress and fever. Heat burned out from the centre of his body, in long heartbeat pulses. Sweat ran from every pore. His bound hands were slippery with moisture. Even the soles of his feet were wet and sticky against the cobble-stones. Worse, he was finding it hard to see. There was a film across his eyes and lights trembled and danced at the edges of his vision. He was half walked, half dragged from the yard, and jostled along the quay. Soon it took all his effort to put one foot in front of the other and he knew that the jungle fever had returned and that he was ill again. If only they would stop and let him lie down. But there was a trial to come. He had to face his accusers, to hold on, to show himself a man of valour.

Mr Frederick Bradbury was much put out to see him dragged back with a crowd in tow. To have an audience to his actions was intolerable, especially when one of the participants was related to his sister-in-law. "We will adjourn to the manufactory," he decided, and turned on his elegant heel at once to lead the way. His office was small but at least it was hidden from the prurient gaze of *hoi polloi*.

They crammed into the dusty space, stood in a semi-circle before Bradbury's presiding desk, with their backs to the neat stack of his account books and Jack, drooping at the centre of their accusations: Mr Jedediah Smith, pinched with fury and delay; Mr Tomson, twisting his hat in his hands; Mr Jerome, puffing rank tobacco smoke into the limited air; a constable, black-clad and sour-faced, wearing his chain of office; Mr Bradbury's surgeon, also in sober black and ready to assist his patron; Mr Cooper and his cohort of musketeers, smug with the success of their endeavours and the certainty of reward.

They were sealed in by the heat of the manufactory. Dust motes bounced against the window like bees. "Well, sir," Mr Bradbury said to Mr Smith, "what's to be done?"

"What's to be done, sir?" Mr Smith said, spitting with fury. "What's to be done? Why the man is to be arraigned and took off to jail. How many more times must I tell 'ee?"

The constable wasn't sure about the practicality of such a suggestion. "We'm full to bursting, sir," he reported, "saving your reverence. On account of we got all those Frenchies a yourn to house and Justice Ford he been a-sendin' down villains to us prodigious the last few days. Now if you could see your way to keep un confined in your cellar, sir, for a day or two, or some such place likewise, then we could get un to court sharpish and squeeze un in afore he goes for execution."

Mr Bradbury quailed at the very idea of having this red-faced, staring stranger under his quiet roof. "Such a course is out of the question," he said. "Have you no room at all?"

"'Tis my opinion, sir," Mr Tomson said, "begging your pardon and so forth, the man is sick."

He was certainly standing in a very peculiar way, leaning sideways as if he were about to fall.

"Are you so?" Mr Bradbury asked. "Take away the gag. I'll hear him speak."

Jack made a valiant effort to stand straight. "No, sir."

"He's an unprincipled villain," Mr Smith pressed on, "and if he's sick, 'tis no more than he deserves." And he pulled out his trump card and laid it into the argument to prove his point. "He thinks niggers are the equal of white men."

There was an outcry at such folly. The constable laughed out loud, but Frederick Bradbury was shocked. "How now?" he said to Jack. "Is this true?"

Self-preservation should have urged Jack to be cautious, to prevaricate, even to lie, but he was caught in the need to show his valour and valour drove him to honesty.

"Yes," he said. "'Tis true as I stand here, sir. I will not pretend otherwise. They are human as we are, they bleed as we do, suffer the same pain, love as we do – sometimes better – die as we do, with the same courage. There is no difference atween us, save that we have guns and whips and are cruel enough to use 'em, and they are poor and naked. There are things done aboard ship 'twould hurt your very soul to see, Mr Bradbury, men and women branded like cattle, chained and left in their own filth below decks for days and weeks at a time, flogged until their backs are raw and they are too weak to stand, children thrown into the sea alive, even the newborn threatened with death, as Mr Smith here knows very well. Ask *him* of it. They are not cattle, sir, nor property. They are human and we make 'em suffer and we'll be dammed in hell for it, every man jack of us. Only a fool or a blind man could fail to see the truth of what I'm saying. Only a fool . . ." Then he was exhausted and panting and too near tears to continue and he had to stop to draw breath and recover what composure he could. He had made his stand and he knew it would cost him his freedom if not his life, but he'd found strength and cleanliness and honour in what he'd said. Despite all the ugly emotions in that tight fly-blown room – the sick excitement that he'd seen so often when the slaves were whipped, the furious incomprehension, the hunger to hurt and punish – he'd told the truth and shamed the devil. Now let come what may.

"Why, the man's mad," Frederick Bradbury said. "I never heard the like. Does he often rave like this, Mr Tomson?"

Mr Tomson admitted that he had spoke so on occasions and Mr Cooper was loud in confirmation. "Stark, starin, raving mad, sir, we allus said so."

171

"He weren't too mad to know how to draw a pistol," Mr Smith said sourly. "He was sane enough then, in all conscience."

The outburst, shocking though it was, had offered Frederick Bradbury an escape from his dilemma. If the man was mad, there was no need to send him to jail. He turned to his surgeon. "What say you, sir? Is he mad, think 'ee?"

"Oh indubitably, Mr Bradbury," the surgeon told him. "There's no question of it. A rising of the mother which has led to delirium extremis. A most interesting case."

"What's to be done with him?"

"He should be sent to Bedlam with all speed," the surgeon said, happily envisaging the introductory fee he would earn from the transaction. "They are experienced in such cases and would know how to treat him." He was already composing his offer to the surgeons there. A man who looked so wild and raved so lucidly would attract the crowds uncommon well. "'Tis beyond our competence to treat him here without the necessary restraints, leg irons and shackles and strait-jackets and so forth. Bedlam is the leading asylum in the country and has the wherewithal for the most intractable cases. I could negotiate the fee and the cost of his keep, should you wish it."

The image of his hated adversary being forced into a strait-jacket and whipped for his intransigence made Mr Smith gloat with satisfaction, but Mr Bradbury was concerned. The thought of paying for an unknown lunatic to be kept in an asylum disturbed him. What would brother George say of it? If only he wasn't so caught up in this wretched wedding and could be sent for to offer advice. Could they afford such an action? And should they? "How long would he stay there think 'ee?" he asked.

"Ah now, sir, as to that," the surgeon reassured, "'tis impossible to say with any accuracy but, in my experience, they rarely see out a year. Most are dead within months. Delirium is weakening."

As if to prove him right, Jack gave a low groan and fell to the floor insensible, his head and limbs shaking uncontrollably, bound as they were, his skin grey and streaked with sweat, his eyes rolling, the very image of a madman.

Mr Bradbury leaned across his desk to look at him. "How soon could it be arranged?"

"As soon as you wish, sir. He could be gone on the noon stage, should you require it."

"You would accompany him?"

At a price. "To the very gate, sir. You have my word on't."

So it was decided. A closed carriage was hired to take the lunatic to the stagecoach, where he was dragged out, more or less unconscious and, after considerable argument with the coachman and a sizeable bribe, was pulled and pushed into an outside seat, held in position by the surgeon and joggled away to London. Such is the price for telling the truth to those who cannot bear to hear it.

Left on his own in the confusion of the quayside, Blue had sat on his heels behind the bollard, carefully hidden by shadow, and watched and waited. It was hard to make sense of what was happening around him because there were so many people about and they all moved so quickly and shouted so loudly and looked so odd with their curled white wigs and their thick canes and sparkling shoes. He realised that Mr Jack was escaping when he jumped off the quay and watched with admiration as he swam across the river and disappeared among the crowds on

173

the opposite bank. Then he wasn't sure what he was supposed to do next, so he sat where he was and went on waiting.

He was miserably upset to see his master dragged back to the quay with blood dripping from his mouth and the top half of his body trussed with great ropes, and very alarmed when he was marched off with all those grumbling men around him and taken into one of the big houses beside the quay. But he went on waiting. What else could he do?

People came and went and presently a carriage arrived, drawn by two black horses, and Mr Jack was carried out of the house as though he were dead and pushed inside. At that he sprang to his feet, ready to follow, but the carriage was off at such speed that it had left the quay and disappeared into all the other traffic on the road before he could catch up with it. He was alone in this bewildering city, without his master and with no one who could speak his language and he would have to make his way by his own devices. But he cheered himself with the thought that there was still his precious paper. What he had to do now was to find someone who would read it to him and tell him where he was to go. Someone who looked kindly, Mr Jack had said. Someone who smiled.

It was easier thought than done, for very few people were smiling on the quayside. They scowled and argued and punched one hand against the other, and smoked pipes with such intensity and fury that they quite alarmed him and sometimes laughed in a rough barking way as though they were dogs – but few smiled.

He tried a gentleman in an odd-looking brown wig, who was writing things in a book with a little wooden stick and seemed a quiet sort of person, but he waved him away with the little stick and told him to be off.

He tried a lady who was walking along the quay with a gentleman in a bright red coat, but she looked at him with such disdain that he knew she wouldn't answer even before the words were out of his mouth. He tried an old man and a young one, but the former merely frowned and the latter turned away as though he was invisible. He tried three possible ladies one after the other but they were smiling at their companions and wouldn't smile or speak to him. It was after midday, as he knew, because the sun had dropped during his search and now he was beginning to feel desperate. What if no one would help him? What would he do then? And at that point, he saw the lady. She was climbing out of a little cart which was loaded with vegetables and driven by an old man in a rough brown jacket, with a black dog sitting bold upright beside him. She had a straw hat on her head and a baby in her arms – a nice fat baby who laughed and chuckled when she settled him on her hip – and she was smiling at everybody, the man in the cart, the dog, the baby. Something in the grace of her body, as she stood swayed against the weight of the child on her hip, reminded him of his mother. He ran to her at once.

Eleven

Mr Jones had taken an unconscionable time to drive his cart to Bristol and Suki was sick with impatience. She'd been up before dawn to pack her bag with William's clothes and gather up her few possessions, and she'd said goodbye to her family and the farmer at first light but the old man had been so tantalisingly slow that it was past one o'clock before they finally ambled on to the Broad Quay. And he seemed to think he'd done well, foolish crittur.

"Here we are then," he said, beaming at her as he reined the mare to a halt. "Broad Quay as ever is. We made good speed, don' 'ee think. You haven't to meet that ol' coach till three, now have 'ee, so you got time a-plenty. Two whole hours. I'd get something to eat if I was you."

Suki looked along the lines of ships crowded into the quay. 'Twould take hours simply to walk from ship to ship. But he meant well and was looking at her so hopeful of a smile that she thanked him and smiled back, despite her annoyance. After all, he didn't know she was here to search for her lover and that every minute was precious. But she *was* here. That was what mattered. She was here and in a few minutes she would know if Jack's ship was in or when 'twas like to arrive. I'll go to the shipping office straight off, she decided, and see what they knows of it. And she sat William on the seat and jumped out of the cart.

What crowds there were on the quay and how strong they smelt and what a great noise they were making, caw, caw, caw, chatter-chatter – just like a flock of crows and maggot pies. After weeks in the quiet of Twerton, she found it quite dizzying. They were fine folk, though, there was no doubt of that. She'd never seen so much gold braid or so many gold buttons, and the ladies were the equal of Lady Bradbury in their silks and satins, especially the one promenading on the arm of that tall redcoat. Her shoes must have cost a fortune. The only drab figure on the quay was a funny-looking man in a brown coat and an old-fashioned bob wig, who was sitting on the wall, busily writing in a green chapbook. There was something vaguely familiar about him, but she couldn't think what it was, not even when he lifted his head and looked across at her. No matter. He was of no consequence. Not when she was so near to finding the Captain. She held out her arms to William and Mr Jones lowered him down to her.

"Who's a pretty boy?" she said, holding him up before her, delighting in his fine fat limbs and his fine brown eyes. "If you'm a good babba and you lets me go a-searchin', you shall have a sugar stick, by an' by. What do 'ee think to that?" And he chuckled and babbled and reached down to catch her hair, as happy as she was. "You'm too much of a weight to hold up for long," she told him, pretending to scold, and she swung him about and settled him on her hip. And at that moment, a black boy ran out of the crowd and came and stood right in front of her. He was dressed in canvas breeches and a smock shirt like a sailor and he had a paper in his hand.

"An't please you," he said. "You read this to me?"

177

She really didn't want to spend any of her precious time reading to a strange boy and opened her mouth to tell him so, but he was looking at her so pleadingly and he had such an open, friendly face and such blue eyes – blue as the sky, which was uncommon odd for a black boy – that she couldn't deny him.

"Later," she temporised. "I can't now, but I will later."

Mr Jones lifted the bag out of the cart and handed it down to her. "I'll be off then," he said. "You'll wait hereabouts, I daresay, till your mistress arrives. There's a good chop house on the corner. Good luck to 'ee."

Suki thanked him, for he *did* mean well despite his slowness. Then she set the bag down on the cobbles next to the black boy. "Stay here an' make yourself useful an' look after my bag," she commanded, as the cart rattled away. "I got things to do. When they'm done, I'll come back to 'ee."

He gazed at her. "You read my paper?"

"Aye," Suki said, scanning the quayside for the shipping office. "Just stay there and wait for me." She could see the door, no distance away.

Blue squatted on his heels beside the bag and settled to wait again, watching as she went swaying away, the baby's bare feet swinging at her hip. He was hungry and thirsty and the quayside was as confusing as ever, but he knew she would come back because she'd smiled as she said so.

The shipping office was in its usual state of excited activity, but this time Suki pushed to the front and made her demands in a loud voice. And was instantly rewarded with the news that the *Bonny Beaufoy* had come in "this very morning as ever is" and was docked at the west quay, ready for unloading. "You can see her from this

178

windy. See? One, two, three – tenth one along. Walk down an' you'll find her."

Walking was too tame and too slow. Even with William's weight on her hip, she ran. He was here. In just a few minutes, they would be together again and her long, long wait would be over. My dear, darling Captain.

The ship was swarming with men unloading the cargo. There was no sign of the Captain but that was of no consequence with so many there who could tell her where he was.

"Have 'ee seen the Captain?" she asked the nearest sailor.

He didn't bother to look at her. "He'm on the quay, Missus. Conversin' with Mr Smith."

She looked, her heart leaping, but she couldn't see him. "Could you point un out to me?"

The sailor stood up and straightened his back. "There!" he said and pointed. To a stranger.

She was cast down. "That arn't the Captain."

"He's the onny one we got," the sailor told her. "How many captains d'you want?"

"Captain Jack," she told him. "He's the one I want."

"Then you'm come to the wrong ship," he said. "There's no one a' that name aboard the *Bonny Beaufoy*. Our captain's Mr Tomson which is him down on the quay. There's no Captain Jack."

"There must be," she insisted, "for this here's the ship he sailed on. I have it on good authority. Captain Jack."

"Do she mean Mr Jerome?" another sailor asked, coming up to join his shipmate. "His name's Jack. An' he were master of the prize ship on her way home, so he'm a captain of sorts. What do 'ee look like, this Captain Jack of yourn?"

She told them happily. "Taller than either one of you, an' a deal taller than me, with broad shoulders an' long legs an' a swaggerin' way of walking. Wears his own hair, thick hair, dark brown like his eyes. White teeth, all lovely an' even. Strong hands . . ."

"That ain't Jack Jerome," the second sailor said interrupting her before she could descend into further raptures. "Except for the swaggerin'. He'm a stocky sort a' fellow with no hair to speak of, brown or otherwise, bein' his head's a-shaven."

"He must be here," she said, insisting because she was beginning to feel desperate. "Captain Jack. You must know him."

But they turned back to their work. 'Twas a wench in pursuit of a lost lover and not worth the waste of breath.

Suki hoisted William into a more comfortable position on her hip and thought hard. He had to be here somewhere. Those men were fools not to know of him, when this was the ship he'd sailed on. She wouldn't give up at the first hurdle. She'd ask one of the others. There were enough of them about and one of them was bound to know.

None did, although she tried more than a dozen. The answer was always the same. There'd been no Captain Jack aboard any of the three vessels, except for Mr Jerome, who turned up as she was questioning a surly fellow with a gold earring, and certainly wasn't her Jack.

"I'll not be beat," she said to William, as she set him down on the cobbles and let him walk. "We'll go back to the shipping office, my 'andsome, that's what we'll do, and see if they got a list of the crew." She should have thought of that in the first place, if she'd not been so quick to get to the ship. They would know.

"No, ma'am," the clerk told her. "Crews are took on by the masters. They'm the onny ones what knows names and so forth. You'll have to ask the master. I can tell you who he is."

"I know who he is," she said drooping with disappointment. "I seen him on the quay. Mr Tomson."

As she trailed out of the office, carrying William on her hip again, she couldn't think what to do next. There were blank walls whichever way she turned and it was nearly time to meet Miss Ariadne. Oh what was amiss with all these foolish people? Why couldn't they tell her what she wanted to know?

The little black boy was still waiting patiently beside her baggage. Poor thing. She'd forgotten all about him and he'd waited all this time. So as she couldn't think of anything else to do, she strolled across to read his paper for him and calm her irritation by a good deed.

He jumped to his feet as soon as he saw her, smiling broadly and holding the paper out. "You read for me now?"

"Yes," she said, and read. "You are to go to the Llandoger Trow and ask there for Quin Cutpurse." The impact of the name made her heart leap. Well here's a thing! Quin Cutpurse. The very man I should have looked for in the first place and here's this nigger-boy been a-sittin' here all this time knowin' where he is. Quin Cutpurse. She had a sudden vivid memory of him: strolling through the Spring Gardens with Jack beside him, laughing together; sprawled before her in that dreadful brothel; scolding her for daring to address him by name, with his commanding voice and his swarthy face and that black eye patch of his. What's

181

this child doin' a-looking for *him*? "Do you know the gentleman?"

"No ma'am," the boy said. "My master, he say to find him. Where I go? You show me?"

Let anyone try to stop her.

She handed him the bag and set off at a great pace. Quin Cutpurse! What luck! Neither she nor Blue were aware that the gentleman in the brown bob wig was following at their heels.

The Llandoger Trow was crowded and there was so much tobacco smoke in the air that it was impossible to see from one end of it to the other. It gathered in dense clouds under the beams, fogged the leaded windows and ribboned about the potboys as they struggled between the tables delivering full tankards and retrieving empty ones. There was no sign of the eye patch but there were plenty of people to ask and most of them cheerful with ale. She took her question to the barman, but was careful not to ask it until she'd sweetened him with custom by ordering a pint of good ale for herself and a platter of cold meats for the boy.

"Quin," he said, when she'd read him the note. "You just missed him. He been in an' out these last three days. Him and his mates. Waitin' for something I shouldn't wonder."

"This boy's got a message for him," she explained. "He been told to wait here."

"Ah well," the barman said, turning to another customer, "that accounts. Yes, sir, what can I do for 'ee?"

She waited until the newcomer had been served, noticing idly that it was the gentleman in the brown bob wig she'd seen on the quay, then she pressed on. "You don't happen to have seen Captain Jack anywhere's about?"

182

"I wish I had," the barman said, frowning. "He got two shillin' on the slate he owe me. No I haven't seen un for months. Went to sea, so they say."

Every road leads to a blank wall, Suki thought, and jumped as the bar clock struck three. "Oh my dear life," she said to Blue. "Look at the time. My mistress will be on the quay and I'm not there to meet her." She led him to the corner of the room and sat him down at the end of one of the long trestle tables. "There's your meat an' there's the rest of my ale to wash it down. You'm to sit here till Mr Cutpurse comes back. You understand? Which he'll do in a while, I'm sure of it, if he'm a-waitin' for something. I'll try an' get back to 'ee a bit later on, but don't depend on't." And with that she left him to vitals and vigil, picked up her baggage and strode off to the quay again.

Ariadne was waiting by the shipping office, looking very grand in a blue silk travelling gown with a stomacher embroidered in pink and gold and a flat bonnet trimmed to match. "La," she said, as Suki came panting up to greet her. "I thought you had missed me. Have 'ee dined? There's a chop house nearby – serves a tolerable meal, I'm told. We've an hour to spare before the coach to Bath. I've *so* much to tell 'ee."

It was actually an intolerable meal, for the chops were burnt and the ale flat, but as they were both too excited and preoccupied to do more than pick at their food, its lack of quality went unremarked.

"We are to be in Bath for seven days," Ariadne reported, "which is little time for all that has to be done. Papa has taken a house in Queen Square. South Parade ain't grand enough for us now that we have a *bride* in the family. 'Tis all for the *bride*. Much good may it do her. She grows more insufferable by the hour. But to

183

return to the matter in hand. You must go the milliner's first thing tomorrow morning, for I mean to have two gowns made up to the most particular specification, the most particular, and it must all be done in secret with none to know of it save thee and me."

"None will, I give 'ee my word," Suki said, gazing at her chop and wondering whether she would have time to slip back to the Llandoger Trow before the coach came. If Mr Cutpurse really was waiting for something, he could be back at any time. He could be there now, this very minute. And if anyone would know where the Captain had got to, he was the man.

" 'Tis a matter of outwitting 'em." Ariadne explained. "If I'm to be shamed before the company, then I'll be shamed in a martyr's gown and let us see how Mamma will enjoy *that*. With luck 'twill shame *her*. Which is a consummation much to be desired. It must be a plain white cambric or a calico if 'tis available, nothing too heavy for I have to move, but perfectly plain and simple, such as a nun would wear."

"Yes," Suki said vaguely. William was asleep on her lap and with any luck would sleep for an hour as he usually did of an afternoon. She might just have time. "Have I got time to run a message afore we catches the coach? If I left William here with you, I could be there an' back in two shakes. He'm sound asleep and he wouldn't be a bit of bother. He could lie in my shawl on a couple of chairs. I wouldn't ask 'ee only 'tis urgent. Jack's come home. His ship put in this morning."

"And you've found him?"

"No," Suki said sadly. "I asked at the quay but they all said they'd never heard of him, which is arrant nonsense. He must be somewheres about an' there's a man at the Llandoger Trow – or to speak true a man as *might* be at

the Llandoger Trow – an' if he is, he might know where
he is. 'Tis all unsatisfactory, I know, but he'm the only
chance I got."

She'd expected instant agreement, even assistance, but
Ariadne was frowning. "How if you miss the coach?" she
said. "'Tis only a matter of minutes before 'twill arrive
and they will be expecting us to travel together. I said
nothing of your visit to Twerton, you understand, and
'twould be unwise to provoke 'em."

"I'll be uncommon speedy," Suki promised.

"But what if you ain't speedy enough?" Ariadne said.
"And what if this man of yours ain't at the inn? You
said he might be, did you not? If he ain't there, 'twill
be a wild goose chase and no good will come of it, no
matter how speedy you are. We must use our wits and
see what is best to be done. Your lover is returned, you
say. You are sure on't?"

"I'm sure on't."

"But you ain't seen him, so he must have some matter
that needs his urgent attention or he'd have sought 'ee
out at once. Or else he's dead at sea and none have told
'ee of it."

"No," Suki said stubbornly. "He arn't dead. I'd have
known if he had been. I'm quite sure of *that*."

"Then we must assume he's alive and ashore," Ariadne
went on thinking. "Ashore and a man afoot, so he will
need his horse, sooner or later. You left word he would
find it at Twerton did 'ee not?"

Suki had forgotten all about Beau. But of course, Jack
would go to Twerton to find him. He might be on his
way there this very afternoon. Why hadn't she thought
of it? And why hadn't she thought to ask for him at the
livery yard instead of trailing off to the inn? "Have I
time to run across to the yard?" she asked.

But the Bath stage was trundling to a halt before the chop house. They could see it from their seat in the window.

"You must write to your farmer," Ariadne said, as Suki picked up her sleeping baby and gathered her belongings. "You must give him instructions, tell him the address of our lodgings in Bath and our address in Cavendish Square, and say he is to send Captain Jack to find you wherever you are. 'Tis the sensible thing to do and, besides, you ain't got time for anything else."

But he could be at the Llandoger Trow, Suki thought as she climbed aboard the stage. Or at the livery yard. And me a hundred yards away. 'Twas too thwarting for words. Anything could be happening and she wouldn't know of it. Quin Cutpurse could be returned and he and Jack could be together. They'd always been boon companions. A pair of rogues both. Oh if only she could have run across to find out instead of being rushed away like this. That was the trouble with the Bradburys. They were always in a rush and Ariadne was just the same as all the others. 'Twouldn't have hurt her to let me run to the inn. I could have been there an' back in two shakes.

" 'Twill turn out for the best, you'll see," Ariadne said. "You couldn't have missed the coach. Just think of the questions there would have been. We must tickle 'em like trout if we're to succeed."

But as Suki settled William across her knees, she was thinking of the black boy with the blue eyes. He could be talking to Quin Cutpurse at this very minute, she thought, instead of me. And the thought made her burn with impatience and frustration.

Blue was standing in a stinking alley alongside the Llandoger Trow, piddling against the wall. He'd sat in

the inn for as long as he could, but Mr Cutpurse hadn't
turned up and the lady hadn't come back, and, finally,
when most of the men around him had finished their
ale and sloped out and there was only the man in the
brown wig and a group of argumentative seaman left,
his bladder was so uncomfortable that he stole out of
the place to find somewhere to relieve himself.

A tall man in green breeches and a dirty black jacket
positioned himself alongside. Blue shifted his feet as
he refastened his breeches but the man hadn't come to
piddle. "You the young un with the message for Quin?"
he said, revealing a mouth full of broken teeth. And when
Blue nodded, he winked and said, "Follow me."

For a second, Blue thought he was going to be taken
back to his seat by the bar but he was wrong. The tall man
led him to a low door at the side of the building and up a
narrow flight of stairs to a low-ceilinged chamber on the
first floor. A man with a black eye patch was sitting by
the fire with two rough-looking men beside him, all of
them smoking clay pipes and deep in conversation.

"Here's your young un at last," the tall man said,
pushing Blue forward. "Found un in the alley a-waterin'
the roses."

"You weren't seen?" Quin asked.

"No fear. I'm sly."

Quin held out his hand for Blue's message and recognised the handwriting at once. "Why 'tis from Jack,"
he said, "an' no news at all. 'Tis instructions to the
nigger and here's us a-thinking 'twould be news of a
good take."

"Then we goes for the weddin' party," the tall man
said. "And takes the stage tonight by way of rehearsal
and for to pay the landlord. That's my opinion of it."

Quin turned to the man on his right. "Charlie?"

"I'm with Spider. I votes for the stage."

"Johnny?"

"I ain't keen," the third man said. "Not with a thief-taker about."

"'Tis only Melluish," Quin said, drawing on his pipe. "An' he's a stick-in-the-mud. You've only to look at him to see that. Him and that old brown wig of his. He'd be hard put to it to catch a cold, leave alone a thief."

"He'm a stubborn man," Spider observed, picking his broken teeth with a broken fingernail. "He been a-sittin' in that there corner all afternoon, a'waitin' for us. He'm a-sittin' there still, I'd lay money on't."

"Let him sit all he likes," Quin said laughing. "He'd have to get up prodigious early to catch me. My vote's for the stage. He'll not trouble us."

"What a' the nigger?" Charlie Moss wanted to know. "What's to be done with him?"

Quin Cutpurse turned to Blue and held out the paper. "What's your name, boy?"

"Blue, sir."

"Well then, Blue, when did our Jack give this to 'ee?"

"Aboard ship, sir."

"And now he'm took to London, accordin' to Spider here. Gone to Bedlam, so he has. So what's to be done with 'ee?"

"Send un packing," Johnny said, spitting in the general direction of the spittoon and missing by inches. "We don't want a nigger along of us. 'Twould queer our pitch."

"We could sell him in London," Charlie Moss said. "There's many a nibbing cull a-lurkin' in the Seven Dials would give their lucre for a sharp lad. Pertickly one small enough ter slip in winders."

"What's your opinion of it?" Quin asked the boy.

"An't please you, sir, I find my master."

Johnny snorted with laughter. "Much good may it do un if he'm in Bedlam."

"Let him find that out for himself," Quin said. "He can stay here till we rides to London an' I say we takes him along. Let him sniff out the lie of the land. See how things stand, in this precious asylum of there'n. If Jack's to be sprung, he'll see how 'tis to be done."

"An' if he ain't?" Charlie asked.

Quin rubbed his thumb against his middle finger to signify the exchange of cash. "Then we'll have us a sale, eh Blue?"

Twelve

By the time Ariadne and Suki arrived at their new lodgings in Queen Square, Ariadne was totally speechless and Suki totally cast down. To be caught in Bath when she knew that Jack *had* to be somewhere in Bristol was so distressing it was all she could do not to weep. But she settled Ariadne into her room, carried William down into the kitchen, inspected the room set aside for his nursery and generally tried to behave in her usual way.

The place was full of servants, but luckily she didn't know any of them, except for Mr Jessup, who was too grand to notice her, and Barnaby, who was too distracted, and Hepzibah, who was too busy lording it because she was lady's maid to the bride and felt she should be given first attention over everything and everybody in the house in consequence.

"I'd have thought you'd have been with that husband of yours," she sneered when she saw Suki. "Or ain't he come home to 'ee yet?"

"I got work to do here," Suki said, huffily. "I've a babba to feed in case you haven't noticed. 'Twouldn't do for all of us to be a-sitting in the kitchen stuffing our faces with sweetmeats all day."

To her delight, Hepzie actually blushed. "I'm tasting 'em for the bride," she said, and carried the little dish out of the kitchen.

190

"If she go on a-feedin' her face the way she do," Cook said, "the bride'll go off bang afore she gets to the altar. I never seen a gel eat so much." She glanced up at the bell board. "There's your young lady a-ringing for you, Suki. You can leave the baby with Abigail."

Ariadne was sitting at the writing desk in her room busily scratching an instruction for the milliner. She signalled to Suki that she was to shut the door and then whispered her orders.

"This is to go to my old friend the milliner," she said. "When 'tis done, you shall write to your farmer and then you can take your letter to the post when you deliver mine. What are the others about?"

"They'm dressing for the Assembly Rooms."

"Good riddance to 'em," Ariadne hissed, signing her name with a flourish. "There! 'Tis done. Now write your letter before Hepzibah comes to spy on us."

So Suki set herself to composition.

> I did not find Captain Jack, but I knows he is returned on account of his ship came in this morning which I have seen. Should he come to Twerton for Beau, which I will pay you for the fodder so soon as I am payed by Lady Bradbury, would you be so kind as to tell him where I am, which is at this address until Thursday morning and thereafter in Cavendish Square number 16 in London. I hopes my father continues well and he don't have no further contree-toms.

Once the letter had been handed over to the postboy, she felt cast down again, for there was so much to remind her of Bristol and her darling. There were gallants everywhere, strolling about in his easy, loose-limbed

191

way, or sprawling in the coffee houses enjoying their tobacco, and, on her way back to Queen Square, she passed the Bristol coach as the last travellers were climbing aboard and wished with all her heart that she had the freedom to join them.

But the days passed and there was no time for anything except work. She woke every morning buoyed up by the hope that this could be the day when she would slip away and look for him, and fell into her truckle bed every night exhausted and disappointed. Ariadne kept to her room and her silence, but she rang for her every minute of the day, sending her to the milliner to bring back off-cuts of the materials she'd chosen or to make arrangements for fittings, fussing over trimmings, ordering slippers, buttons, ribbons, feathers.

"I must have perfection," she said when Suki sighed. "You'll not deny me that, surely. This could be the last service you will do me. 'Tis little enough when you think how Melissa is disporting herself."

Which was true enough, for the bride had the entire household in uproar, with gowns to be fitted, a new necklace of fine pearls to be admired, special meals to be cooked to accommodate her growing appetite, wedding lists perused and the wedding breakfast chosen dish by dish in consultation with the cook and her mother, for, as she explained – entirely unnecessarily since they were both well aware of it – "my husband has the most delicate constitution and must not be put to the least inconvenience."

And as if all this fussing over food and clothes weren't bad enough, Lady Bradbury was determined that before she returned to London every single one of her Bath acquaintances should know of her daughter's great triumph, so the family attended every important ball, gave elaborate dinner parties every afternoon and even held a public breakfast, in the Harrison Rooms no less, as though they were gentry born. And, of course, William's presence was required in the drawing-room before and after every event, so that his progress could be displayed and applauded.

"Never a minute's peace in this house," the cook complained, thumping her mixing bowl down on the table with displeasure. "Why she got to have a dish of coddled eggs in the middle of the afternoon I cannot imagine. I shall be glad when we all go back to London again and can have this wedding over an' done with." Suki agreed with her wholeheartedly.

"The week's nearly up," she whispered to Ariadne as she helped her undress on Tuesday night, "an' I've not heard a word from Farmer Lambton, nor gone to Bristol."

"'Tis my last fitting tomorrow," Ariadne whispered back.

She thinks of nothing save gowns and ribbons, Suki thought sadly, whilst *I*'m a-wondering if my lover is alive or dead, and there'm no way I can find the truth on't.

But the very next morning a letter arrived from Twerton addressed to Miss Brown. She paid the postboy with trembling hands and took William and the letter to the nursery, her heart leaping with hope. At last! Now she would know. Had he gone to Twerton for that horse of his? Oh he must've done. And if he had, he'd be coming to Queen Square to find her. Maybe that very morning. She tore the seal, bright-eyed with expectation.

It was a flat, dull, disappointing letter. Captain Jack had not arrived to collect his horse, which was in fine fettle. Her father was well. Her mother sent her fondest love to her and to William. *"There is,"* he

193

wrote at the end of the first page, *"only one thing left to say."*

Suki couldn't think of anything at all, except her misery at his lack of news, but she turned over the page to read what it was.

Since my dear wife's death, I have been giving thought to what is to become of the farm, which needs a woman's presence and a woman's care. I hope I do not trouble you too much if I say that it do seem to me that 'tis possible that your lover may not return to you, there being many hazards at sea and you having heard no word of him. Had he returned on the ship you saw, I am certain he would have met with you or come to the farm in search of his horse. That being the state of affairs at present which, believe me, I hope may change to your better satisfaction, I have a proposition to put to you which I hope will, if not meet with your approval, not displease.

I have asked your father for your hand in marriage. He is agreeable to it and said I might broach the matter when I wrote this letter. I do not expect an answer immediately for this is naturally a matter that you must consider carefully and I know you are not one to act on the gad. Howsomever I urge you to consider the advantages. The farm is known to you, on which account the running of it would present no difficulty. You are young and strong. The baby could be farmed here while you are still his nurse, should you and the Bradburys wish it. You would be near your father should he need your care. You have my assurance that

I would be a considerate husband to you. You would want for nothing.

Your Obedient servant,

Constant Lambton

She didn't know whether to laugh or cry and in the end did both, to William's consternation. How could she possibly answer such a letter? Oh the foolish, foolish man! But then she remembered that odd moment in the kitchen when they'd looked at one another and been caught up in all the wrong emotions. Or had she imagined it? No. She was sure she hadn't. It *had* happened and happened to them both. And yet he'd never referred to it, either then or now. Oh how confusing this was. And what a long time 'twould be before she could talk to Ariadne about it and hear what she had to say.

Ariadne was trenchant. "You'll not agree to it," she said, so annoyed by the news that she forgot to whisper.

Suki had been fluctuating all week between a determined hope that she would find her lover again, somehow or other, and that all would be well, and a growing and unhappy fear that he was lost to her, either at sea or through sickness, or maybe even through loss of love, which was the worst and deepest misery of all. "He offers me a home," she said, "and if I don't find Captain Jack, I shall need a home of sorts, if I'm to keep my William." 'Twas uncommon hard to be torn between your baby and your lover, but that seemed to be the size of it.

"But you don't love him."

"I like un well enough."

"Liking ain't love," Ariadne said firmly. "You mustn't do it."

"I'll write an' tell un I'm considerin' it," Suki temporised. "'Twill wait till after this wedding, when I might get a chance to visit Bristol and see Mr Wenham. There's no need to rush. He said so."

Ariadne wondered whether she should say something comforting because it was plain that Suki was beginning to doubt whether she would see her lover again, which was an uncommon painful state to be in, as she knew only too well, but at that moment they heard the thump of footsteps on the landing and Sir George bellowing, so their conversation had to stop.

"'Od's teeth!" the gentleman roared. "Hermione! Where are you? Such news!"

Lady Bradbury was in Melissa's room helping her to decide between a pair of white satin slippers and an identical pair in cream. "What's amiss?" she said calmly, opening the door to him.

He had a *billet* in his hand and waved it at her. "Such news," he said happily.

"Another addition to the guest list," she said. "I do wish people would not leave things to the last moment. Who is it this time?"

"Guest list," he bellowed. "There's more to life than guest lists. This is trade, ma'am. Trade. Our merchant-man is back from Lisbon and we've made a splendid profit. Quite splendid. I have it first-hand from Sir Humphrey. How say you to *that*?"

"Had he no message for me?" Melissa asked petulantly.

The question puzzled her father. "What message should he have dammit? You're to be married a' Wednesday."

"Which is why," Lady Bradbury told him acidly, "a wedding list is of some consequence."

Sir George was too busy planning his return journey to pay attention to such a puny barb. "We will start at first light," he declared. "We three will travel in the coach and four with Ariadne and the goods and household shall take the wagon. We'll harness six horses to the wagon and then we shall be well provided for."

"I trust we shall not leave too early," Lady Bradbury demurred. "Arabella tells me there are highwaymen abroad. Two coaches were robbed on the new road, only last week. Would we not be wise, my love, to wait until full daylight."

Sir George was scathing. "Are we old women, to be frightened of a shadow? Tush wife, where's your courage?"

"We do have a bride to consider," Hermione said. "You would not wish her to be discommoded on her way to her wedding. 'Twould be heartless."

His answer was immediate and dismissive. "We will travel the old road by way of Laycock. 'Twill be safe enough there, in all conscience, even for a bride." Then he was off down the stairs, roaring for Jessup.

"I shall be *so* glad to be married, Mamma," Melissa said.

The next day dawned bold as summer and bright with sunshine. Sir George was up earlier than his servants, and seemed to be everywhere at once, supervising the packing, checking the horses, bellowing at Barnaby and chivvying his womenfolk.

"I've a mind to make you travel in the cart," he told Ariadne, half teasing, half serious. "You'd soon be cured of all your nonsense in that event." But she climbed into the coach as silent as ever, and didn't look at him.

"You two had best sit facing me," Lady Bradbury decided as Melissa yawned from the house to join her sister. "There is room for my dear Benjy beside me."

That arrangement didn't satisfy Sir George at all. "'Od's teeth!" he roared. "I'll not have that cur upon the seat. The floor is good enough for dogs, ma'am."

"You are to be spurned, I fear, poor dumb creature that you are," Hermione said, lifting her corpulent animal and settling him upon the floor.

But that didn't please her loquacious daughter. "Pray do sit the horrid creature somewhere else, Mamma. If 'twere to shit, my petticoat would bear the brunt. You know how unreliable it is. Let it sit in the corner next to Ariadne. She'll not mind, being she can't speak and she ain't the bride."

As she climbed reluctantly into the open cart with William on her hip, Suki glanced across at Sir George, irritated by his plump face and his plump complacence. He moves us all about, she thought, whenever he feels like it, all on the gad and with no thought that we might have opinions on the matter, that there might be people we don't want to leave behind. Then it occurred to her that this was the first time she'd been near him since that awful morning when she'd hit him, and now they were to spend two and half days travelling together. What if he were to see her again at one of their overnight stops and recognise her?

But they were all settled and ready for the off and he didn't seem to be looking at her, or at anybody else if it came to that, so maybe he'd forgotten. Jessup climbed up beside the postilion, and their journey began, up the slow hill to Bath Easton, leaving the city behind. Rich men have short memories when it comes to favours asked of serving girls, she thought, and Ariadne is always saying that women are less than cattle to him. But he shouldn't be dragging me away from Bristol all the same.

After a few miles, William became fractious and began to grizzle and complain, as he always did when he travelled anywhere. And really the way the cart rocked and juddered, she couldn't blame him. By the time they reached London, they would all be covered in bruises from head to toe. Fortunately, their lead horse cast a shoe outside a village called Box, so they had to stop and wait while the limping animal was led off to the nearest smithy. "We will take the air while we may," Sir George decreed. So they all climbed obediently from coach and cart and stood about uncomfortably on the uneven road. This time Sir George looked straight at her and obviously didn't have the faintest idea who she was. Which was rather a relief.

Presently, Lady Bradbury and Melissa took a short promenade, dragging the unfortunate Benjy behind them like a grunting cushion, but Suki and Ariadne sat on a tussock of rough grass with their backs against a dry stone wall while William amused himself plucking the stone crop. The road was lonely and silent, save for the occasional birdsong, and now Suki could understand her mistress's fear of attack, and see that the promenade was a nervous, watchful business and entailed much craning of necks and many abrupt turns. There was some sense of security inside their vehicles, but out in the open they all felt exposed and vulnerable. She was relieved when horse and postilion returned and the journey could continue, uncomfortable though it was.

At ten o'clock they crossed a low stone bridge over a brook and came to a little old-fashioned village called

Laycock, where the houses were a higgledy-piggledy collection, small and low and much in need of repair. As they trundled through a narrow street, past the glow of the smithy and an ancient inn where two mud-spattered horses stood waiting, Sir George stuck his red face out of the window and told the coachman to stop at the Red Lion.

"We will take breakfast here," he said. "Rest the horses, Sam. Bowden Hill ain't a jaunt for an empty stomach."

The Red Lion was a modern building, set right on the edge of the village. It was three stories high and made of brick, with a fine classical balance about it, seven windows to each floor, three on the central bay and two on either side, and all finely graded and neatly curtained. Behind it was a courtyard shaded by a fine horse-chestnut tree, where there was a new pump for watering the horses and very fine stables. Inside it was still old-fashioned, with low beams overhead and a great stone hearth at the far end of the room. But they served a good strong cider in the servants hall and the food was wholesome.

The postilion was too full of gloom to eat well. "Time to take our ease when we'm atop of Bowden Hill," he said dourly. "Why we couldn't've took the new road, I cannot imagine. But there 'tis. You can't tell 'em nothing, not that lot. I hopes they has the good sense to walk up the hill."

"I shall speak to Sir George about it," Jessup promised.

At the foot of the hill, the coach and cart both stopped and Sir George and Jessup got out to discuss conditions with the coachman while the household waited. Warblers were singing shrilly in the reeds beside the river and the sky was as blue as a thrush's egg.

"''Tis a fine fair day," Sir George said when he came back to his womenfolk, "so we will walk to help the horses."

"My love!" Hermione protested. "Our shoes will be worn to shreds! Have you considered the distance?"

"Shoes!" he said. "''Od's teeth. Are we to consider shoes? If you wish to be at the White Hart by nightfall, you were well to do as I say."

"I shall be ill!" she said leaning back in her seat and clutching her kerchief to her bosom. "Have you no care for the delicacy of my constitution?"

He snorted and scowled, but eventually gave way. "Very well, ma'am," he said. "Stay where you are, ma'am, and if we are forced to travel by night in consequence, we shall know whose folly to blame."

She protested his heartlessness, but stayed in the coach, and so did Benjy, who was snoring in an evil-smelling heap at her feet. But everybody else got out or down, and prepared to climb. And a long hard climb it was, with the coachman leading the horses, up and up and further and further away from civilisation, between dense trees that creaked and whispered ominously, and over ruts and hollows hardened by sunshine and brutal to the feet. Half-way up, they passed a solitary farm house, settled under the rim of the road, and the farmer came to the gate to touch his cap to Sir George and wish them goodday. Then they toiled on past a bend in the road and the farm was lost to view among the trees. It was very hot and they were all footsore, and William grew heavier by the minute. Sir George walked ahead of his womenfolk, with Jessup and the coachman, the postilion walked with his horses, but Ariadne and Melissa and Suki dropped further and further behind.

"How far we shall see once we'm at the top," Suki said

to encourage her panting companions. At that moment, she could see very little except the road under her feet and a few inches of foliage on either side of her.

"'Tis a view I could well do without," Melissa grumbled. "It takes a deal too much effort." She was watching the road as she spoke, so Ariadne was able to glance at Suki and smile.

"We shall soon be there," Suki said, returning the smile. There was a sudden sharp noise behind her, and she turned her head to see a black shape running out of the trees towards them. Then, almost before she had time to realise how frightened she was, three more figures followed the first. Four men, in black and green, masked men brandishing pistols and shouting in loud harsh voices, dark threatening men crouching under the branches and leaping into the road. Highwaymen!

The first caught Ariadne about the neck and had his pistol pressed into her side before she could scream, the second seized Melissa with such force that she fell, squealing like a stuck pig. At that, Sir George turned and began to run down the hill.

"Stand where you are, sir!" the leader yelled. "Stand still damme, or the girl is dead!" And Sir George stopped as though he had been frozen to the spot, and was instantly and totally in control of himself and the situation.

"Very well, sir," he said. "You may take what you please. You'll not be hindered, if the ladies are not molested."

"In that case, I'll trouble you for your purse, sir," the leader said equally coolly. "You will all be bound, sir, that's understood, but pervidin' you do as you'm told, you'll come to no other harm. You have my word as a gentleman of the road. Stop the cart!"

Now Suki could see that the four men were not identical black shapes at all. They were all different and they all had different jobs to do. The one tying Ariadne's hands was young and fair-headed, with awkward bony wrists like her brother John; the one pulling the cart-horses to a halt was tall and skinny with long angular limbs; the one sitting astride Melissa was the shortest of the four and wore bottle-green breeches and a green cocked hat; while the leader was a stocky man, with an undeniable presence, a watchful man, his wits as quick as his movements and his voice familiar to her, although in the panic of the moment she couldn't think why. She was noticing so much, but in a disjointed way, and without effort, as if her vision were no longer capable of sustained sight, but was fragmented, so that she saw events in a series of sharp brief glimpses. They passed so quickly they were gone before she could understand them, and yet they were hard edged and indelible and in the sharpest focus.

Melissa lying on the road where she had fallen, with Fair Hair sitting astride her, the barrel of his awful pistol jammed against her throat. There was a red hand mark on her cheek, and she was struggling to cry without making a sound. Fair Hair binding her hands behind her back, tying her into a squirming bundle, rolling the bundle into a ditch as if she was of no more consequence than dirty washing.

Ariadne tied to a tree, her face totally withdrawn, and her expression as mild as the saints in the church window.

Sir George stripping off his coat and tossing it to the leader, skimming his hat after it as if he were throwing pebbles across water. Green Breeches behind him, pulling his wig from his head and hurling it into

203

the nearest tree, where it hung, like a huge dead duck. Sir George smiling as though he found it amusing. And there, on his bald pate, the dull red scar where she'd hit him.

The coach rolling backwards, as the horses scrambled and slipped, trying to turn sideways to recover their balance, then set free and slithering down the hill, foam flecked and showing the whites of their eyes, with the traces trailing behind them. The coach tipping over slowly and gracefully, grinding as it came to rest in the ditch, with one wheel still spinning uselessly in the air.

Jessup and the coachman back to back against a single slender tree, bound with grey rope and trembling like leaves. Jessup coughing.

Skinny climbing the sides of the fallen coach, all straggling arms and legs, making a grab for the postilion's fowling piece.

Benjy scrambling from the upturned coach, growling. His jaws clamped about Skinny's legs. A sudden blow, the pistol descending. The dog twitching in the road, dark blood trickling from his ear.

The master handing over purse, rings, watch. Brown hands grabbing. Lace torn from a pink sleeve. White face at a window. Black mask before her. Hard eyes. Hard familiar eyes. William burrowing into her neck, clinging to her hair with both hands, "Mamma! Mamma!"

"Your hands! Quick! Show me your hands." Holding up one hand, then the other, stupidly. "Purse?"

"No. I haven't any money." She only possessed one article of any value and that was Jack's silk kerchief. She'd taken to wearing it tucked into the top of her bodice like a fichu and it was so creased and crumpled that it no longer looked the part. With luck, he wouldn't notice it.

"Buttons?" How vilely he smelt! His sweat strong and hot and acrid, reminding her of the Spring Gardens.

"No." And then realisation, spoken at once, before she could think how dangerous it was. "I know who you are! You'm the one they call Spider."

Then fear, filling her throat, and making her heart leap and struggle as he pulled her to her feet, baby and all, and pushed her ahead of him, to where his leader was standing, bouncing the breath out of her body with every step. She was aware that there were black legs following them along the ruts of the road and then, breathlessly, she was in a grassy clearing and surrounded by sweaty black clothes, hard limbs and harder eyes. Four fine horses were tethered to a bush, their fat rumps like polished chestnuts and there was a black boy standing beside them, his blue eyes wide. Blue eyes!

"She knows who we are," Spider said.

Green Breeches spat. "Shoot her," he said. "She'll 'peach, sure as fate. Shoot her, Quin."

"She'm Captain Jack's wench, Charlie," Quin Cutpurse said, considering her. "We can't shoot the Captain's wench."

"She'll peach."

"Bind her legs!" Quin Cutpurse ordered, and Green Breeches bound her, very roughly indeed, and sat her beside a bramble bush, with William still in her arms, still burrowing into her neck, but miraculously not crying.

She could see the wide valley below her, stretching back and back until the detail was lost in a blue vagueness of distant hills. Ploughed fields as brown as ginger, shimmering lakes of winter wheat, pasture dotted with the small humped shapes of cattle, a vast, wide reassuring landscape, patched into comfortable irregularity by dark hedges and darker copses. She gazed as though she were

205

sitting in the Spring Gardens and had nothing to fear, and, as she gazed, an odd quiet courage grew in her breast like an opening rose, so that her heart steadied and her mind cleared.

"You need have no fear of me," she said and her voice was calm. "I shan't 'peach. You've only to tell me one thing an' you have my vow, I'll not breathe a word of this to any livin' soul."

"Do she mean it, Quin?" Green Breeches said, wiping his nose on Sir George's fine brocade. "What do 'ee think?"

"Tell me what you want," Quin Cutpurse said. "There's money a-plenty. Your master keeps a fine fat purse."

"Not money," she said. "Just tell me where the Captain is. That's all I want."

"And *that* will buy silence?"

"Yes."

"Tell her, Quin, in heaven's name," Green Breeches urged. "We'll not have control of 'em much longer." He had his foot in the stirrup of his horse and was watching Fair Hair who was covering the prisoners with his pistol, standing legs astride in the middle of the road below them.

"Mount!" Quin Cutpurse called, untying his horse.

There was a scramble of feet and hooves and all four were on horseback and the horses were wheeling and snorting and as eager to be off as their riders. Quin swung the black boy up into the saddle before him, and then they were galloping out of the clearing and across the fields, and he was calling back to her, "Bedlam. That's where you'll find un. Bedlam-in-Moorfields." Then they were gone.

She realised that she was exhausted and that her legs

were shaking. But she knew where to find the Captain at last! At last!

"Gorn!" William said, looking for the horses. Now that they were on their own, he was perfectly cheerful. She answered him automatically. "All gorn! Horses all gorn!" as if they were back at Twerton and he had been watching the cows come in for milking. My hands are free, she thought, watching them as they patted the baby's back. I'd best go and untie the others. But she didn't have the energy. The Captain was alive and in London, in Bedlam-in-Moorfields. That was all that mattered. She knew where he was and now she could find him.

She set William down on the rough grass and slowly untied her legs, stopping half-way through to remove an ant that was climbing on her petticoat. After the noise and speed of the attack, everything was extremely slow and peaceful. She strolled back down the hill like a member of the ton languidly taking the air and untied the master, slowly and painstakingly, without saying a word. Then she was exhausted again and had to sit against the tree because all she really wanted to do was to crawl into bed and sleep for hours.

She was aware that the master was running about untying ropes and giving orders in a quick clipped voice that she hadn't heard him use before, but none of it was really interesting. Jessup mounted one of the recaptured horses and trotted off downhill, Barnaby was untying the cook, Melissa was crying, Lady Bradbury eased herself out of the upturned door of the coach and walked past the dead body of her pet and didn't even notice him. Her face was a terrible grey-white, her left sleeve was stained with blood and she tottered as she walked, but Suki was too tired to feel any sympathy for her.

The cart was turned round and the ladies climbed into

it and sat with their feet on the dirty straw and didn't complain. Then they all went down the hill, slowly and without speaking, with the master and Jessup walking behind them, and the postilion leading the horses, down to the river and the Abbey and the gentle human society of Laycock. The warblers were still singing.

Thirteen

The landlord of the Red Lion was most concerned by their bedraggled return, and ran out into the road to assist the ladies from the cart with his own hands.

"'Tis a scandal!" he said to Lady Bradbury, sympathetically, spurred on by altruism and hope of profit. "Highwaymen in broad daylight! And on Bowden Hill! I thought we were rid of 'em. My poor dear lady, how you must be suffering. Come in! Come in! We are here to serve you!"

The lady held up her blood-stained sleeve so that everybody could see the cuts she'd sustained when the coach overturned. "Fiends!" she said, raising her eyes to heaven as if the highwaymen were already there and being judged. "Heartless fiends! Look 'ee here. See what they've done!"

"They will end at Tyburn on the triple tree," the landlord promised. "Have no fear!"

The lady turned to her husband. "Did I not particularly warn you of this very eventuality, my love?" she asked. "Oh, how right I am proved!"

"No more of that!" Sir George said mildly, handing Melissa out of the cart. "The danger is past and no life lost."

"But consider what is stolen!"

"Money. Trinkets. Nothing of consequence," Sir George

209

said, dismissing them. "We can soon replace 'em. I've done it once, damme. I daresay I shall do it again." And ignoring his *déshabillé*, and Melissa's protest that her pearls were *not* trinkets, he herded his ladies through the front door. Then he gave instructions, in a voice of such massive authority that smeared, bald and half-naked as he was, he was obeyed without question. He would require a private room, in the front of the house, grooms were to be dispatched to find his horses, and a boy to retrieve his wig, the coach was to be mended, a surgeon sent for, he would need warm water, mulled wine, aqua vitae, tobacco. He stood in the middle of the room radiating activity. Even Suki had to admire him.

Soon bellows were being pumped into the kitchen fire and black coals were glowing into life, all three mullers were in use and every kettle in the house had been filled with water and set to heat. The family were ushered into a side room, with Jessup, Mrs Sparepenny and Hepzibah to attend them. Lady Bradbury was provided with cushions and a footstool, and the wise woman arrived, in lieu of a surgeon, and was soon administering sage tea to her blood-stained patient, and cleaning her cuts with a distillation of hound's tongue and moonwort, binding the torn edges together with newly gathered gossamer.

"'Twill do well enough, milady," she promised as she gathered her simples ready to leave, "do 'ee but consent to rest and keep 'ee warm. Take only soothing foods for a day or two. Honey an' arrowroot, a chicken broth. But no red meat nor wines, nor spices, vinegars, strong sauces. I give 'ee good-day."

"We will send payment to 'ee as soon as we arrive in London," Sir George told her. "We are, as you will understand, a trifle discommoded at present."

As she took curtsying leave, there was a clatter of hooves outside the window and presently a newcomer was introduced into their privacy. He headed straight for Sir George, who looked up and scowled at him to indicate that his intrusion was not welcome.

He wasn't the least abashed. "My dear sir," he said, holding out his hand. "I'm uncommon sorry to hear of your misfortune. I came post haste expressly to prevent it, but I fear I am too late. John Melluish, sir, thief-taker. Pray allow me to serve you."

"We've met before, I think," Sir George said, squinting at the man's old-fashioned jacket and his brown bob wig.

"We have, sir," Mr Melluish agreed as they shook hands, "but more of that later. You were attacked nearby, I believe. Did you get a good look at the villains, sir? If they are to be caught and your goods returned to 'ee, a description would be of inestimable value and, I need hardly point out, the sooner and more accurate it can be given the better."

"They were masked, sir," Sir George told him, "and wore black."

"Their usual habiliment, I fear. Did you see more, ma'am?"

"I was in the coach, sir," Hermione said, "and positively torn to shreds as you see. I fear I was too distressed to take cognisance of any man's appearance."

"Quite so," Mr Melluish soothed. "What of the servants? Would any of them have had a closer look, think 'ee?" He looked round at the three in the room, all of whom shook their heads.

"You could try the wet nurse," Sir George suggested. "They carried her off. Spent quite a while conversing with her as I recall."

"An't please you," Hepzie put in, "whatever they spoke on, 'twas to some purpose, for they forbore to tie her hands the way they did to us. She was the one what came down and untied the master when they'd ridden away."

Her information had the desired effect. "Did she so?" Mr Melluish said. "Then pray let her be sent for."

Suki was in the stable yard, holding William out over the dung heap so that he could empty his bowels without soiling his petticoats. "They'll have to wait till he'm finished," she said, when Hepzie came to fetch her. "This arn't no job to be rushed, is it my 'andsome?" She knew from Hepzie's smug expression that, whatever they wanted her for, it wouldn't be pleasant. And when she arrived in the private room and was introduced to "Mr Melluish, the thief-taker", she remembered him from the quayside at Bristol and knew she'd been right.

"You were taken away by the highwaymen, I believe," the gentleman said.

She stood at the centre of the room with all eyes watching her and had to admit it.

"You spent some time conversing with 'em."

That had to be admitted, too.

Mr Melluish gave her a shrewd look. "Why was that?"

She had to find an explanation for him and it had to ring true, so why not tell him part of the truth? A little truth wouldn't be peaching. "I recognised one of 'em," she said, "an' told un so. 'Twas a man called Spider. He tried to pick my pocket once in the Spring Gardens in Bath. I'd have knowd un anywhere. He took me up the road to where the others were on account of he wanted 'em to shoot me but they wouldn't."

Mr Melluish wrote it all down in his green chapbook. "What else did they want of 'ee?"

"Little else," Suki said. "They were after money an' jewels an' such like."

"They did not tie your hands, I believe."

"No, sir. They couldn't on account of I was holding William, as I am now. I s'ppose they thought to leave me a fair way off from the rest, to give theirselves time to escape."

The interrogation went on. Had she recognised any of the others? No indeed, sir. What could she remember about them? They were dressed in black and wore masks. Were any other names mentioned? Oh no, sir. Eventually she was dismissed.

"She could be an accomplice," Mr Melluish warned as soon as she'd gone. "'Tis my opinion she should be watched and noted."

Lady Bradbury rolled her eyes to heaven. "I cannot credit such a thing!" she said. "She is my wet nurse."

"What are your plans, sir?" Mr Melluish asked Sir George.

"We must travel on," Sir George said, "as soon as the coach is repaired. This afternoon if possible. We have a four-day wedding toward."

"Then I must trouble you no further," Mr Melluish said courteously. "If you would be so kind as to provide me with an address to which I may write, I will report progress to you."

The address was given with the assurance that he would be welcome there at any time and the hope that he would be successful in his endeavours.

The thief-taker bowed. "Your sarvant, sir."

"Send all thieves to the gallows," Sir George told him cheerfully. "That's my opinion on't. And accomplices

too, damme." But as soon as the man was gone he turned
to his daughters with a very different expression on his
face. "Take a turn in the air, me dears," he ordered,
dismissing the servants with a wave. "I've a word to
say to your mother."

They went obediently, Ariadne empty-faced, Melissa
frowning, the servants curious. Hermione held a kerchief
to her forehead and closed her eyes against whatever was
to come.

"Your wet nurse, ma'am," he said, "is a fraud. I've
found her out, damme. I thought her face looked familiar
when she climbed into the cart this morning, and now I
know the reason of it. 'Tis the wench that hit me with
the clyster."

Hermione sighed heavily and held up her right arm
so that her injuries were towards him, but she didn't
argue.

"I gave strict orders, as you will recall, ma'am, strict
orders that she was to be dismissed on the spot. On the
spot. And what do I find? She is still here. Still a member
of our household and an accomplice to highwaymen to
boot. 'Ods bowels! What is the world coming to?"

"She is a good nurse, my love," Hermione said
weakly, "and good nurses are hard to come by. I could
not find another and thought . . . I am sure you would
not have wished to put your son at risk."

Her husband roared at her. "'Od's teeth we're *all* at
risk! She's an accomplice, damme. You heard what the
man said. An accomplice. You have nurtured a tongued
viper in the family bosom. A tongued viper. Well don't
blame me if we're all murdered in our beds. That's
all I've got to say on the matter. 'Od's blood and
bowels, I never heard the like. To keep such a one
in our service when I expressly forbade it. She's to

214

be dismissed, ma'am. She should ha' been dismissed
long since."

"I give 'ee me word—" Hermione began weakly.

"Aye and so you should!" he roared. "Dismiss her,
ma'am, and let that be an end on it."

"I give 'ee me word," Hermione pressed on, "'twill
be done the minute the wedding is over. I can hardly
spare time to find another wet nurse with Melissa's
wedding to arrange. Allow me that at least."

"Well," he grumbled, "you have the right of it in that
regard, I daresay. The wedding takes precedence. But
not a minute after, for I won't hear of it."

Hermione waved her kerchief at him to signify sub-
mission.

"I'm off to attend to the coach," he told her. "We
travel in an hour. Make up your mind to't."

In fact, it was late afternoon before the coach had been
mended to his satisfaction and their journey could be
resumed. But this time they negotiated the dreaded hill
without mishap and, even though storm clouds gathered
over their heads as they rattled on towards Calne, nobody
minded. The coach and cart were stopped briefly so that
William could be carried across and settled on Ariadne's
lap to keep him out of the shower but, apart from that,
the journey was uneventful. They reached the Red Lion
at Hungerford before dark and, although it was cramped,
it was comfortable enough for one night's stay. And
the Bear at Slough, where they stayed for their second
night, was quite palatial, even though the food was
indifferent.

As far as Suki was concerned there were only two
things wrong with the journey. One was that it was too
slow, but nothing could be done about *that*. 'Twas the
way of travel everywhere. The other was that Ariadne

had to share a room with her sister so, even though
she went to her night and morning to help her undress
and dress again, and to bring her water to wash with,
there was no chance of any conversation. And she did
so want to tell her about the Captain.

But 'twill all come right in the end, she thought,
as she settled to sleep on that second night. Now I
know where he is. Bedlam-in-Moorfields. Moorfields in
London. And I shall be in London tomorrow. There was
still William – how was she going to explain about him?
But she was full of hope. I will find the Captain first,
she decided, letting the thought fill her with optimism,
and then we will go to the master and confess together.
I will tell him how much I love my little 'andsome and
how I couldn't be blamed for the death of the other
poor little mite, on account of I wasn't there when he
died, which he must see the truth of. Which I might
even remind him of. He'll be fair about it, surely. One
way or t'other. There's good in the man. He arn't all
roaring an' pushing 'ee down on beds.

The last day's journey took far, far longer than it
should have done. The horses were parlously slow
and just before Cranford Bridge the coach got stuck
in a ditch and it took nearly an hour to get it out
again. But by early afternoon they were bowling along
the London Road towards Tyburn and Suki could
smell the smoke of the city. They were nearly there,
praise be!

Fine coaches passed them as they progressed and the
road grew more and more crowded. Soon they could
hear the growling of a throng of people, and the air
wafting in through the open window smelt of sweat
and body heat and perfume. And not long after that,
the coach ground to a halt.

Sir George filled window with his bulk and called out to the coachman to know what was amiss.

"'Tis a hanging day, sir," the coachman's voice replied. "I doubt we shall get past."

"Turn her sideways on," Sir George ordered happily, and he turned himself sideways on to announce the good news to the family. "Here's good fortune. We're to see a hanging. An' if that ain't the best medicine for a mute and the best warning for an accomplice, I don't know what is, damme."

So the coach and the cart were turned for the entertainment, and Sir George ascended to sit with the coachman, happily if ponderously, taking Ariadne with him, and leaving Melissa and her mother to watch from the windows.

"Be sure the wet nurse has a good view," he called across to the cart. "I want her to see this. Mark, learn and inwardly digest. That's the style on't."

The order sounded ominous. 'Tis on account of me being taken off by that wretched Spider, Suki thought. But she would have watched in any event for she'd never seen so many people gathered together in all her life. The road was packed from one side to the other, with coaches becalmed here and there within the mass. Even as she watched, their own coach was completely surrounded, and an orange seller arrived, pushing her way through the throng by dint of striking violently to right and left with her basket.

"Be good sport today, yer honour," she called up to Sir George. "Sweet China oranges?"

He called back cheerfully. "Who's to go?"

"Jimmy Cade," the woman told him. "The highwayman. Peached by his mistress, so they say. A terrible black-hearted villain."

"And the other?"

"I couldn't say. Any sweet China oranges, sir?"

A little ahead of them on the left-hand side of the road was a high grandstand packed with the busy wigs and fine clothes of the gentry, and immediately in front of it, the famed triple tree of the Tyburn gallows, three gaunt beams weathered black and joined at the top by three equally forbidding cross beams set in a triangle. Nooses already hung in position on two of the beams but there was no sign of the death cart as yet, so the crowd was in a state of excitement almost as high as the gallows.

Sir George bought oranges for them all, which made a welcome diversion, and presently while they were still moistening their dry throats with the juice, the crowd beyond the gallows began to cheer and catcall, and Suki could see the death cart rocking slowly through the mob towards its destination.

"I haven't never seen a man hung afore," she whispered to Barnaby.

"Nor I," he whispered back. "Be a bit of sport, eh?"

"That's Tom Turlis, that is," the orange seller told them, nodding her head in the direction of the hangman. "Best Jack Ketch we ever 'ad. 'E'll send 'em off like ninepence, you see if 'e don't."

The cart had reached the gallows and was being manoeuvred into position beneath the beam, and now Suki could see that the highwayman was young and handsome, like Jack. He was wearing a long white shirt of some kind and his own thick fair hair, which looked shocking somehow, among all the wigs around him, like nudity.

"Look at that 'air," the orange seller said. "Growd that in jail. Make a fine wig after, that will."

The hangman hauled the young man into position under the noose, pulling on the ropes that bound his arms, and tugging him by his fine hair, and Suki suddenly realised, with a shock that made her spine tingle, that the long white garment he was wearing wasn't a shirt at all but a shroud. Then the crowd near the gallows shushed for silence and he began to make a speech. His thin voice echoed in the vast space before him but the Bradburys were too far away to hear the words. However it appeared to be a good speech, for the crowd cheered when it was done, and cheered again when the young man bowed. Then they held their breath while he stood meekly under the noose and the hangman removed rings from his fingers and took a purse from his trouser pocket and finally fitted his white neck into the grey snake of the rope. Then they grew gradually and terribly silent.

Poor thing, Suki thought, to have to stand there waiting to be killed, and she just had time to wonder what it would feel like to be hung when the horse darted from under the gallows, taking the cart with it at some speed. The crowd gave a great guttural roar, and the young man fell, his legs kicking the air. It was so quick and horrible that she couldn't bear to look any more and buried her face in William's body while the crowd roared and cheered and threw their hats into the air. There was a lump in her throat and her heart was pounding against her ribs as though she was afraid. How fearful to be alive one minute and choking to death the next. No wonder Quin Cutpurse told her not to peach.

By the time the tumult had died down and she dared to look again, the body had gone and another cart was inching towards the gallows. This one contained a plump, solid-looking woman with a billowing bosom and a very red face. She was dressed in her best, with a fine feathered hat and a blue cape with gloves to match.

Not for her modest speech and the terrible acceptance of a shroud. She was shouting at the top of her voice, running from one side of the cart to the other to attract attention, and struggling all the time to break from the ropes that bound her hands. Her voice was so loud that Suki could hear every word she was saying. "I never killed 'im. Never! I loved that babby! 'E could a been one of me own. I never killed 'im. 'Tis a lie, you unnerstand."

"We shall 'ave some rare old sport wiv this un," the orange seller said, licking her lips.

The sport began before the cart reached the gallows, for the lady suddenly wriggled her hands out of the ropes, whipped her hat from her head and tossed it into the crowd, to delighted cheers. The hangman made a dive for her hands but she was too quick for him and caught him such a blow in the stomach that he fell back against the side of the cart, momentarily winded. She had her gloves off immediately and then her cloak, and both were tossed to her friends before he could scramble to his feet and stop her. "You ain't making money out of me, mate," she shouted at him. "An' don't you think it!" And the crowd applauded all round her, as her friend held up the cloak and waved it like a triumphal flag. "You ain't stringing me up neither!" she shouted at the hangman, squaring up to him with her fists bunched like a prizefighter. Her audience was thrilled by her, and gave her another round of vociferous applause.

Could she fight him off? Suki wondered, admiring her. How proper and sensible to put up a struggle. That's

220

what I'd do. 'Tis the natural way. And she willed the woman on.

It was a riotous fight, for the woman was a heavyweight and knew how to punch and, even though the hangman was strong, she was almost a match for him, kicking and thumping and squirming out of his grasp when he tried to tie her hands again, and on one occasion flailing him with his own rope. But at last he pinned her into a corner of the cart and tied her legs into a bundle with shreds of her own skirt. And the crowd, being an extremely sporting lot, applauded him to show how even-handed they were. Even then she went on struggling, so that he was forced to sit astride her heaving body in order to tie her hands. And that provoked much cheerfully ribald comment, and several impossible suggestions, given the present state of her legs.

It was all so good humoured and noisily cheerful that Suki found herself enjoying it, excited by the struggle and the applause. It didn't seem possible that this strong, determined woman would actually die. Even when the hangman was finally dragging her towards the noose by her hair, there was an unreality about it, like a Punch and Judy show. It was a brutal display, no more, and she half expected the two participants to stop and take a bow. But the noose was tightened about the woman's neck, the hangman stood back from his handiwork and the crowd grew silent again. And the woman suddenly flung herself forward off the edge of the cart. Her neck snapped with such a crack that they could all hear it quite clearly, and then her head jerked upwards and red blood spouted out of her mouth like a fountain, and the crowd groaned and then cheered. And Ariadne fainted away.

Suki handed William to Hepzie at once and climbed

out of the cart to help her but it took a tremendous effort to struggle over to the coach and, even when she finally reached it, it was a very long while before she could get her mistress to come round, for her body was wedged against the coachman's seat and the crowd was so densely packed around them that there was no way she could be lifted down and set on the ground. Suki eased the poor girl's head between her knees and frotted her hands and wished she had some aqua vitae about her.

Sir George pronounced it an uncommon good thing. "She'll speak now! You'll see!"

How little you know of her, Suki thought, lifting the Ariadne's head. It made her quail to think how heartless he was being.

Below them, two women were talking about the execution, their voices clear, and their sentiments unequivocal.

"She was still a murderer, whatever you might say."

"Such a fighter! Does yer 'eart good to see a fighter. I don't 'old with they meek ones!"

"She killed that babba, don' you ferget. Stole it from her ladyship an' then killed the poor little soul."

"'Tis true enough. Aye! She never 'ad no business stealing a babba. That I'll allow."

Fear trailed icy fingers through the centre of Suki's body. Could you be hung for pretending your baby was somebody else's? Surely not. Not if you'd cared for it and loved it and kept it healthy. But then she remembered that other baby, that poor little long-forgotten baby, lying on the kitchen table, pale as wax and tiny and innocent. What if Sir George accused her of killing that baby? He was heartless enough to do it, in all conscience. Please God, she prayed, don' 'ee let nothin' like that happen to me. Out there, in the bloodthirsty crowd, with Ariadne unconscious, and Sir George callous, she felt horribly vulnerable.

At last Ariadne groaned and opened her eyes. She saw Suki but, much to her father's annoyance, she didn't speak. The worst of Suki's fear receded now that her mistress had recovered, but she was still troubled, and it seemed more important to her than ever that she should find the Captain and get him to acknowledge their baby. She must go to Bedlam-in-Moorfields the very first chance she got.

But as she was soon to discover, life in London was even more frenetic than life in Bath. The house in Cavendish Square was enormous and the work there so demanding that, even though there were scores of servants, they were all hard at it from early morning until they slept at night. It was late on Sunday afternoon before Suki even discovered that her old friend Bessie was working in the kitchen. She scarcely saw Mr Jessup and Mrs Sparepenny who were distant gods in this great household, although their orders came through endlessly to each and every one of their hardworking subordinates. Every single room had to be made ready for bridesmaids or wedding guests, and the kitchen was under such pressure, feeding the household and preparing the wedding feast, that the housekeeper and the cooks barely had time to talk about anything else – and were certainly in no mood to give permission to the family wet nurse to go off on some wild goose chase to the other side of London.

"Vastly entertaining, I daresay," Mrs Sparepenny said disparagingly, when Suki finally plucked up the courage to seek her out and ask her, "viewing the lunatics, but 'tain't for the likes of you. Nor me neither. We've got other matters to attend to. 'Twill need to wait till this wedding's over and done."

It was a disquieting answer. Was Bedlam a lunatic asylum then? Surely not. What would the Captain be doing in a lunatic asylum?

"Oh yes!" Barnaby said, when Monday came around and he and Bessie were helping Suki to prepare the guest rooms. "That's what 'tis, right enough. Famous for it. They opens it up every afternoon an' people come from all over to see 'em. Very comical they are, by all accounts. I wouldn't mind going mesself."

"I s'pose you don't happen to know where 'tis?" Suki asked, as casually as she could.

"I do, as't happens," Barnaby said, pleased to be the one with the information, for once. "Me an' Dick was at an inn over there one time. 'Tis right over the other side a' London. Miles away. Took us hours to get there."

So I'll never get there an' back while this wedding's a-going on, Suki thought. I'll have to wait till it's over. Mrs Sparepenny was right about that. But what was he doing in a lunatic asylum? Surely he hadn't taken a job looking after madmen. He was too full of life and fun. Yet Quin Cutpurse had said that would be where she'd find him. And she did so want to find him, dear, dear Jack.

He was lying on dirty straw, on a stone-flagged floor, struggling to focus his eyes, and wondering where on earth he was. He knew that his mouth was dry from long fever, that his hips were sore from lying on the stones, that he was achingly hungry. He could see that his arms were thin for lack of sustenance, and that he was dressed in rough canvas breeches and a filthy cotton shirt. And he realised that, wherever he was, it was a dark stinking place and full of fiercesome noises. But he'd been struggling with nightmares for so long that it was hard to tell whether he was awake or asleep.

Hideous faces swam into his line of vision, now a man with a bulbous nose and one eye lower than the other, here a mouth full of broken teeth, black with decay and green-edged, there a man with a shaven head and cheeks criss-crossed with scars, grinning and cackling. If this *was* a nightmare, it was of another kind. It wasn't like the dreams that had racked him through the long days and nights of his fever – the dreams of formidable women who'd beaten him and starved him, who'd told him he was worthless and thrown him into the holds to stink and suffer with the slaves, who'd tossed him to the sharks to be torn apart alive.

I must speak, he thought, trying to clear his throat. If he could hear the sound of his own voice, he would know that the nightmare was over. "Where am I?" he said and was ashamed to hear how weak he sounded. "Where am I?"

The question sent the grinning creature into hideous paroxysms of laughter and soon three more shaven heads pressed down towards him to grunt and cackle. He closed his eyes because he couldn't bear the sight of them. When he opened them again, there was a new face before him and this one was showing concern. "Am I dead?" he asked. "Is this Hell?"

"You got the right of it there," the face said. "'Tis the nearest thing this side a' the Styx. But look cheerly. You ain't dead yet. You're in Bedlam among the lunatics."

The knowledge made Jack's heart shrink. I must escape, he thought, be sprung, bribe a guard, now, this minute. I can't live with lunatics. But he barely had the energy to sit up and had to rest his back against the wall.

"That's the style," his new friend approved, squatting beside him. "Try some broth." He had a bowl full of the stuff on the straw beside him. It was grey and unappetising and full of gristle, but Jack was so hungry he ate it.

"Name a' Gurney," his new friend said, "an' atween these four stinking walls, no more mad than you are."

But you are unprepossessing to say the least, Jack thought, with that filthy jacket and that shaven head. And he put up a hand to his own head to comfort himself with the softness of his own thick hair, and was shocked to find that it had all been shorn to stubble. He spat a lump of gristle into the straw. "Then if you ain't a madman," he said, "why are you here?"

"Had some sort of fever," Gurney explained. "Much like you. Raved somewhat, so I'm told. Took a knife to someone or other, so I'm told. Nothing of any consequence. But they don't take no account of what *I* say. So here I'm stuck and here I stays. 'Od rot 'em!"

The cackling man slothed towards them and made a grab for the bowl.

"Stow that!" Gurney said, swiping him round the ear. "Unless you wants yer skull caved in."

"Gi' us a mouthful," the man whined. "Tha's all I wants. A mouthful for pity's sake. You got plenty."

"That's on account of I've worked for it," Gurney said, slapping him again. "If you wants food, beg for it like the rest of us, 'stead a' lying around all day." And when the man had sloped away, he added, "Now that one *is* mad. He reckons he's the King a' Spain."

"Are we let out to beg?" Jack asked. If that was the case, there was hope of escape.

It was quickly dashed. "Out?" Gurney laughed. "No fear 'a that. They keeps us locked up night an' day. Oh

226

no, 'tis folks they lets in that pays us. Pays handsome some of 'em, if you goes about it the right way. You wasn't ever an actor by any chance? They're the ones what does the best out of it in here."

"I've been a good many things in my time," Jack told him with a return of pride. "Seaman, horseman, actor, gentleman of the road, slave master. I've seen some parlous things at sea, men whipped and branded, babies thrown overboard alive, hundreds of slaves thrown into the holds to stink. 'Tis a living hell on a slave ship, I can tell 'ee."

Gurney slapped his tattered breeches with delight. "That's the style!" he said. "You tell 'em *that* when they comes round a-gawping an' you could earn a pretty penny. Act up for 'em. They likes to be frighted. I tells 'em how I stabbed six men in a single night, or throttled a young female, that sort a' thing, an' threatens I shall stab 'em an' throttle 'em likewise. They screams prodigious. That's the style of it."

"Who are these people?" Jack asked. "Are they visitors? Or do madmen have friends and relations?"

"Relations?" Gurney said with some scorn. "Not they. You never see relations hereabouts. Only too glad to be rid of us, relations are. No, they comes to see the sights. Weekday afternoons and twice a' Sundays. Scores of 'em. We're an entertainment for 'em."

"And they pay us, you say?" If they paid enough, he might scrape a bribe together.

"Showers us," Gurney told him. "Farthings, pennies, groats. I got a gold sovereign once."

Jack handed him back his bowl. Foul though it was to be incarcerated here, there was hope. "I can tell 'em some prodigious fine tales," he said, "for I've seen more than most and much of it ugly. I shall tell 'em

227

of fights at sea and blowing a man's brains out with a pistol, of legs smashed by cannon balls and the stumps dipped in boiling tar, red-hot brands and whips and cat-o'-nine-tails, jungle fever and the pox and the flux, storms that could break the back of a ship in seconds. Let's see how well they like that. If there's money to be made, I'll make it, damme. I'll not stay here for the rest of my life to be made mock of."

Fourteen

Melissa's wedding day began with a shower of rain, but fortunately there was so much to do that hardly anybody noticed it, and those who did were far too tactful to let her know, for now that her moment of importance had arrived, she was in a state of such nervous apprehension that she was beginning to stutter.

The house was in uproar from the attic to the kitchen. There were more wedding guests than anyone could count, and each one had brought at least two servants, so every room was noisily occupied. To add to the crush, six under-cooks and more than a dozen scullery maids had been hired to help prepare the wedding breakfast, so the kitchen was full to bursting and hot with roasting spits and boiling tempers. Lady Bradbury was determined that the breakfast should be a very grand occasion, and had ordered twelve different dishes for the meat course – including roast sirloin, three mutton pies, two beef stews and a whole roast lamb – ten for poultry, ten more for fish, to say nothing of custard creams, ices, jellies and pastries. So the cooks and their assistants had arrived the previous evening and had been hard at work all night long, under the irritating supervision of Lady Bradbury herself, who was in a state of frantic anxiety and had stayed up all night to make sure that everybody knew it and shared it. By dawn, she had infected everyone in the kitchen and as a result one of the scullery maids had burned her hand on the griddle, a dish of scallops had been dropped on the floor and, in the heat and chaos, quarrels had grown swift and sharp, even though she was present to witness them. Cook was in a towering temper.

"If I was you, ma'am," she said at last, tight-lipped and formidable, "I should take myself off to my chamber and have a nice lie down or you'll be in no fit state for the wedding, which you wouldn't want now, would you, saving your reverence? We can manage here."

"Well," Hermione dithered, scanning the food on the table for possible misdemeanours, "I might retire for an hour or so. I am sorely fatigued. You will make sure that everything is done according to my instructions, will you not? Appearances are so important." She put one long white hand before her mouth to conceal a yawn. "How I shall survive this day, I truly do not know. My sensibilities are positively lacerated already. Positively lacerated. Howsomever a short rest would be within the bounds of possibility, I believe."

"Take as long as you like," Cook said, acidly, when the lady had drifted away. There were still far too many dishes to prepare and far too little space to prepare them in. "I've had enough of your sensibilities to last me out the week. Now let's see to that lamb or we shall have 'em all a-ringing bells for their breakfasts afore we knows where we are."

The guests had started to arrive the previous afternoon and had spent the evening gambling at cards and wandering from table to table, gossiping and picking at the food provided to sustain them. Now, mercifully, they were sleeping off their exertions. But their servants were up and about, setting fires and brushing shoes and laying out clean clothes in the various dressing-rooms, so the upper floors of the house were abuzz with whispers.

Suki was in Ariadne's bedroom and they were on their own at last, and able to talk – as well as they could with William riding his little hobbyhorse on the carpet between them.

"Are you sure 'twas Bedlam he said?" Ariadne asked. She spoke in a whisper for, even though the door was shut and William's chortles were loud enough to give them cover, she was wary of being overheard.

"Positive," Suki whispered back. "What do 'ee think to it? Mind the coal scuttle, William."

Ariadne confessed that she didn't know what to think. "Howsomever, now that you are here, I must warn you . . . Mamma means to dismiss you. Papa recognised you at the inn."

Suki was so upset it took her a second or two to absorb what she'd heard and longer to recover from it, but she wasn't surprised. She'd been expecting trouble ever since the hanging or why would he have said "Mark, learn and inwardly digest," the way he had? "How do 'ee know?"

"Hepzibah told the bride. They imagine I am deaf because I do not speak – poor fools – so I hear a deal of gossip. You're to leave as soon as the wedding is over, so you'd best find this lover of yours the first chance you get."

"I shall," Suki said earnestly. "I've every intention. But with this wedding a-going on, I shan't get the chance till Sunday afternoon."

"Aye," Ariadne sighed. "We are captive in this house till the hurly-burly's over. I shall be glad of the end of it, too. Four days is a parlous lengthy time to have to endure."

Suki understood how she felt. " 'Twill be easier once your dance is over an' done."

"I am quite prepared for it," Ariadne told her, calmly. "The gown is made to my specifications, which is a comfort, and I daresay the trough is ready. I shall do well enough. If all goes according to plan 'tis even possible I might be in a position to help you."

Her expression was so mischievous that Suki took hope from it. "What do 'ee plan to do?"

" 'Tis a secret," Ariadne said, "and must remain so or 'twill spoil. Keep patience until the final ball and," she paused, "all will be revealed." Then, as if her words had amused her she began to giggle and had to hold a kerchief to her mouth to muffle the sound.

She arn't a-going to tell me, Suki thought, watching her closely. Not with that look on her face. It irritated her to be kept out of the secret. "I'll bring 'ee breakfast presently," she promised. "I dursn't stay longer or they'll come a-looking for me. Hepzie's on my back every second of the day."

"I don't doubt it," Ariadne said. "Now you know why. See if you can bring me a cup of hot chocolate."

As Suki crept down the servants' stairs with the hobbyhorse under her arm and William on her hip, her heart was constrained with misery, despite Ariadne's hint of help. She'm whistling in the dark, she thought, for she'm as powerless as I am. If ought's to be done 'twill need to be by stealth and cunning. But she couldn't think of a single trick that would help her now. Her mind was too full of the terrible certainty that if Lady Bradbury dismissed her, she would never see William again, and that was something she simply couldn't allow to happen. But she could hardly go running off to Bedlam on the very day of the wedding either, no matter how much she might want to, not when her presence could be required at any time to show her "noble charge" to the wedding guests, and bring him in to the wedding breakfast, and the bride-bed ceremony, and all the other occasions that would fill the day. It was parlously difficult.

As she passed the dining-room, she noticed that the servants' door was slightly ajar so she stopped, settled William more comfortably, and put her head cautiously round the edge to see what was going on inside. If the master was there and on his own, maybe she could catch his eye and speak to him. Beg him for help maybe. 'Twas a desperate thing to think on, but she was in a desperate position.

He was sitting at the centre of the table surrounded by half a dozen cronies – Sir Arnold Willoughby, of course, that funny little Mr Smithers, and on Sir George's left hand, a quiet man he was calling "brother Frederick", who was keeping an anxious eye on two greedy little boys who were sitting at the end of the table stuffing their faces with cold beef and quaffing beer as though they were grown men.

"No, no," Sir George was booming. "You did the only thing open to 'ee in the circumstances. If a man runs distract, he has to be restrained. Stands to reason, damme. 'Twas commendably done."

"The expense . . ." his brother demurred.

"Tush man," Sir George said, whacking him between the shoulder blades. "Expense is of no consequence. We can withstand expense. Eat up and you shall join us at Thames side and see what profits are to be made in our trade to Lisbon. We're meeting with Humphrey at ten o'clock to check the next cargo."

"Wools and silks," Sir Arnold said, smacking his lips as though he were tasting them. "Tableware, silver,

233

wallpapers. All uncommon fine, damme. You must see 'em Frederick. They'll sell like hot cakes."

They're surely not leaving the house this morning, Suki thought. Lady Bradbury will be furious. But what a diversion 'twould cause. Maybe I could slip out after all. She'd hardly notice that I was missing if he . . .

There was a ripple of air in the passageway behind her and Hepzie materialised at her shoulders.

"Were you sent for?" she whispered, acidly, "or are you just playing the spy?"

Suki bristled. "You'm a fine one to call the kettle black, the way you goes on. Which I knows all about."

"What I am is of no account," Hepzie told her haughtily. "You should be with your mistress, while you are still her servant. The bridesmaids are to be dressed by noon. Lady Willoughby's daughter has been ready this half-hour to my certain knowledge. I wouldn't wish to be tardy were I in *your* shoes."

"But then you arn't, are you?" Suki said crossly. And she stomped off to the kitchen to find Bessie and take a bit of breakfast, determined not to be given orders by a mere lady's maid.

The servants' table was full of breakfast dishes which had been prepared for the guests and were being served to them in their rooms, as and when they woke. So the servants were eating whatever they could find. Suki and Bessie helped themselves to a platter of cold meats, bread and ale and took them off to the nursery to dine in peace.

"Lady Bradbury's still abed," Bessie reported, as she forked up a slice of cold beef. "Lying on her back an' a-snoring fit to break the rafters."

"Let her stay there," Suki said with feeling. "Then we can have a bite to eat afore they'm on to us again."

But the hope was soon dashed. They'd barely taken the edge off their hunger before bells were being run again and they could hear people running from the kitchen, calling and giggling. Sir Humphrey's retinue had arrived with four trunks of clothes, three wig stands and his personal mattress, valet, *frisseur*, surgeon, two valets *de chambre*, pet squirrel and all. Soon half the household was crowded into the hall to witness the spectacle and Mrs Sparepenny was rounding up the chambermaids so that they would be ready for the ceremony of the marriage bed the minute the mattress had been hauled into position. Suki was sent to fetch the bridesmaids and to see that Ariadne carried the bowl of rose petals that were to be sprinkled on the sheets to bring good fortune to the bride and groom. So there was no possibility of running off to Bedlam or anywhere else.

William found the whole business wonderfully entertaining and hid under the sheet as it was lowered across the mattress, and ran off with the rose petals, and romped on the bed so that the fresh sheets were crumpled – which the chambermaids said was a very good omen – and finally got tired and cross, and had to be suckled back to good humour, also on the bed, which was the best omen of all. So the job was done to everyone's satisfaction.

But it was growing late and Sir George was still out inspecting his cargo and Lady Bradbury was still asleep and the carriages were beginning to arrive to take the guests to church.

"You must wake her, I fear, Hepzibah," Mrs Sparepenny said. "You shall take up a cup of hot chocolate and a platter of dainties. Rouse her by degrees. She must not be agitated. Not today."

Hepzie scowled and tried to refuse. "What of the

bride?" she said. "I'm *her* maid now. Surely I must care for her."

"Suki can look after her for the time being," the housekeeper decided. "Dress Miss Ariadne first, Suki. You've time to do both. Well look lively, the pair of you. Jump to it."

Charlotte Willoughby was already dressed and sitting in Ariadne's bedroom. She was most distressed to find her old friend still speechless.

"Don't she speak a word?" she asked, as Suki lifted Ariadne's blue gown from the cupboard and laid it on the bed. "'Tis mortal hard to be struck dumb."

Suki agreed that it was. "We'm to be quick," she explained as she laced Ariadne's stays, "for Hepzibah is sent to look after milady and we'm to look after the bride."

So Ariadne was arrayed in her bridesmaid's gown, with her hair *au naturel*, and topped by the smallest of lace caps and the longest of embroidered blue ribbons, and she and Charlotte tiptoed along the corridor to see Melissa.

She was still sitting at her dressing table in her chemise and under-petticoats. Because this was a state occasion, she was wearing high-breasted stays and consequently had to sit bolt upright and keep her shoulders well down. She looked as uncomfortable as she felt, for the stays pinched her sides and made it impossible for her to breathe deeply enough to satisfy a panicking need for air. Her face had been painted with white lead powder to cover her bruises and her cheeks were reddened with two round circles of rouge. At that moment she was submitting to the attentions of the *frisseur*, who was dressing her hair in the very latest French style, the front hair being drawn up into a tall padded mound above her forehead and stuffed with an abundance of prickly black wool, the back being tortured into curls. Four separate curling irons were warming quite viciously upon the hob, and the heat they required from the fire was making the room excessively stuffy and adding to the poor girl's breathing difficulties.

"How do I look, think 'ee?" she asked anxiously when her bridesmaids came into the room, with Suki and William behind them.

Privately Suki thought she looked like a wooden doll, but Charlotte said the right thing like the kind girl she was. "As fine as ever I've seen you, Melly."

Melissa picked up her looking-glass and eyed her extraordinary image from every angle. "Aye," she said doubtfully.

"You shall have the tallest head in the church," the *frisseur* promised, wielding his curling tongs like a baton. "When your toilette is complete, you will be *amazed*, I promise you."

And amazed she certainly was. For what with the height of her hair, the weight of her blue brocade gown and the stiffness of her embroidered petticoat, it was impossible to move more than half a pace at a time, and as she had to carry a fan, a cane, a handkerchief and a bouquet, there was no part of her body that wasn't either tightly controlled or required for some ritual purpose. Except her eyes. And the eyes looking back at her from her looking-glass that morning were far too afraid for comfort. To be the centre of attention had seemed so desirable when all this began, but now she was wondering how on earth she would ever sustain it, through all the hours and days ahead of her. To say nothing of the nights!

There was a commotion in the corridor outside her

room and they could hear Lady Bradbury's voice. "How could you *do* such a thing? I wonder at you, sir, upon my life I do. On your own daughter's wedding day. When you know what a tender constitution she has."

Sir George was fighting back. "'Od's bowels, woman. It's come to a pretty pass when a man may not inspect his own cargo, damme."

"A man," Hermione told him acidly, "may inspect his cargo on any day of the year, not on his daughter's wedding day. You have no heart, sir. I have always thought as much but now I am sure on't."

"Heart! Tosh!" Her husband roared. "I'm here am I not? These are my legs, my hands."

"Abate your tone, sir. Do you wish the household to hear us?"

"Hell's teeth! Am I to be told how to speak now? Is that the humour of it?" And he flung open the bedroom door and strode forward into the heat. "Ready are yer?" he boomed to his daughter.

"Have a care, sir," Hermione warned, "lest you make her swoon."

"She'll not swoon," he said. "She's marrying one of the *ton*."

So Lady Bradbury left the house with the two brides-maids, and Sir George lay on his daughter's bed and fell asleep with his mouth open, and Melissa stood by the window, stiff with fear and ceremony, and watched as her servants giggled off along the street towards the church and the coaches trundled her guests from the door one after the other.

The rain had stopped, at least temporarily, so the servants gathered on the pavement outside the church to watch the last arrivals. Suki and Bessie were right at the front of the

238

crowd, with Barnaby between them, and all three were enjoying the time-honoured occupation at such nuptial gatherings of being catty about the appearance of the guests, for Suki had decided that as she had no choice but to attend this wedding she might as well get as much fun out of it as she could.

"Do 'ee look at those legs!" she giggled. "That's never his calves! You can see the padding from here."

"If I 'ad a bosom as wrinkled as that," Barnaby observed, "I should keep it covered so I would."

"I'd like to see you with a bosom," Bessie teased him. "We could sell you to a freak show. Make a mint a' money that would."

The carriages were almost as much fun as the guests, for they too had been decked with ribbons and given a thick coat of paint, and they carried so many liveried servants that Bessie said it was a wonder the poor horses could pull them all through the streets. It was fun to try and identify the coats of arms painted so boldly on the sides of these splendid vehicles. Suki surprised herself by the number she knew, and Bessie had become an authority.

"That's Lady Home," she said, "An' that's Mr Beckford. He's the richest man in England, so they say. An' that's the Duke of Errymouth. I seen that one, many and many's the time."

Jessup had been detailed to greet the arrivals at the church gate, and a pompously important job he was making of it, opening doors with a flourish of new lace cuffs and bowing and scraping as if he were welcoming royalty. Many of the guests knew him and spoke to him by name, so that he coughed and smirked with mock modesty before their faces and looked mightily pleased with himself behind their backs.

"Now who?" Bessie said, as the next coach rolled splendidly to the gate. It was drawn by four greys and had the largest and brightest coat of arms – blue stars on a field of gold, a silver helm, three red martlets, and a fierce wild boar, running.

"I know this one!" Suki said.

"Well course you do," Bessie said. "Seein' 'tis Lady Bradbury's very own family. Daventry arms, that is!"

But that wasn't the reason, Suki thought, struggling to remember where she'd seen it before. 'Twas nothing to do with Lady Bradbury. She was quite sure of that. But there wasn't time to think about it for the Daventrys were descending from their flamboyant coach and making an entrance. And very impressive it was.

They were dressed in the height of fashion and so highly perfumed that they scented the air all the way to the church door. Sir Francis was in blue satin, with so many gold buttons on his jacket that they were almost close enough to touch each other. His wig was a delicate shade of pink to match his velvet shoes, the fullness of his billowing shirt sleeves and the embroidery on his waistcoat. He carried a white cane, on which he leant himself, sideways, and with the air of one almost too fatigued to stand.

But if he was a sight to stop crowds, his wife was even more splendid. She had a sharper nose than Lady Bradbury, and an expression of such supercilious disdain that she could barely focus her eyes on anything more than a few inches above her chin. She was dressed in the very latest fashion, in a cream silk mantua, embroidered all over with a delicate tracery of flowing tendrils, green leaves and the smallest rosebuds imaginable, in red and pink and saffron yellow. Her trained skirt was looped up on either side of her petticoat in curves of material

240

that matched exactly the curved curls of her powdered
hair. Above the curls was a small swathed turban,
which supported a confection of pink and yellow ostrich
feathers and three huge bows of embroidered ribbon. In
short, she was every inch an aristocrat. When her three
children stepped out of the coach behind her, she didn't
even glance at them.

Jessup rushed forward to grovel and cough before her,
and she squinted at him for a second and, then, to Suki's
amazement, actually spoke to the man. "Ah! Jessup, ain't
it? Goin' along are yer?"

"She knows him," Suki said, much surprised.

"'E was a Daventry servant to start with," Bessie told
her. "'E come with Lady Bradbury when she married.
Cook told me."

Which is why he runs errands for her, Suki thought.
I might've known. But there wasn't time to think about
that either, for there was Lady Bradbury herself, running
down the church path to greet her distinguished guests,
huge-eyed with anxiety.

"I am *so* glad you were able to attend, cousin Francis,"
she gushed. "We are all so *honoured*. Indeed we are.
I was only making the observation to Sir George this
morning. Such an honour! I trust I see you well."

"Tolerable," Sir Francis drawled. "Ain't the weather
for standin' about, though, damme."

Hermione took the hint at once, and with increased
distress. "Pray to step inside," she begged, bowing her
entire body before them. She looked so subservient that
Suki really wondered at her. Why was she so anxious to
please? They were her own family, yet it was almost as
though she were afraid of them. It was another puzzle in a
puzzling afternoon, but there wasn't time to consider that
either, for a red-faced Sir George had arrived with the

241

white-faced bride and the bridal procession was shuffling into position beside the church gates, their stiff petticoats swinging like bells.

And Suki suddenly remembered where she'd seen that coat of arms. It was the one embroidered on the Captain's kerchief. She wore it round her neck at that very moment, washed and pressed for the occasion. But Jack wasn't related to the Daventrys, surely. She'd always known he came from a good family. But not the Daventrys. He'd not be living in a lunatic asylum if he were part of a family as grand as that.

"Come on!" Bessie urged, pulling at Suki's sleeve. "If we don't get inside this minute, the service'll start without us an' we shall miss it."

So they crammed into the back of the church behind the pews and settled to be entertained by the wedding. To Suki, used to the ornate splendour of the Abbey at Bath and the sombre heaviness of the little church at Twerton, entering the Church of St James in Piccadilly was like walking into light. It was so bright and modern, and full of echoing sound, from the white marble under her feet to the high white ceiling over her head. White columns with heavily gilded architraves supported the roof and the gallery was decorated with a line of complacent cherubs with golden wings; the side windows were made of clear glass, so that sunshine shone through the panes and made the gilding shine like coins; and in front of the high altar was a rich wooden screen where clusters of grapes, fruit and garlands tumbled like brown curls, and a superb mahogany eagle held up the gilded lectern. A rich man's church without a doubt.

The space between the front pews and the high altar was wide enough for a theatre and every bit as dramatic. Here the wedding party were grouping themselves, in an argumentative semi-circle facing a golden priest. On his left stood the painted statue that was the bride and, on his right, her extraordinary groom. He was dressed from head to foot in pure white satin with gold buttons on his jacket and waistcoat, and gold buckles on his white satin shoes, and a pale yellow wig on his elegant head, dusted with white powder so that it glittered like snow in the sunlight. He looked like a creature from a fairy-tale, and as unlikely a bridegroom as Suki had ever seen.

But for the moment, he was upstaged by the furious argument that was being conducted in hissing stage whispers by the Daventrys and the Errymouths, both of whom felt they should have pride of place at the centre of the group. Lady Bradbury was nearly in tears, Sir George was trying to be diplomatic, and the golden priest was wringing his hands.

Such a to-do, Suki thought, watching them bristling anger at one another. As if any of it is of any consequence. Miss Melissa will marry her ridiculous bridegroom no matter where any of them stand. And much good may it do her. I only wish they'd hurry up, for the sooner the wedding is done, the sooner we can get back for the feast. I only had a bite from that cold beef an' a bite arn't sufficient on a day like this.

But if the service was slow, the wedding breakfast was taken at a snail's pace, for the carriages had to queue to discharge their occupants at the door, and then the guests had to be greeted one by one, and there was so much wine to drink and so many impressive acquaintances to meet that it was more than an hour before the party sat down to the first thirteen sizzling courses.

The bridegroom brought his squirrel to the table and fed it on tit-bits and was prevailed upon to take a sip from every single dish himself, so as to bring good fortune to

243

the marriage. He actually ate one or two of the choicer
offerings and seemed to enjoy them. His guests were
most impressed and his new mother-in-law almost sick
with relief. But then the toasts began and soon they
were all comfortably drunk and the fish course could
be served.

"I gather that your eldest is to dance in the hog trough,"
Sir Francis said to his cousin.

"I fear so, sir," Hermione murmured. "Poor child."

"Waste no pity upon her, ma'am," Sir Francis advised.
"If she's too plain or too curst to catch a husband, she
must take the consequences of her folly, damme. 'Twill
make some sport for us."

That was the opinion below stairs where the Bradbury
servants were gathered about their own table, enjoying
the remains of the first course.

"Eat up!" Mr Jessup commanded happily, sitting at
the head of the table, as befitted the steward of such
an important household, and drinking his third glass of
wine. "And a good health to all the company – krmm,
krmm – your good selves included."

"'Twill soon be time for Miss Ariadne to dance in the
hog trough," Hepzibah said. "She'll be a-ringing for you
presently, Suki Brown. I can't wait to see it. 'Twill take
her down a peg or two and not afore time. All this silly
nonsense of not talking. 'Tis play acting to my way of
thinking. She's a deal too hoity-toity for her own good."

Suki sprang to her defence. "She've suffered cruelly,
poor lady," she said. "I feel a deal of pity for her an' so
should you."

"Which is why," Hepzie said in her superior way,
"you're still a wet nurse and maid to a total failure and
I'm to travel with the bride on the Grand Tour."

Mrs Sparepenny looked sharply at both girls, ready

to forestall a quarrel but Mr Jessup was on his feet proposing another toast and the moment passed.

But Ariadne's humiliation was still to come and, although it was delayed by the wedding breakfast which went on for nearly four hours, eventually the party left the table and retired to their rooms to dress for the ball and Ariadne rang for Suki.

Her special white dress was taken out of the cupboard and lowered over her head. Her jewellery was removed and her hair brushed into careful curls. Then she sat by the bed and waited to be summoned.

"We been told we may watch from the minstrels' gallery," Suki said, adding with feeling, "I shall applaud when you'm done."

Ariadne begged she would do no such thing. "'Tis a punishment," she said, "and must be endured." But then there was a shuffle at the door and she had to resume her silence as Jessup came in to collect her and take her down to the ballroom.

The guests were gathered about the dance floor where the pig trough stood in smelly isolation, trailing dirty straw and still smeared and stained by the drool of its former users. There was a ripple of surprise as Ariadne appeared in her cambric gown, but as she signalled to the musicians to play and lifted her long skirts to step into the trough, surprise turned to shock, for her feet and ankles were indecorously bare.

"How lewd!" Lady Carstairs said behind her fan to her good friend Lady Fosdyke. "Don't she know she's being indecent?"

"She has style," Lady Fosdyke said. "I'll give her that. To dress in the height of fashion and all in white cambric is masterly. But I should say she's a deal too cunning still."

She was also, it had to be admitted, moving with great dignity and a total lack of emotion. She stepped into the bran as though she was stepping into the baths, and then danced so well and with such careful rhythm, that the wedding guests burst into spontaneous applause when she finished, and even the servants, who had packed into the gallery and were watching ghoulishly, had to admit that she'd taken her punishment well.

But then it was time to bring the bride and groom to bed and, that, as they all told one another as they rushed up the stairs after the groomsmen and the squealing bundle they were half carrying, half dragging, was the best part of any wedding. The chambermaids made a very thorough job of undressing Melissa, removing every single pin from her elaborate gown, and holding each one up to the company for ribald comment. "No prick of misfortune for *our* bride," they said. And "here's another sharp little prick." And "here's the biggest prick of them all." And the company cheered, and offered advice, "Lie still now, me dear, for you won't get another chance till morning." And the bride blushed and giggled and begged them to desist, and was teased and tickled and rolled about in the bed until she was stripped to her chemise and her stockings.

Then the groom arrived, carried shoulder high by his leering groomsmen, but cool and elegant even then. Not for this exquisite, the rough and tumble of a public stripping. He was disrobed, holding up an arm or a leg as required, but noticing every move his drunken friends were making and ensuring, by the severity of his glance, that his clothes were folded and hung away in the wardrobe, uncreased. When the sack posset was brought, he drank his in one draught, wiped his lips elegantly upon his handkerchief, and turned to look ardently upon his bride as she struggled to swallow hers.

"Go to it, Humphrey!" his friends encouraged him.

"You need have no fear of *that*, me dears," he said, and pushed the bride down upon her back.

"Draw the curtains damme," Sir George roared in delight, "or we shall all be shamed."

"Patience, son-in-law," Lady Bradbury said archly. "You have forgot the stockings in your ardour."

"Then you'd best be quick about it," the gallant said, "or breed daughter's that ain't so tempting."

So the order was given and all young guests made a rush at the bed, the girls to attack the groom and the young men leaping amorously and noisily upon the bride. For a little while arms and legs flailed with abandon, the mattress sagged under the weight of such a tangle and there was much cheerful tickling and groping. But at last four flushed bodies detached themselves from the muddle, triumphantly waving the four discarded stockings. The cheering and laughing died down as the two girls took up their positions at the foot of the bed and, with their eyes closed, tossed the stockings over their shoulders. One caught the bridegroom across the chest, the second landed on Melissa's shoulder. Then the applause began and the chant went up, "Who hits the mark over the shoulder, must married be ere twelve months older."

Then it was the turn of the young men and while they were taking up their positions at the foot of the bed, Suki glanced across at her silent mistress and winked. Ariadne, looking quite impish, winked back. So the second pair of stockings were thrown and, as neither of them hit their targets, the throwers were mocked and teased. Then the bed curtains were drawn, and the guests retreated to the landing to sing the wedding song, to the accompaniment of as many members of the band as could squeeze into the crowd on the stairs, and the bridal couple were left to their own devices.

It had, they all agreed, been a splendid wedding and there were still three more days of festivities to enjoy.

Early the next morning a *billet* arrived from Bristol for Sir George. And the news it contained set the second day breakfast off with a roar. The last sugar cargo had returned to port under the safe escort of the *Yorick*, and proved to be of better quality than expected. So the groom, who had taken a share in the venture by virtue of his part ownership of the privateer, was cheered for a double triumph and the bride who had come down to breakfast in a new gown and with her face scrubbed clean, kissed her new husband, blushing almost prettily, and declared she must have brought him luck.

When the meal was over, Sir George retired to Lady Bradbury's boudoir to enlarge upon his success.

"Good news, what?" he said, hopefully. A high profit might bring him forgiveness for his misdemeanour of the previous morning. "I shall buy you a jewel to mark the occasion."

"A pretty thought," she said and actually managed a smile.

The smile reminded her husband of the amorous activity that had been taking place under his roof during the past twenty-four hours, and gave him a happy idea. "Oblige me, my love?" he suggested mildly.

"Of course," Hermione agreed equally mildly. "If I may just have a moment or two to prepare myself." She had foreseen the possibility of such demands and was ready for them.

He waited beside the bed, slowly unbuttoning his breeches, while she found her library book, Mr Fielding's latest and most scurrilous offering, *Amelia*, and arranging herself comfortably upon the pillows, lifted her skirt into neat folds over her bosom. Then she opened the book and her legs, and inclined her head graciously towards him to give him permission to begin. He fell upon her at once, and soon the two of them were more or less happily occupied, he humping vigorously towards his pleasure at one end of her anatomy, she enjoying Amelia's adventures at the other. Taken all in all, weddings were really quite agreeable occasions, and this one was going well.

Fifteen

The second day of the wedding passed without incident. Dinner was served late but that was only to be expected when half the house party had stayed in bed until noon, and those members of the gentry who had agreed to attend didn't arrive until well past the suggested hour. But the ball began on time and was much enjoyed, for by now Sir George had forgotten his transgression and was his cheerfully rubicund self again, and his guests were all well into the spirit of the thing.

The dancing continued until three in the morning when a cold collation was served before the visiting guests departed. And once again they all slept on until midday on Friday, when they woke to dine and dance all over again.

By the morning of that third day, the huge ongoing party had established a routine and a pecking order, in which Lord and Lady Fosdyke held court at one end of the social scale and Ariadne crept into the dining-room to take her silent place at the other. She was so quiet and withdrawn that Suki grew concerned about her.

"'Twill soon be over," she encouraged as she eased her mistress out of Friday's finery. "Sunday's a-coming."

Ariadne's reply was enigmatic. "And Saturday precedes it."

Saturday was to be the grandest day of them all, since

all the important guests were returning for the final ball, including Sir Francis and his wife, so preparations for the feast kept the cooks and scullery maids up all night for the second time that week. But on this occasion, Lady Bradbury left them to it and didn't interfere, so there was a deal less fuss in the kitchen, even though there were more dishes to prepare for this dinner than there'd been for the wedding breakfast.

But every minute of this last day brought Suki closer to the moment of her dismissal, and her need to find Captain Jack grew more and more urgent as the final feast and ball approached. I shall see un tomorrow, she said to herself, as she carried William into the drawing-room for yet another inspection as the guests began to gather. I shall set off first thing in the morning, while they'm all busy speeding the bride and groom and standing in line for vails and so forth. And she tried to work out how many hours it would be.

"Sixteen," Ariadne told her, as though there were no doubt of it, "for 'tis two o'clock now and 'twill be eight in the morning when you leave the house, if all goes according to plan."

Suki was lacing her stomacher, but she paused to laugh, the laces dangling between her fingers. "You speak as though 'twere ordained," she said. "How can you be so sure on't?"

Ariadne was wearing her teasing expression. "I have foreknowledge, perchance."

"Would you did," Suki sighed, "for if I don't find the Captain tomorrow I don't know what will become of me an' William. Even if I married Farmer Lambton I doubt if he could prevail upon 'em to keep us together."

"Take heart," Ariadne said and her voice was so warm that it brought a rush of tears to Suki's eyes. "We are both in the lap of the gods and the gods are kind on some occasions." She looked at her image in the pier glass. "Am I subdued enough for the bride's final triumph, think 'ee?"

"You look well," Suki told her, blinking her tears away.

Ariadne grinned. "Appearances," she declared, in her mother's voice, "are *so* important."

So the bride and groom were applauded into the dining-room and their sister took her place at the foot of the table and the final feast began. It soon became rowdy and inebriated. So many toasts were proposed and so many bumpers drunk that the company rapidly lost count and balance, and even Frederick Bradbury began to enjoy himself; the bride ate so much that her face grew puce coloured and she had to unfasten her stomacher; the squirrel was given a long rein and ran across every plate on the top table, to the amusement of all those who were beyond its range; and Sir George told scurrilous tales to both his neighbours and was roundly chided and admired.

But Ariadne sat silent and ate little and watched everything, and when the ladies retired she went straight upstairs to her chamber when her mother wasn't looking. Which was where Suki found her, lying on the bed, stripped to her chemise and reading one of Lady Bradbury's three-volume novels.

"Yes?" she said, when Suki had knocked and entered.

"You didn't ring," Suki said, feeling she had to explain her presence.

"No. I didn't, did I?"

"Are you ready to be dressed?"

"No. As you see."

"Am I to come back later?"

This time Ariadne didn't even look up from her book. "No."

She was in such a peculiar humour that Suki couldn't think what to say next. "Well then . . ."

Ariadne turned over a page and assumed her insouciant expression. "I have decided that I shall dress myself this evening," she said. "Go down and enjoy the ball. There will be much to enjoy, I promise you."

It was unheard of for a young lady to dress herself. But she was plainly in no mood to argue about it so Suki left her. She'm a-goin' to cut it, she thought, as she went back to the kitchen, an' I can't blame her, for she'm suffered enough, what with Melissa crowing an' giving herself airs, an' Hepzie being rude to her, an' her mother an' father ignoring her. I'd do the same. 'Tis a pity she won't see the ballroom though, for 'tis uncommon fine tonight.

The household had been busy all morning preparing the place, sweeping the dance floor, clearing out spent candles, gathering up dirty glasses and smeared plates, polishing the chandeliers, setting new fires, bringing in the new decorations. Now the walls were hung with green boughs, which had been bent into curving shapes which looked uncommon pleasing against the blue wallpaper and shone in the dazzle of candlelight from Lady Bradbury's splendid chandeliers as though every leaf had been polished. To complete the picture, each green confection had been entwined with gold and white ribbons and hung with long strings of tiny golden bells that were threaded so close together and had been gathered up in such profusion that they tumbled and curled like swathes of mythical hair. Suki and Bessie were very taken with it, especially as the band were to be dressed in green and gold to match the decor and the supper tables were heavy with greenery, too.

" 'Tis a shame Miss Ariadne won't see it," Bessie said, "poor lady. But we will, won't we? We can stand in the gallery, same as last time. Mrs Sparepenny said."

They managed a good position right at the front, where they had a clear view of the doors and could watch every entrance. And as they had come to expect, the entrances were spectacular.

Lady Home was in royal purple, with gold cock feathers in her hair, and Lady Fosdyke, not to be outdone by her rival, was dressed in equally regal scarlet with a bejewelled turban to set off her snow-white wig. Sir Francis wore a jacket embroidered in gold thread while his wife was caparisoned in saffron yellow with a head-dress made of peacock's feathers. Lady Bradbury, standing beside her husband to greet their guests, was insignificant beside their splendour, for *her* new gown was pale blue, trimmed with pink embroidery, and looked decidedly out of fashion.

"She'll give that to Hepzibah presently," Suki said, enjoying the discomfited expression on her mistress's long face.

"Here's the bride and groom," Bessie said.

They were standing just inside the door, looking round expectantly and waiting for their applause to begin. The bride had put on weight since the start of the wedding and was waddling in a very unbecoming way, and the groom was leaning backwards at such a precarious angle that it really was a wonder he didn't topple over. But they were the cynosure of all eyes and that was what mattered.

There was the usual polite ripple of applause and those nearest to the newly-weds told them how fine they were looking, and then the master of ceremonies announced that the ball was about to commence and begged that the company be upstanding for the opening quadrille.

And just as Sir Humphrey was swaying his bride on to the floor, the door was pushed open and Ariadne stood in the doorway.

She had little kid slippers on her feet and wore long kid gloves to her elbows, but apart from that she was stunningly and triumphantly naked, for the dress she'd had made up for the occasion was a mere wisp of gauze and apart from a *cache sexe* of green leaves that was tastefully stitched to her skirt and matched the chaplet of green leaves that encircled her dark hair, it was completely transparent.

The sussuration of indrawn breath was like a gale. Then there was an outcry as her mother staggered and seemed about to faint, crying, "Oh the abomination! How could she do such a thing? At her own sister's wedding!". The ladies exclaimed in horror at her behaviour and the gentlemen advanced towards her, eyes gleaming and mouths moist.

Suki was so thrilled by her daring that she clapped her hands together in delight. What style she has. So this is what she meant by "all will be revealed", she thought. And what courage! No wonder she had to keep it a secret. She tried to catch Ariadne's eye to show her how well she understood and how much she approved. But Ariadne was busy catching other eyes, as she advanced gracefully into the ballroom, smiling to right and left at the gallants who crowded around her, eager for a closer look and the chance to partner her – in one way or another. She knew she had the pick of the bunch and would choose the richest who offered, and she was happily aware that there were little dramas being played out in every corner of the room because of her – that her sister was red-faced with anger and stamping her feet, that Jessup had retired to the furthest corner, coughing fit to crack his lungs, that her mother was swaying and preparing to swoon, that her father actually had his hands over his eyes. Oh 'twas a perfect, flesh-tingling, parent-defeating, absolute triumph.

Hermione was weeping on the shoulder of her dear friend, Arabella, there being no adequate or comfortable space into which she could swoon. "I am shamed before my family," she sobbed, "and I had such hopes of this wedding. Such hopes. I shall never hold up my head again. Somebody send for Mr Jessup and tell him to deal with it."

"Sir George will see to it," Arabella soothed. "Never fear. He'll not permit a scandal."

But Sir George was so shocked that for a few seconds he was completely speechless and could do nothing but hurrumph and splutter while his daughter continued her procession and his brother tried to reassure him.

Then he removed his hands and found his voice. "How could she *do* such a thing?" he wailed. "She's no better than a whore, Frederick, a common whore making a public exhibition of herself and she always had the best that money could buy. The best."

"You mustn't blame yourself, my dear feller," Frederick said, patting his arm. "Indeed you must not. There ain't a thing you could have done to gainsay it. Women are a breed apart and that's the truth of it. Given to vanities and follies of all sorts. Ain't we always said so?"

"She's no daughter of mine," her father groaned. "I tell 'ee that. Where's Jessup? He'll know how to deal with her. She must be moved before too many people see her. I'd not want any of my friends—"

But his young friend, John Smithers, was already standing before the shimmering flesh of his errant off-spring, mouth agape with admiration and lust. And in the second shock of the evening, the lady spoke to him.

"La Mr Smithers!" she said, her voice high and clear and ringing like a bell. "I thought you a theatre-goer, sir, upon me life, yet one would think you had never seen a gauze before."

There was another intake of breath and another outburst of amazement: "She speaks!", "Did you ever hear the like?", "She ain't dumb after all."

"She does it a-purpose," Melissa wailed, "to spoil my wedding."

"Ignore her," Sir Humphrey advised, covertly watching her pretty flesh. "Remember that you are my wife."

"I hate her!" Melissa howled, stamping her feet with distress. "Hate her, hate her, hate her."

"Pray do not discommode yourself, my love," her husband said, trying to restrain her, "for we are to open the quadrille." And he tried to send a signal to the band. But they took no notice of him, being fully and happily occupied watching the naked lady.

"Five pounds says my old feller is the first to squire her," Lady Fosdyke said, offering her challenge to all the ladies grouped around her.

There were plenty of takers, there being nothing more attractive than a gamble for high stakes, especially when there were so many married fools to back.

But Lord Fosdyke was already at Ariadne's elbow and winning his wife's bet for her. "We have seen many a gauze in our time, my dear," he said, "but never worn so becomingly, if I may be permitted to say so."

"You turn a pretty compliment, sir," she answered, smiling into his eyes. Oh such a fine rich man! And wouldn't his wife be cross if she chose him.

"Perhaps you will honour me with the pleasure of the opening quadrille," the noble lord suggested.

"Do you ask me to stand up with you before all these people," she teased. "Fie, my lord, we should cause a scandal."

"I stand up for you already," he said, acknowledging his wife's calculating glare with a wry half-smile. "And as to causing a scandal, we are above such considerations." And he offered her his arm.

So Miss Ariadne Bradbury and Lord Fosdyke opened the quadrille instead of the bride and groom. And Lady Fosdyke won her bet.

From then on the ball was one titillatingly scandalous moment after another, for the triumphant lady danced every measure, and each one with a new enraptured partner, who dared the experience even though they knew they would have a hard time of it explaining themselves to their wives when they returned to their seats.

After the third measure, Sir Francis sought out his cousin, striding down upon her with a face bright with such mischief that she looked up quailing with fear at what he was about to say.

"I congratulate 'ee, ma'am," he drawled, "You've bred a corker, upon me life. Ain't seen such cracking entertainment in months. She'll do well with old Fosdyke. He might even get her into court."

She was so surprised it was all she could do to summon the words to thank him.

"I'd stand up with her messell," he said, smiling at the temptation, "if Virginia would permit me."

"Which she won't," Lady Fosdyke said, stepping up to join them. "Leave her to my old feller. He'll see her right. 'Twon't last more than a month or two – his light a' loves rarely do – but he'll see her right. She's made a fine choice, Hermione. You should be proud of her. Won me a pretty penny, too. Whatever else, she's a sight better than that mimsy-pimsy sister of hers."

Hermione's head was beginning to spin at such un-expected compliments. "I'm obliged to 'ee," she said faintly.

"So you should be," the lady said. "Your dance, I think, Sir Francis. I've a mind to tread the boards for once and my husband is otherwise engaged."

Towards one o'clock, Jessup announced that supper was served and, at that, Ariadne looked up to the gallery and signalled to Suki that she was to come down.

"Bring me my travelling cloak and my chemise and a day gown for tomorrow," she ordered. "The blue if you can find it. We mean to leave while they are supping."

"I'm so—" Suki began.

But Ariadne put a hand over her lips for Lord Fosdyke was walking towards them through the crush. "I will send to 'ee at eight tomorrow," she whispered. "Pack the rest of my things tonight and bring 'em with you then. And William, too, of course, for you can travel on to Bedlam when you've delivered 'em. Did I not tell 'ee the gods could be kind? Now make haste or I shall be forced to travel as I am."

So the few and necessary clothes were packed in Ariadne's smaller travelling bag and rushed downstairs to be handed to her as she left the house, wrapping the cloak around her as she went. There wasn't even time for Suki to wish her luck. Not that she needed it.

Sixteen

On Sunday morning, the Bradbury household rose early, for the bride and groom intended to set off on the Grand Tour – complete with their peculiar retinue – as soon as they had taken breakfast and their mattress had been packed for transport. And although most of the guests had stayed on to pelt them from the doorstep with the traditional shoes and rice, they, too, would be taking their departure and distributing vails not long after that. But Suki Brown wasn't concerned with any of it. She was up and out of the house before Cook came yawning down to prepare breakfast, for Ariadne had been true to her promise and had sent a carriage to collect her at eight o'clock.

For once, William endured the journey without complaint, partly because he was still sleepy but mostly because it was such a short and easy ride – across the empty Oxford Street, through two sleeping squares and into a long elegant terrace where they stopped before a house with a black door and two very white doorsteps. Suki and William were admitted by a housemaid in a blue gown, who asked them kindly to step this way and led them upstairs, while the wicker skip containing Ariadne's clothes was hauled from the luggage box and carried into the hall.

Ariadne was sitting up in a very grand bed, in a very

grand bedroom. She was wearing her cream chemise and, to Suki's relief, she was on her own.

"He left at daybreak," she explained. "I've ordered breakfast and some porridge for William. He's having bread and meats sent over and he promised 'twould be here by nine. We have plenty of time. Bedlam don't open until eleven – I've made enquiries – and the carriage will take 'ee there and bring 'ee back again. What do 'ee think to this house? 'Tis all mine, so he says."

"'Tis uncommon fine," Suki told her and as Ariadne was smiling, she ventured to ask, "Are you happy here?"

"Happiness don't come into it," Ariadne said easily. "'Tis a job, no more, no less. I've made my choice and now I will make the best of it. 'Tis a deal better than being forced to marry whatever popinjay my idiot father might have chosen for me. At least I don't belong to the gentleman. There's no question of obeying him or any suchlike nonsense. 'Tis a business arrangement, no more. He's a demanding lover for an old un, I'll say that, but I daresay I shall find someone younger and more handsome to pleasure me, and in the meanwhile I shall live well enough. I'm to have a carriage of my own and horses, and fine clothes and jewels – he says I've only to ask for 'em – and whatever servants I require what's more, which is why I sent for you. How would 'ee like to be my lady's maid? If you don't find your lover." And when Suki hesitated, "You know my ways so well and I could depend upon 'ee to be discreet, could I not? 'Twould suit us both I believe, and 'twould be a deal better for you than marrying that dreadful tell-tale of a farmer of yours."

"I must go to Bedlam first," Suki said. "If I can find the Captain—"

That was understood. "Nothing need be decided yet. I have written my address on this paper – you see? – so you can write to me as soon as you know what you intend. Ah, here is our breakfast come. I trust you have an appetite."

So they sat on two comfortable chairs beside a pretty little round table and ate the bread and meat provided and took it in turns to spoon porridge into William's mouth. Suki was too excited to eat much, but she made an effort and, although her heart wasn't in the conversation either, she talked to Ariadne like the old friends they were. When the blue-gowned maid returned to inform her new mistress that the carriage was waiting for her friend, they were still re-living the shock that Ariadne had caused the previous evening, and giggling with delight at the memory of it.

But now it was time for Bedlam and the moment of discovery. As Suki stood to leave, she was trembling so much she had to hold on to her gown to still her hands.

"You must visit again soon," Ariadne told her, "even if you *do* find that lover of yours, which I do truly hope for 'ee." And in a moment of happy impulse, she seized Suki's hands and kissed her on the cheek as though they were sisters. "I wish 'ee good fortune, Suki Brown."

"As I do you," Suki said, lifting William on to her hip.

Outside the house, the street was still empty, although rather more smokey than it had been when she arrived, and this time her journey was a great deal longer and more complicated.

First they travelled east along endless roads until they reached a wide street called Cheapside where there were terraces of shops on either side of them, each with its own shop sign hanging above the pavement like a stiff tin flag. Then they turned north and edged through a series of narrow lanes which were all excessively dark and dirty and smelt of piss and decay. Here the houses leant towards one another as if they no longer had the strength to stand erect and slatternly women gossiped in dark doorways, peering out at the carriage in the most alarmingly suspicious way. Suki felt decidedly uncomfortable there, especially as the overhanging houses pushed darkness into the carriage so that she could barely see where she was. And then, just as William was beginning to grizzle and climb over her lap, they were out in the light again and the coachmen called down to her that they were at the London Wall and would soon be there.

Presently he pulled his horses to a halt. "There's your asylum," he said, pointing to it with his whip, as Suki stuck her head out of the window. "You've arrived."

It was a long, stately, splendid building, like a palace, with two perfectly balanced wings on either side of a central tower. At the top of the tower was a curved tiled roof, above the roof a balcony of grey stone surmounted by a decorated clock tower, surmounted in turn by a cupola as bulbous as an onion, and topped off by the gilded statue of a flying dragon. There were rows of fine carriages waiting in the road outside, so the first visitors had obviously arrived already, and the entrance was marked with a painted placard. A flight of two stone steps led to a gate, the gate gave way to a gravelled path, which led, in turn, to a narrow door guarded by a liveried attendant in a grey tie wig. It all looked extremely fine and elegant. In fact if it hadn't been for two doleful statues brooding on either side of the gate, Suki would have had no qualms about visiting the place at all. That is until she walked up the front steps.

Then she knew she was entering a lunatic asylum because of the smell of the place. It stank of vinegar which had obviously been used by the bucketload to sweeten the air. But beneath its cleansing fumes, there were residual smells that were all too familiar – of shit and stale piss and human sweat. It reminded her of Sir George's chamber-pot. Oh, she thought, how can my dear, fastidious Captain live in such a place? What on earth is he a-doing working here? The sooner she found him and persuaded him out of it, the better.

She lifted William on to her back, tying the ends of her shawl tightly at her waist to support him, and walked boldly up to the attendant.

"Penny to see the lunatics," he said, holding out a hopeful palm.

"I haven't come to see no lunatics," she rebuked him. "I come to see the Captain."

"Captain who?"

"Captain Jack," she said. "I don't know his other name but everyone calls him the Captain."

"No one a' that name 'ere," the attendant said. "Leastways, not so far as I know."

"There must be," she insisted. "I have it on the very best authority." He must be here. He simply *must*. She'd waited so long and come so far. Her face was so fierce with distress, the attendant took pity on her.

"Stay there a tick," he said, "an' I'll ask Mr Todd."

Mr Todd wore the same livery, but with rather more gold braid attached to it. He was sitting in an office beside the front door, demolishing a meat pie with total disregard for the stink around him, and with such

264

vigour that scraps of it flew into the air as he chewed and spoke.

"The Captain?" he said. Munch, snort. "Yes, we 'ave got a Captain, Joe." Munch munch, gobble. "Number sixty-nine, east corridor." Snort, crunch, smack, smack. "That's where."

"That'll be a penny," the attendant said. But she was already running down the corridor, with William bouncing on her back. He was here! He was here! Just a few yards away. Her dear darling Jack. "I'll pay on the way out!" she called.

It was a very long corridor and full of extraordinary creatures: old women, shrivelled as witches, mumbling and tottering, their eyes wild; old men, muttering and twitching, their wigs matted and their faces spiked with stubble; women in weird costumes, posturing; and men in loincloths, scratching; and creatures so deformed and smeared with filth that it was impossible to see what sex they were. In the numbered rooms they crouched on their haunches in dirty straw, rocking or spitting or lying mute as corpses. It was a terrifying place. And walking in among the wild and lunatic were groups of gentlefolk in their best clothes, scented and powdered and superior, exclaiming with mock horror at the awful sights around them, and enjoying every one of them.

Which was more than Suki could do. "Soon be there," she said, speaking to William but encouraging herself. "Forty-nine, fifty. Soon be there."

Room sixty-nine was a shattering disappointment. There was nobody in it except a half-naked lunatic with a shaven head and a scabby face, who was sitting on the floor, staring at the wall. She was so upset that the tears sprang to her eyes, and she let them fall, standing in the dirty doorway, at a loss to know what to do or where to go, or what to say.

The attendant came panting up beside her. "Penny," he gasped. "Penny fer entry!"

She took a penny miserably from her pocket and put it in his palm. "Where is the Captain?" she said. "You told me he was in room sixty-nine. So where is he?"

And the lunatic lifted his head and looked up at her, with the Captain's eyes.

The shock was so profound that it drained all colour from her face and took the strength from her legs. She sank to the stone flags of the corridor with William clinging to her neck, and groaned, "No, no, no! Oh my dear Captain! What have they done to 'ee?"

"Who is it?" the Captain said, dully, peering at her. And although his voice sounded thicker than she remembered, it *was* his voice, and the sound of it made her weep again.

She leant forward into the room and took his hands, and he allowed the touch, but seemed puzzled by it. "Who is it?" he asked again, blinking his eyes.

"Oh my dear Captain," she said. "'Tis Suki. Your own Suki. Come all the way from Bath to find 'ee."

"Polly Anna, is it?" he said, peering at her again.

The name angered her. How dare he confuse her with another woman! How dare he tell her there ever *was* another woman! "Suki," she said firmly.

"I fear I do not know you, ma'am," he said. "Perhaps you mistake me for another."

"No sir," she told him. "I do not mistake you, for you fathered my child."

He scowled slightly as if she had presented him with an enigma. "I have no memory of it," he said at last. "But I confess to you, ma'am, my memory is

266

fleeting since I came to this place, and most uncertain."

"You said I was your one true love," she said. "Did you lie to me?" She was surprised by how calm she was being.

"All men lie to their wenches, one time or another," he said sadly. "'Tis the way of the world, I fear."

"You said you loved me."

"Love!" he sighed. "What is love? We seek it all our lives but I fear 'tis only folly, when all's said and done."

She undid her shawl and lowered William very gently until he was standing in the corridor behind her. "Your folly made a son," she said, picking him up in her arms and turning him to face his father. "A fine child, look 'ee. And yours. Now what do 'ee say to that?"

He glanced at the baby and scowled again. "What can I say? I am no longer free to speak as I will. They incarcerate us here and feed us pap and laudanum until our brains are numb. If you look to find a husband and a father for your child, you must seek elsewhere. We may not woo, nor wed, nor father, and there's an end on't."

The words burned into her brain, shattering her calm and returning her strength. She rose to her feet and roared at him in an extremity of disappointment and rage. "Don' 'ee dare speak so. That's your child I carried, an' bore, an' fed, an' lied for. An' all for the love of you, poor fool that I was. All for the love of you! And now you say you may not wed. Where's your valour, sir? 'Od's bones it makes me sick to see 'ee."

An attendant was behind her pulling at her arms and begging her to desist, but she was too angry to hear him and his touch was an irritant she simply shook away. She strode into the dirty straw with William in her arms and aimed a kick at her lover's scabby legs.

He scrambled to his feet in alarm and backed away from her, holding out his hands to deflect her, as she lifted her foot to take another swing at him. But at that moment, and without any warning, he looked up, staightened his spine and began to declaim – in a bold unnatural voice as if he were an actor – and turning she saw that a group of ladies had gathered in the corridor to watch them and that several of them were applauding as if her anger had been part of a play.

"Shall I tell 'ee of Africa?" he called to them.

And they nodded and called out, "Pray do."

"Where the great chief Wan Four sells men like beads," he said, "and flogs 'em with a cat-o'-nine-tails until their backs are raw, and the crocodiles lie in wait at the water's edge to eat 'em as they fall. Such creatures as you would never believe. They are tall as a house and with skins like armour and they can swallow a man whole – bones, brains, blood and all, with a snap of their great jaws." He mimed the closure of those jaws with both arms, clapping his hands together so sharply that he made several of the ladies jump with delighted terror. "How would 'ee like to see such things as that?"

They shuddered happily and threw coins at his feet.

"Shall I tell of a sea fight when the muskets shoot like hail and cannonballs fly towards 'ee, red hot, and each one capable of ripping off your arm or tearing off your leg? And what thereafter, I ask 'ee? Shall I tell 'ee? You lie on the deck in a pool of your own blood and the pain of it too great to bear, and the surgeon takes your stump and holds it down in a tub of boiling tar, and you may scream all you please but 'twill be done though you die of it, for you will die without it, when your limb turns green and gangrenous and the poison rises to your brain."

The shudders increased and more coins were thrown and Suki turned her head to glance at their enraptured faces while he took breath for another story. But there were no more words. Instead he gave a sudden, high-pitched, howling scream, that made them all jump with alarm. It frightened William so much that he clung to his mother's hair and began to whimper. Suki turned her head again, annoyed by such an exhibition and ready to rebuke him, but then she saw that this wasn't part of his act. It was too extreme and he was too visibly shaken, his eyes staring at some horror behind her, one finger pointing. And she turned again to see what on earth it could be to frighten him so, and found herself looking into the startled face of Lady Bradbury.

"Are you come here to taunt me, lady?" he cried. "Or are you some ghost from my past, risen to torment me. Speak to me!"

The crowd were delighted by his appeal and turned to the lady to see how she would respond, the regulars declaring that this was the best display they'd ever witnessed.

Hermione was caught in two minds whether to swoon away or to face him out with some flippant remark. The corridor was so crowded that it would be difficult to swoon in any comfort, even with Arabella beside her to ease her to the floor, so she decided on speech. "Tush!" she said, addressing her remarks to her companion. "What nonsense these poor fools do talk. Do I look like a ghost, think 'ee?"

She should have chosen a fall, for he recognised her voice and was enraged by it.

"She's the one!" he screamed. "That painted lady in

her silks and her rouge. That lady is my mother, the Lady Bradbury. My mother! If you seek to see who brought me to this pass, look 'ee there. She's the one. 'Od rot her! Farmed out, kicked out, naught but a bastard, so help me, and 'tis all her doing. You may call yourself a mother, ma'am, but you have no sense of the meaning of the word! No sense at all. Reckon your ream pennies, now, you'd best, for your sins have found you out. 'Od rot her! Rot her!"

Out of the corner of her eye, Suki could see Mr Todd hurtling down the corridor towards them, and behind him a chattering crowd of lunatics and gentry. And then her eye was caught by a sudden downward movement and she saw that Lady Bradbury was falling. Suki realised that for once this was no pretence, but a genuine swoon, for Lady Bradbury was toppling sideways and extremely heavily, knocking the people behind her into awkward positions by the weight of her body and groaning in the most alarming way. The two attendants were considerably hampered by her collapse, for she took up a great deal of room in the crowded corridor and soon gathered a crowd of her own, but they pushed past as well as they could and reached out to catch the flailing arms of their half-naked captive, who was still screaming abuse at the top of his voice. It was all so sudden and violent and terrible that Suki could do nothing but cry, the tears cascading down her cheeks and dripping off the end of her nose. But it wasn't until another attendant arrived with a canvas strait-jacket and a bottle of laudanum, that any kind of order was restored.

The three men worked together so quickly and brutally that everybody stepped away from them. First they flung the Captain to the ground with such violence that his head hit the wall with a crack, then they forced his arms into the stiff sleeves of the jacket while he was still stunned. Then the first bound his arms and the second chained his legs while the third poured laudanum down his throat, despite his groans. Then they gagged him with a dirty cloth, picked up the coins and pocketed them, and left. And Suki was caught up in such an overpowering rush of pity that her entire body ached with it, pity for him to be cast down so low and treated so cruelly, pity for William who would never have a father now and might lose his mother, too – Oh how could they bear it? – and pity for herself to have come so far and tried so hard and waited so long, only to be reduced to this. 'Twas too cruel!

Now that the exhibition was over, the gentlefolk were moving on. The corridor was full of swishing skirts and happy conversation. Lady Bradbury was left propped up against the wall, looking putty pale, with Lady Willoughby kneeling beside her, rubbing her hands and murmuring to her. One of the attendants was carrying a chair towards them, and following him through the crowd was a small black boy in a sailor's smock and canvas breeches – a small black boy with blue eyes.

The sight of him was such a surprise it stopped Suki's tears. "How now," she said to him. "What are *you* doing here?"

But he walked straight past her, and dropped to his knees beside the Captain, calling to him, "Mr Jack! Mr Jack!"

The attendants were lifting their rich patron from the floor and easing her into the chair, profuse with apology.

"A poor sick fool," Mr Todd said. "You mussen pay 'im no mind, ma'am. They don't know what they're a-sayin' half the time. Laudanum you see, ma'am. Weaned on it he was an' now 'tis the only way to sweeten 'is foul mind."

"This man," the black boy said clearly, "is my master. I tell you, he has the most sweet mind of any man. He save my mother's life. I'll not hear him spoke of so."

"What's this? What's this?" Mr Todd said, frowning at him. "Are we to be told our business by a blackamoor? Be off with 'ee, wretch, afore I takes a whip to 'ee."

"He speaks true," Suki said, standing up for him before she'd stopped to consider how dangerous it might be. "He is not a child to lie. I met him in Bristol and know him for an honest crittur. If he says he'm Jack's slave, then so he is."

"He may be what a' will but he'll not stay here," Mr Todd said, "for I've no room for him. Be off with 'ee. You heard what I said."

Blue looked at his master, then at Suki, then at Lady Bradbury who was looking down her long sharp nose at him. "I stay with my master," he said stubbornly. And to Suki's delight, he untied Jack's gag and removed it gently from his mouth.

"Fetch me a whip!" Mr Todd roared. But there was a gloved hand on his arm restraining him.

"We must be sorry for these creatures, sir," Lady Bradbury said. "I will pay you a crown for his keep if you will agree to let him stay an hour or two. I am too unwell to stay longer, as you will appreciate, but I will send my man to settle accounts with you. Suki, you will kindly assist me to my carriage. Good day to 'ee, sir."

Suki looked back at her lover but he had his eyes closed and seemed to be asleep. The black boy was unfastening the strait-jacket and wiping the dirt from

272

his face. There'm nothing I can do for him, she thought. I may have found him but t'was all in vain. And she lifted her mistress gently from the chair and she and Lady Willoughby led her away along the corridor. Whatever is to happen now, she thought as they stumbled forward, will happen whether I wills it or no.

Seventeen

It was a miserable journey back to Cavendish Square. Suki needed to cry, and to cry for a very long time, but with Lady Bradbury watchful in one corner of the carriage and Lady Willoughby concerned in the other, there was little she could do to relieve her feelings, except keep her head down and cuddle William. But her mind was spinning. Now that she'd got over the initial shock of seeing her lover locked up as a lunatic, she was remembering what he'd said. "Lady Bradbury, my mother!" Could it be? Or was it mere raving? If he spoke true, 'twould explain the kerchief and Jessup's knowledge of Nowhere Lane. He'd been delivering money to someone. Why not the Captain? She looked at her mistress, wondering, and Lady Bradbury opened her brown eyes and looked back at her, hard and straight and forbidding. How much had she heard afore she fainted? Suki thought fearfully. I was yelling so loud, an' I know I said the baby was his. Over and over again. She must have heard it. I shall be punished as sure as fate. What will she say? And worse, what will she do? But Lady Bradbury's eyes were closed again and just for a moment and mercifully, she wasn't saying anything.

They were all relieved to be back in Cavendish Square which was echoingly empty and seemed a great deal larger without its guests.

"What a blessing to be returned to civilisation," Lady Bradbury said, gazing at the well-ordered balance of her hall. "Life at this end of London is so much more polite, would you not agree, Arabella?"

You can be dismissed politely, Suki thought, as she followed the two ladies into the hall, and I daresay I *shall* be.

"Ah," Lady Bradbury said. "Jessup. I've an errand for you to run. Where is the master?"

Sir George was at his club, apparently, and Cook wished to know when she should serve dinner and for how many.

"Are you well enough to withstand a meal?" Arabella wondered, her face full of concern.

"Indeed yes," Hermione said airily. "I am *quite* recovered, as you see. 'Twould be too foolish to allow oneself to be discommoded by such a trifle. Tell Cook she will oblige me by serving dinner for two at four o'clock. I will send for you later, Suki." It was said in such a calm way and with so little expression that Jessup didn't see the import of it. But Suki did, and it made her stomach shake with apprehension.

So Jessup went off on his errand and the ladies dined and Suki waited. The hours passed and as there was little for her to do, she sat in the nursery and darned her stockings and presently Bessie appeared with her own mending and sat down to work beside her.

"You missed a treat this morning," she said. "You should've seen 'em go off. What a to-do! That ol' squirrel of his got out the cage an' we was all chasin' it for hours an' hours . . ."

Suki let her run on but she was too worried to listen. And when the stockings had been mended and William had been settled for his afternoon nap, she was relieved when Bessie took herself off to help in the kitchen. But she'd not been gone more than a quarter of an hour before she came panting back again to say that Lady Willoughby had gone home and the mistress was in the parlour and would like to see Suki straight away.

Please God, don't let them take my William away from me, Suki prayed as she climbed the back stairs to the drawing-room. Anything else, but not that. He'm all I got now the Captain's shut away. All I got, an' I love him more'n I can bear. I'll never tell another lie in the whole of my life if you only let me keep my William. I promise.

But the only answer she got was the steady ticking of the grandfather clock in the hall below, and the alarming rhythm of her own heart, which was pounding in such a frantic way she was finding it hard to breathe. She gave a timid knock on the parlour door, and while she was waiting to be told to enter, she offered up her prayer for the last time.

The room was full of afternoon sunlight, which shone through the high windows in columns solid enough to touch. There'm so much gilt and glass in this room, Suki thought, wincing away from it, and 'tis all so dominating and hard. The frames glowed around respectable portraits, the mirror threw back dazzling reflections, the brass fender winked and sniggered, even the curtains were as bold as grass. How could she hope for mercy in a room like this?

Lady Bradbury sat by the fire at the far end of the room beside the marble fireplace, with the tea things on a low table at her elbow, and a mound of cushions behind her powdered head. She seemed quite herself again, and far from being angry was affable and gracious – and thoroughly terrifying.

"I sent for you," she said as Suki hesitated into the room, "on a literary matter. You *do* read, I trust."

"Oh yes, ma'am."

"A most agreeable distraction don't you find? You must give me your opinion upon a novel I have just been reading. A romance. Of great delicacy. It made the tears start to my eyes." She gave Suki a faint smile and waved a languid hand towards a high-backed chair. "Pray, do sit down."

Suki perched on the edge of the appointed chair and waited. The silence in the room was painful. What will she say next? she worried. She'll dismiss me now, she'm sure to.

But Hermione went on talking about the novel, gazing into the distance, as though into memory. "'Tis a pretty history but fanciful," she said. "A tale of love requited. Young love, you understand, headstrong and, sad to say, unsuitable. She was the daughter of a duke, poor creature, and he the son of a gardener. But a pretty passion and uncommon sweet for all that, and all the taste of love she ever had. He told her she was all in all to him, sweeter than springtime, his own dear love, his own for ever. You know how fulsome men are when they woo."

"Yes," Suki agreed, breathlessly. Oh yes, how well she knew.

"She believed him, poor fond foolish child that she was. We are much deceived in matters of the heart, I fear. There was a child. A son. A pretty boy, with fine brown eyes, as I recall. But there," she sighed. "Her father railed at the disgrace, her mother took to her bed. The girl begged permission to marry, but 'twas out of all question and disallowed. I told 'ee 'twas a dismal story. The gardener was dismissed and sent away, and his son with him, to a foreign country, as I recall. The lady never saw him again." She paused to refill her cup and drank tea, calmly, her face perfectly controlled. "So here you have the crux of the tale," she went on, "a daughter ruined, a lover fled, the child in the womb. What should be done, think 'ee?"

"Were I that daughter," Suki said. "I would keep the child, come what may."

"Aye, so you would. I do believe. And lie for it, if t'were needful."

Fear tightened Suki's throat, but she told the truth. "Yes, ma'am, I would."

Hermione sipped her tea. Then she put down her cup and continued. "The duke was adamant, you understand. His daughter had no choice, poor foolish lovelorn soul. The child was farmed to a labourer's wife in Ba . . . the – um – nearest town. And later sent to school, and lodgings found. The lady married as her father wished. A good man, to be sure, but passionless. How think you of her story? Could she do other, given the circumstance?"

"The saddest tale, poor lady," Suki acknowledged. "She had no choice, ma'am. I can see that plain." Then she paused, wondering whether she dare speak further. If milady could speak in parables why not follow her example? "Should you care to hear it, ma'am," she offered. "I could tell *you* a tale."

"'Tis a pleasant fancy," Hermione said, "and no harm in't. Pray proceed."

"How of the child grown to a handsome man. With fine dark eyes 'an a merry way. Full of such passion. How of that?"

"It sounds most like."

"How if he found a foolish wench of his own, who loved him true, an' bore his child. How if she then took service in the town with a fine family. The best, ma'am, if you'll allow."

Hermione smiled to signify that she would allow it. "What then, child?"

Suki licked her lips and hesitated for just a second. Then she spoke the truth again, but quickly before it could frighten her into silence. "How if the mistress had a baby, too? A fine child, and very like the other. How if the lover nursed it as her own, and loved it, too, and lost it, suddenly?"

"In death?" Hermione asked, and her expression was calculating.

"In death."

"Then she would have a choice, too, would she not? To tell the truth and lose all, or lie and keep her child in the household? Was't not so?"

"Yes, ma'am. T'was exactly so." What else could she say? There was only the truth now.

The silence that followed was long and thoughtful. Hermione gazed at the embroidered firescreen, with her chin in her hand, brooding and scowling.

"The child is a fine strong boy," Suki offered, "worthy of any family, even the highest. If 'twas a fault to keep him in the household, there are those who might not wish to see the fault undone."

Hermione looked at her for a long fraught minute. "I believe I would be of their number," she allowed, "were I to be asked. I must confess I would rather be a mother than a grandam, in all conscience, although I dare swear son-in-law Humphrey will alter that, if the deed ain't done already." She stood up and walked to the window and stood for a while looking down into the garden. "My advice to the girl," she said, "if 'twere sought in this matter, would be to say nothing but to

279

leave matters as they are. The child will thrive, given his heritage. 'Tis a fine child, as you say. Why should the world and his wife be told such a tale? Some things are better left unsaid."

Suki was finding it very hard to breathie.

"Besides," Hermione went on, "there is a husband in the case, is there not? A good man, as men go, and doubtless fond of the child he thinks his son. We would be churlish to harm his faith, or deprive him of an heir."

'Tis settled, Suki thought, her head spinning with the wonder of it. I'm to keep my William, after all. She was smiling so widely she could feel the skin stretching beside her eyes.

"If I were asked for advice," Hermione continued, "I should say, 'Find a good husband. Be known as a wife.' A country husband, a farmer or smallholder for preference, where the child could stay, for rest and fresh air and suchlike, when his parents were elsewhere, where he could visit when he reached the age to be sent away and educated as a gentleman. As sent away he surely must be at the right age and the right time. That you'll allow."

'Twill have to be, Suki thought sadly. She couldn't keep him for ever. She was lucky to keep him at all. She knew that. And eventually he would have to go to school, like all young gentlemen. That was the way of the world. "Yes," she agreed. She would have to give up all hope of the Captain and marry Farmer Lambton, after all. 'Twas not impossible. If Ariadne could make the best of *her* situation, then so could she.

Lady Bradbury stood up, smoothed her gown and pulled the bell rope, but when Suki rose, expecting to be dismissed, she waved her back to her seat again. "Stay where you are," she commanded. "I have someone I wish you to meet."

This was so extraordinary that Suki didn't know what to make of it. She sat where she was and waited obediently and presently Jessup appeared and was sent to fetch "the young person". Which after a minute or two, during which time Lady Bradbury contemplated the fire and appeared to be deep in thought, he did.

The young person turned out to be a gentleman in a white bob wig. He wore black buckled shoes, a green coat and buff breeches that didn't fit him at all well and seemed ill at ease, for he was coughing nervously as he was ushered into the room. So Suki kept her eyes down, like a good servant, and didn't look at him after the first quick glance.

There was a brief silence. Then Lady Bradbury held out her hand to receive him and he bowed to kiss it, murmuring "your sarvant, ma'am". And Suki recognised his voice and looked at him again, this time with such wonder on her face that he smiled at her, almost as if he knew her.

"This gentleman," Lady Bradbury said, "is Mr Daventry, a kinsman of mine and grandson to the Duke of Daventry. He has been much abroad of late, and being returned was incarcerated in an insane asylum, through no fault of his own, where I discovered him by pure good chance this morning, and where he should never have been sent, in all conscience, not by any stretch of the imagination whatsomever. He is here to rest and recuperate and to conclude his business with Sir George."

Suki dropped a curtsey, as that seemed to be expected, but she said nothing, there being little she could say. This is how 'tis to be, she thought. He'm here and accepted and excuses found for un. He'm to be family and we'm to be kept apart. She was powerless before the speed of so many changes – and all in one short day. Still, at least he looks more like himself, she thought, now that he'm properly dressed and he got a wig over that awful shaven head. An' that's a comfort. But she winced when she looked at his face, for his lip was split and his cheeks bruised and his eyes were empty of any love or recognition, although he was looking straight at her.

"I believe I saw you this morning," he said. He spoke politely but there was doubt in his voice.

She answered equally politely, as a servant was bound to. "You did, sir."

"You must forgive me if I do not recall as I should," he said courteously. "I have been unwell, I fear, and given a deal of laudanum, which do clog the brain uncommon hard."

He doesn't know me, Suki thought sadly. I could be any wench to him. Or any servant for that matter. But she did her best to sympathise. "I don't doubt it, sir."

There was a discreet tap on the door – a Jessup tap – followed by a deprecation of coughing. The master was returned, he reported.

"Ask him if he will be so good as to join me," Lady Bradbury said. "Tell him I have a piece of news for him, which I know he will be anxious to hear."

For a confused second, Suki thought the butler was going to speak out of turn, for he stood where he was, hesitating and pondering and giving Jack the oddest look. But then he recovered himself and coughed away to do his errand.

"You may leave us," milady said to Suki, "but stay within call for we may have need of you. There is a spot just beyond the door which will serve, I daresay.

It usually does if the scuffs upon the boards are anything to go by."

So they know they'm spied upon, Suki thought, as she curtseyed and left them. I might ha' knowd it. There arn't much goes on in this house that she don't know about. Still at least I got leave to listen this time. Not that it made much difference. She'd have eavesdropped anyway, with or without permission, for this was a conversation she simply couldn't miss.

Sir George made his usual weighty entrance and flung himself into a chair with such force that the castors groaned beneath him. "How now, wife!" he said, cheerfully. "I hear you've a piece of good news for me. Well speak on, me dear! Good news makes good appetite."

"Your factor is proved a villain," the lady said in her cool voice.

To be told such a thing and with so little ceremony baffled his brain with distress and disbelief. He struggled to comprehend, taking temporary refuge in teasing. "You jest me, dear," he hoped.

"No, sir," she insisted. "'Tis as true as I stand here. Which this gentleman can confirm. Your slave master, sir, Mr Jack Daventry, and a kinsman of mine, as I daresay you will recall."

Sir George flicked a limp hand towards the young man, who was standing politely waiting to be introduced, but he didn't look at him. "Sarvent, sir!" he muttered and continued to stare at his wife. "If 'twere true I should have known of it," he protested. "Frederick would have told me."

"Frederick knows nothing of it," Hermione told him. "I should have known nothing of it myself had it not been for Mr Daventry. He was the one who saw all and noted it, being your slave master."

The fog of incomprehension began to clear. "My slave master ran mad," he said. "Stark staring raving mad. Sent to Bedlam, damme. Frederick told me so."

"No, sir," Hermione said. "Your slave master was sick of the fever and sent to Bedlam at the behest of your purser, that abominable creature, Mr Jedediah Smith, who, I might tell 'ee, sir, knew of the villainy and said nothing. How you ever came to employ such a man is beyond my comprehension. Howsomever Mr Daventry could tell you more of this than I can, should you wish to hear it."

"Speak," Sir George said weakly. "'Twill all be iniquity, I do not doubt." And he sighed with the approaching misery of it.

So Jack told his tale, beginning with an account of how the surgeon chose the six strongest slaves, explaining what became of them and how they were discovered, and ending with a description of the secret hoard of cut cane that he and Blue had been shown by the slaves in the fields. "He purloins a tenth of your crop, sir, with every harvest. Your slaves were sure of it."

Sir George listened with increasing anger, at first drumming his fists on the arms of his chair, then on his feet prowling and scowling but heavily attentive. By the time the full story was told, he had reached roaring point. "'Od's bowels!" he yelled. "The man's an arrant knave, 'od rot him. I never heard the like. Wants hanging, drawing and quartering, so he does. And I'm the man to see it done." It was time for decision and action. "I'll go to Nevis myself on the first ship, damme." He rang the bell so furiously it was a wonder he didn't pull it from the wall. "I'm obliged to 'ee, Mr Daventry, sir," he said, remembering his manners. "Uncommon grateful. There'll be a bounty in it for 'ee, you have my word on't."

"Well as to that," Hermione said acidly, "you'd best think of paying him his wages first. He ain't been given a penny piece by that rogue Smith."

"Is this true, sir?" Sir George asked.

Jack looked him straight in the eye. "I fear so, sir."

"Not a penny piece?"

"Not one, sir, though the purse was agreed upon before we sailed, as your brother will tell you. Fifty-one guineas, as I recall, to be divided between Mr Tomson and myself, he to take two thirds."

"'Od's blood!" Sir George said to his wife, as Jessup materialised through the servants' door. "I despair of human nature. We are into abomination here. Ah, Jessup. Pack up seven suits of clothes and so forth and lay out my travelling coat. I'm off to Nevis in the morning." He turned to Jack, and added casually, "You'd best come with me, young feller-me-lad, since you know the ins and outs of this affair."

The order took everyone by surprise and, out on the landing, where she'd been standing right up against the door so as not to miss a word, Suki caught her breath so suddenly she was afraid they would have heard her and stepped back towards Ariadne's empty room in case she had to hide in a hurry. Was she to lose him again so soon?

But Lady Bradbury was the mistress of any contingency. "Far be it from me to contradict you, my love," she said, taking breath to contradict him soundly, "but is this wise? I make this observation for your own good and the better accomplishment of your plans, which are too admirable to put to any hazard."

Sir George's brain lurched with annoyance and

renewed incomprehension. "Hazard?" he said. "I see no hazard. Mr Daventry will be invaluable, don'tcher know. Invaluable."

"Indubitably," Hermione agreed. "To arrive with a witness in hand would certainly add strength to your case. Howsomever, to be seen arriving with Mr Daventry might warn your factor that his conduct is to be investigated and in that eventuality you might find – indeed I dare swear you *will* find – that all evidence would be destroyed or hidden before you could bring it to light. 'Tis a matter you will doubtless wish to consider."

"Aye!" Sir George admitted. "'Tis true, deuce take it. But if such is the case, what is to be done?"

"I could offer advice, my love, should you wish it," Hermione said, adding modestly, "such as it is."

He waved a weak hand towards her. "Pray do."

The plan she outlined was neat, simple and entirely to her purpose. Mr Daventry would mark the position of the slave compound and the illicit sugar store on one of Sir George's maps. He could then carry his evidence with him secretly and would be free to travel with a trusty servant, who being unknown upon the island would give no cause for alarm to its dishonest inhabitants, "until you burst upon 'em sword in hand."

Sir George was stunned by its practicality and its self-enhancing drama. "Capital!" he roared. "Upon me life! Couldn't have planned it better myself."

Jack cleared his throat discreetly and prepared to put in his own happy penn'orth. "If I may make a suggestion, sir?" he offered. And when permission was granted with a lordly wave, "It seems to me, sir, that the ideal companion for your adventure stands in this very room before us. I refer, of course, to Mr Jessup. I know from Lady Bradbury that he has been her most loyal servant these many years but now that all her children are – um – settled, there will be less for him to do. Is that not so my lady? Consequently . . ." And he looked at the butler with a triumphant, insolent boldness, daring him to argue or refuse.

The two men bristled at one another, Jack cool with revenge, Jessup dark-faced with suppressed anger, while Hermione watched them and Sir George roared that it was "Capital! Capital!" and declared that Jessup was "just the man." Eventually the butler dropped his eyes and Jack permitted himself a smile and the matter seemed to be settled.

"You'll need to pack two trunks, what," Sir George said jovially as Jessup frowned from the room. He beamed at Jack and Hermione. "Now for the maps, Mr Daventry. We'll see to 'em here and now, what. No time like the present."

Hermione held out her hand to prevent Jack from rising. "There is still the matter of the bounty," she said.

Sir George had lost interest in such matters. "'Twill wait till my return I daresay," he said vaguely.

But Hermione insisted. "I'd not wish you to travel with a bad conscience, my love," she said, "there being no worse companion on any journey than a pricking conscience."

"I'll give 'ee my note of hand," Sir George suggested.

She persisted, as Jack and Suki listened with rapt attention. "I believe we could do better than mere note of hand," she said. "I believe we could make this a matter of property."

Suki caught her breath, Jack's heart was racing, Sir George looked interested. "How so?"

"You will remember the manor farm at Appleton, my

love. You have always intended it for a stud farm, have you not? Very well then. How if you were to offer the property to Mr Daventry in lieu of capital and by way of bounty. 'Tis in parlous bad repair, I'll grant you. The house is past rescue. But there's a deal of good land attached and with hard work and a new owner – a man of bottom and enthusiasm, a good judge of horses, and a gentleman you could trust, I need hardly add – 'twould soon be brought to profitable order. In a year or two I dare swear 'twill be a model of self-sufficiency and outshine all stud farms in the country. How say you to that?"

It seemed an admirable plan. "Would you be agreeable, sir?" Sir George asked. "Could 'ee take to the farming life, think 'ee?"

Land of my own, Jack thought, flushed with surprise and pleasure, a home, property, a new life as a gentleman, the very thing I've always known should be my portion. He understood little of farming, but none need know it. He could learn, and quickly, as he'd learned to be a slave master. And if 'twere to be a stud farm, he would be working with horses for the most part, which would be sheer reward. He might even breed another Beau. Oh yes indeed, he would be most agreeable.

"Then the business is concluded," Sir George said. "Now perhaps we may proceed to our cartography."

He reached the door so quickly that Suki only just had time to avoid him, skipping into Ariadne's room as his first broad foot splayed out on to the landing, and she'd barely reached the servants' door before Lady Bradbury was in the room and signalling to her to stand still and say nothing.

They waited until they heard the library door open and shut. Then Lady Bradbury gave rapid instructions.

"You will have heard all, I do not doubt," she said. And when Suki nodded. "You are to make ready to travel to Appleton with Mr Daventry and master William within the week. The tailor is ordered for tomorrow morning but I doubt if Mr Daventry's new clothes will be ready much before five days. Possibly more. Tailors are uncommon tardy. You will take one maid servant to assist you – Bessie would do well, I think – and Barnaby shall drive the carriage and look to the horses. He is a dolt when it comes to curtains, I fear, but he has some sense with horses and should do well in a stable. You will stay at Appleton until Mr Daventry's new house is ready. I will send a letter to that effect to Mr Norris. Nothing need be rushed, you understand."

Suki dropped a curtsey and murmured, "Yes, ma'am," but her mind was in such a turmoil she felt as if her brain was boiling.

"Be of good cheer," the lady advised, nodding her powdered head. "All will be well. T'ain't the best of all possible worlds, in all conscience, but we must make what good of it we can. Ask Mrs Sparepenny to attend me directly." And she swept from the room, straight of spine and determined.

The buzz of gossip in the kitchen was so loud that when Suki stepped through the door it was like walking into a hive. Not surprisingly, William was very much awake, but perfectly happy, sitting on Bessie's lap beside the table, chewing a sugar plum. He turned as Suki swished towards him and held out his arms to her, calling "Mamma-Sue! Mamma-Sue!" but she barely had time to pick him up before she was surrounded by every servant in the place, all eager for the latest news.

"Is it true the master's off to Nevis?", "Have 'ee met the young gentleman? He come here with jest a blanket

289

round him, half in a swoon he was. Do 'ee know who he is?", "Mr Jessup's got a face like a thunder cloud and won't tell us a thing."

No matter what may become of me now, Suki thought, as she held her baby's lovely warm familiar body close and safe in her arms, even if Jack don't remember me, an' arn't like to wed, an' is come home changed to a distant stranger I barely know, I still have you, don't I my little love, an' that's a deal to be thankful for. And your life's safe an' provided for now. You shall have fine clothes and good food an' grow to be a gentleman, with rich toys to play with an' money in your pocket an' a pony to ride an' all. She could just see him on a pony. He'd be a fine rider. Like his father. And she suddenly remembered the splendid sight Jack made astride that great horse of his. But of course, she thought: Beau. There's still Beau. He haven't been told a word about Beau. He don't know I've a-rescued un, and kept un safe. A deal of good could come of *that*. Why hadn't she thought of it before? I must write to Farmer Lambton and tell him we shall be in Twerton as soon as may be and promise him that he'll be paid at last.

But meantime there was milady's message to deliver to Mrs Sparepenny, and after that the pressure of all those questions to answer, which she did as well as she could, prevaricating a little and ignoring those that had to be avoided. And then the chores of the day carried her along and there was no time for hope or regret or even thought. When she finally fell into bed at a little after midnight, she was so tired she slept as soon as her head touched the pillow.

Eighteen

S ir George left for Nevis early the next morning with a
great hullabaloo and the promise to return in triumph
"as soon as I have apprehended all villainy, what!"

His wife waited for an hour in order to be quite sure he
was clear of the house and then, suitably attired in a new
and splendid day gown, attended by a new and superior
lady's maid, and with enough clothes to sustain even the
most anxious three days, she set off for a well-earned
visit to her cousin, Sir Francis. Before she left, she
handed Jack his earnings, paid in full and in gold coin,
with the instruction that he was to take the second coach
and four to Appleton when he was ready and meantime
was to provide himself with clothing suitable for his
new position. "Do not stint yourself," she instructed.
"Appearances are *so* important."

For the next five days, Jack Daventry lived between
luxury and terror. By day he was treated like a lord,
with abundant food to eat, a tailor to provide obsequious
service, tradesmen to offer new wigs, buckled shoes and
fine linen, and Blue to wait upon him hand and foot.
By night he fell into a sleep hag-ridden by nightmare,
where fierce women thrashed the child he had been, and
asylum keepers threw the man he had become against
walls and gratings and tied him in a strait-jacket so that
he could barely breathe. He was tossed into the sea to be

eaten by sharks and crocodiles. Muskets beat his face. Cannonballs tore off his limbs. He woke groaning, with the sweat running down his spine and falling from his eyebrows, so that he had to shake it from him like a dog, and was glad of Blue's comforting presence to call him back to the day.

In the afternoon he and Blue took a stroll in the gardens at the centre of the square and Blue told him how he had found the Llandoger Trow and travelled to London with Quin Cutpurse, and how they had held up coaches and robbed all manner of gentry and finally how the Spider had taken him to Bedlam, "because I ask and ask. He say, 'You come back to Seven Dials after. We got gentleman for you to meet.' But I find *you* so I do not go back."

That information made Jack suspicious, knowing how Quin liked to operate. "What sort of gentleman was that? Do 'ee know?"

"He got cats," Blue reported. "He is . . ." He struggled to remember the name. "Cat burglar."

"I have saved you from a life of crime," Jack said, ruffling the boy's woolly hair. "And not a minute too soon."

"What is lifacrime?" Blue asked.

But he never got an answer because at that moment Suki came out of the house leading her toddling William by the hand and, at the sight of her, Jack took flight and headed off for the opposite end of the garden to avoid her. There was something about her red cheeks and those bright eyes that triggered the most uncomfortable memory, and as he couldn't determine whether it was a nightmare he was recalling or some actual and painful occasion, he simply removed himself from the pressure of it.

So when his last new jacket had been delivered and

his journey was finally about to begin, he was very much put out to discover that she and the child were to travel in the carriage with him. He stood with one foot on the step, uncertain how to proceed.

"Do you go far?" he asked, wary but making an effort to be polite. But when she told him they were to travel all the way to Appleton together, he forgot his manners completely and rushed back into the house to find himself a book to occupy him on the road. The thought of sitting opposite those bold blue eyes for such a long journey was so disquieting that he had to have a barrier that could be held up between them whenever need arose.

His deliberately averted eyes made Suki ache with sadness. She felt rejected, especially after days when it had been painfully clear that he was going out of his way to avoid her. But she tried to cheer herself by observing that he looked a deal better than he'd been when she saw him in Bedlam-in-Moorfields and reminding herself that she would soon be reuniting him with his horse. He was immaculately dressed, in a brocade coat very similar to the one he'd worn on that first love-dazed summer of theirs – Oh what an age ago that was! – the cut on his lip had almost healed, his bruises were fading, his skin was a healthier colour and his head was covered with the thick dark stubble of returning hair. It only needed his memory to return and all might yet be well. 'Twas foolish to blame him for unkindness if he could not remember her. Meantime she had taken pains to be well prepared for the journey, with one basket packed with bread, cold meats, beer and pickles to sustain them on the first leg of their journey and another full of toys to keep William amused. And she'd written to Farmer Lambton to warn him of their arrival.

It had been a difficult letter to compose, for she had

to let him know that the Captain was returned without allowing him to think that they were already married or even like to be. She pondered for more than a day until she found the diplomatic words she needed, but when they were written she knew she'd done well and was pleased by her delicacy. "Captain Jack," she'd said, "has been uncommon ill and is still a deal too weak to plan his future or even talk of it. 'Twill cheer him to see his horse again, but we must be mindful of his feelings which are a deal too tender at the moment. I would be obliged if you would say as little to him as you may and if you would advise my parents that I hopes they will do likewise." Now it was simply a matter of waiting and hoping.

Her letter to Ariadne, on the other hand, had been an easier task altogether. She had written to her at length and freely, recounting everything that had happened and describing her feelings in detail, from the shock of seeing her beloved as a lunatic in Bedlam, through the amazement of Lady Bradbury's story of his birth – "which must be a secret atween us for I have given my word not to tell it to a living soul" – to the relief of knowing William's position was ensured and the embarrassment of being forgotten and unrecognised "which do break my heart I can tell 'ee, having loved him so long and so true."

Ariadne had sent an answer the same afternoon to say how greatly she was surprised by Suki's news and how much she sympathised. "Do not lose heart, my dear," she wrote.

> Allow time to heal him, as it surely will. When his memory is returned I do not doubt that he will love you as truly as he ever did. I cannot wait to visit with you at Appleton, which I shall do at the first opportunity, you may be sure, for

I am full of curiosity about this new brother of mine, especially as Mamma must not know that I know his circumstances, and would dearly like to meet him, particularly if he has the good sense to marry my dearest friend. Write to me at the very next opportunity for I long to hear how this matter will turn out.

But there was a deal to be lived through before that could be done and a long road to travel. Fortunately, the first part of the journey went well, for although Jack spent his time gazing moodily out of the window or pretending to read his wretched book, she managed to keep William amused with the cup and ball and the monkey on a stick and the jack-in-a-box, and fed him a sugar stick when he started to grizzle, so the time passed relatively easily.

When they stopped that evening at The Bear at Slough, Jack realised, rather belatedly, that they were on the road to Bath.

"How now?" he scowled at Suki. "Does our coachman not know the road?"

"We are to travel by way of Lambton Farm at Twerton," she told him. "Milady's orders." And her heart lifted for now she could tell him about Beau and the telling might restore his memory.

But he was already turning away from her. "'Twill be a matter of livestock, I daresay," he said casually, and strode into the inn to make sure of a good room.

She realised that she was shivering with the cold of rejection. Oh how easily he could cast her down. And how thoughtlessly. It hurt her that he was so unaware of her and turned away from her so quickly, for it showed how little she meant to him. And there were still two more days to journey before they would reach Lambton

Farm. It was uncommon hard to have to wait so long, especially when it wasn't in her nature to be patient. But patient was what she had to be, notwithstanding. There was nothing for it but to travel on, keep her secret and feed her remaining hope as well as she could.

William was less well behaved on the second day. He grizzled and complained and climbed over the seats and smeared the windows with his sticky fingers. In the end she had to suckle him to get him to settle. But on the third day he was exhausted and slept all afternoon, sprawled across her knees and growing heavier by the mile, as the sky coloured with sunset, the horses laboured and the carriage grew dark. She was very relieved when they turned in at Lambton Farm at last, to the usual cacophony of affronted farm animals, and Barnaby drew the horses to a halt.

Jack sprang out before the step was down. "We must make haste," he said to Barnaby, shouting above the din of squeals and squawks, "if we're to return to Bath and find good lodgings for the night. Who am I to see?"

"Well as to that, sir," Barnaby shouted as he unfolded the step, "'tis Suki you must ask. She's the one what knows."

She was carefully carrying her sleepy baby out of the carriage, as Blue and Bessie scrambled down from their perch on the driving seat. "If Bessie will take him," she said, "I'll show 'ee the way. Let un see the pigs, Bessie. He'll like that. Give him a little stick so's he can scratch their backs. 'Twill stop 'em a-squealing." Somebody was opening the door of the cottage and she could see Mrs Havers' inquisitive face framed in the window, but fortunately Farmer Lambton was already on his own doorstep and waiting for them, so she led the Captain across to make the necessary introductions.

"Mr Daventry, this is Farmer Lambton, who been a-caring for your property since April. Mr Lambton, please to meet Mr Jack Daventry, a kinsman of milady's."

Property? Jack thought, staring at her. 'Twas a curious word to use of livestock. But there was no time to question her, for the farmer was leading him towards the stable yard.

"He's all ready for 'ee, sir," he said. "You'll find him in fine fettle."

The stable was dark with dusk but there was no mistaking the horse that stood in the first stall, pricking his ears at their approach.

"'Od's teeth!" his master cried, running to fling an arm about that splendid neck. "'Tis my Beau! My Beau! How now, my beauty. I never thought to find 'ee again." He was so close to tears he had to duck his head into Beau's mane, and the horse pawed the straw and twitched his flanks. "Let me look at 'ee."

He had been most carefully groomed, his bay coat brushed till it shone, not a single tangle in mane or tail, his hooves new shod.

"I had the smith look him over, so soon as I received our Suki's *billet*," Farmer Lambton explained.

So she arranged this, Jack thought, glancing across to where she stood in the shadows. She's known about it all along. The more he heard about this girl the more intriguing she became. "I'm beholden to 'ee, sir," he said to the farmer. "He'll have cost 'ee a deal in fodder, I fear. I trust you have kept accounts."

He had. "Written up week by week, sir, as is my custom."

Jack said he was glad to hear it and promised to settle with him, "Forthwith. You have my word on't. I'll ride him first. Aye, I must ride 'ee, must I not my beauty." He

297

was already hauling his saddle from its hook, impatient to be up and away. "You cannot know what it is to find my horse, sir. I thought I should never see him again and here he is, large as life and twice as handsome and raring to go, ain't you my charmer."

And that's the way of it, Suki thought sadly, as she watched him saddle up and ride – oh so happily – out of the yard and off along the bridle path, easing his great stallion from trot to canter to full rippling gallop. He remembers his horse but I'm forgot. She felt bleak to the point of tears.

"I see I must cease my suit," Farmer Lambton observed as they stood in the yard together, "since your lover is returned to 'ee."

She was confused by his directness. "Not that I didn't take your proposal serious," she hastened to assure him. "Nor that I wasn't grateful to 'ee. Uncommon grateful. 'Twas just—"

"You're a good girl, Suki Brown." he said. "And I wish 'ee joy. Indeed I do. Now you must go and see your mother. She's been a-waiting for 'ee all this while."

Which was plainly true, for Mrs Brown had been standing in the doorway of her cottage, with Tom and Molly owl-eyed beside her, ever since the carriage arrived.

"So he came home again," she said, as Suki walked towards her, "this Captain of yours. He'm a fine figure of a man, I'll grant 'ee that. Uncommon handsome, which anyone with half an eye can see even if she arn't disposed to think well on un, which I arn't. Have he put a ring on your finger?"

Such straight disapproval made Suki wince. "Well as to that," she said, trying to make light of it, "he's been

ill an' aren't recovered yet. Time enough for rings and
things when he'm back to health."

"He looks healthy enough to me," Mrs Brown said,
watching as he sprang from the saddle and strode into
the farmhouse. "Got a good firm step on un, I should
say. A deal too firm for an invalid."

Suki's control was slipping. "I tread on ice," she said,
her mouth trembling despite a mighty effort to keep it
under control. "And whether 'tis thick enough to support
me or will break under the next step I cannot tell."

"What ice?" Molly said, examining the ground at her
sister's feet. "I can't see no ice, Suki."

And at that Mrs Brown called her youngest daughter
a goose – and changed the subject, asking after the
babba and the Bradburys and so giving Suki a chance
to recover. And by the time she'd told them as much of
her news as she could, Jack was out of the farmhouse
and back in the saddle again, calling to her and eager to
be off. So she kissed her family goodbye, promising she
would see them again in the spring, and returned to the
carriage and her sticky baby.

"I shall ride into Bath," Jack said, patting Beau's neck.
"Bessie and Blue can take my place in the carriage to
keep you company." But he didn't look at Suki at all. He
only had eyes for his horse. "We'll not be parted again in
a hurry," he said to the animal, "eh, my charmer." And
was off and out of the yard before Barnaby had time to
put up the step.

There was so much power about him, up on that great
horse, so much pride and so much happiness. He led
them into Bath as if he were at the head of a triumphant
procession, looking about him like a conqueror. He'd
barely walked ten yards along Stall Street before he was
surrounded by old friends, calling out to him and to one

another. "Why look-ee here. The Captain's back." "Well damn my eyes, where have you been, you varlet? 'Od's bones, 'tis uncommon good to see 'ee, damme if it ain't. You must come and have supper with us. We won't take no for an answer, damme."

I am home, he thought, as they trooped after him to the inn. Back where I belong. I've money in my pocket, friends at my side, fine clothes on my back, land to farm and Beau in the stable. What more could I want? The horrors are over and done.

That evening, Suki had supper with Barnaby, Blue and Bessie, who was bubbling with the excitements of the day. "What a lovely horse Mr Daventry's got," she said. "He's a thoroughbred, I'd lay money, the size of him. And what a lot of captings you do know, Suki."

Suki had been eating sleepily, worn out by travel and disappointment. "Do I?" she asked.

"First your brother," Bessie explained. "He's a capting, ain't he? The one we was looking for that time. And Mr Daventry. They was all calling him Capting out there in the street. I heard 'em. And your husband. He's a capting, ain't he?"

"Yes," Suki agreed sadly. "He was."

Bessie's kind heart was touched to see her friend so melancholy. "He'll come home sometime," she comforted. "You'll see. They all comes home sometime or other."

Suki gave her a bleak smile. "No," she said. "I don't think he will now. I've a-waited too long for un. I'm afeared he'm lost to me now an' I must face up to it."

"'Tain't like you to speak so," Bessie said, most surprised to hear such pessimism. "Never say die."

"You may have the right of it," Suki admitted, although in her present dejected state she didn't believe it. "So

I won't say die. Not this evening, leastways. I'll say goodnight to 'ee and hope 'ee sleeps well. We've a long day tomorrow and a deal of travelling to do."

But sleep came late to Suki Brown that night. The mattress was cold and lumpy and, no matter how much she turned and sighed, she couldn't find a comfortable hollow upon it. And then, when she finally drifted into a chill-footed sleep, she was plagued by a torment of dreams. She and Jack were strolling in the Spring Gardens but when they stopped to kiss, he wouldn't look at her and when she tried to put her arms about his neck, he melted into air and was suddenly on horseback and riding away from her. She ran and ran, calling his name, as he leapt from the horse into a bucking carriage and from the carriage into a fast running river. She plunged into the water after him, but he swam away from her and was lost, leaving her to struggle in a current she couldn't withstand, weeping and yearning.

When she woke it was grey daybreak and rain was pattering against the window. "'Twill be a bad day," she said to William as she held him over the chamber-pot to piddle.

In the next room, Jack was waking from a nightmare, too. This one was so fraught and complicated that he was determined to forget it as soon as he could. "We'll make an early start," he said to Blue, "for the weather is against us."

It was a sensible decision, for the next and final leg of their journey was the hardest of them all. Rain fell from the sky in sharp white rods all day, whipping the horses, penetrating coats and breeches and reducing the road – which was in a poor enough condition in dry weather – to a slime and slurry of mud. They got stuck in deep ruts on two rain-driven occasions and all five of them had to get out and put their shoulders to the wheel to heave the carriage on again. Streams of water poured from Jack's new hat and dripped from the toes of his new boots, Barnaby grumbled that he was wet to his skin, his passengers were so jolted and flung about that they were bruised beyond caring, and William did nothing but wail and wouldn't be comforted by anything, not even a sugar stick, which he bit and flung away from him until shards of it were stuck to every surface in the carriage, from the seats and windows to Bessie's skirt and Suki's hair.

They were all heartily glad when they came to Appleton at last and could get indoors to a warm fire and clean clothes. Mrs Norris bustled into the courtyard to welcome them, dispatching servants right and left to carry in their baggage and lead their horses away to the stables to be groomed, fed and watered.

"I got a good ol' rabbit stew a-boiling for 'ee," she said. "Three jack rabbits. As plump a set of fine furry fellers as you ever saw. Been over the fire since mid-morning so they have. I reckoned 'twould be today, when we got milady's *billet*. 'Twill give 'ee a good stomach lining, rabbit stew. What we all needs on a night like this, which arn't a night to travel in and that's the truth on't. I never saw such rain, not since last Michaelmas. Come you up to the fire so soon as you'm ready."

It was such a warm welcome and the stew smelled so enticing that Suki forgot that she had once thought the house old-fashioned, dark and draughty. Now she was simply glad to be indoors, aware of the heat of the fire, leaping and crackling in the hearth, and of the rich glow of the candles that flickered in the sconces on the wall and burned most warmly in the three triple-headed candlesticks upon the kitchen table, casting golden light on Mrs Norris's new bread and patterning the pewter platters and tankards and the two great flagons of cider with lustrous stripes of amber.

That night she slept easily in the bed she'd used during that first impatient winter and woke refreshed and restored and eager for the day. The rain had stopped, there was a pale sun lighting the courtyard and the dawn chorus was in full-throated song.

As she was stirring the porridge pot, and gossiping with Mrs Norris, and assuring William that she'd not be a minute and then he could have his breakfast with a bit of patience, Bessie came yawning into the kitchen with a message from Mr Daventry.

"He's goin' up to Home Farm, seemingly," she said, "for to see his property. Mr Norris is a-driving up in the cart and he says will you join him. Mr Daventry, I mean. Not Mr Norris. Though you'll be a-joining 'em both in a manner a' speaking. I'll feed the babba if you like."

The request was so unexpected after everything that had happened on their journey that Suki was bemused by it, but she put on her bonnet and wrapped her shawl round her shoulders and went out to obey it, notwithstanding.

Mr Norris was already in the driving seat, sitting bolt upright with his old black dog bolt upright beside him but there was no sign of Beau and that was a surprise, too, for she quite expected Jack to be in the saddle. But, no, he climbed into the cart and sat down beside her. And off they went, following the bridle path east without a word being passed between them.

It was Mr Norris who did all the talking. "'Tis a mile and a half or thereabouts," he said, "and I'd best to warn 'ee, sir, 'tain't in the best of conditions. Sir George keeps up the orchards wonderful, as you can see, sir, and the

Appleton House is a model to the county, though I says it as shouldn't, but Home Farm – well now that's a different matter. 'Twas rented out to Mr Chomondley, you see, sir. He ran it for years, and since he passed on there's been narry a one to care for un so 'tis . . . Well, you'll know how 'tis, sir."

It was a ruin. The farmhouse was built of wattle and daub and thatched in the old style, but the thatch was so old it was dust grey and full of great holes where the mice scrabbled and the small birds nested and twittered, and the house itself was so dangerously out of alignment that it looked as though it would tumble over at a sneeze. And as if that weren't bad enough, the fields were no better. Most of them were clogged by burdock and nettles, the hedgerows were knotted for lack of husbandry, the ditches clogged for lack of clearing and one field so badly waterlogged that there were pools of water shining like blue skies all over it.

Suki's heart sank at the sight of it, but Jack was determinedly cheerful.

"'Twill need a deal of work," he said, "so 'tis as well I'm a man for a challenge. Let's see the stables, Mr Norris, since they will be my main concern."

The two men walked round the house to the yards behind it, with Suki trailing after them, wondering what purpose she served by being one of the party. He'd handed her out of the cart but he hadn't spoken a word to her since they left Appleton House. In fact, he was speaking to Mr Norris again as she entered the yard and saw the stables.

"Now these are a deal better built than the house," he was saying. Which they were, being made of stone with a firm brick floor and a tiled roof. "What do 'ee think to 'em, Suki?"

She said she thought they would serve.

"And so they will," he agreed. "Uncommon well."

"I must be on my way now, sir," Mr Norris said, "if I'm to be at the mill betimes. If you don't need me no more, I'll bid 'ee good-day."

Am I to stay here, Suki wondered, or leave with Mr Norris?

She was answered at once. "We will take a look inside the house," Jack said, "and walk back presently. That will suit, will it not, Suki?"

So they took a look inside the house, which was full of dust and much decayed and according to Jack "not worth the ground it stands upon. I shall build a new house on that mound across there. In the new style, with fine windows and a good bold door, and a drawing-room on the first floor where it ought to be. What say 'ee to that?"

She said it sounded handsome, since that was plainly what he wanted to hear and was true besides. But she was still puzzled and unsure of herself and wondered what they would talk about on their long walk back to Appleton House.

At first, he spoke at length about his plans for the home farm. "I have always hoped to farm," he said. "I shall need a manager, I daresay, for to tell 'ee true, Suki, I know little of farming as yet, but I mean to learn. I knew little of slavery when I first set sail from Bristol but I learned that trade well enough and 'twas a deal more difficult than any farming life could be. Besides I shall be breeding horses and there's an occupation I have in my very blood. And Beau to put to stud what's more."

As no answer seemed to be needed, Suki walked beside him and kept her eyes down and said nothing.

It was a bitter-sweetness to be so near to him and yet so far from his thoughts.

They walked on in silence for several hundred yards and then he suddenly spoke again. "I am much beholden to 'ee, I think," he said. "For you were the one who found my Beau, I believe, and bought him from that rogue Wenham and rode him to Lambton's farm."

She admitted that this was so, but did not look at him.

"Then I owe you the price you paid for him."

"No," she said, looking at him at last and smiling because she was so pleased by what she was about to tell him. "The money was your mother's. She sent me a note for five pounds to pay for William's new clothes. 'Twas in my pocket at the time, so I spent it. Though what she'd have said had she known I do not dare to think."

"And what of William's clothes?"

"I made over his old ones."

"You are a sterling creature," he said, touched to think that she would put the care of his horse before clothes for this child she loved so much.

"I could hardly stand by an' see un beaten, poor crittur," she said, and as his expression was encouraging, she told him the story.

"Then I truly *am* beholden to you," he said when she'd finished. The more he talked to her, the more strongly she was attracting him, with those fine rounded arms and that pretty bosom and her dark skin glowing in the sunshine and those blue eyes looking at him with such candour, reminding him. But of what? The curse of it was that he couldn't remember, although he sensed it to be important. Echoes rose to disturb him but faded away from him as if they were slipping into the untidy hedges. "I must make amends to 'ee."

"There's no need."

"Were my mother to be believed, there is a pretty way to do't," he said, smiling at her.

She was alerted by the smile and annoyed by the change in his tone, but he didn't notice and pressed on. "She maintains," he dared, "that a farmer is twice the man with a good wife."

Oh the misery of it. To be so near to a proposal from this man she'd loved so much – still loved so much despite his faults – and all for the very worst of reasons. "That, sir," she told him as coldly as she could, "is no concern of mine."

"But it could be, could it not, were we to marry?"

She straightened her spine, and moved two paces away from him, her face set. "Then my answer's no," she said. "And you'd best know it now afore you ask. I'll not have my life arranged for me by any milady, no matter who, and no more should you. 'Tis belittling. Insulting. We should be above such things. If I marry 'twill be for love, not for an arrangement. I thought better of 'ee, sir, indeed I did."

Her fierceness was burning away the mists in his mind. "When you found me in Bedlam," he reminded them both, "you said you loved me."

"That was then and in the heat of the moment," she told him furiously. "A deal has happened since. I arn't a pawn in Lady Bradbury's game nor do I ever intend to be."

"You said that William was my child."

"Aye, so he is," she said. "But they arn't no reason to marry neither, since I've birthed un and cared for un on my own and now he'm to be brought up as milady's son and sent to school as a gentleman and to inherit Sir George's estate and we'm to keep our secret."

This time, to be told that he was indeed a father filled him with an unexpected pleasure – and some hope.

"Then perhaps," he said, "we should keep our secret together as man and wife."

"No, no, no!" she cried, stamping her feet. "I won't marry for convenience. I could have took Farmer Lambton months since if I'd meant to marry so. And I won't do it. Never, never, never. 'Twill be love or nothing. Don't 'ee understand?"

"What a firebrand you are," he said admiring her. But then he saw the gleam of tears in those wild eyes and realised that her anger was caused by pain. "I did not mean to hurt 'ee, upon my life," he said, putting his hands on her shoulders to turn her towards him. "I thought 'twould please you."

The touch of his hands was more than she could bear. "Then you thought wrong," she said, and tried to twist away.

The movement triggered a memory that spun in his drug-tamed brain, caught, held and edged into focus. "The Spring Gardens," he said, staring at her. "The Spring Gardens in Bath. You wore a pink gown and little red slippers and I stole six pinks from the border and put 'em in your hair. You are Suki from Twerton. We went to the theatre and saw the silliest play. Oh how I do recall."

To be remembered was such an exquisite pleasure after so much hurt and disappointment that she caught her breath and stopped struggling. "You said I was your one true love," she rebuked him. "And then you forgot me. You recognised your horse and didn't know me from Adam. Your one true love."

He was so caught up in the power of the memory that he missed her rebuke. "And so you were," he said.

"How I do remember. You rode before me on the saddle with your hair blown about and your bonnet on your shoulders. I loved you more than I could say."

Her answer was bitter. "And have forgot me since."

"No, indeed, truly. I thought of 'ee on board ship and in the slave camp, even in Bedlam. I could not put a name to 'ee in Bedlam because of the laudanum. 'Od rot it. You were my comfort in the worst of times. I dreamt of 'ee in Bath not two nights since and a cruel dream it was, for I thought to hold you and lost you at every turn."

"You said nothing of it in the morning," she said, yearning for him. Oh if only he had spoken then.

He winced. "Fool that I was, I did not know who you were in the morning."

Love was stirring in them both, pulling them together by its magical cords. "And do you know now?" she asked breathlessly.

He caught her in his arms and held her so close she could feel his breath in her hair. "You are a sterling creature," he said. "A wench of pure gold. My one true love."

She knew he was exaggerating but it was sweet to hear the words even so and she put up her mouth for his kiss as though they were still the lovers they had been all those months ago. And the kiss was sweeter than any words could have been and a deal more true.

"How I remember now," he said. And he did indeed. Those arms about his neck, those blue eyes growing languid with desire, that sweet breath playing against his lips before he kissed her again. He was restored – full of strength and hope in a world rich with colour and possibility – and confident enough to tease.

"A thousand pardons," he said as their third kiss ended. "I had forgot. You do not wish to marry me."

She could tease, too. Now. "That was afore your memory returned to 'ee."

"How say you now that it has?"

"Now that it has," she told him with mock seriousness, "I will give your proposal thought, sir."

"And in the meantime I may hope?"

She knew she would marry him, although he was no longer the dashing gallant she had loved in Bath all those months ago, but a man a deal more complicated, changed by suffering, made vulnerable, needing help and support as much as she needed it herself. But, oh, a man she loved more than ever. "In the meantime," she said, putting her arms round his neck in her old easy way, "we will try what a little love may do."